SHADOWS OF THE NIGHT

CHARLIZE K. KELLY

First paperback edition printed by Amazon, October 2023
Cover design by Artscandare
Map design by Natalia Junqueria
Editing by Agatha Whitechapel
Interior book design by Natalia Junqueira

To my favourite murderous vampires—
David, Dwayne, Marko, and Paul.

The muses of this story, because without you, I wouldn't have been able to bring this divinely blissful and blood-stained world to life.

Author's Note

Before you indulge in the world of Celacali, it's important to understand that *Shadows of the Night* isn't for the faint of heart and shouldn't be read without warnings or the understanding that this is a *dark romance*. I don't condone the behaviour depicted on these pages, I just find writing from the darkness … enthralling.

Shadows of the Night contains: Alcohol and drug usage, assault, attempted rape, bestial violence, blood, death, divorce, emotional and physical abuse, fire, gore, gun violence, hallucinations, flashbacks, hostage and kidnapping situations, murder, profanity, PTSD, religious metaphors, sexism, sexual harassment, sexually explicit scenes, torture, violence, polyamory, BDSM, stalking, voyeurism, corruption, age gaps, exhibitionism, degradation, character deaths, threesome, knives, consensual and non-consensual biting, dubious consent.

Now, if you've read all those warnings and have still decided to continue reading, welcome to the malignant city of Celacali. And if you're family or friends reading this (even after the warnings), I warned you, and I'm not going to apologise—I won't hide because I'm afraid. I stand to lose nothing by sharing the darkness I created, gaining more than I thought I ever could. So, if you can handle the unorthodox and controversial topics within, then … *Initiation's over … Time to join the club.*

Charlize K. Kelly

"Come with us, Michael."

David, Kiefer Sutherland—The Lost Boys.

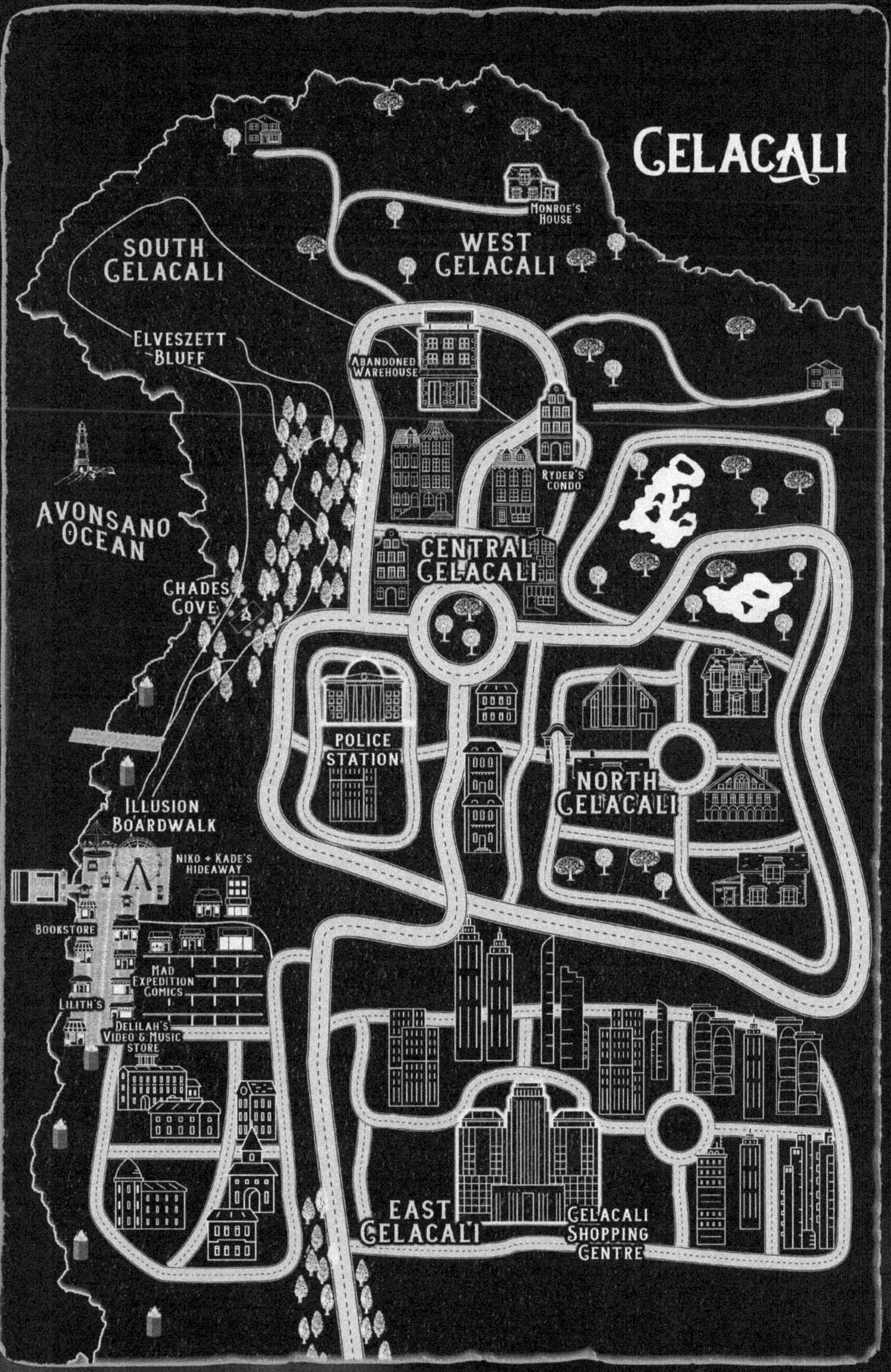

CELACALI

MONROE'S HOUSE

WEST CELACALI

SOUTH CELACALI

ELVESZETT BLUFF

ABANDONED WAREHOUSE

RYDER'S CONDO

AVONSANO OCEAN

CENTRAL CELACALI

CHADES COVE

POLICE STATION

NORTH CELACALI

ILLUSION BOARDWALK

NIKO + KADE'S HIDEAWAY

BOOKSTORE

MAD EXPEDITION COMICS

LILITH'S

DELILAH'S VIDEO & MUSIC STORE

EAST CELACALI

CELACALI SHOPPING CENTRE

LINE DO NOT CROSS POLICE LINE DO

CRIME SCENE DO NOT CROSS

CRIME SCENE DO NOT CROSS

IME SCENE DO NOT CROSS

CRIME SCENE DO NOT CROSS

CRIME SCENE DO NOT CROSS

LICE LINE DO N

O.

July 2024.

Death's forlorn presence stalked her, its scarred and foreboding hand wrapping around her throat until she knew she was going to die with every shaky breath past her lips that burrowed the knowledge deeper into her bones. Thunder resounded ominously above the churning ocean, white-capped and as unforgiving as the frigid wind that buffeted her fear-riddled back.

Pressing and plucking at her beige crocheted jacket, her heart pounded against her ribcage as she walked, mouse-brown tresses whipping her face. Loose blue-metal stones skittered over the cracked and desolate alleyway as she squinted back over her shoulder, hazel gaze scouring the shadows. Her childish fears of what prowled the inky darkness, as she made herself walk faster, seemed more like a premonition than an innocent fear now. Death was directing her to calamity, forcing her to fight for her next breath or relinquish it to him.

It was a risk you always took, and one that hung heavily over the coastal city of Celacali. Like a constant brewing storm, always on the cusp of wreaking havoc and despair upon those unlucky—*foolish*—enough to be out wandering the streets. Or the alleyways that bordered and backed the suburban areas, forking off like dark tree roots. She had been foolish enough to venture out, despite her husband's warnings, in search of him and their sons when the first flash of lightning split the sky.

The stagnant stench of mould and wet bitumen filled her nostrils with every panicked inhale. Her breath rang harshly in the eerie silence that blanketed her hearing. A startled yelp raked up from the depths of her chest as she rounded the corner of the alleyway and her stare clashed with a banefully grinning blond. He leaned with his shoulder pressed into the bricked building, grin stretched so widely as to be unnatural. His teeth glinted in the moonlight.

The man pulled his hand from a pocket before waggling his fingers in a taunting manner, black leather hugging the muscles of his calves and thighs as he withdrew and pushed himself off the wall. As he advanced towards her, brushing his long-fingered hand down the front of his charcoal-grey Metallica singlet, she whirled and disappeared down the dankly lit alley to her left.

Her sneaker-clad feet pounded the ground, thumping as obnoxiously as her pulse, now roaring in her ears. She stumbled, eyes wide and frantic as her gaze darted over her shoulder and sinister jeers rippled off the brick walls surrounding her. The resounding and haunting quality reminded her of a pack of wolves howling at the moon—predators on the prowl. She urged her legs to move faster—to run faster—rounding another corner into another back street. A tattooed arm with varying patchworked designs grabbed hers, spinning her towards a different darkened pathway, one she wasted no time darting down. Even if her instincts screamed at her that she was going the wrong way. She couldn't hear them, nor process the panicked thoughts, through the billowing cloud of terror that clutched her heart like a vice.

As her feet carried her along the moonlit street, her heart slammed against her ribcage as if to tear itself from the caverns of her chest and she steadied herself rounding the next sharp corner, fingertips digging into the grooves of the brickwork. A soft sob of relief spilled from her lips as she recognised her surroundings. She registered the blinding flash of lightning blearily, ears ringing with the deafening rumble of thunder, as the first drops of rain pattered against her skin. Her pace quickened as she neared the shadowy junction, heart rate spiking at the sight of a towering brunette in the centre of the left alleyway.

His chest was bared through the unbuttoned front of a black denim jacket, ebony-brown locks falling to the middle of his biceps, and a dark tattoo shading his hip and lower abdomen. His imposing presence was haloed by the flickering light of a lamppost. She tore her eyes from him, whirling as the echoing crunch of feet ghosted her ear, and dread curled through her blood. Her hands trembled at her sides, budding hysteria weaving itself up from the tips of her toes to her throat like barbed branches of a rosebush. Two blond males grinned with unsavoury delight as she swung around once more.

The first of the two winked, knocking his shoulder into his sandy blond companion's, who grinned like the Cheshire Cat, arms covered in intricate designs. His white tank top was cropped, revealing more lines of ink across his stomach, shoulders, and collarbone before they disappeared below the waistband of his denim jeans. The enigmatic duo feigned sympathetic smiles as they looked at the woman. The dirty-blond with wild, shoulder-length hair shook his head, mocking her as terror dragged its talons across her chest. She turned ever-so-slowly towards the brunette, who surveyed her with his dark eyes and the barest tilt of his head.

"It's not wise to be out after dark," crooned a honeyed voice from her right.

She longed for the ground to open beneath her and swallow her whole as her eyes traced over an ivory-skinned man with hair as white as snow-capped mountains and eyes as blue as glaciers, longing for death to come swiftly so she could escape his ungodly smirk. He watched her hungrily, the darkness of his aura seeming to bleed out into his clothes, dark as the shadows in which he lurked. His pale brows lifted, prompting her to speak as he surveyed her from over his leather-clad hand and the grey-white smoke of a cigarette. When she didn't speak, he exhaled, tendrils of smoke curling around his diamond-shaped face.

"You never know what lurks in the shadows," he said. His dark chuckle reverberating off the walls, lightning bathing his face as he corrected himself, "You never know *who* lurks in the shadows."

The clattering of a rubbish bin startled her, her head whipping towards the source as the blond duo stepped closer and she subconsciously backed away. Her retreating steps didn't discourage them. Instead, their grins glinted wider and they crept closer. Their movements were all lithe ease, the promise of violence rippling off them like heatwaves as the platinum blond man watched her idly. They circled her like wolves, dragging their fingertips across her jacket-covered arms.

"I … I was looking for my husband," she said, swallowing the anxious lump in her throat and clenching her fists at her sides, hoping to hide their trembling from his uncanny gaze. "He should've been back with my sons by now."

The frigidness of the ivory-skinned man's gaze burned her skin.

"Like I said. It's not wise to wander Celacali at night," he cocked his head, passing his cigarette to the brunette without removing his gaze from her as he seemed to consider her—recognise her. "*You,* of all people, should know that. Shouldn't you?"

"Please …"

The duo drew closer, hands latching around her forearms before she could attempt to flee. The sandy blond with hazel eyes like her own tutted mockingly, drawing closer. Her gaze locked on the brunette's, who exhaled a perfect ring of smoke. The dirty-blond traced the fingers of one hand down her arm, his bracelets skittering, whilst his other clamped around her bicep.

"*Niko,*" warned the brunette.

Niko sighed with exaggerated annoyance. Lifting his hands palm-up to the brunette, a goading smirk upturned the corners of his lips as his cyanic gaze dragged away from his companion and to her.

"It's a little late to beg now. Don't you think?" he said.

"Please! I have two sons." Her voice trembled as she pleaded with the men, desperation clouding her tone as the blond duo shared a look. "I have a family. Please, don't do this!"

"Family or not. *You* walked into the night. Into *our* domain," Platinum Blond barked, ensnaring her within his glacier irises, something resentful and malicious flaring in the dark tinges of his eyes. "I'll admit, it's been quite hard to find … *sustenance* tonight. And you, sweetheart, walked into our domain willingly."

"I didn't *know*—"

"You *didn't know*?" He chuckled without humour, shaking his head whilst he rubbed his stubble-smattered jaw with a gloved hand. "Isn't your last name *Montes*?"

Her eyes widened before she shoved her surprise aside, but the man's lips curved in a smirk that did little to hide the danger behind it, catching her flicker of surprise with keen eyes.

"How?" she whispered.

"How … do I know?" he mocked.

She nodded, words failing her as his leather-clad hand subtly gestured towards her with a swift flick of his wrist, and Niko and his sandy-haired counterpart took a final step. Their hands latched around her arms and waist, trapping her between them. Niko's dirty-blond hair brushed against her shoulders, the taller blond's hands latching around her arms as he pinned her to his chest, and his hazel-eyed companion released her, Platinum's response now forgotten as he skated his fingers along her collarbone and brushed her hair from her throat. She struggled against Niko's grasp, bucking and thrashing wildly in his arms, trying to tamp down the sobs building in her throat.

"It'll all be over in a couple of seconds," Niko urged, his musical voice taking on a soothing edge. "Kade's just a picky eater."

The sandy blond, *Kade,* lifted his fuscous gaze from her collarbone to glare at his counterpart. "I might be *picky,* but at least I'm not messy."

Niko shrugged, tightening his grasp on her forearms when she shoved against his arms, the *tha-thump, tha-thump, tha-thump* of her heartbeat deafening in her eardrums.

"Please ... don't," she pleaded.

Kade paused, holding her stare before his lips pursed and he crouched ever-so-slightly. "It'll only hurt for a second. I promise."

Tha-thump, tha-thump, tha-thump.

Her struggle grew as the plains of Kade's face distorted, the bone structure sharpening and furrowing like something from nightmares and dreams alike. His eyes bled into an eerie shade of white that gradually faded into a golden-yellow, the pupils of his eyes lined by a crimson-red ring. She bucked against Niko's grasp, tugging frantically as her terror-filled pleas were drowned out by the ominous rumbling of thunder. Tears streaked her face, wetting the apple of her cheeks in the same moment Niko tore into her throat. Her eyes screwed shut as her scream rang out across the inky depths of the night sky and Kade moved in, sinking his elongated teeth—*fangs*—into her soft flesh.

As her grip on their clothes slackened, it occurred to her that Celacali was many things and none at all; wrapped together in perfect harmony with chaos and serenity. Effortlessly twined together with life and death.

A duo you either loved or hated.

A duo that blurred within the heart of Celacali; forgotten by those it governed.

Tha-thump, tha ... thump, tha ... thump.

The coastal city was said to be a city for runaways. For the lost who wished to find a place amongst the blinding lights of its popular tourist attractions, some even blamed the siren call of *Illusion Boardwalk* for the title the city upheld. But she knew, just like every local knew, that it wasn't the boardwalk that whispered of something more.

Something dark and sinister.

It was the men—*monsters*—who she'd been foolish enough to assume were myths who lured and herded unsuspecting locals and tourists to their demises. And she, like so many before her, had fallen victim to Celacali at night. Believing she wouldn't meet the same fate as the hundreds of missing person posters plastered upon the boardwalk's noticeboard. This foolish notion brought a fresh onslaught of tears as her heart pulsed sluggishly in her chest and her eyelids grew heavy, her body weight supported by the two men who fed upon her.

Tha ... thump, th ... ump, th ... ump.

As the feeling of her strength waning and ebbing seemed to matter less, Niko shifted his grasp upon her, deftly twining his long fingers in her hair to pull her head back, and bare more of her throat to his deadly ministrations. Her eyelashes fluttered and her vision blurred, and his elongated incisors tore painfully into the middle of her throat. A cry of agony tumbled from her lips, her fingertips digging into the flesh of Kade's arm as her weak struggles floundered in the daze of her blood loss. Niko's grip around her waist tightened, the hand in her hair tugging her head back further. Like he couldn't satisfy himself, even as the blood from his previous incision trickled down her neck and stained the black fabric of her T-shirt.

She knew what Celacali was said to be. Even as that very thing was slowly being drained from her. *Life;* the boardwalk, the music, the food, and the lights, thrilling all who spent a night there beneath the stars. It was the city of dreams, built on the foundations of the life of its tourist attraction, luring everyone into its heart for centuries.

But with life comes death.

And Celacali was the City of the Dead.

PART ONE

Agathokakological (adj);
Composed of both good and evil.

POLICE LINE DO NOT CROSS POLICE LINE DO

CRIME SCENE DO NOT CROSS

CRIME SCENE DO NOT CROSS

CRIME SCENE DO NOT CROSS

CRIME SCENE DO NOT CROSS

ICE LINE DO NO

I.

July 2037
Nyx

"Two local women were found murdered this afternoon in Celacali's northern suburbs, and chief of police, Isaac Silvia, has yet to comment on the ongoing investigation and why renowned detective Azeil Monroe has returned to the city—"

The wind ruffled Nyx's hair through the open window of the car door, tangling loose curls that didn't cling to her sun-warmed skin. The saline breeze filled her nose as she reached forward and abruptly changed the radio station, casting a weary glance towards her father from her peripherals. Leaning back in her seat, she turned her gaze to the abundant flora outside her window.

The drive from Malor to Celacali had been filled with soft, almost indistinct music from the radio and the brief conversations between them, neither daring to mention the ongoing case that'd partially resulted in their move. Or the permanent return for Azeil, who'd been living part-time in Celacali for five years.

She supposed it made sense that conversation came awkwardly. Even her father wasn't sure how to proceed after the days that had followed her parent's divorce— a divorce that'd dragged on for months— and the announcement of a murder case centred in the heart of his hometown. It still seemed selfish to her, to feel grateful that the days of hearing her parents fighting and their hushed arguments drifting up the staircase of their Malor home were gone.

But in the echoing silence that followed, came the swift move to Celacali.

Nyx's father, Azeil Monroe, had assured her that there was plenty to do in Celacali, though he always conveniently steered the conversation away from what exactly it was he'd done whilst living there those twenty-five years ago in his youth, and heavily emphasised that she was to be careful in her exploration of the coastal city. Giving her just enough to understand the appeal of the place, boasting of concerts he'd dragged his younger brother, her Uncle Asher, to. But he left just enough out that, funnily enough, it made Nyx want to explore whatever Celacali had to offer more, despite the risk of being spotlighted by its recent murder cases.

If not for her parent's divorce and the imminent investigation her father had been hired for, Nyx Monroe believed that her mother would've eventually divorced her father anyway. Blinking as if she had thought Azeil would start laughing and reveal that he was joking about where they were moving to, or back to, as the case may be. Alyvia, Nyx's mother, had been livid at first, throwing question after question at Azeil about how he could be so stupid as to move back there after everything that had happened.

But Azeil had brushed it off with a simple, "They're gone, Via. There's nothing to be afraid of in Celacali."

Nyx's older adopted brother had watched from the kitchen table, seemingly unbothered by whatever had gotten their mother so worked up. Although, that might've just been Xander. Not much seemed to faze her brother, but Nyx knew better than to assume that he wasn't thinking about it, knowing that if Xander had mastered one thing in his early thirties, it was a mask of disinterest. And even though he maintained a poker face for most things, Xander doted on his baby sister. He'd promised Nyx he'd come and show her his favourite things in Celacali, a comic bookstore being at the top of his list.

Xander had always been her reliable, dependable older brother. It had been his shoulder she'd cried on when she'd been afraid. It had been him she'd told about the golden-eyed beasts who lurked in the shadows on her way back from school or the late nights spent with her small circle of friends. Or even the nights when eyes seemed to glare back at her from the darkness of the streets. Always waiting. Always watching.

"Dreams," Xander had always urged, brushing a reassuring hand down her back. "They're just dreams, Nyx."

A soft sigh tumbled from her lips as she recalled the look Xander had thrown their mother, filled with reassurance and certainty. He had convinced Alyvia that everything would be fine and that whatever she was so afraid of was twenty-five years gone. Nyx furrowed her brow in mild confusion, wondering what unnerved her mother so much about Celacali. Was it the beasts Nyx swore she saw in her dreams? Or something else? She turned to look at her father, his dark brown hair tangling in the wind, just like hers.

Not much had changed about her father's fashion sense from the photos she'd seen of him in his younger days. Even now, he stuck to his neutral-coloured T-shirts, denim jeans and worn out Converse shoes. The grey crewneck T-shirt he wore was faintly creased, and his denim jeans looked in dire need of ironing. Nyx couldn't remember seeing him in anything else. The only difference was his hair, cut short to the nape of his neck, and the faint scarring along his left earlobe from the ghost of an earring.

"Hey, Dad," she called; the silvery tone of her voice laced with the lining of a tease. "How much longer do I need to be stuck in this car?"

A smile spilled across her father's face as he threw a glance in her direction, his blue-grey eyes straying from the road long enough that she saw him roll his eyes.

"Another ten minutes or so."

She pursed her lips in mock distaste, fighting the urge to smile. The colourful sign that read 'Welcome to Celacali' coming into view just as they rounded the next bend. Nyx watched with poorly concealed excitement as the sign grew closer until it passed by, and she was forced to crane her neck so she could glimpse its wooden backing. Stone tombstones and bouquets were scattered haphazardly beneath the sign, drawing a gasp. Her unease grew at a moss-green sign reading 'City of the Dead' in all white text, thriving narcissi at its base. She couldn't decide what unnerved her more, the tombstones or the green sign. She wondered whether her mother's worry *had* been misplaced after all.

"Just out of general curiosity. Why is there another sign that says, 'City of the Dead' *after* the welcome sign?" she said. The warm leather seats of the car stuck to her skin as she turned away from the open window, "And what is that smell?"

A tangy, salt-filled fragrance twined with something unpleasant, engulfed her senses, making her screw up her nose as her father's deep chuckle filled the car. Azeil shook his head in amusement.

"It's the ocean and the narcissi that grow wild around here, Nyx. That smell is the salt in the air and the flowers," he explained.

"It smells ... weird," she said.

"You'll get used to it, eventually."

Nyx arched an eyebrow doubtfully, the tension in her shoulders easing despite her father successfully leaving the first half of her question unanswered, before she turned back around in her seat. The dark brown, A-line tank top she wore stopped just above her belly button and stuck to her skin in the warmth of the tropical lowlands. She grinned as she recalled the stumped look Xander had given her this morning—his only request being that she needed to grab a jacket so she wouldn't get cold. Her low-cut boyfriend jeans, paired with black Doc Martens, had warranted her mother's approval, who'd quickly pulled Nyx into her arms and told her to be careful.

Nyx remembered the pointed look her mother had thrown her father. She would miss her mother's fiery concern and her flawless instincts, seeming to know what Nyx felt whenever she couldn't voice her thoughts aloud, but she couldn't dispel her excitement of moving from city to city—of something new.

"You know, you never answered my question about the sign," Nyx pointed out, resting her head on the headrest.

Her father turned his attention away from the sweeping bend for a few moments, his gaze tracing Nyx's face as though he were searching for something that would deter him from answering her. He turned his head back towards the road and Nyx waited.

"It's nothing but a bit of a joke. The sign and tombstones were there when Asher, your grandmother, and I moved here in 2012," he said, off-handedly.

Nyx hummed softly in acknowledgement, dragging the coin-like charm of her necklace absentmindedly, her interest piqued as her gaze caught hold of a blinding neon sign down by the water. It was too far away to make out the words but she made a mental note to find out more about it later, even if she had to go down to the shoreline of Celacali herself.

She briefly wondered where exactly they were supposed to be moving to and if it was within the major town of Celacali nearest to the beach, highlighting her lack of knowledge of the city. Nyx knew two things for certain. Firstly, her grandmother, Niamh Monroe, had left the house they were moving to in her will to either Asher or Nyx's father. She also knew that her great-grandfather had left the house to her grandmother before he had died almost twenty years ago. Secondly, she knew for certain that Uncle Asher had clarified that he didn't want the house and had told his brother he'd keep Leo, the dog, and Azeil could have the Woodland Mansion.

As Nyx recalled her father and uncle's antics, she thought of her grandmother's sweet and nurturing nature, the adoration she had used to shower on Nyx and Xander before she had passed away in the earlier months of 2025. Nyx had been seven, but her grandmother's bright smile and cheerful voice remained etched into every childhood memory Nyx had of her. Her great love of books, and the concern etched across her face whenever Nyx vehemently swore she'd seen golden-yellow irises staring back at her from the tree line, and the stories she'd read to Nyx, imparting beliefs of a reader living a thousand lives in the span of one. Though she hadn't understood it at the time, Nyx did now. Whilst her grandmother's two sons had been nothing but a handful from the moment they had moved to Celacali—a fact they both vehemently denied to this day— Grandma Niamh had always kept their best interests at heart.

So, it'd come as no surprise when she'd left everything to her sons. The house she'd inherited and made her own, was given to them with the same open-hearted nature she'd been remembered for. As the never-ending greenery washed over the scenery outside, Nyx supposed she had her grandmother to thank, as her irises flitted from cloud to cloud, for this new opportunity.

This chance at freedom in the city her father immortalised. Or the promise of new beginnings that clung like honey to her tongue, engulfing her mind with enthralling perspectives, and satisfying the deeply shattered shard of her being that seemed to perk up at the name of a city *jokingly* dubbed the 'City of the Dead' as her fingertips brushed the pale scars across her knuckles.

Almost like it found comfort in the sinister and morbid nickname.

* * *

As her boots crunched upon the gravel stones beneath her feet, Nyx marvelled at the house before her. The few bags she'd grabbed from the backseat dug into her shoulders, the slight niggling pain seeming to taunt her whilst she approached the front steps. She fought to hide a faint smile at the metallic *clinking* of her father fumbling with his keys, trying to remember which one would unlock the front door. Nyx's fingertips smoothed over the wooden veranda's solid and intricately carved pillars, admiring the jarrah-wooded house and the veranda that wrapped around much of it.

A small outdoor setting and chairs were covered by a sturdy canvas to her left, taking up the large expanse of decking overlooking Celacali and the Avonsano Ocean, its dark waters sprawling as far as the eye could see before it disappeared along the horizon. Pots, both hanging and not, decorated the veranda with plants that seemed to flourish from the time that Grandma Niamh had passed away and her father had inherited the house. Nyx's grin grew as she thought back to the number of times her father had travelled from Malor to Celacali just to make sure the house was properly maintained whilst he rented a condo within the central suburbs of the city. A defiant *click* of the lock now drew Nyx's attention away from the veranda and back towards the front door.

Her father's eyebrows screwed together as he pushed the door open carefully, as though he was afraid of breaking the beautifully stained-glass panels at its centre. A stale, musty smell greeted them, as well as the fading scent of paint as he held the wooden door open, gesturing with his head for her to go ahead before he followed. Most of the raw-wooded walls had been painted over in a soft, homey cream colour, masking the once subtle grain detail, but the contrast with the sections her grandmother had left unpainted worked well. Old sheets covered the furniture, protecting the TV, indoor couches, tables, chairs, and lamps from the salt-riddled air.

Nyx looked at her father; forehead creased as a question bubbled to the forefront of her mind. "Why did Uncle Asher call this the *Woodland Mansion* when it's clearly not?"

Azeil smiled and a soft laugh spilled from his lips as he grasped the first grey sheet covering the couch and pulled, uncovering a three-seater couch. Then he repeated the process with the coffee table and another couch.

"When we first moved to Celacali, my grandfather lived here and that room over there—" Nyx followed his direction to see a beautifully renovated sunroom that appeared to connect to a pre-existing room. Light grey cloths covered the glass table and metal chairs.

He removed another sheet from the TV, continuing, "Was once his man cave of sorts. My grandfather had a certain ... love of insects."

"Like butterflies, right?" she said.

He chuckled, "More like *dead* insects that he kept in jars or pinned to corkboards. I think *entomology* is the correct word for it."

Nyx stared at him for several moments, blinking as she waited for him to tell her he was joking. But when he merely stared back at her in response, she knew she had the answer to her next question.

"You're telling me my great-grandfather used to collect *bugs* in his spare time? For fun. And *completely*, unironically?" she said.

Her father nodded as he moved to pull off cloths covering lamps, "Pretty much."

"That's … peculiar," she muttered, toying with the straps of the bags across her shoulders.

"That's one word to describe it, but your uncle took one look at that room and declared it the 'Woodland Mansion.' And he's never let me forget it, either."

Nyx noted the way his eyes darted to the sunroom beside her, a nostalgic smile spreading across his face as he walked towards it. Stopping within the doorway with the tips of his shoes at the edge of the threshold before he seemed to force himself to turn back towards her; eyes brewing with memories.

"Bedrooms are upstairs," he uttered, distracted. "The only door on the right is yours."

She nodded, shifting the straps of her bags on her shoulders as she watched her father turn back towards the sunroom, lost in a haze of memory. Nyx turned on her heel, leaving him to it, and crossed the lounge to the wooden staircase. The occasional stair creaked beneath her feet as she trailed her hand across the wooden handrail, glossy like the hardwood floors and stairs. She paused at the top, peering down the sundrenched hallway to her left. The wooden beams that spanned from the precipice of the balustrade to the wall on her left acted as a type of railing that reminded her of a balcony.

The first door on the left side of the hallway was cinched firmly shut, barring her entrance as the door handle rattled loudly in her grasp. With a disgruntled huff—frustrated by the locked door—she continued down the hallway, incandescent light filtering in through the sheer curtains obscuring a medium-sized window. The second door on the left was open, revealing a white-tiled bathroom floor, spotless except for a faint reddish hue to the grouting. A claw-footed bathtub with a showerhead sat at the far end of the room, sleek bath taps almost unnoticeable behind a pane of frosted glass, artfully shrouding half the tub from view. A single sink with glass shelves perched upon silver bracketing beneath its basin, and a toilet occupied the rest of the medium-sized room. She stepped away and continued her investigation.

The pads of her fingers pressed into the cool wood of the door before her, pushing the door open as she entered the deceptively large room. A queen-sized bed sat tucked almost in the corner, two wooden bedside tables perched on either side. An empty wardrobe with sliding wooden doors had been left open, revealing spacious clothing racks and simple, faux oak draws. Sunlight spilled in through two large windows, taking up a wall each, their silver hinges enabling them to swing open and shut.

A faint ticking reached Nyx's ears as she walked further into the room and dropped her bags onto the bare mattress. Her onyx-brown irises looked back at her through the glass front of an analogue clock mounted on the wall. The brief inspection of her room promptly urged her to unzip one of her bags, pulling a light, granite-grey jacket from one bag and, stuffing her arms through the sleeves, she walked back out into the hallway.

The boxes in the U-Haul aren't going anywhere, she reminded herself, hurrying to the wooden staircase. Determination took hold of her as she skipped the last few steps, her boot-clad feet connecting with the hardwood floors with loud *thumps.* Nyx wanted—craved—to see what Celacali offered, and something told her that the neon lights down by the beach would give her answers.

"Hey, Dad," Nyx drawled as she rounded the right baluster of the staircase and walked into the kitchen, her fingertips clinging to the grooves of the door frame.

Her father's head turned away from the open door of the fridge and to where she stood with a pleading smile.

"What exactly is there to do around here?"

Nyx's father eyed a clock on the wall beside the doorway, letting the fridge door swing close with a gentle thud. "You know the Ferris wheel you saw on our way in?"

She nodded, recalling the rounded structure she had seen along the shoreline, and gestured with her hand for him to continue talking.

"That's the famous boardwalk of Celacali," he said.

"Famous, huh?" she jested. "Can I go down to said boardwalk during an ongoing murder investigation, or should I dig my grave for when I inevitably die of curiosity?"

His lips twitched, arms folding over his chest. "Don't you want to unpack first?"

"Not really. It's not *exactly* on the top of my to-do list."

Azeil let out an amused sigh as he shook his head; an almost default response to the vast majority of things Nyx said. "I'll tell you what, if you can get your bike off the trailer without my help, you can go down to the boardwalk. *During* the city's homicide investigation."

"That's all I have to do? There's no catch?" she questioned hesitantly, disbelief marring her face as she waited for the inevitable curfew or warning to come, despite her adulthood.

He gestured to the front door with a carefree wave, fortifying her thoughts, "You're only nineteen for so long, Nyx. Enjoy yourself."

That was easy, Nyx thought, half of her subconsciousness waiting for him to discourage her from exploring for her safety.

"I mean it, Nyx," he said. "The past three months have been rough on both of us, but I don't want that to be the reason you don't get to live your life."

She dipped her head in a curt nod, letting what her father had said sink in. He was right. The past few months before her parent's divorce had been finalised had been rough, filled with a constant back and forth of paperwork, arguments, and tension. Even on the quieter, more peaceful days, well … some had always been worse than others.

"Thanks," she breathed, making for the front door.

"You're old enough to make your own decisions, Night. There's no need to thank me!" he called, following her out into the lounge, "I was joking about making you get your bike off the trailer. I already did it."

"Anything else I should know?" she asked over her shoulder.

He appeared to mull over her question for several seconds, chewing his bottom lip between his teeth before he seemed to settle on one thing. "Be careful."

Nyx arched an eyebrow, glancing towards the faded, red Honda 250 that rested against a pine post by the veranda. "I thought you said there was nothing to be afraid of in Celacali?"

"There isn't, but that doesn't mean it's any less dangerous after dark for a girl by herself. *Especially* with the ongoing murder investigation."

"We both know I can handle myself," she grinned, showcasing her teeth. "You made sure of that."

"Ah, that's right. Celacali should be more worried about *you* after you took such an interest in learning how to punch things, and not the recent murders."

Nyx shrugged, a Cheshire-Cat-like grin spreading across her face. "Hey, it was *your* idea to teach me how to defend myself. It's not my fault that I took a liking to it."

His chuckle filled the house as she stepped through the front door and onto the veranda, calling, "I might not be home when you get back but try to be home by sunrise."

She frowned, a grim smile quirking her lips. "Work?"

He nodded, returning it. "Work."

Nyx traipsed down the small set of stairs, shuffling through her pant pockets in search of her keys as she crossed the short distance to where her bike leant against a pine pole. Her handle grips were cool to the touch as she threw her leg over the seat and started the engine with her foot resting upon the floor, squeezing the clutch twice before she cast a last glance over her shoulder at the lodge-like house. The sun's waning rays bathed the darkly wooded house with a farewell golden glow as she pushed in the choke, spraying gravel and leaving nothing but a trail of dust behind her.

II.

Azeil

The sharp ringing of phones accosted Azeil's eardrums, puncturing the chatter filling the police station as one phone call ended and another one started. Azeil's dark brows furrowed, his silvery gaze raking the room with an air of calm to rival the activity in the building and the nervous energy in his chest. Tucking his key card into the front pocket of his jeans, he manoeuvred his way around the desks and through a pair of swinging doors to the back of the room, glancing over his shoulder to ensure no one recognised him. The bustling life of the central offices quieted as the doors swung shut and his footsteps echoed down the empty corridor, passing conference and interrogation rooms before he rounded a corner and continued down the next, swiping through a locking mechanism slot.

As Azeil pressed his palm flush against the metal door, the morbid thought that he spent more time around the dead than the living flitted through his head, as he entered the morgue. White fluorescent lights bathed the room in a way he always found unsettling. The ghostly yet clinical lighting refracted off the silver surfaces of the evenly spaced mortuary tables in the centre of the room as his footsteps echoed off the concrete floor.

Donovan Carter leant upon a central mortuary table. His slight beach wave curls cut to the nape of his neck, the black ink of his sleeve tattoo peeking out from the cuffs of his forensics jacket, black jean-clad legs crossed over boot-clad feet.

"I see you're busy as always, Donovan," Azeil said, gesturing at the emptiness.

A wide grin spread across Donovan's youthfully square face; the lightness of his blue-grey eyes accentuated beneath the overhead bulbs. He shrugged his broad shoulders, pushing off the table and adjusting his cinerea shirt. "There's nothing quite like being the living dead amid ... the dead," he said.

Azeil cocked his head, eyebrows raising as his lips pursed with uncertain amusement, "That's a bit ... grotesque. Even for you."

"For me? Don't act like you don't think the same thing whenever you walk through that door," Donovan pointed out, a knowing look on his face.

He chose not to answer Donovan, directing his gaze to the mortuary chambers spanning the back wall and the many cabinets, some left open and empty, whilst others remained latched closed, labelled with whoever laid within. Azeil knew from his connections within Celacali and the officials of the city that whatever bodies occupied the police morgue were part of an investigation and, despite how many bodies he'd seen since starting his detective career thirteen years ago, he'd never gotten used to seeing his victim's bodies for the first time. So, whenever he was hired to work on their case and received the briefing file, it was difficult.

He would never forget the cries of agony and desperate pleas, or the tight press of fingertips across his forearms as mothers clutched at his shirts whilst their husbands stood unmoving and disbelieving, gazes locked upon him with their newfound reality. Those pain-filled moments blistered his insides, festering into the flesh beneath his skin until he obtained the unanswered clues left to rot and he had enough evidence to lock the guilty behind bars—never to see the light of day again.

Donovan's gaze weighed heavily on his face as Azeil cleared his throat and looked at the twenty-eight-year-old, his tone implying the jokes were over.

"What do we have, Carter?"

"You already know the basics from the files I sent you; two women, murdered in North Celacali," Donovan explained, straightening and walking towards the mortuary chambers. His fingers brushed the solid handle as he turned to peer over his shoulder, argentine irises appraising. "I hope you're not squeamish."

Azeil's eyebrows furrowed, lips parting as he deadpanned the younger man. Ushering him to open the cabinet with a curt wave of his hand, he approached the silver-doored mortuary fridge as he spoke. "Who do we have?"

A hissing noise filled the room as Donovan pulled the mortuary chamber open, frigid air skating over Azeil's skin. For a moment, he blanched at the body lying there as Donovan dragged the inner drawer out. The shape was wrong. His misgivings turned to horror as Donovan pulled back the white sheet covering the body, revealing a dirty-blonde-haired woman with discoloured skin and mutilated limbs, her right arm cleaved from her shoulder and her left forearm a shredded mass of torn flesh. Azeil swallowed the bitter taste coating his tongue, accepting the latex gloves Donovan offered him. He grasped the woman's chin carefully between his thumb and forefinger before angling her head away from him to bare the macabre wounds marring her throat and shoulders.

The sound of shuffling paper dragged his eyes away from what was left of the dead woman, and up to Donovan, releasing her chin and re-covering her with the sheet.

"Eleanor Hayes. Twenty-three years old. Lacerations to the throat and shoulders. Mutilated and severed arms. Distinct bruising and discolouration over the left bicep. Like her attacker pinned her in place whilst they killed her," stated Donovan, closing the file in his hands and sliding the mortuary tray back into the cabinet. The heavy thud of the drawer door closing filled the room as he continued, "and she's missing copious amounts of blood, possibly from the injuries sustained before her death."

"What's the relation between the two victims?" Azeil questioned, following Donovan as he moved to another mortuary chamber three down from Eleanor, and pulled the cabinet open with the same pressure-releasing hiss as before, recalling the devastated couple who'd hired him.

"I think they were childhood friends," Donovan responded, grasping the handle of the sliding tray before pulling it out and removing the sheet covering the second body. "This is Abigail Dawson. Twenty-two years old. Again, she lost a lot of blood, possibly from the lacerations to her neck and wrists, which seemed to target her major arteries."

Azeil's latex-clad fingers grasped the bleached-blonde's chin between his fingers, angling her head to the right so he could *attempt* to make sense of these two murders. Whilst Eleanor's arms had been severed from her body, Abigail's were intact and discoloured with ugly bruising, as if she'd fought hard. His fingertips released her chin, trailing over the mangled cut across her forehead, the violet bruising to her right temple and eye socket. He lifted his hand from her forehead, curling his fingers into his palm and rising back to his full height, a frown etched into his face, grey eyes troubled.

"Was their blood loss sustained before their deaths? Or were they ..." He hesitated, eyeing the woman as Donovan grasped the mortuary tray and pushed it back into the cabinet. *Hiss. Thud.* "Were they mutilated before they died?"

"It seems like they sustained the blood loss *before* they died, but that it was inevitably a way to keep them on the precipice of death whilst their attacker severed limbs and lacerated vital arteries, keeping them alive for however long it took their hearts to fail from lack of oxygen in the bloodstream." Donovan's gaze lifted from the case file between his hands, surveying Azeil and the notepad he held with analytical interest.

"Seems like?" Azeil arched his brows, prompting elaboration as he tucked the notepad beneath his arm and peeled off the latex gloves.

Donovan shrugged; his expression sheepish, "I haven't had the chance to perform their autopsies, so their exact cause of death is still unknown."

"They're still in rigor mortis, aren't they?"

As Donovan opened his mouth to respond, the mechanical unlatching of the morgue door echoed across the room. Azeil turned his head to see the silver-flecked brown hair of a man who strode towards them with hard-set determination. His white dress shirt, gold plating of his police badge hanging from his neck, black slacks, and dress shoes were all in impeccable condition. The pristine white of his rolled-up sleeves bared silver-white and puckered scarring over his forearms. *Knife wounds,* Azeil reminded himself as he turned towards the chief of police, a man who could ensure his investigating clearance was suspended or revoked.

"They are still within rigor mortis, Monroe," Issac Silvia confirmed before directing his next words to the forensic scientist who doubled as a morgue technician. "I need you to get onto the two women's autopsies as soon as possible, Carter. I can't keep the public updated if I'm not aware of their COD to provide a statement."

Donovan dipped his head in a curt nod, straightening and tucking the case file beneath his armpit. "On it, Chief."

Silvia raised his chin, acknowledging Donovan's compliance before turning back to Azeil with a grim set to his jaw.

"I'm assuming you've been tasked with following leads connected to one of the deceased's parents, Monroe." Silvia's brows arched, daring him to disagree. "I think we have a copycat on our hands."

"I was." Azeil's frown grew, deepening the creases on his forehead as he retrieved his notes from his armpit. "What makes you say that?"

Silvia *thwacked* the file onto the nearest surface, documents sliding out and peeking over its protective edges. "Because it matches *this* case file from 2024." His blue-green irises studied Azeil intently as he continued. "A case *you* were hired for, and your *big break* as a detective."

Azeil lifted his hand to rub his jaw, approaching the table and the case file scattered over its metallic surface as if the contents would bite him. His fingertips brushed the documents, tidying the disarray as he picked it up and flicked through it. A sick sensation cleaved his chest, rankling over his skin like a thousand tiny insects. It reminded him of a time he'd tried to forget, *moments* he wished to erase. Azeil masked his unease behind a well-practised disguise of calm.

Silvia watched him with an air of authority. As if satisfied with whatever he found, he turned and made towards the double doors of the morgue. "Don't do anything I'd have to report to the board, Monroe."

"No, Chief."

"I'd wish you luck, but we both know nothing about this case, or your involvement will be about luck."

"It never is," Azeil murmured, heeding the chief's warning as Silvia offered him a grim smile and disappeared through the swinging doors.

His gaze dropped back to the case file. Chewing his bottom lip, he leaned against a mortuary table and sifted through the documents, scanning the familiar paperwork as though it would give him the answers he sought. Azeil raised his head, looking at Donovan.

"What are you thinking, Monroe?" Donovan asked, eyeing the file.

Azeil sighed as he rubbed his face before he cupped the back of his neck.

"Killers always have a type, don't they?" he mused and Donovan nodded, waiting for him to continue. "And I'm thinking these two women might be the killer's type. They're both blondes, whether it's their natural colour, or dyed, and they're both between the ages of twenty to twenty-five."

"So … our killer has a thing for twenty-year-old blondes?"

"That's one way to put it."

Donovan gestured at the case file, arching a blond brow as he squinted, trying to make out the tiny text. "Was … Sophia Montes a blonde?"

"No, she wasn't," Azeil said, replacing the documents. "That's just one reason the chief's theory is wrong."

"The murders. They don't match like a copycat would, do they?"

Azeil shook his head, confirming Donovan's perception. "The lacerations and severed limbs match Sophia's condition, but the bruising and the harsher, almost methodical way that the killer went about murdering the women are too … rehashed. Plus, the timelines don't match."

"What are you saying?" Donovan questioned.

"It's like the killer waited, perfecting their craft without murdering anyone for thirteen years. And now that they have, they're back to finish what they started."

"Why would they wait thirteen years?"

Azeil pursed his lips, fighting to push the blinding flash of platinum blond hair to the depths of his mind and the crumbling warehouse it dredged up memories of. The stomach-churning flicker of blood-stained teeth distorted into a malignant smirk filling his mind, a wetly rasped chuckle ringing in his eardrums—haunting him with the presence of a past that clung to him like superglue. Despite everything good Azeil had done since that day, he couldn't dispel those memories from the caverns of his mind or the orotund voice that taunted him still.

"Maybe the killer had unfinished business," Azeil offered, trying to shake the echoes of his past as he reminded himself that those ghosts were dead—they couldn't harm him. Just like he'd told Nyx whenever she ran to him with terror in her eyes and begged him to believe that *something* was watching her.

"You think these are … *revenge* murders?" said Donovan in disbelief.

"Revenge festers, unlike any other emotion, eating away at you from the inside out. Until one day something snaps—some crucial piece of us that can't be mended—and the only way you can soothe that bitter pain is with murder."

"Careful, Monroe. It sounds like you know what you're talking about," Donovan teased, lips curling.

Azeil's gaze shuttered, forcing a playful grin across his face as the slight familiarity of his response sent déjà vu coursing through his chest and his instincts bellowed at him to abandon the comradeship he found with Donovan—a kindred soul with a bloodied path and death on his hands. "I'm no murderer, Carter. I'm just someone who spends too much time thinking like a murderer to answer client's questions."

Donovan shrugged, toying with his necklace. "Whatever works, I guess."

As his words hung in the morgue, that orotund voice crooned in Azeil's head. He remembered *why* he'd chosen the path of being a detective, foolishly hoping it'd be enough to wash the stain of his past from his skin—from his memories. Just as Donovan had begged Azeil to vanquish his criminal record so he could pursue a career his sister would have been proud of ... had Donovan not gotten into a fatal car accident that had claimed his sister's life, things might've been very different. Yet Azeil knew Donovan spent his days punished by his sister's memory. Azeil promised he wouldn't be a murderer, that he'd protect innocents from the likes of the men who haunted him.

"But you are *a murderer,"* that malignant drawl said, reminding him of everything he wished to forget. *"... At least, now you are."*

Nothing could erase that inky blackness from his skin. At least, not with Nyx—a blazing star in his night's sky of dark memories—by his side.

III.

Nyx

The sun dropped beneath the depths of Celacali's horizon, plunging the city into the grasp of night's allure. Blue-metal stones crunched beneath the soles of Nyx's boots, the screams of adrenaline-filled enjoyment flitting across the star-flecked sky as she parked between two cars, and the neon-lit sign of *Illusion Boardwalk* beamed in a brilliant arch of cherry-red. She killed the engine as her gaze settled upon the retro lights. Pulling the key from the ignition, she wandered towards the arch of the boardwalk.

Screams of unconcealed excitement rippled past her, her eyes tracking the paths of sugar-hyped kids running between their parent's legs, tugging with sticky hands for attention whenever they spotted a ride or game stall that captured their interest, whether it was the Ferris wheel, the carousel, or a stall that sold show bags. Nyx's lips twitched, side-stepping a boisterous young boy whose attention seemed fixated on the Twirling Teacups. His parents rushed to keep up with the small child that pulled at their interlocked hands.

The neon-red sign of the boardwalk bathed Nyx's skin in an unsettling light as she passed beneath the archway of the entrance and drank in the vibrant atmosphere, exhaling. A store—functioning as a video and music store—caught her eye as she slipped past a group of people and into the quieter shop.

DVDs took up most of the movies available to buy, only seconded by an extensive collection of vinyl and CDs, but upon further inspection, Nyx noted a decent collection of VCR tapes of varying genres. An electric blue sign bathed a rack of rock CDs in its luminescent light, mounted upon the wall behind the cash register that read 'Delilah's Video & Music Store.' And, as her gaze trailed over the nostalgia-imbued store, a young woman with a smattering of freckles and auburn-coloured hair absentmindedly toyed with the cash register from behind the counter. Her eyes lifted from the ancient register to survey the store and its inhabitants for the briefest of moments before her attention dropped to the DVDs and tapes stacked in neat boxes beside her.

Nyx wandered around the small aisles of DVDs, CDs, vinyl, and VCR tapes for several minutes, alternating between running her fingers across the sleeves and plucking whatever caught her eye from off a shelf. As she bent down to pull out a DVD, the bold lettering of 'Horror' hanging above her head from the ceiling, the sudden, gruff barking of a dog startled her, and she dropped the DVD. The plastic cover clattered loudly on the polished concrete floor before she hastily ducked down and tucked the case back onto the shelf. Brushing a stray piece of hair behind her ear, she surveyed the store.

Nyx shook her head as though it would rid her body of the sudden surge of adrenaline, winding her way back through the small aisles, and disappearing through the front door and out onto the bustling boardwalk. The balmy breeze kissed her skin, seeking to smooth over non-existent hackles that rose in the presence of the drunken men leaning heavily upon the opposing storefront, jostling each other as they cat-called any woman that walked past them. An unimpressed glint sparked dangerously, rankling her as their drunken comments met her ears, their whistles and slurs flitting by as Nyx's stride carried her past them and into the first store that caught her eye.

Pleasantly surprised, she appraised the modernised comic bookstore like she knew Xander would, rattling off the name of each comic and its worth, rarity or franchise with ease. An array decorated the tiered tables at the centre of the store, stacked neatly and by what she assumed would be genre or franchise. A string of wire ran from one pillar to another above the tiered table, selected comics cinched by wooden pegs. A grimace contorted Nyx's expression, her uncle's vehement voice echoing distantly in her mind, a loyal comic enthusiast, even now.

Sparing the rusted cash register and the paint-chipped counter a fleeting glance, she made her way through the store and its U-shaped layout as though Xander had dragged her here himself. She wondered—as her gaze skittered over the shelves encasing the wall to the left of the counter, collectables and special editions of figurines and statues situated neatly upon the black-painted wood—if this was the comic store Xander had told her about, and if he'd still delight in showing it to her if he knew she'd already seen it.

She exhaled softly, knowing that Xander would still drag her to the store a million times over if he had the chance. Nyx could picture his animated happiness as he rambled on about the various comics before her, mouse-brown hair falling in his face when he leaned down to pick one up. How he'd hastily brush it away from his face, a sigh of annoyance spilling from his lips, mumbling about wanting to cut it. With that, Nyx took a last, longing look around the store, and slipped back outside. Raking her fingers through her curls in hopes of taming the uncooperative mass, her gaze drinking in everything as though it'd be the last time she'd ever see it.

Food stalls seemed to pop up as the coastal fairground opened, and extended beyond the last few storefronts, giving way to the lively games sector that beckoned locals and tourists alike. The neon lights decorated twirling, swinging, and rocking rides, almost blinding Nyx's gaze as she looked from ride to ride before stopping on the carousel in the middle of the boardwalk, tucked within the heart of the bustling stretch of wood like a beacon haloed by ornate and lavish allure. Her interest was caught by the hand-painted plastic horses that children and adults alike clambered upon, the soft, less harsh white lights casting angelic shadows across the places the light couldn't reach.

Nyx paid none of the passers-by any attention—content to gawk at the beauty and life that filled this rickety arena like a true tourist. Which, she supposed, she was. She couldn't pinpoint, as she halted several metres from the carousel, what exactly held her so entranced. But as she looked around, she couldn't shake an almost nostalgic feeling that engulfed her. The energetic nightlife filled Nyx with something akin to comfort; the kind that came with a good book, or rainy days spent curled up in a plush chair, watching water droplets streak down the windowpanes.

Her chest swelled with content as she soaked in every detail of the wooded boardwalk before tearing her gaze from the shifting passers-by, and beginning anew on her trek past the rides. Wandering past the screams of terror and glee from the rollercoaster on her right, she crossed to the part of the amusement sector barricaded by fire-lit barrels.

Tourists held up their cameras, snapping countless photos of the rides around her, delighted smiles dancing across their faces as they thronged to another ride or stall whilst the teenagers of Celacali shook their heads in amused disinterest; the initial thrill of the boardwalk now dim to them, but still not gone completely.

Nyx chuckled softly as the distant sound of music drifted to her ears, calling to her. She wove between the haphazard thrill seekers in search of the source of the music, which grew louder and louder. Slipping between two barrels alight with orange-yellow firelight, the haphazard people turned into a crowd, seamlessly leaving the rides behind her and entering the arena of a large stage, where cheering, screaming, singing revellers danced to the music filling the night sky. The stars above glinted in the inky depths, a waxing moon shining down upon the boardwalk as the thrill of the night seeped into all who were brave enough to stay out past sundown—when Celacali truly came to life.

Nyx sucked in a lungful of air as she pushed past people, weaving between the shifting crowd, and situating herself at the top of the stands surrounding the stage. Ignoring the glares or sneered comments from those disgruntled by her path, she was unable to care about what perfect strangers thought. The breeze off the ocean caressed her skin, her fingers wrapping around the frigid railing that pressed into the middle of her back, tipping her head back until her hair cascaded down behind her and the moonlight bathed her in its silvery light.

Her curls danced in the sea breeze as she closed her eyes. A wistful smile spread across her face when she straightened and surveyed the crowd below her, the lights of the boardwalk stretching on for roughly three-hundred metres, noting the way people lost their inhibitions to the wind. A faint rumbling of motorcycles flitted past her ears, swept away by the band on stage as she hummed along to the music, the drums, bass and electric guitars interlacing with the lyrics, making it easy to get lost within.

And maybe Nyx never wanted to be found but stay stuck here beneath this star-flecked sky and the ambience of the night.

Within the heart of Celacali.

* * *

Nyx rounded the doorway into the kitchen, a wide grin pulling at the corners of her lips, as the sweet fragrance of pancakes permeated her nose and she pulled out a chair to sit at the wooden table. Her dark stare flickered over scattered pictures, documents and police reports strewn across the surface of the table beside her father, whose gaze trapped hers as her fingertips brushed a glossy photo nearest to her. *Unauthorised documents compiled from his connections,* she thought, gaze darting to his.

"*Nyx,*" her father warned.

She sighed, fingers retreating from the image and files splayed over the table. "I know … *personal boundaries.*" The chill of the morning clung to the seat pressed into Nyx's legs, her black tennis skirt not quite reaching her mid-thigh. Her olive-green, long-sleeved shirt revealed a small triangle of skin from her belly button to the skirt's waistband, with small buttons adjoining the shirt from its triangle cut at the hem to the neckline. "To be fair though, if you didn't want me to see your files. Don't leave them in plain sight."

Azeil's eyebrows screwed together, lowering the document he was reading to ensure his full attention was on Nyx. "That would suggest that I don't *trust* you, Night."

The nickname traipsed over her, reminding her of how she'd garnered it back when her parents had found her sitting on the rooftop of their Malor home, head tipped up to the night sky as her curtains danced in the breeze. The name had stuck like the ties her name held to the Greek Goddess and Nyx's love of the night, a true nyctophile who loved everything about the night's shadows.

"And that's not what I want you to think—because I do trust you—just please ... *try* to curb your curiosity," Azeil said.

Her bare feet brushed against the floor tiles, eyes straying from her father as she plucked a pancake from the stack and doused her plate with maple syrup. "I'll try."

"That's all I ask." A mirthful grin spread over his face, his granite irises sparking with interest. His own curiosity palpable. "So, what'd you think of the boardwalk?"

Nyx's onyx irises flared, "If you can't find me one day, and I seem to just ... *vanish*. I'll be at the boardwalk."

His lips pursed at the mention of her *vanishing,* and she briefly regretted her poor taste of words before her father seamlessly recovered.

"It couldn't have been *that* good," he said.

She nodded, eyes widening as if his assumption was absurd—blasphemous even. "It's just ... different." Frustration pinged in her chest as she struggled to describe the feeling the boardwalk evoked in her. "It gives me a feeling almost like home. Like I'm *supposed* to be here."

Her father's eyebrows rose in surprise, gaze swirling with interest as he adjusted the red and black sleeves of his flannel shirt. Surprise registered in Nyx's gut as she noticed his clean attire, and chose to ignore the tired circles beneath his eyes.

"The boardwalk feels like home?" he prompted as though he didn't think he'd heard her correctly.

"I know it sounds weird, but I can't shake that feeling," she said. "It feels like it's a right in this world of wrongs."

He nodded slowly, accepting her explanation. "Did you find any shops you liked?"

"There was a cool video and music store stocked with *heaps* of classics."

"What is your idea of classics, exactly?"

"Labyrinth, Scream, Flatliners—" Nyx leant forward until her elbows rested upon the table, expression utterly serious as her tone suggested the obviousness of her responses. "*—The Lost Boys.*"

"Are you ever going to let that movie go?"

She furrowed her eyebrows, dropping her gaze to the tabletop and appearing to mull over his question. A wide grin tugged the corners of her mouth upwards when she met her father's gaze. "*Nope.*"

"Really?" Azeil questioned; a fond smile playing across his lips.

"It's a *cult classic,*" she said, her head cocked to the side, considering her father. "And are you really going to *try,* and convince me that those stories of 'golden-eyed beasts' weren't derived from that movie?"

"Not everything is always a story, Nyx. Sometimes they're realities no one wants to believe."

"… *Right.* I don't buy it. They're just stories you tell children to scare them into behaving. Not reality," she stated, unbelieving.

Even as her mind betrayed her with a memory of golden eyes watching her through the high-arched windows from the alleyway between two houses back in Malor. Once she'd tried to follow, to investigate, go looking. But they'd remained as elusive as the shadows, gone like a waking dream you tried to remember. On closer inspection, the window was just that … an empty window. Nothing there. From that point on, she'd tried to dismiss it.

They weren't real, she reminded herself. *They never were.*

"And how do *you* know that?" Azeil challenged, bringing her back to the present as he arched a dark brow.

"Because, just like the Lost Boys, they're not real."

"Whatever you say, Night." He drawled, choosing to change the subject as he continued. "Is there still a comic bookstore?"

Nyx nodded, the nameless comic bookstore entering her mind. The tiered tables, hanging comics and rusted cash register drifted to the forefront of her skull as she tried to recall if she'd seen the store's name or not.

"Yep. I went in there for a little while, looked around and then I left," she said. "I almost bought something from the video store though, so it wasn't a complete loss."

"Almost? Why didn't you?"

She scoffed, recalling the barking that'd startled her enough to drop the DVD. "Some dog started barking and scared the crap out of me."

Nyx's father laughed, picturing her impromptu departure from the video store. "I thought you said you could handle yourself?"

"I can. I just wasn't expecting... barking," she shrugged her shoulders, toying with her fork. "Besides, after that, I went to a concert."

"Sounds like an... eventful night. Would it be worth going down there again tonight?" He paused, a teasing grin on his face. "That's if you want to go down there with your old man."

Nyx raised an eyebrow, a soft smile across her face that rivalled her father's. "Are you sure it's not going to interfere with your bedtime, *old man*?"

His deep laugh resonated within the otherwise empty house, a happy glint that Nyx hadn't seen for a long time revealing itself.

"What do you say, Nyx? Me and you down at the boardwalk for some good, old-fashioned father-daughter bonding?"

"Sounds like a plan," she said.

* * *

The neon kaleidoscope of the boardwalk lights reflected off the glass-windowed storefronts they passed, a beguiled grin plastered across Nyx's face as she continued to side-eye her father, whose gaze darted from storefront to storefront as if he'd never seen it all before.

Azeil paused, his footsteps coming to an abrupt stop beneath the striped awning of the coastal arcade, searching for something that reminded him of the past.

Nyx surveyed her father as he turned slowly towards the bustling amusement sector and took in the games, rides, food stalls and shops of the boardwalk for the first time in his years spent living part-time in the city. The nostalgic look that crept across his face was almost comical, a dark-haired man soaking up the life of Celacali's boardwalk—committing it to his memories. His wistful expression seemed to darken for a few seconds, but Nyx shrugged her shoulders as she craned her neck to peer over the ever-moving passers-by and to the few stores lining several metres of the lively fairground she hadn't ventured to.

"Hey, Dad?" she began, waiting as his attention fell back to her and away from the boardwalk. "I'm going to go see who's performing tonight, okay?"

"Yeah, sure," he uttered offhandedly, gesturing to the arcade behind him with his hands. "We'll meet back here at twelve."

She smiled, finding his distracted tone amusing as she turned and called back over her shoulder. "Don't have too much fun while I'm gone."

His laughter echoed behind her, carried upon the crisp, saline wind as she weaved through the patrons wandering the boardwalk. Jarring herself when she stopped abruptly to peer up at the glowing green sign of the store. The grotesque font reflected in her gaze, a faint frown of bewilderment marring her face as she recalled the comics her uncle had shown her, and the stories inside them—golden-eyed beasts that ruled over a lavish city by murdering its citizens, a popular tale from her childhood.

Nyx stood beneath the glowing green halo for a few more seconds, trying to dredge up the memories at the edges of her mind—the faintest memory of two mousy-brown-haired boys flittering across it. A huff of frustration passed through her teeth when she couldn't pinpoint it before she whirled on her heel and continued down the wooden boardwalk, her tennis skirt brushing against her legs.

Boardwalk-goers of all ages flocked to the coastal fairground beneath the stars. Teenagers lounged with their arms draped over the metal railings of the boardwalk, some passing cigarettes back and forth whilst others scrutinised passers-by with mild interest. Adults were scarcer but still scattered about, throwing disgruntled looks in the direction of shouting teens or those they didn't like the look of. As if the rowdy youth expressing themselves through clothing, art, piercings, and tattoos were the problem of the world. She appreciated that courage—to be whoever they wanted to be without fear.

A buttery scent drifted on the breeze, mingled with the smell of the ocean and fried food stalls of the boardwalk as Nyx wandered over to a small cart selling popcorn. Shuffling through her pockets to pull out a couple of dollar bills. The elderly man behind the counter accepted the money she handed him with a soft smile, passing her a small tub of popcorn before she thanked him and walked away, gaze landing on the carousel.

Angry shouting and the loud scuffling of boots on wood made her tear her gaze away from the strange merry-go-round and towards the railing off to the side of the Ferris wheel. Landing upon a group of Ivory Skulls—a notoriously dangerous and ego-driven gang who believed they *owned* Celacali—shoving against the chests of three young and yet imposing bikers. Their fingers grasped the younger trio's clothes as they scuffled, Nyx craned her neck to see over the small crowd that loitered around the carousel. The fourth biker, a platinum blond with steely irises and a spiky mullet, smiled cruelly down at the dark-haired Ivory Skull who gripped the collar of his black shirt as if he were merely a fly, leaning closer to the dark-haired man, lips curled into a derisive smirk.

The gang of men ceased their scuffling and shoving against the younger bikers, their eyes wide and expressions drenched in mild horror, as if the dark-haired gang member had agitated the wrong snake. Nyx watched on as the man's eyes widened in fear and his tattooed hands released the collar of the platinum blond's shirt. He hurriedly stepped back and away from the other who adjusted his leather gloves, obsidian ink curling around his right wrist and forearm like a scaled serpent. The pale-haired man dusted the front of his shirt, a pleased but frigid smile on his face as his stare-scanned the ever-changing crowd upon the boardwalk.

Dark zeal danced across his three companions' faces, their gazes trailing after the Ivory Skulls as the gang members hurried away from the group of four and disappeared amongst the patrons. Seeming to enjoy the fear they evoked in the men, two of the bikers nudged each other with smiles on their faces. The taller blond with wild, rockstar-like hair traipsed beside his smaller companion, the black mesh of his shirt shifting with his movement. Nyx could see a black-inked cheetah that began at the nape of his neck and crawled across his right shoulder, curling down onto his pectoral where it stopped. His legs were clad in black jeans slit at the knees, leather combat boots, a strange and yet befitting combination that complimented the colourful threaded and leather bracelets around his wrists and piercings.

The smaller blond, whose arms, chest, and abdomen were decorated with patchwork tattoos, pulled his companion into a playful headlock. The hem of his white, cropped T-shirt rose over his abdomen, dangerously low-cut jeans and slightly faded boots shifting with the movement. His sandy blond curls brushed the nape of his neck and a Cheshire Cat-like grin stretched across his face as the taller blond shoved him.

The final biker's dark gaze tracked his tussling companions with a bemused expression, shaking his head at their antics. His ebony-brown hair fell below his shoulders in thick tresses, black denim jacket open, revealing the toned planes of his chest and stomach, illustrated by a wolf that started above his left hip and dipped down to the defined planes of his V-line. His almond skin was displayed proudly for all to see, like the necklace that hung from his neck, the earring that brushed against the left side of his throat, and the bracelets around his wrists. The charms on his jewellery were indistinguishable from where Nyx stood, but she still couldn't help but stare.

She watched the group for several more moments as her eyes trailed after them with startled curiosity, and the three men walked over to four motorcycles staggered in a line beside the railing of the boardwalk. The platinum blond pulled a lighter from the pocket of his jeans, clasping a cigarette before he lowered his head and lit up, inhaling a lungful of smoke in one long, languid moment.

With some effort, Nyx tore her gaze from the group of bikers, forcing herself to turn away, despite the peculiar sense of familiarity ravaging her insides, and to continue in the direction of the stage—her intended destination before she'd grown distracted. Her brows furrowed in annoyance, frustrated by the curiosity that'd upended her path to the concert venue of the coastal fairground, weaving and ducking through the throng of people before she slipped through the fire-lit barrels and climbed to the top of the stand beside the stage, just like before.

Leaning back onto the metal railing, her forearms pressed into the chilled metal whilst she peered down at the people who danced and sang along to the music around her, oblivious to the set of eyes that watched her from beside the Ferris wheel, wisps of white-grey smoke curling around his face.

IV.

Nyx

Guitar riffs and the lulling pulse of drumbeats engulfed Nyx's senses, stealing her breath, and replacing it with something addictive that seeped into her bloodstream—seeking to keep her trapped in the city's siren call. The soles of her shoes met the wooden planks beneath the concert stands, her beach curls dancing in the alkali wind. Nyx wasn't sure how much time had passed since she'd left her father on the boardwalk. The stars above continued to glimmer as she wove and sidestepped the tide of people, making her way to the meeting place.

Disgruntled glances met her as she stopped in front of an old, almost antique, bookstore and peered up at the worn sign. Rust decorated much of the metal signage; its writing stained, illegible, and peeling. The exterior bellowed 'decrepit', and the glass windows were murky and dust-covered, the brickwork of the building was now chipped and weather-beaten but something about the warm, xanthous lighting drew her in. Like that tantalising comfort that came hand in hand with the beauty of entering a fictional world. A soft chime followed Nyx into the store, the ornate door swinging closed behind her on silent hinges.

Bookshelves lined the opposing walls in neat rows, varying genres filling the shelves with their different colours and designs, paperback or hardbacked spines, leather-bound or wax-wrapped pages. A small slice of paradise of words crafted together in stories as riveting and thrilling as their neighbour. The shelves were staggered sporadically, bracketed at their ends by more piles of books, and plush chairs and lounges were tucked into every crevice. Nyx trailed her fingers across the spines of the books as she walked further in, noticing small plants, both hanging and potted placed beside chairs and shelves, or fastened to the arched windows beside the front entrance.

The soothing scent of ink and paper filled Nyx's nostrils and calmed her soul, like aloe vera-scented balm on the reddened skin of sunburn. Her fingers ghosted above the title of a purple-spined book and she pulled it from its shelf, turning it over in her hands so she could glimpse its white cover. The spine, like the bold text upon the cover, was a dark mauve and filled Nyx with a swell of disbelief. *Inkheart* had first been published in 2003, and had later been adapted into a movie in 2009—filling parts of her childhood with silver tongues that whispered fiction into reality and leaving her with the longing to be transported into worlds she'd been cursed to only read about. Over the years, the book had vanished like the magic contained within its pages, becoming as elusive as the author who had written the story. Proving to be harder—almost impossible—to find in the thirty-four years after it'd been published. Still, she wondered if it was pure luck that she'd stumbled upon this store and the book in her hands but, as her gaze found the price upon the cover, she decided luck *was* on her side.

"Find something you like?" a timbred voice asked.

Nyx startled as her head snapped in the voice's direction, the book in her hands almost clattering to the floor. "You scared the crap out of me!"

The curly-haired blond's laughter flickered through the room, stray curls brushing against high cheekbones and framing his oval-shaped face before coming to rest at the nape of his neck. His hazel-brown eyes rippled with mischief—and something told Nyx that the warm, beige-skinned man delighted in causing trouble—appraising her with a small incline of his head that jostled a silver, feather-shaped earring. Nyx's palm pressed against her chest, thundering beneath her hand as her eyebrows came together and her gaze fell upon his intricately drawn tattoos with an undertone of familiarity cusping her mind. A descending hawk—captured mid-flight, like an ancient painting of old sat on his arm. His denim jeans, colourfully threaded bracelets and faded boots made her wonder if his style matched his personality. Bright and somewhat welcoming. A soft grin inched over his face as he watched Nyx study him, as if he was used to such blatant curiosity and interest.

"Sorry about that. I forget how quietly I walk," he said. "Kade Artus, fellow browser," he offered his hand, an air of uncertainty bleeding into his introduction. "I might as well introduce myself after scaring you like that." He chuckled softly whilst she surveyed him, unnerved by his silent appearance. An exhalation of breath passed his lips when she shook her head, a mirth-filled grin brightening her face as her gaze lingered on the silver hoop piercing his left eyebrow.

"Don't worry about it," she said, brushing his apology off. "I'm Nyx, Nyx Monroe. You might as well know the name of the person you scared."

"Monroe?" Kade questioned—rolling her last name over his tongue as his almond-shaped eyes narrowed with interest, the silver of his hoop piercing catching the light. "Like the famous detective of Celacali?"

"Exactly like that one," she said tersely.

His eyebrows knitted, eyes trailing across her face as he noted the curt edge to her tone, and curiosity seeped into his hazel irises.

"Are you new to Celacali? Because I don't think I've ... *seen* you here before."

Nyx eyed him warily, weighing up whether it was safe to tell him when she'd moved here. His brow quivered, noting the way she hesitated. His eyes seemed to lighten with understanding as he waited patiently for her response—*if* she decided to answer.

"I moved here a few days ago," she offered vaguely, noticing the subtle shift of his weight from one foot to the other.

Kade nodded, accepting her answer before he gestured to the book in her hand. "Are you going to buy that?"

She glanced down at the book, weighing it in her palm like a pair of scales. "Inkheart's ... *elusive*. I'd have to be a fool to let the first copy I've come across slip through my fingers."

Kade shifted his weight and cocked his head like a bird, seeming to consider her in a new light. "Something tells me that you're anything but a fool, Nyx."

Nyx narrowed her eyes suspiciously at him as his statement bordered on something else. "What makes you say that?"

He gestured to the book again, a surety taking hold of his entire posture as a smug smirk curled his lips. "Judging by the way you're holding onto that book, I'd say you know *exactly* what would happen if you put it back on the shelf."

She eyed him with partially feigned distrust, wary as her father's warnings echoed in her head. "And when did you become a book expert?"

He shrugged, lifting a hand to toy with the earring in his left ear. "I'm not, but one of my friends is a sucker for *elusive* books."

"*You* have friends? I thought you sneak up on girls in bookstores for fun."

"I'll admit that it's a habit I'm having a hard time breaking," he replied jokingly.

Nyx rolled her eyes, fighting to stop the grin threatening to creep across her face. Turning her back to Kade, she wound her way through the shelves of the store and to the front desk, where a cash register perched atop the mahogany surface.

A bored cashier lifted her head, her falsely pleasant smile stretching her mouth when she saw him, "Hi, Kade."

Kade paused at Nyx's right shoulder, lazily dragging his gaze over the cashier and nodding briefly before looking at Nyx for a long moment, his gaze lingering. Then, as if deciding on something, he grinned, continued past her and exited out the front door.

The cashier took the book from Nyx's hand with slanted eyes, bringing it up on the till before snatching the twenty dollars Nyx passed her. As Nyx picked the book back up off the counter—plastering a sickly-sweet smile over her face—she thanked the disgruntled woman and strode to the door.

Kade pushed himself off the front of an empty storefront when Nyx walked outside, grinning. "How much of Celacali have you seen, *new girl*?" he asked, drifting to her side.

She squinted, mentally cringing at the softness of her drawn-out reply, "The boardwalk?"

His eyebrows rose as if Nyx's answer surprised him, eyes brimming with mischievous delight as his arm draped over her shoulders. "What would you say about a personal tour of Celacali?"

"From you?"

"Who else, love?"

Her eyebrows rose, peering up at him, his height pipping hers by a couple of inches. "Pet names already? Careful, Kade."

His hazel irises glinted; perfect crescents embedding the soft flesh of his cheeks. "What do you say, *angel*? Game enough for a little night tour?"

"I probably shouldn't, blondie." She cautioned, worrying her lip between her teeth.

"Because of the murders?"

She shrugged as they wove through the bustling boardwalk, tipping her head back to look into his eyes, admiring the Romanesque planes of his face. "It's not exactly an … enticing incentive, to disappear somewhere with a perfect stranger."

He whirled to face her, clasping his hands over her shoulders, the tiny, silver bird earrings in the helix of his right ear glinted, drawing her gaze from his face for a moment as his hawk-like stare searched her eyes.

"What if I can prove that I'm *not* the killer?"

Nyx frowned. "You want to … prove that you're … not the murderer?"

"Exactly," Kade replied, grinning from ear to ear like a dog praised for doing something good.

"And how are you going to do that?"

He opened his mouth, frowning as he shut it and rubbed his jaw. "I … don't know."

"Let's just, for argument's sake, assume that we're both the murderer," she said.

"You," he gestured to her with a lazy flick of his wrist, "want me to believe that you're a murderer?"

"Everyone's capable of murder."

Kade shook his head, a laugh spilling from his lips as his head tipped back and he pulled Nyx back into his side. "Touché, angel. Touché."

Passers-by eyed him warily, glancing out of the corners of their eyes whilst others pulled their children to their sides, unease in their gazes. Nyx's brows pinched together as confusion flickered within her—Kade narrowed his eyes at those brave enough to utter insults directly to his face.

"Somewhat of a celebrity, are we?" she asked.

He looked down at her, those hazel eyes warm and inviting, unlike the narrowed and cold stare he'd thrown the passers-by. "More like a trouble magnet."

Nyx nodded, accepting what he said without surprise—even if his airily uttered response should've discouraged her. But the slight crookedness of his nose seemed to cement his answer like he'd been in one too many fights over the years. Kade's grin slinked back over his face, his arm strong around her shoulders as he led her through the throng of people. His sepia gaze scanned the surrounding patrons, searching for something as he seemed to thrum with something akin to pride. Like a hawk preening its feathers after a successful hunt. She frowned as she followed his gaze towards the Ferris wheel; the ride was ablaze with shades of greens, yellows, blues, purples, and pinks as people eagerly lined up in front of the ride. Kade manoeuvred them, cutting through the line of queuing people—his arm never leaving her shoulder—and beyond.

And, like Moses and the Red Sea, the boardwalk-goers parted to let Kade through. Nyx's brown-eyed stare landed upon four familiar bikes—vacant of their riders—parked beside the Ferris wheel and the steps that led down to the beach.

"You're one of *those* guys?" she said.

"What?" Kade breathed out, confusion etched in his silvery voice.

"One of the guys stirring up the Ivory Skulls earlier, near the Ferris wheel," Nyx clarified, recalling the quartet and the rowdy tussle earlier that night between the notorious gang members her father had warned her about.

Kade's stride slowed, eyebrows raised as he glanced down at Nyx quickly, and a crease carved his forehead. "You saw that?"

"I saw two guys mucking around after they'd picked a fight. The smaller one, which I assume was you, had the taller one in a headlock," she explained, turning her head back to the motorcycles and their riders, who now lounged against the metal railing, staring out across the shoreline and to the horizon.

Kade threw her an unreadable look and led her to the trio of bikers—his companions. He stooped down beside her ear like he was telling her a well-kept secret, "The element of surprise gets Niko every time." He shook his head, biting back a smug grin, "And between me and you, we ended that *fight* before it even began."

"Who's Niko?" Nyx said.

"The taller guy in the headlock and the one on that bike," he said, pointing towards the motorbike nearest to the steps.

The taller man's Atlantic-blue gaze locked on their approaching forms as he turned from the rolling waves along Celacali's shoreline and a slow grin crawled across his square face. His wild, dirty-blond hair was chopped at the top and fell to his shoulders in a mullet, his black mesh-like shirt rode up to his belly button as he ambled over to them; his stride lithe. He stopped several paces from her, restlessly tapping his fingers against black-clad thighs, peering down at her with open interest—excitement akin to a puppy rippling off him in waves.

"Who's this, Kade?" Niko drawled, his voice musical and husky.

Kade glanced down at Nyx before lifting his gaze to Niko, "This is Nyx."

Niko's gaze lit up as he wrapped an arm around her shoulders, knocking Kade's arm off, and leading Nyx towards their motorbikes and the remaining nameless bikers, she found his confidence enthralling.

"Hello Nyx, I'm Niko," he drawled languidly. "And that over there is Kotori," he said, pointing to the dark-haired biker with a black-metal lip ring in the shadows.

Kade tutted, a sound spurred with mock displeasure before a feigned glare hardened Niko's brow as he peered over Nyx's head to his friend.

"Nyx!"

Nyx turned towards the exclamation of her name, searching the boardwalk for the dark-haired head of her father; his voice recognisable amongst the chattering and shouting. Her eyes widened, realising the time as she slipped from Niko's grasp—the tall blond frowning with confusion.

"I'm sorry, I've got to go," Nyx said, an apologetic grin extending across her face.

She found her father waiting patiently beside the arcade entrance at the edge of the hundred metre or so stretch of the retail sector. His granite gaze trained upon Niko and Kade with narrowed, suspicious eyes.

"Do you have to?" Niko whined, pouting.

Nyx smiled softly, "I do, but how about we do this tomorrow night?"

The pout disappeared in a flash, perking up like a watered flower and Kade grinned as the two shoved each other.

"See you tomorrow night, angel."

"Where should I meet you?" Nyx said.

A cheeky grin curled Niko's lips, his husky shout carrying over the bustle of the boardwalk. "We'll find you, *chica*."

And, though his words had been playfully uttered, she couldn't shake the ominous feeling that clung to her skin like mist.

The deafening rumble of motorbike engines drew her attention from her father as she wandered to his waiting figure and he met her halfway.

"Who are they?" he asked.

Niko, Kade, and Kotori disappeared down the stairs of the boardwalk, their whoops of joy echoing in the night. As they passed, the nameless biker lingered, dragging an icy stare over her father with the prowess of a predator sizing up its prey before his eyes slid to Nyx. He revved the bike before he disengaged his kickstand and followed his friends, his lights dimming along the shoreline.

"Nobody to worry about."

V.

Nyx

Clouds obscured the inky depths of the sky, stealing the softly, twinkling stars from sight. The harshness of the boardwalk lights lightened the crisp whiteness of Nyx's shoes and the dress shirt she'd commandeered as a makeshift jacket, the warmth of the night brushing against her stomach like a gentle caress. Her black, cropped tank top contrasted with her honey-toned skin, the fabric of her baggy, ripped skater jeans brushing against her knees.

A soft huff of annoyance slipped past her lips as she brushed an offending fallen curl behind her ear, eyes darting from person to person. The salt-riddled breeze carried the heady, floral perfume of the native narcissi and something else—something foul. A dank, almost dead smell like the rotten underside of a fallen apple.

Footsteps echoed off the wooden planks, drawing Nyx's attention away from the passers-by and to the approaching dirty-blond-haired biker, weaving through the people on the boardwalk with feline ease. She hadn't noticed before but, unlike Kade, Niko's stride was filled with boundless energy that resonated off him in waves. His bright, cheeky grin and playful, Atlantic-blue eyes dared you to not smile in his presence—like ambrosia that plunged delight and life into your bloodstream. Nyx's eyebrows raised as he came closer, his black jeans slit along the knees and black mesh shirt unchanged from the night before. A charcoal-black suit jacket embellished with gold-bronzed steampunk charms and chains was draped over his shoulders. Niko peered down at Nyx, his chiselled features riddled with mirth, fingers twitching at his sides like he was fighting the urge to fidget. His excitement skittered off him like lightning striking the earth—powerful. His silver dagger earring glinted in the neon lights, swinging from his left ear. She noticed he was taller than her and his companions by at least an inch or two, the five-foot-nine blond reminded her of a restless golden retriever as he fought the urge to rock on the balls of his feet.

"You know, you remind me of Paul from The Lost Boys," she mused, tilting her head to the side. There was something else about him she couldn't put her finger on. A strange sensation of … memory tugged at her, trying to lead her somewhere. Gone.

Niko glanced down at himself, blond brows furrowing as though he couldn't make sense of her words. "I … remind you of a *vampire* from an eighties movie?"

"You've heard of it?"

He scoffed, shaking his head as his lips tugged into a cheeky grin. "It might surprise you … but I don't live under a rock. Of course, I've heard of it."

"Right," Nyx drawled, narrowing her eyes in mock disbelief. "When you said you'd find me, I didn't think it would be this fast."

Niko's grin seemed to grow as he draped his arm across her shoulders and Nyx found she liked his bold advances, beginning to lead her towards the Ferris wheel—their unofficial meeting spot.

"You made it quite easy, *chica*." Niko glanced down at her, grinning, before returning his attention to the people on the boardwalk. "Easy enough that you took the fun out of finding you," he finished playfully.

Nyx shook her head, lips pulled up into a soft grin as Niko lead her through the ever-busy boardwalk. Stares, like the ones directed at

Kade, were thrown at Niko. And in their silent wake came whispers and taunts. Nyx peered up at Niko from beneath her lashes, mind turning with a multitude of questions—like who was older, Niko or Kade? Why did the locals vocalise their disgust and simultaneously veer away from him? She assumed, the longer she stared at him, that Niko was the youngest of the two, purely because of his personality, but her intuition whispered that he was the oldest.

"So, Niko, how long have you lived in Celacali?" she asked, pace never faltering. Niko's cyanic gaze darted to her for a few seconds, as if her interest was unusual to him, and they slipped past the ever-growing line of the carousel.

"I'm just one of the many runaways of Celacali. I've been here for years ..." he trailed off, snickering like something about his reply was amusing. "How about you, new girl? You couldn't have been here long if Kade offered you a tour of Celacali."

"I haven't," she replied honestly. "I moved here three days ago; this is my third night on the boardwalk."

"And your father isn't concerned that you spend your nights here?" Niko queried, the Ferris wheel looming above their heads, as he ignored the people that pushed past them with little thought.

"No more than any other parent would be."

"Even with the ongoing murders?"

"As bad as it sounds, our lives can't stop because others have ended," Nyx stated, recalling her father's similarly phrased urgings.

Niko nodded slowly, surveying her carefully as though he was letting the pieces of her response sink in. And, with carefree ease, his Atlantic-blue gaze left hers and lit up when his stare fell upon his companions beside the Ferris wheel. His pace quickened and his long-fingered hand clasped hers, leading Nyx through the line beneath the Ferris wheel, ignoring the murmurs of disapproval. Nyx wondered—as Kade's beaming face broke through the chattering crowd—if she should be following Niko so blindly or if, in her pursuit of finding herself, she'd latched upon the first thing that seemed to cinch with every unspoken desire she possessed. Her unsurety irked her, poking at the depths of her being that longed to throw her cautions to the wind as she squared her shoulders beneath Kotori's, the nameless biker's and Kade's stares as he scrambled off his bike and he traipsed over to the approaching duo.

"Nyx!" Kade exclaimed, dislodging Niko's hand from Nyx's, and pulling her into a friendly hug. "I was worried Niko wouldn't find you."

Nyx frowned at Kade, returning his hug somewhat awkwardly, briefly noticing the familiarity of his clothes. "Why wouldn't he?" And, like it was an afterthought. "You're very ... touch-oriented, you know that, right?"

Kade pulled away with a soft smile, rubbing his palm against the nape of his neck. "I do. I've always been like that," he explained, rushing his words in a way that made Nyx grin, almost like he couldn't get the explanation out fast enough. "Niko has a *slight* tendency to get distracted."

"I'm not *that* bad," Niko muttered, his brows screwing together, gaze narrowed in mild annoyance.

Kade chuckled, patting Niko's shoulder. "You're not, but you always get *so* wound up."

Niko scoffed and the pair laughed, reminding Nyx of siblings who revelled in the other's annoyance and frustration. Kade's laughter rang out across the cloud-plunged sky as he fluidly moved out of Niko's reach. He grinned from ear to ear and traipsed towards her, slinking around Niko, and lazily slinging his arm across Nyx's shoulder before he continued leading her to the intimidating duo lounging astride their bikes.

"Are you coming, Niko?" Kade called out over his shoulder, grinning wickedly when Niko's mumbled insult reached his ears.

Niko caught up to the duo in a few strides, pausing beside Kade, who halted in front of their bikes and the two bikers who analysed the people on the boardwalk with frigid interest—like they were storing anything and everything they noticed for later. The two men eyed the two blonds, glancing between Niko and Kade before their gazes drifted to Nyx—noting every shift of movement she made without moving from their places.

Kade breathed out sharply, frustrated by his silent and imposing companions before he glanced at Nyx and introduced the platinum blond biker. "Nyx, meet Orion," he said before gesturing to the dark-haired man. "You've already been introduced to Kotori."

Nyx found herself reluctant to break the imposing duos' gazes as she appraised them and noticed the subtle, but still familiar, changes to their clothes. And now that she was closer to them, her gaze trailed over the intricate serpent that curled around a cross hanging from Orion's left ear, his ivory skin contrasting unnervingly with the obsidian trench coat and the cigarette tucked behind his right ear, before she turned to Kotori.

The brunette's dark gaze studied her intently. Unlike the previous night, Kotori brandished a fearsome wolf etched into his skin, peering down at her through his ebony eyebrows, the black-metal of his lip ring glinting in the light, his ring-clad hands draped leisurely over his handlebars, muscular thighs sinfully bracketing either side of his stripped-down motorcycle in a way that spiked her heartrate.

Kade's lips curled into a mischievous smirk as he eyed the two and Nyx glanced towards him, her brows arching with confusion as he continued.

"Or, if it's easier, the blond is Orion and the brunette is Kotori," Kade's voice lowered conspiratorially. "The *kill them with silence* duo."

Niko's choked laughter rippled in Nyx's ear, and she cast a wary glance at Orion and Kotori, grimacing as the pair levelled Kade with simmering stares. A muscle in Orion's jaw twitched, his almond-shaped eyes narrowing at Niko, who staunched his laughter and peered up at the Ferris wheel.

"You've done it this time," Niko muttered, as he meandered over to his bike.

Nyx wanted to follow him if only to hide behind his broad back. "Something tells me you should be a little less smug, Kade."

"And why is that?" Kade said.

Nyx's eyes widened, wondering if he had lost his mind or merely had a death wish. "Do you want my answer?"

"Why not? What's the worst that could happen?" he questioned airily, hazel eyes locked on his companions.

"For starters, and I might be wrong," she cautioned. "It *might* be because they look like they want to murder you."

"Anything else, angel?"

Nyx blinked once. Twice. Stunned by his offhandedness. "I don't know about you, but I'm not sure *killing* someone with silence is a bad thing."

"But—"

Nyx sighed, rubbing her face. "There's worse ways to go than silently, trust me."

"Are you threatening me?" He teased, grinning a tantalising grin like the thought amused him.

"I will hit you if you don't wipe that grin off your face," she said.

Niko tipped his head back, his husky laughter breaking through the bustling boardwalk as Kade stared down at Nyx with surprise—whether, at her warning or the unwavering edge to her tone, she didn't know. A deep, diverted laugh rumbled from Kotori's bare chest, his umber gaze glinting with satisfaction at Kade's expense. His thick, unbound hair fell down his back as the neon lights of the boardwalk glinted off the silver crescent moon by his left ear.

"*Silently* or not. I *will* smack you upside your head for that comment," Kotori assured, smiling tauntingly at Kade, dwarfing Kade's five-foot-eight frame. As the dark-haired biker strode towards Kade and draped his arm across his shoulders with a wolfish grin, Nyx crept silently to Niko's side—safely outside Kade's spotlight.

Orion's upper lip twitched. He sported a spiky mullet, something Nyx silently applauded him for. It was definitely a look to remember. And decked out in all black from his boots, pants, T-shirt, and trench coat—he radiated an air of intimidation. A dark aura that demanded her attention, whether it was out of fear or respect, she didn't know but she suspected he'd be smug about it, regardless.

"For the runt of the litter. You'd think goading me wouldn't have crossed your mind," Orion drawled from his bike.

"I'm not the *runt,*" Kade retorted, ducking out from beneath Kotori's arm.

Orion hummed mockingly, quirking his brow, daring Kade to disagree with him. Niko's eyes glinted with mischief, watching as Kade sidestepped Kotori and came to Nyx's side. He reached for Nyx's hand and led her to his bike, side-eyeing Orion, and Kotori.

The weight of someone's gaze nestled into her back as she neared his bike and she turned, searching the crowded boardwalk, a frown embedded along her forehead. Her eyes snared upon the grotesque sign and pair of eyes that watched her from the doorway of the comic store, and she realised that she recognised the mouse-brown-haired twins. *Tobias and Alexander,* she reminded herself—the twins she'd grown up with.

They peered at the four bikers sitting astride their bikes. The shorter, coffee-eyed twin's gaze studied Nyx intently—almost like he recognised her but couldn't believe it.

"Problem, Nyx?" Orion questioned, his steely gaze skittering to the twins.

Nyx peered back over her shoulder, shaking her head quickly as she glanced back to where the twins stood in the open doorway. "No. I just … know them."

Orion frowned. "How do *you* know the Montes'?"

"My dad and uncle used to live here."

Orion's eyebrows arched—the barest indication that she'd captured his interest—before he schooled his face and leant forward, resting his forearms against the handlebars of his bike. "What did you say your last name was?"

Nyx turned and accepted the hand Kade offered her, assisting her onto the back of his bike—the movement smoother than if she'd done it without his shoulder as leverage. Nyx craned her neck to see over Kade's shoulder, her thighs pressing against Kade's hips when she met Orion's eyes.

"I didn't," she smiled softly from behind Kade's shoulder, teeth gleaming. "And I'm sure you'll forgive me if I don't tell you, what with the murders and all."

Niko let out a low whistle, "Careful, Nyx. 'Rion doesn't like evasion."

From the corner of her eye, Nyx saw the others disengaging their kickstands, engines rumbling to life.

Kade bit his bottom lip, trying to hide his grin. His amber eyes brimming with devilry as he started his bike engine, and his voice reached her ears over its thunderous rumble. "Unless, of course, it's *him* evading the questions."

Orion shook his head, his cold, irked chuckle carried over the sound of his bike's engine as he took off down the concrete stairs, disappearing along the shoreline of Celacali in a blur of sand and blinding headlights.

Kotori turned to Nyx, shaking his head with that same amused grin. "You're brave for such a small *krijger*."

"You speak Dutch?" Nyx blurted, eyes widening as she recognised the language she'd studied and become fluent in after she'd learnt Xander was Dutch. Her teenage years spent with a private tutor had paid off, even if most nights coming home she'd felt like she was being watched—being followed—the entire two-block walk home.

A soft, almost unnoticeable smile lifted the corners of his mouth. "Amongst others," Kotori replied, sparing Nyx a last considering look before he took off down the stairs and onto the beach.

Niko waggled his eyebrows excitedly, revving the engine of his bike once. Kade chuckled, twisting the throttle, revving the engine until a loud rumble filled her ears and she almost missed his mischievous warning. "Hold on tight, *angel*."

The high-pitched whine of throttled motors barked, coughed and then chuckled, disappearing along the shoreline of Celacali in a blur of sand and blinding headlights.

Barrels of leucous firelight spotted the shoreline, dotting the sand with dancing shadows that rippled over Niko's broad features as he sidled up beside Kade's bike and winked cheekily. Nyx craned her neck to peer over Kade's shoulder, tracking Niko as he recklessly wove around the fire-lit barrels, his howls of delight left to ghost the night sky. In one moment, Nyx glimpsed the wooden beams of a pier, and in the next, she buried her face in the white fabric of Kade's shirt to avoid the gritty dust cloying in the air.

Kotori disappeared into the looming tree line branching across the beach. Nyx's curls whipped around behind her, tangling as Niko followed him and they steadily approached the dense forest. Adrenaline sparked its way up her chest, the bike headlights their only guidance, as they wove their way through the forest. Her grasp tightened around Kade's waist, fingertips clutching his T-shirt when he swerved to avoid a fallen tree branch and then smoothly righted himself. Like he'd known it'd been there all along.

The breeze grew colder the deeper they drove; the scent of salt and narcissi filling the air and their lungs. A faint brush of sea spray misted Nyx's skin, pairing with the rumbling of nearby waves, sooty clouds coating the sky in a never-ending blanket of darkness. Kotori and Niko's lights flickered in and out of sight as they manoeuvred their way through the trees with ease, avoiding rocks, bushes and fallen branches with an air of practised calm. He glanced back over his shoulder, dimples nestled in his cheeks, before he turned his head and disappeared over the crest of a small sloping hill, eyes dancing with delight.

Panic seized Nyx's heart when the rocker-like blond vanished from her sight, worry lashing her gut as the crisp oceanic scent grew stronger. The crashing of waves was deafening, like thunder ominously rolling through the clouds. Kade chuckled to himself; the vibrations rippling from his chest and into her own. As he sped up with a quick twist of his wrist, and Kotori vanished over the hill, Nyx's grasp tightened, her heart jolting in her chest as they cleared the hill with a small, easy jump.

Niko's amused grin remained etched into his face as he and Kotori waited, lounging astride their bikes, wind ruffling their hair.

Nyx's stomach rolled with unease, the crashing of waves now thunderous in her ears as her gaze skittered several metres away from Kotori and Niko to where the earth disappeared abruptly. Kade swiftly pulled up beside his companions, quickly killing the engine as he watched Nyx stare down at the impassable drop. She tore her eyes from the edge of the cliff face and frowned as she studied a lone bike, vacant of its rider.

Niko all but pranced to where Nyx sat, helping her off the back of Kade's bike and across the rocky terrain until they reached a set of old, weather-beaten stairs that clung to the cliff face. Her grip tightened then, clutching Niko's hand as he dutifully led her down the rickety stairs. The wooden staircase groaned and creaked beneath her feet, the faint sway of the steps plunging terror into her heart. And, like he could sense her distress, Niko's hand squeezed Nyx's, his thumb smoothing over her hand as he glanced down at her with a sense of surety in his eyes that she was grateful for. Kotori and Kade followed behind, talking amongst themselves in voices too low for Nyx to hear over the crashing of the waves.

Anxiety crept steadily into her veins when Niko let go of her hand and slinked through a gap in the rock face. Nyx's senses kicked into overdrive; one half of her mind screamed at her to run whilst the other urged her to stay. She hesitated, gaze narrowed upon the gap. Kotori brushed past her shoulder, sparing her an encouraging look over his shoulder before he disappeared into the hole.

Kade's arm brushed Nyx's shoulder as he rounded her and paused beside the entrance, leaning his shoulder into the rocks. "Are you coming?"

Nyx paused, eyeing the cliff face with unease whilst she contemplated turning around and walking back ... through the forest ... to the boardwalk? That was miles away, who was she kidding?

Kade waited for her answer, patient as though he had all the time in the world. She threw a lingering look up the wooden stairs behind her, the crashing of the waves against the cliff face filling her ears as she breathed in deeply.

"Lead the way," Nyx breathed out with as much courage as she could muster.

Kade's eyebrows rose, doubt seeping into his hazel irises. "Are you *sure*? Because I *can* take you back to the boardwalk if you're uncomfortable."

"You'd take me back to the boardwalk? Just like that?" Nyx asked, clicking her fingers together as though to emphasise.

"You've only got to say the words, Nyx, and I'll be more than happy to walk you back up those stairs and take you back to the boardwalk."

"Just like that?"

He nodded his head, a soft smile across his boyish features. "Just like that." He paused, gnawing at the pad of his thumb as his eyes studied Nyx intently before he lowered his hand. "I promise you we'll never hurt you, not now or even in the future."

Her brows furrowed at his strange choice of words.

Kade waited, appraising her and the hesitation that cloyed thickly in the air like it coated her tongue, disarming and conniving.

With a swift dismissive shake of her head and a deep inhale, Nyx knew, somehow, that he meant what he said, and that soothed the anxiety clawing over her ribcage.

You shouldn't be doing this, she thought; her gaze flickering to Kade's. *But what if I regret* not *doing this?* she answered herself, challenging her subconsciousness.

Deep down, Nyx knew that the four men *could* be the killers her father's case stemmed from, but some deeply warped and shattered piece of her didn't care if they were—refusing to shy away from the dangers of the unknown. Not again.

Moonlit blue-metal stones and splatters of blood.

She trailed behind Kade when he turned and slipped through a sizeable gap in the rock face. Unlike him, she didn't look back.

Dank darkness engulfed her senses when she followed him into the cave, squinting in the darkened tunnel, fingers skittering over the coarse wall. Small stones skittered across the floor, echoing through the dimly lit tunnel as Nyx's shoes sent them tumbling over the sand-smattered ground. She could make out the outline of a wooden door and Kade's silhouette in the darkness as he traipsed over to her and clasped her hand in his, enticing an uncharacteristic skip of her heart, leading her closer to the faint light illuminating the end of the tunnel and the voices, music, and laughter rippling off the rough walls. Her eyes widened in pleasant surprise, a pang of bewilderment spreading through her chest as the tunnel opened into a large, spaciously lit living space.

Nyx gasped, delighted by the external illusion of the cave and the decrepit and unwelcoming entrance that contrasted the lavish room before her. Kade's grasp tightened on her hand as he carefully led her down a set of sloping marble stairs, her eyes roved, greedily soaking in the Victorian-styled cave, spliced with something ancient and yet modern. Like an ancient temple of Greece that had been rebuilt within the crevices and fissures of the cave, tying with the askew chandelier hanging from the ceiling and its ornately designed crystals that refracted the moonlight from the scattered holes in the ceiling.

Nyx marvelled at the firelight illuminating the cave walls, its reddish-orange flames licking the metal eagerly. Kade gently released her hand and wandered across the illusionist-like hideaway. A large map sprawled across the rock face, cities and towns depicted in a dialect she didn't understand, the edges of a vast empire frayed and yellowing. Varying trinkets scattered the cave's crevices, stacked, and arranged upon the natural shelving with perfect precision. Two intricately carved columns bracketed the rock face to the left. A large two-seater hanging chair secured by silver chains resided nearest to three mismatched couches, a fraying map lay on the floor in a semi-circle where Niko and Kotori lounged comfortably. Niko sat sprawled over a plush grey couch next to an obsidian statue of Cerberus that rose over the armrest. An old, ancient-looking throne of black steel loomed several paces from the one-metre-high statue, the firelight glinting off Orion who spared Nyx the fleetest of glances before he turned to continue his conversation with Kotori.

Nyx's gaze found Kade's from across the room. He sat off to the right, further back, a messily arranged bookshelf and book stacks scattered around him. She approached him silently, past an old stereo on a small jutting out ledge playing softly, the sheerest of curtains wisping against the boombox as the faintest breeze blew through the cave. An unused and seemingly forgotten four-poster bed lay behind Kade and then, as she sat down beside him, her gaze fell upon the red-tailed hawk perched upon Kade's thigh. His fingers ran gently across its cream and white mottled plumage, as he grinned at her.

"It's beautiful," Nyx breathed out softly, gesturing to the yellow-eyed bird.

Kade's grin widened, his head angling towards her. "He is, isn't he?"

"Does he have a name?"

"Aloys," he replied, pausing as the leucistic hawk nibbled at his fingers affectionately. "It's a French-originated name meaning a quick thinker and a warm-hearted individual."

She glanced up at Kade, unsurety etched into her eyes. "May I?"

Kade nodded enthusiastically, coaxing the hawk onto his forearm as the bird of prey keened softly. Aloys' head cocked, yellowed irises surveying her uncertainly before Kade's fingers brushed her hand and he gently moved her hand to the hawk. "If he likes you, he'll nibble your fingers like he did with mine before."

"And, if he doesn't like me?" Nyx questioned, watching the bird with wonder.

"Don't worry about that," Kade said after a beat of silence.

She opened her mouth but quickly silenced herself as the hawk leant forward and gently nibbled her fingers. Aloys' sleek, soot-coloured beak scratched happily over the soft flesh of her fingers and palm. Without removing her gaze from him, Nyx's voice ghosted across the cave, drawing Niko, Kotori, and Orion's attention to her, "How'd you find this place?"

Orion's voice rang out, raising both Nyx and Kade's heads from Aloys in unison.

"This used to be a popular tourist attraction about forty-five years ago." Orion paused as he scrutinised the cave and the slight dusting of sand over the ground. "It's a shame they built the lookout along the limestone cliff face. Because, when the big one hit Faycairn and the aftershocks ravaged the coastline, the lookout and the tourist centre within the cave took a header straight into the Avonsano Ocean, crumbling away from the cliff face like limestone tends to do."

Niko, Kotori and Kade each grinned with bemusement, like siblings who'd heard the same explanation repeatedly.

Nyx arched a curious eyebrow, ceasing her gentle caresses over Aloys' feathers. "So … you live here? In a cave?"

Orion nodded his head, his glacier gaze filled with a sense of frigid calm. "We do."

"What about your parents? Aren't they worried that you live here? In the abandoned ruins of a *tourist destination,*" she questioned, glancing around the cavern.

They laughed at her then, soft chuckles and wide grins as Nyx's brows furrowed with confusion.

"Our parents couldn't care less, Nyx," Orion began. "Then again, they never were too concerned about us, and now that we're gone, it's one less thing they need to *worry* about."

Nyx nodded her head slowly, considering. "So … it's just you four?" As she said the words, that strange sensation of grasping at straws descended upon her, seeming to cool her nerves. Trying to hold her in memory. Remember. *Remember what?*

Four of them.

Niko's movement jolted her, his eyes alight with pride as he pushed himself up from the couch and crossed the room, taking her hand in his own, and leading her over to the couches nestled around a large firepit.

"Now it is," he replied, turning as they sat down on the soft couches.

Nyx frowned, "*Now* it is?"

"We used to have some ... companions, but that didn't work out," Kade piped up from his spot in front of the bookshelf.

Nyx hummed in acknowledgement, before Niko broke the silence with his muttered comment, "Because of some guy."

"A guy?" she pressed, angling her head to peer up at Niko.

"Yeah, he seemed like he'd fit in well with us, you know? We hung out with him, showed him around Celacali and everything but it just ... fell apart after him and Orion had this big argument," Niko rattled off airily, seeming to miss Orion's stony glare.

Niko shook his head, rubbing a hand down his face with exasperation. Nyx watched—a faint smile playing across her lips—mildly amused as Orion peered up at the ceiling like he was praying for a *semblance* of patience. Kade grinned, shaking his head as he coaxed Aloys onto a driftwood perch and crossed the room to sit down beside Nyx and Niko.

"And what a mistake *that* was," Orion muttered, tearing his icy stare from the ceiling.

Nyx frowned as she caught the tail-end of Niko's hushed retort. Kade and Niko started in on each other once again and she watched the two interact—every little thing they did reminded her of siblings fighting amongst themselves.

"Thanks to Mr. Future CEO and his *impeccable* judge of character over there," Kotori gestured to Kade, a goading edge to his voice as Kade paused, hand poised to whack Niko once again as his hazel irises hardened and he turned ever-so-slowly to the wolfishly grinning brunette.

"I'm sorry, *oh wise one,* but I don't recall *you* doing anything," Kade said before he leant down and picked up a small pebble.

"Was I supposed to? I thought you had it *under control.*" Kotori's zealous gaze held Kade's as Nyx blinked in mute shock beside the mischievous blond; trying and failing to hide the amusement creeping into her expression with their combined antics.

"I did," Kade said.

"You didn't," Niko snickered, ignoring his companion's glare. "It was a shit-show."

"No, it wasn't," Kade protested.

Kotori scoffed, shaking his head. "It *was*. We couldn't go to the boardwalk for *weeks* after that. Not unless we wanted to ... incriminate ourselves further."

Kade rolled his eyes as he tossed the small pebble at Kotori's chest then leant back into the couch, throwing a mocking wink at Kotori.

"Kade, food. It's your pick," Orion ordered smoothly, stare never straying from Nyx.

Kade huffed, glancing down at Nyx quickly before he stood from the couch and disappeared up the marble stairs and down the dimly lit tunnel. His footsteps echoed throughout the cave along with the snitching of a door. Niko twirled a pre-rolled joint between his fingers and lit the joint, sweet-smelling smoke filling the air.

"Tell me, Nyx. How long have you been in Celacali?" Orion asked from his steel throne, breaking the brief silence.

"About three days now," Nyx answered honestly.

"What brings you to Celacali, of all places? Not a lot of people have heard of the famous *City of the Dead*," he drawled.

Her nose scrunched up, disdainfully. "My parents divorced. Mum stayed in Malor with my older brother. Dad and I moved to Celacali."

Niko nodded, resting his head upon the back of the couch and inhaling another lungful of smoke, his arm draped carelessly behind Nyx's back as he trailed his gaze lazily over the stalactites on the ceiling—following the discreet wiring attached to the lights hidden within.

Kotori shifted upon the couch he'd claimed, elbows coming to rest on his thighs,

"How old are you, Nyx?" he asked softly; the deep timbre of his voice calming and pleasant to hear.

Nyx hesitated as the weight of their eyes settled upon her. "Nineteen."

Kotori hummed; a low sound that corralled in her mind like thunder. "And your father lets you wander the boardwalk alone? During an ongoing murder investigation?"

"We have a mutual understanding of each other's lives, and it works for us. He keeps busy with cases and clients while I live my life how I want to, what's not to like?"

"That doesn't bother you?" Kotori asked.

She frowned. "Why should it?"

"It's dangerous after dark in Celacali," he said, coolly.

Nyx arched an eyebrow doubtfully, Kotori's serene admission sending a jolt of déjà vu through her—reminding Nyx of what her mother had said before they'd left for Celacali. But, just like her father, she plastered a self-assured smile over her face and spoke, "There's nothing to be afraid of in Celacali."

Orion's disdainful laughter echoed through the cave, his steely irises alight. "Nothing to be afraid of? Oh, sweetheart, there's *always* something to be afraid of after dark," he drawled, drumming his gloved fingers on the black-steeled armrest of his chair.

Nyx shrugged, mentally tossing Orion's warning to the churning waves below Elveszett Bluff. It didn't occur to her, as Orion's expression turned stony and he bristled from her dismissal, that her father's connections wouldn't reach the shadows of Celacali's night. Or that the glint that flashed in Orion, Niko, and Kotori's gazes *wasn't* surprise.

Nyx's head turned towards the cave entrance as Kade returned—a large brown box in his hands.

"Who's hungry?" he asked in a sing-song voice.

"Me!" Niko exclaimed, jolting up from the couch in a rush to get to the food, his shoulder knocking Nyx's as he scrambled, snatching the box from Kade's hands.

Kade shook his head without surprise and followed Niko back to the couch and pulled out a carton of Chinese takeout.

"Chinese? Again?" Niko said.

Kade ruffled Niko's hair as he sat down, pulling the cardboard box from Niko's lap, and into his own. "Quit your whining, Niko. You know it's the only restaurant open on the boardwalk after dark," he scolded, pulling two cartons of Chinese from the box before he tossed one carton towards Kotori and carefully passed another to Nyx.

The mouth-watering scent of Chinese spices and sauces engulfed her senses as she pried open the cardboard's white flaps. A hushed laugh tumbled from her lips, mind dredging up flashes of scenery and movie dialogue. *Déjà vu, anyone?* she thought with a shake of her head, the special fried rice eliciting a rumble from her stomach.

Kade and Niko grinned, sparing her a glance before they turned back to their food and dug in, nudging each other playfully whilst they ate.

Orion watched Nyx closely, his icy eyes trying to decipher her.

"What'd you think of Celacali so far, Nyx?" Kade asked around a mouthful of food.

Niko snickered, garbling a noodle-filled answer for her. "*There's nothing to be afraid of in Celacali*, Kade."

Kade's eyebrows arched, gaze flickering between Niko and Nyx. "Is that so?"

Nyx shrugged, toying with her spoon. "It's true enough."

Kade nodded, letting silence descend upon the cave for several seconds before he continued. "Still, what do you think?"

"It's been ... different. Malor isn't like Celacali," Nyx said.

"So, you didn't like Malor?" Kade prompted, his head angling with hawk-like curiosity, chopsticks left forgotten in his food.

"It was okay," she paused, worrying her bottom lip between her teeth as she pondered how to explain herself, flashes of memory appearing unbidden.

Split and bloodied knuckles.

"It's just ... something about Celacali is *inviting*. It seems to appeal to everyone that comes to the city. I don't know if it's the boardwalk, but it's—" she began.

"Like you're supposed to be here, right?" Niko finished, lifting another forkful of noodles to his mouth as he awaited her response.

Nyx nodded, chewing her mouthful of rice and swallowing before she continued. "Oddly enough, yeah. The boardwalk has a type of allure where something captures your attention and then there's always something to quench that interest."

"Sounds like a siren's call to me," Orion uttered from the throne-like chair, his mouth wide open, noodles dangling between the wooden utensils.

Nyx chuffed out a light laugh, musing over the response as she ate. "Maybe you're right, but something tells me that Celacali is a city for the lost."

"City of the Lost. City of the Dead. It's all the same thing, different but still the same," Orion stated confidently.

"I think people come to Celacali in search of a place to belong. And they either find what they're looking for on the boardwalk and in the city, or they become one of the many missing persons of Celacali." Nyx paused as she mulled over her own words. "And maybe that's why it's the City of the Dead."

Orion lifted his eyebrows, fascination seeping into his face. "What do you mean?"

She sighed, fingers raking through her hair whilst her mind scrambled, trying to find another way to describe the way she thought Celacali worked and what made it the feared 'City of the Dead'. "You come to Celacali in hopes of something new. Something better, right?"

Orion nodded, his interest seemingly well and truly peaked as he leant forward in the ancient throne. "Right."

"And you either find what you're looking for, or a piece of you dies when you realise that nothing in this world can bring you happiness, surety *or* a sense of calm and belonging."

Orion hummed, his eyes brimming. A darkly satisfied smile crept across his face, trickling over his stubbled jaw like water down a windowpane. The intimidating aura that surrounded him eased as if he had suddenly seen Nyx in a new light—one of intrigue, that he *needed* to know more about. "A piece of you *does* die when you enter Celacali, Nyx," he said. "The question is just whether they can save you or not before you flatline."

VI.

Nyx

Sunlight streamed in through the sheer curtains of the windows, bathing the wooden floorboards in softly golden rays, and warming the end of her bed. An irritated groan emitted from the back of Nyx's throat before she grasped the soft quilt and tugged it over her head. Then, finally rubbing the sleep from her bleary eyes, she sat up. Inkheart's white cover glared up at her—as her gaze trailed lazily across her room—left forgotten on her bedside table since she'd bought it. As she swung her legs over the edge of the bed, and her sock-covered toes grazed the floorboards, her fingers raked through her tangled curls—trying to tame the unruly tresses.

She remembered Kotori had driven her home and a soft smile tugged at her mouth, at the memory. She turned towards the two large windows on the left wall and the first bedside table. The sun dared to peek through a gap in the blanket of grey, illuminating her room as though clutching onto the last of its hopes, fighting to keep itself alight and visible as the clouds tried to swallow it whole.

Then, like a thought, it vanished behind the darkening clouds and plunged the world into a duller, less welcoming place. Nyx crossed the room, pulling the sliding doors to the wardrobe open, groggily staring at the drawers and clothes hanging above her shoes. The faint ticking of her analogue clock seemed muffled to her ears before she pulled open one drawer, then another, retrieving a red singlet top and a pair of distressed jeans. Nyx peered over her shoulder and out the window, worrying her lip whilst she contemplated the dreary weather of the tropical lowlands of Celacali—did she need that black flannelled shirt? With a soft sigh, she decided it was better to be prepared. Several minutes later, she walked out of her half-unpacked bedroom and down the dimly lit hallway.

As she reached the top of the staircase and craned her neck to peer down into the lounge room below, her gaze found her father's in the doorway of the sunroom—his head tilted up to the glass-paned windows, soaking up whatever peace he had found in that darkening sky—as she descended the stairs and crossed the lounge room, diverting to the kitchen to find something to eat.

"How was your night?" Azeil asked, turning to her when she crossed the threshold to the sunroom, an apple in her hand.

"Eventful," she replied, her gaze appraising. "How was yours?"

"It was good. Quiet but good," her father answered with a sigh. And, as though he had just remembered where she'd been and the murders of Celacali whilst he'd been in the city's Central suburbs, his eyebrows furrowed. "When did you get home? I didn't hear you come in."

Nyx noticed the dark circles beneath his eyes as she wondered how he could've missed her return—Kotori's motorbike was anything *but* silent. "Sometime this morning?"

"This morning?"

Nyx rubbed the nape of her neck, nervousness prickling it with goosebumps. "Yeah, sometime around two."

Azeil nodded slowly, his granite gaze shifting like the ocean. A crease marred his forehead, fingers digging harshly into the metal chair until his knuckles bled white.

Nyx guessed where his thoughts were going. To those ruthless beasts her entire family all seemed to fear and, as a child, Nyx had once feared too. Those terrifying stories of murderous beasts with nightmarish fangs. As time passed, Nyx had dismissed the tales as mere myths, burying them in the depths of her mind—where they faded. And yet, she could never dispel the ghost of her uncle's voice in her head or the concern that singed her chest when she saw her father's fingers flex around the armrests. *Demons,* she thought. *We're all battling demons.*

Nyx discarded the apple on the table and placed her hand on her father's shoulder—to break him from his silent anguish. The tensed muscles coiled beneath her palm as she crouched down before him and gazed up at him, heeding his warnings correlated to his PTSD and the gentle advice her mother had given her to help with the memories that haunted him. "Dad?"

Her father blinked once. Twice. The glazed glint to his eyes clearing when his eyes lowered to hers. A strained but grateful smile passed his lips before he gently grasped Nyx's hand and pulled her up from the floor. Pushing himself out of the chair and wrapping his arms around her, he inhaled shakily.

"Are you okay?" Nyx asked, worried.

Azeil sighed, his arms dropping to his sides before he stepped away, turning his back, posture tense beneath the weight of her question like a broken record. He sucked in a calming breath of air, facing Nyx, his hand-crafted mask gilded with clarity and calm. She knew that he *hated* her seeing him like this.

"I'll be okay."

It was Nyx's turn to sigh as she trailed behind him into the lounge room and sat upon the armrest of a couch, waiting patiently for him to sit down. She opened her mouth, prepared to speak, but quickly closed it when nothing *right* came to mind. A beginning pitter-patter of rain droplets echoed through the house, momentarily distracting them both.

"That's not what I asked," she said softly, her stare tracing over the silent and sullen lines of his face.

His gaze met hers. A look of pain brimming his earthen irises, as he grasped Nyx's hand and gently squeezed. "I know."

Silence engulfed the room, cocooning father and daughter in an eerie void. The rain patter had become a downpour, suddenly almost deafening as Nyx turned and watched water course down the glass panes of the sunroom.

Please be gone by nightfall, she thought. Like some unbidden sliver of thought shunted to the forefront of her mind—desperate for another night upon the boardwalk.

"Asher's coming to Celacali in a week," Azeil stated quietly.

Her eyes lit up at the mention of her uncle, excitement imbuing her tone. "A week?"

"He mentioned something about checking up on the comic bookstore the Montes' own," he said. "They own *Mad Expedition Comics* on the boardwalk."

Nyx's eyebrows raised, thinking back to the twins who had watched her from the doorway. "The Montes'? Like Tobias and Alexander?"

"Exactly like those ones." Her father peered over his shoulder at the falling rain with a look of disdain before he turned back to Nyx. "Movie day?"

She smiled, shifting so he could reach the remote sitting on the small table beside the armrest. "Rainy days and movies … sounds good to me."

As they focused on the TV screen and the opening scene, Nyx realised that for the first time in a long time, they were sitting together, comfortable and calm—satisfied to just watch movies as rain poured down outside. And as much as Nyx missed her mother's laughter and the crinkles on both sides of her eyes whenever she smiled, she basked in the serene mood between herself and her father.

She dared to hope that maybe, just *maybe*. Celacali was exactly what he needed.

What they *both* needed.

* * *

Two years earlier ...

Terror jolted through Nyx like a bolt of electricity, fizzling through her bloodstream as her heartbeat yammered in her eardrums and a pair of hands grasped her forearms. The rumble of a motorbike engine faded as its dark-haired rider tore off down the street, leaving her in the aftermath of a very close call with a ringing in her ears and a disconnected sense of reality.

It'd happened so fast. One moment she'd been crossing the street, starting towards the winding trails of Malor's largest park and her favourite spot beside the lake where the black swans lingered, and in the next, a masked man on a motorbike had tried to haul her onto his bike, seeming to brush her struggles aside as if they were nothing, before another man, a blur of blond hair, had swiftly stepped in and pulled her from the masked man's grasp.

As her mind recalled her saviour and her adrenaline fled her bones, Nyx turned to thank him. Her brows furrowing as she pivoted in a slow circle, dazed and confused when she couldn't find him. She stood alone, park patrons tossed glances her way before continuing about their day like they hadn't almost witnessed an abduction. *He'd been right there,* she assured herself as her thoughts whirled and the ghost of his hands prickled her forearms. *Hadn't he?*

Her hands trembled as she grasped the coin-like charm of her necklace, dragging it back and forth along its chain in hopes of soothing her frayed nerves, repeating her grandmother's assurances that it'd protect her from harm. With a shaky exhale, she started towards a nearby bench, slumping against the wooden chair as her gaze roved the greenery around her. Her sneaker-clad foot tapped anxiously against the path, hand leaving her necklace to rub against her thigh, plucking at the denim before she adjusted the hem of her T-shirt.

"Are you okay?" came a gravelly voice.

She turned towards a man with luscious curls framing his face, dark eyes skittering over her in concern as he stood several paces away with his hands tucked into his jeans, his polo shirt creased in some places.

"Uh ... I guess," she said, raking a hand through her hair before a disbelieving laugh tumbled from her lips. "As good as someone who was almost kidnapped can be."

The man grimaced at her response, eyeing her with an unsure expression. "Do you need me to call someone for you?"

"Not right now. I want a few minutes of peace before I call my dad."

His lips quirked with a knowing grin. "Protective father?"

Nyx chuckled. "Something like that."

A calm silence stretched between them, the barest whiff of cigarette smoke carried across the breeze along with the sensation of being watched before Nyx straightened and hurried to introduce herself once the unnamed man shifted uncomfortably, scuffing his shoes against the pavement.

"I'm Nyx," she offered with an awkward smile.

The man returned her smile, a soft chuckle emanating from his chest as he reached out his hand towards her. "*Kai.*"

VII.

Nyx

Dark, thunderous clouds roiled as purple-white bolts of lightning struck an angry ocean, deterring many from venturing outside. Braver boardwalk-goers soaked up the gravid unease for a night upon the neon-plunged boardwalk, dodging the puddles of water dotting the wooden planks, and dripping onto the sand below.

Nyx tipped her head up and silently wished the rain would stay out at sea; at least for now. A frigid breeze crept across her skin—carrying a salty twang of ocean and the now recognisable opulent-sweet fragrance of the narcissi to her senses—she pulled her black flannelled shirt closer, hoping to trap her body heat to her skin.

Water droplets clung to the neon signs of the rides and stalls, refracting tiny rainbows over the wooden planks before they fell, leaving no trace. Nyx found Orion, Kotori, Niko, and Kade moments later; the quartet scattered around their bikes beside a water-bathed Ferris wheel.

Orion smiled at her as his gaze trailed over her sanguine singlet and distressed jeans. "Four nights in a row, Nyx. Do you like us *that* much?"

As one, they stared at her almost insolently, half-mockingly, waiting.

Nyx shrugged, smiling as she glanced around the quieter boardwalk and then to Orion, the charcoal sleeves of his shirt rolled to his elbows, a cigarette tucked snugly behind his left ear. "That depends," she murmured, angling her head, "you're always on the boardwalk, aren't you? So, how many more nights are *you* planning to grace it with your presence?"

Niko grinned cheekily, pulling Nyx into a hug filled with the jangling of his bracelets. His cheetah tattoo peeked out from beneath the neckline of his KISS T-shirt, dotted with artful holes as he answered her question without missing a beat.

"Every night, chica, for as long as we shall live."

"Wouldn't you get bored of it?" she asked, glancing down at his black attire.

Kade joined them, the silver of his earrings flashing in the brilliant lights.

"Celacali is many things, angel. But you'll find that boring isn't one of them," he assured her smugly.

They looked to the carousel, a tantalising air of calamity hanging above the motley group. Niko's hand grasped Nyx's, and they approached the slowly turning ride. Water droplets clung to the elegant arches of silver and white, sparkling like tiny stars, a halo of white light illuminating the ornate ride. Nyx craned her neck, peering over her shoulder at Orion and Kotori, who followed them, like two wolves on the prowl for their next meal, their eyes flitting from person to person with shifting interest.

It occurred to her then, that Kotori and Orion upheld a leader-like position in the quartet. She turned towards the carousel with the knowledge—instinctual confirmation—that out of the four, Orion was the one in charge. And, as if they were confirming her suspicions, Niko and Kade glanced back to Orion before they sidestepped the metallic barrier and climbed onto the turning ride, hoisting her up onto the wooden base with lithe ease.

Stares seared into Nyx's skin, like a dozen branding irons in her back as Niko's fingers laced with hers. They wound through the plastic horses until they found an empty section.

"Don't be shy, angel. Hop on," Kade urged, leaning his hip against a chestnut-coloured horse.

"You want me to … get on it?" Nyx stated unsurely.

Niko chuckled, shaking his head as he gestured to the darkly painted horse. "C'mon, Nyx. It's just a ride."

With feigned annoyance, she sighed and dragged a palm down her face. But her dark eyes flickered with delight as she climbed onto the onyx horse.

"Satisfied?" Nyx challenged, shifting in the uncomfortable plastic saddle.

Kade shrugged, "I'd be lying if I told you I wasn't." He cocked his head to Niko, grinning mischievously, a pleasant shiver enticed by his grin trailing down her spine, "What about you, Niko? Are you satisfied?"

Niko's hands wrapped around a metallic pole on either side of him, reminding Nyx of celebrities posing for fancy magazines, a lifeful grin splitting his face.

"Immensely."

Nyx turned to Kotori, who'd silently crept onto the carousel, leaning against a faded pearl-white horse, his arms folded across his bare chest before his gaze narrowed and tracked Niko's past her shoulder. A group of Ivory Skulls lingered beside the metal barriers of the carousel as she turned to follow their gazes, and a bell-like warning tolled in Nyx's mind—an omen that resonated in the marrow of her bones. Her gaze darted from person to person, surveying those upon and around the carousel as flashes of a lion stalking an antelope blitzed in her head.

Kotori angled his head, ebony hair mussed from the wind. His necklace dangled hand-crafted charms that Nyx couldn't decipher and the neon-white lights of the carousel glinted off his crescent moon earring. Orion stalked closer to the rival gang leaning against the carousel's barricades, a predatory grin tearing his face.

"Stay here," Kotori murmured, glancing at her before he strode to the edge of the carousel and jumped down.

For a moment, she considered climbing off the plastic horse just because she'd been told to stay put—her fingertips pressed into her thighs, and the muscles in her back tensed and prepared to flee whilst the carousel continued to spin in a slow circle. Passers-by tossed uneasy glances at Kotori, who joined Orion as Niko and Kade moved in unison, leaving her alone. Then, Orion's gloved hands clamped down on the shoulders of a dark-haired man, shunting him backwards.

"I thought I told you to stay off the boardwalk?" Orion drawled.

The other man's lips curled, scoffing as he dragged his gaze patronisingly over Orion. "The boardwalk is *our* turf, not yours," he said.

Orion clicked his tongue, "Is it now?"

Nyx missed what happened next—as the ride slowly turned and she lost sight of them—she only saw Orion step closer, brushing his leather-clad fingers over the cheek of a woman who shadowed the man's shoulder. The blueness of his eyes ablaze as the rival gang member launched himself at Orion, his hand slipping from the woman's face and her companion gripping Kotori's necklace in a white-knuckled fist. Kotori's features contorted with revulsion, teeth clenching together, eyebrows narrowing into a displeased frown. Niko and Kade bristled and shoved the Ivory Skulls away from them as easily as shooing away two flies.

The usually silent and docile biker bristled, angrily shoving the dark-haired man away before Kotori whirled back around and wove through gaping passers-by, revulsion and disdain etched firmly into his face as he pulled himself up onto the carousel and approached Nyx. Thinly veiled rage on his features as he visibly fought to calm himself, fists clenching and unclenching at his sides as he leant stiffly against a pole. Kade and Niko snickered, knocking into each other's shoulders playfully as they traipsed over to Nyx, shadowing her on either side as she climbed off the plastic horse and eyed the three men.

"You weren't lying when you said you were a trouble magnet," she mused, brushing her hands down her thighs.

Kade grinned, "I lied about the magnet part," he explained, glancing conspiratorially around the carousel, "We tend to find trouble ... or make it."

Nyx nodded, a teasing smile tugging at the corners of her lips. "You don't say."

Niko chuckled before his eyes narrowed upon something over her shoulder. His serene smile fled as Nyx turned, peering through the people on the carousel and the lingering boardwalk-goers. She spotted Orion being dragged away from the ride by a young security guard—his lips a sneer.

"Hey, Kade," Nyx murmured, her eyes on Orion.

"Yeah," he said.

"He's not being dragged away by that security guard, is he?"

Niko chortled, boot-clad feet thumping upon the wooden planks in an odd, yet even rhythm. "*Nope.* He's humouring the oaf."

Nyx watched as the rain began to fall haphazardly and the thunder returned, rumbling ominously over the ocean—nearer. They looked on as the security guard released Orion and he gestured to their bikes with a wave of his hand.

"Hey, Kade?" Nyx murmured, parroting her earlier words.

"Nyx?" Kade responded in kind, grinning down at her.

"I'm going to go," she said.

Niko spun on his heel towards her. "Already? But the night's only just begun!"

Nyx chuckled, "I'll be back tomorrow night, hopefully the rain'll be gone by then."

"Do you promise?"

"I promise," she confirmed, grinning up at the tall, retriever-like blond.

She watched Orion, whose gaze lingered malignantly on the security guard as she wandered further down the boardwalk—unaware of the weight of Orion's gaze. Lightning rippled through dark clouds, as Nyx shouted farewell over her shoulder and she passed Orion on her way to the neon arch of the boardwalk's entrance.

She quickened her pace from a brisk walk to a rushed jog—the faded-red paintwork of her Honda calling to her as she ducked through the parked cars. Her leather seat was sodden with water, and squelched as she sat down. Her fingers drumming impatiently upon the handlebars as she waited for the well-loved bike to warm up. And, when she deemed it was, an elated laugh tumbled from her lips, like a babbling brook as she twisted the throttle and the bike jolted forward.

VIII.

The steady thrum of rain pattering against bitumen echoed in the air, rivulets of water rushing through cracks in the desolate parking lot, like the foundations of a formidable dam had burst and cascaded down the coastline of Celacali. The thunder and the waves were an incessant moaning backdrop against the boardwalk. Despite the endless storm that lashed the coastal city, little could discourage the four figures within the shadows—waiting like a pack of wolves on the prowl.

Everyone knew monsters didn't lurk under your bed in the city of Celacali; they lurked in the serenity of the night, slinking through the shadows without disturbing the silence.

Anticipation jolted the quartet, blue and brown eyes brimming with restless energy, like a horse pawing at the dirt. The leader of the group, a man with clothes as dark as his hair was eerily white, tracked each light of the boardwalk as they turned off. Each one diminished to the darkness, another nail in a coffin, plunging prey deeper into an awaiting fate. They delighted—like the predators they were—as each light went out and the darkness crept in. The thunder in their eardrums as blackness bathed the boardwalk in shadow; now darkness reigned supreme over the storm-plunged city.

An unspoken understanding passed between them as they dipped their heads, water droplets clinging to their eyelashes and soaking their clothes, beginning to move—to hunt. Laughter echoed hollowly; a kind that embodied everything holy and not. They shoved each other playfully, knocking and bumping into the light-starved alleyways, hiccupping flashes of light punctuating their steps like last, wavering appeals.

As the alleyway opened into the deserted car park, a pair paused within the shadows, waiting like wolves steadily herding their prey. And, as if the Goddess of the Hunt commanded it, a beige-uniformed security guard crossed the parking lot. The rich, redness of the boardwalk's archway was blanketed by the shadows that seemed to skirt behind the young man walking across the vacant lot, his stride an uneven jaunt.

Though Celacali's boardwalk was a place brimming with light and life; a duo so intricately interwoven that it was almost impossible for it to be unravelled, it was also a place blanketed by darkness and death; two malign forces that uncoiled those beaconed bindings with ease, slicking the coastal city with its moniker 'City of the Dead'.

Kotori approached Kade and Niko from the darkness, followed by Orion who seemed to appear from thin air, and together, they followed the security guard's movements with sinister eyes. They were eager to quell an eternal hunger, one they didn't need to quench often but needed to maintain. The consequences of going without always loomed at the back of their minds, ever-present. If they waited too long—a month without sustenance—they'd become trapped in their unconscious bodies, unable to wake themselves unless someone gave them blood. Orion seemed content to wait for the perfect moment to strike, exhaling a cloud of smoke as his companions turned to him expectantly, waiting for confirmation that the hunt could begin.

These men, they knew what lives were defined as. *Moments:* fleeting junctures in time, in a place like Celacali, ruled by monsters like them. Some passed quickly, urged along by their doings as they revelled in the kill, while others dragged out like they were never going to end; those inexorable moments so many dreaded. But truthfully, lives were like sliding doors to these men; when one closed, another opened.

It was just a matter of *which* ones needed closing before another could open.

The undivulged knowledge ghosted over the security guard's head, who continued on, oblivious to the gradual closing of his door. It didn't matter to them. It never did. Not with the ease and mastery that they blended into society, or the fear they instilled in the locals of Celacali. There was nothing inherently *good* about the four men—monsters, who watched the security guard, waiting eagerly for the hunt to begin—but there was a darkness to them. An indelible stain forever etched into their beings that coated their skin with ghostly memories of blood and terrified screams; their favourite sound to hear.

Orion grinned maliciously as he turned to Kade, Niko and Kotori. A smoothly drawled order fell from his lips as he crushed the dregs of his cigarette beneath his boot.

"Let's go, boys."

Howls of delight rippled over the parking lot. Devilish sounds of glee as the guard spun in search of the source. Dread clouded his heart when he turned to meet them, a hitched pause before he turned and ran. His heart thudded loudly in his chest, as he fumbled his keys from his pockets, his fingers trembled and sweat beaded his brow, short pants of air fanning his car's window.

The distinct *click* of the car's locking mechanism tolled in his ears; attainment fluttered within the man's gut as he wrenched at the car door. His heart stuttered and leapt within the caverns of his chest when a gloved hand clamped around the door frame, preventing him from pulling the door open. Undiluted fear leeched his bloodstream as he gasped at the blue-eyed man, who peered down at him nastily.

"Beautiful night, isn't it?" Orion drawled; a crack of thunder ricocheting across the sky as if in answer.

The man gawked, terrified as he spluttered out half sentences and gibberish. Kade and Niko snickered, leaning against the side of the car with chins propped on their hands, fingers curled around the necks of spirit-filled bottles. Fear keened in the young security guard's chest, as every one of his instincts screamed at him to run—to live.

His black shoes scuffed over the bitumen, stumbling away before he collided with a solid chest. Kotori.

Orion clicked his tongue mockingly. "Not so fast," he taunted, gloved hand grasping the man's shoulder in a bruising grip before he stooped to the security guard's height. "It's not very ... *polite* to kick people off the boardwalk. You know that, right?"

"But ... I ..." The man spluttered; his brain too fear-drenched to think properly.

"You, what?" Orion challenged, his fingertips digging painfully.

The man grimaced in pain, hands grasping Orion's forearm as desperation bubbled within his chest and he shoved at the gloved grip.

Kade and Niko laughed and they upended the bottles of alcohol, pouring sharp-smelling liquid over the car seats.

Orion feigned sympathy as he stepped closer to the trembling man. "I really should apologise for my behaviour earlier," he gestured lazily to Kade and Niko, "and theirs now. But I'm *not* sorry, and neither are they."

The guard swallowed audibly; a foolish, cornered deer. Herded and trapped. He looked at the young men surrounding him. Like himself, but not. *Monsters* who hid behind the masks of men, out of sync with humanity, or emotions like regret and empathy. Unless they sought to fool their victims with a flicker of likeness dredged up from memories of their past—then they *seemed* human.

As Orion's face morphed into something from legend and nightmare alike, the guard visibly withered. Once glacial eyes were now a shocking fire-yellow from the iris' outer edge, his pupil defined by a perfect, crimson ring. His cheekbones sharpened, jutting beneath his skin in deep grooves near his eyebrows, the bone structure prominent beneath his ivory skin. His canines and incisors elongated, honed to lethal points that pressed against his bottom lip. He stepped closer, and pulled the quaking man to him in one swift motion, a snarl tearing from his throat at the thrashing and struggling.

They always did that, thought Orion.

His grip on the security guard tightened, gloved hands fisting the man's shirt before he sunk his fangs into his throat, rending skin with abandon.

The man shoved at Orion's chest, a gurgled scream becoming a gargle as his efforts weakened with the agonising and terrifyingly quick loss of his blood. Much like fighting through quicksand: you cannot pull yourself out. His blood stained his beige uniform as his jugular tore and his heart pumped his life out in a red spray, splattering his parted lips and making a gruesome Pollock parody of him. He suffocated on his own blood.

Kotori, Niko, and Kade poured whiskey and vodka over the fabric of the man's car seats, their eardrums filled with the distinct, and steadily waning, thump of his heartbeat. Until, eventually, it ceased to beat at all, and their senses were plunged into silence. The trio paused their ministrations, the astringent alcohol stinging their nostrils when Orion pulled away from the man's throat and the soft *drip-drop* from the soaked car seats masked the *drop-drip* of the corpse in his arms.

Blood trickled down Orion's chin, staining his stubbled jaw and throat, gloved hands holding the lifeless body at arm's length before he shoved it into the back seat of the car and slammed the door. He pulled a silver lighter engraved with a coiling serpent from his pocket and gestured for his companions to step back. His thumb struck the lever and the flare flickered as he tossed it into the car with the body. Flame licked at the spirit-soaked seats, igniting and spreading, engulfing the interior. The fire fed on the ethanol just like Orion had fed on the guard.

Orion turned away from the burning car, his lips curled into a salacious grin.

"What'd you say to a bonfire, boys?" Orion questioned, delighted by his companions' hollers of zeal.

Niko beamed with unsavoury delight; bracelet-covered wrists jangling as he rubbed his hands together. "I heard it'll be to *die* for."

Orion looked at Niko, "How long have you been waiting to say that?"

Niko fidgeted, "Do you *really* want to know?"

"Not particularly," Orion laughed, shaking his head with a soft smile playing across his lips. He inclined his head in the direction of their bikes and started towards them, calling back over his shoulder to his companions. "Let's go, boys."

IX.

Nyx

Kaleidoscopes of colour glinted off the wooden planks of the amusement park, the early morning light refracted in the shimmering water droplets dotting the rides and store alcoves; a stark but welcome change from the previous night's frigid and dreary storm.

As Nyx meandered past the neon-lit archway, her fingers toying with the inky hem of her T-shirt, curiosity and intrigue drove her through the smaller crowds of harried and awed patrons. Her curls—tied half-up, half-down—danced in the salt-riddled breeze, stray pieces of hair tickling her face and the sliver of skin along her waist. A startled yelp tumbled from her lips as a small boy with lush, wheat-coloured curls and hooded, forest-like irises collided with her plaid-clad legs. He peered up at her, wide and fearful before his small hands shoved at her khaki-coloured pants and he hurried away, disappearing amongst the shifting tide of passers-by. Smoke addled the blueness of the sky, clogging her nose with a distant unsettling stench, her mind racing as it tried to place it.

Nyx stopped outside the comic bookstore, glancing down the slower-paced sector lined with small stores and hidden alcoves with seating areas for those seeking a reprieve from the bustle. She thought, for a moment, to continue further into the coastal fairground's centre, to the rides a hundred or so metres away, but then, she thought of Xander and went inside.

The U-shaped layout of the store and its fresh-printed scent greeted her. She browsed the extensive collection, the thin tomes packed in plastic sleeves for protection, the price handwritten on small stickers. She flipped through a few under the alphabetised section "P", until one cover caught her eye. A gore-spattered, bad-tempered looking… elf? With twin blades. "*Poison Elves* by Drew Hayes," Nyx muttered.

She put it back and turned slowly to the store's register, her fingertips leaving the colourful and elaborate comics. She wondered, as her gaze locked on the mousy-haired twins, if they remembered her like she remembered them.

The taller of the two, *Alexander*, she reminded herself, rested his hip on the paint-chipped counter, arms folded over his black-clothed chest as he scrutinised her. His shorter brother, Tobias, lounged lazily, nose ring and array of chunky finger rings, with subtle curls pushed up and out of his eyes. And, like Alexander, he appraised her.

Coming to some sort of decision, the brothers pushed off from their respective counters and approached Nyx. Alexander's look was condescending, like he knew how out of her depth she was. Recognition sparked suddenly and he gestured to the glossy comics. "Do you know what you're looking for, *Night*?" he asked, light and teasing.

She shook her head, mirroring his grin at the use of her nickname.

"Not in the *slightest*, Alex."

"You haven't changed one bit," Tobias drawled, before he stepped forward and engulfed her in a hug.

"Neither have you two," Nyx murmured, stepping out of Tobias's arms and into Alexander's. "How long's it been anyway?"

Alexander pulled away, releasing her, "Too long."

And Nyx found that she couldn't disagree. It'd been years since she'd seen the Montes twins, not since her grandmother had passed away and they had travelled to the coastal city for her funeral. Nyx remembered the havoc they'd wreaked on the boardwalk as kids, darting between patrons' legs in their pursuit of the carnival rides. She knew, like Alexander and Tobias knew, that her uncle had mildly regretted bringing them together, realising too late that together they were trouble.

"The terrible terrors," Nyx said out loud, recalling her uncle's nickname.

Tobias's gaze flicked between the comics and Nyx. "What *are* you looking for? Is it something particular?"

Nyx pursed her lips, bristling at her mind's botched attempts at recalling the comic Xander never shut up about. "You'd think I'd know," she sighed, "but I *can't* remember the name."

Alexander chuckled, ignoring Nyx's frustration, a Doppelgänger to the frustration she'd had when they were children, and she couldn't find them in a game of hide and seek. The brothers shared a look before Alexander leant over Nyx's shoulder to pluck a turquoise-blue comic from the tiered table, extending the glossy book towards her. The startling-red title 'Vampires Everywhere' scrawled across the cover, with a depiction of vampires tearing people to pieces, bats and a cloaked man clutching a bloody stake in his hand.

Nyx arched her brow, eyeing the two like they'd both just grown another head. She glanced at the twins, gingerly accepting the comic from Alexander. "Is this—?"

"—An *exact* replica?" Alexander finished for her; a lopsided grin curving his mouth as he feigned contemplation. "It is."

"How'd you get *this*?" she said, raising the comic with a slight tremble in her hands. And, as if suddenly realising how illusive the replica was, she pushed it back to Alexander. "I can't take this!"

"Take it, Nyx. *It could save your life,*" Tobias drawled; a taunting smirk quirking his lips as he dared Nyx to take the comic from his brother.

"I'd say, give it a read and if you don't like it, bring it back tomorrow, but I think we both know that won't happen," Alexander stated, pressing his fingertips to Nyx's forearm, and pushing her arm towards her chest.

Nyx sighed, feigning annoyance as she flicked through the colourful artwork on each page. "Happy now?"

Tobias grinned. "Extremely. Time to go now, Nyx," he stated before he ushered her out of the store with Alexander trailing behind. He playfully saluted her from the store's threshold, lingering for a moment before they both turned and disappeared back inside.

Nyx stared at the open doorway, lips parted as people brushed past her. She blinked once. Twice before turning on her heel and clutching the turquoise-green comic closer to her chest. She meandered towards the car park, stopping for a moment to survey the boardwalk map split into four sections; the carpark flowing into the stores and boutiques sector, the neon archway depicted as the entrance. The storefront section seemed the quietest, where people were content to wander at a slower pace for a hundred metres or so, before the walkway opened to the carnival rides and food stalls, spanning several hundred metres before the final sector above the ocean, the stage with its stands of seating.

She turned away from the directory then, to continue her path, a light and blissful sensation cloying in her chest when a flash of white hair darted across her peripherals. She paused beneath the parking lot entryway, turning her head in search of Orion. But, after a moment, her attention was drawn instead from her faded-red Honda to the blackened remains of a car.

Something keened in her head, shrill and like the warning cry of an eagle. She saw the charred wreckage of the car's body and cautiously glanced at her bike, just metres away. Nyx wondered how she could have missed it, how anyone could have missed it, when it was so out of place, a fire-lashed blot amongst the life of the boardwalk. That horrid stench she'd smelt earlier engulfed her senses now, choking her the closer she got to the burned wreck. Her steps faltered at the blood-puddle beside the driver's door, the sight unsettling her quaking nerves. She mustered up the courage to peer through the shattered windows and when she did, a disfigured scream tore from her throat. Her gaze locked onto the charred and blackened outline of a body before she stumbled back. Pressing her hand firmly against her mouth with wide and panic-filled eyes, she turned on shaky legs and staggered away from the blackened remains.

* * *

The soft rustle of pages turning ghosted her ears, soothing her frayed and shaken nerves as sunlight filtered through the gap in her curtains. As Nyx's eyes trailed over the glossy sheen of the comic's pages, her bedsheets wrapped around her snugly, she fought to shove the charred and rancid body from her mind. Her stomach churned with unease; her mind throwing flashes of seared and disfigured flesh to the forefront of her thoughts. She couldn't shake the images, no matter how hard she tried, and it unnerved her despite how quickly her father had picked her up after she'd rang or the questions she'd had to answer when Azeil notified the police and a pair of officers sat across from her in the kitchen.

What were you doing at the boardwalk? Did you notice anything unusual or anyone out of place? What led you to the car?

Inkheart lay face down on her bedside table, seeming to glare at her as she became enthralled by the turquoise-blue comic instead, combing its contents with interest and nostalgia. As she turned the pages, her gaze drinking in the detailed drawings and texts of the vampiric horror comic, she mentally thanked the twins for such a gift.

The door to her bedroom swung open on silent hinges, and her father's sheepish gaze appeared in the doorway.

"You scared the crap out of me." Nyx breathed out. She lowered her hand from her chest, resting it in her lap as her eyebrows furrowed, keen observation missing nothing. Her father had changed since she'd retreated to the safety of her room, he now wore a crisp, white dress shirt, black slacks and dress shoes paired with the metallic glint of his detective badge secured to his belt. It seemed foolish to her now, that she'd deluded herself into thinking she'd never stumble into the intricate web of death and despair racking this city. She knew now, that she'd *never* been safe from the case her father had been hired for.

So, what'd changed? she wondered, lowering the comic.

Azeil chuckled, "Where'd you get that?"

"Tobias and Alexander gave it to me."

"Ryder's sons?"

Nyx *mmhmmed,* barely hearing Azeil's shocked tone. Her gaze strayed from him and back to the sheened pages. Azeil's gaze lingered on Nyx as he seemed to weigh up the need to ask her if she was okay after today, or if he should let it go for now. He sighed.

"Go." She urged, smiling softly. "It's your job."

"But—"

"I'll be fine," she frowned before correcting herself. "I *am* fine. I'll be right here when you get back, I promise."

"Are you sure? Because I can stay if you want me to."

"*Go,*" she repeated, firmer than before.

"If you need anything, call me. Don't hesitate, okay?"

She nodded, noting the way his slate eyes churned with unease. "I will, you know I will."

"Don't open this door for anyone, Night, okay?" He urged softly, turning to leave with his hand on the doorknob for emphasis. "And ... lock it behind me, please."

Nyx's frown deepened, as she heard the front door close and the magnitude of her father's worry settled in her chest. It occurred to her, as she nodded dutifully and her father closed the door behind himself, that she'd never seen him *this* worried for her during a homicide investigation—his preferred field of investigation. Nothing seemed to faze her father amid the sleepless and tension-filled nights of his cases, not even her parent's divorce.

She tossed the warm sheets off her legs, rising from the bed to lock her door as he had requested, the soft *snick* of the locking mechanism sounding extra loud in the room. In the now empty house.

Her mind raced with a million thoughts as she glanced towards the gap of her blinds, and the vast, cloudless sky. The sunlight shone down upon Celacali as the morning drew on, bathing the city in warmth. She thought of the promise she'd made to Niko—that he'd see her again tonight. Thoughts of the four men who would wait for her on the boardwalk as the sun set; the promise she'd made to the Atlantic-blue-eyed biker unfulfilled. A broken promise—forever damning and irreparable.

X.

Azeil

Flimsy police tape crinkled in Azeil's hand as he lifted it and ducked beneath its flimsy barricade, his slate irises darkening at the clamour of voices and flashing lights of the press behind the boundary. His name echoed across the parking lot, desperate shouts accompanied by a series of questions from various news companies, each devoid of empathy, despite the crime scene he steadily approached. *Vultures,* he mused with a fissure of disdain, gaze flickering to their bodies lining the yellow band. Azeil neared the inferno-eaten arches of metal, side-stepping a team of forensic scientists and police officers, who tossed glances and exchanged whispers as he passed, clustered around the driver's side before he spotted a blond head of hair amongst the bustle emanating within the barricaded area.

As Azeil wove through the team tasked with the recent homicide, Donovan straightened, shaking his head with mock disappointment whilst his fingers toyed with the navy-blue hemline of his forensics jacket. A lopsided grin on his face, "You know you're not supposed to be here *fashionably* late, right?"

"I'm aware," Azeil said, his tone wiping the grin from Donovan's face.

Donovan frowned. "But—"

"It's not the worst thing I've done for a case. Surely *you* know that? Considering I removed manslaughter from your record so you could keep this job."

"You know I live with that regret, the agony of being the reason my sister is dead. You know that, don't you?" Donovan said anxiously.

Azeil arched a dark brow. "Did I say you didn't?"

"Well, no," Donovan spluttered.

Azeil sucked in a deep breath and exhaled in a sigh as he retrieved his notepad from his jacket's pocket, pointedly changing the subject. "Who do we have?"

Donovan jokingly rolled his eyes as he led Azeil back to the remains of the car. "Twenty-seven-year-old Connor Rhodes; local security guard on the boardwalk."

A low hum emitted from the back of Azeil's throat, acknowledging Donovan's response as he scrutinized the blackened and foul-smelling remains of the vehicle. An eerie silence descended over the parking lot as inch by inch of the discoloured and blistered corpse was carefully removed from the backseats and into a dark coloured body bag atop a gurney. Daunting flashes of camera light discoloured and highlighted the harshness of the blackened and sloughing skin, baring the charred flesh to his stare like a scene in a horror movie.

Except, Azeil *lived* in a horror movie, where the victims piled up on top of each other.

"What's the suspected COD, Carter?" Azeil murmured, angling his head towards Donovan, who flanked his shoulder. His eyes trailed after the coroner, a balding man and his assistant who manoeuvred the gurney to the coroner's vehicle.

"You'd assume it was being thrown into the backseat of a burning car, wouldn't you?" Donovan drawled. "But that's not the case."

Azeil sighed, pulling a pen from his pants and clicking the end. *"Donovan."*

"Always *so impatient,*" Donovan taunted, raising his hands in mock surrender. "It appears Connor died of blood loss before his killer loaded him into the back of his car and struck a match."

"So, this," Azeil gestured to the smoke-stained car before jotting notes, "is all just an attempt to get rid of a body?"

"A lousy attempt, but an attempt nonetheless, yes."

Azeil's eyes narrowed on the forensic scientist. "What trauma to the body suggests that?"

"The left side of his throat was torn into, the jugular brutally severed with an almost … animalistic quality." Donovan's lips pursed, confused at his own explanation.

Azeil scoffed, scuffing the toe of his shoe against the bitumen as he drew a line through a bullet-point. "There goes the theory of the killer's type being females."

As Azeil lingered beside the fire-riddled car, he mulled over what he did know and how this murder linked to the others. He knew that the killer seemed to enjoy draining their victims of blood before death, making the harsher and more grotesque lacerations and disfigured limbs articulate. Almost like they revelled in the final display.

He stepped away from the vehicle as a tow truck appeared, striding towards Donovan as his mind scrambled at anything that'd explain or link Connor to Eleanor and Abigail. Their unexplained blood loss was one, what happened to all the blood? Along with the nature of their deaths. But Azeil couldn't decipher *why* the killer had suddenly disposed of Connor, a security guard who worked most nights at the boardwalk. His fingers toyed absentmindedly with the silver watch around his left wrist, drumming his fingertips upon the glass face as he worried at the details. He knew he would've been fine, that this would've been just another case; if Nyx hadn't been the one to stumble upon the body.

His worry must've been obvious, as Donovan lightly tapped his shoulder and inclined his head towards Azeil's sleek, black 2021 Toyota Camry.

Before Donovan could open his mouth to ask if he was okay, Azeil got there first, "You get any evidence?"

Donovan paused, surveying Azeil intently before he sifted through the bag slung over his shoulder and retrieved a clear bag labelled 'Evidence' from its many pockets. "Just this lighter. It was found beside the body and the backing of the seats."

"May I?"

Donovan nodded, extending the bag towards Azeil. As Azeil's fingers grasped the plastic bag between them and his granite irises trailed over the marred metal of the lighter, his eyes widened a fraction, a sick feeling engulfing his stomach, plunging like the steep drop of a rollercoaster. With a harshly inhaled breath of air, his grasp tightened on the evidence bag, crumpling the top half in his white-knuckled fist whilst he fought to suppress trembling hands, pulling his phone from his pants pocket to take a picture of the lighter. He tried to remind himself, like a broken record or a haunted mantra, that it wasn't the same lighter that flashed in his mind's eye. That it didn't belong to those ghosts who haunted him. That they were dead, and it had been *years* since that truth became a reality.

But it didn't work, a memory flickered, the silver glint of a serpent-engraved lighter catching the neon lights of the boardwalk as its owner brought it up to the cigarette perched between their lips. Azeil's heart pounded in his chest as he forced his gaze to focus, scanning the lingering crowd. A flash of platinum blond hair before it disappeared around a corner into an alleyway. *Had he really seen that?* His skin prickled with goosebumps, a shiver tickling up his spine as he clenched his hands into fists, waiting for the ache of his fingernails digging into his palms to recentre him in the present.

"Azeil?" Donovan called unsurely.

Azeil focused on Donovan's voice. "What? Did you say something?"

Donovan cocked his head, eyeing Azeil with concern. "Azeil, are you okay?"

Azeil dipped his head in a curt nod, clearing his throat, "Why wouldn't I be?"

"You don't *look* fine. Plus, I thought I'd lost you for a minute there," Donovan gestured airily towards the shadowed alleyway with a pointed glint in his eyes. "You seemed distracted."

"I'm fine, Donovan."

Donovan opened his mouth to argue but closed it with a shake of his head. His reluctance did not escape Azeil's notice, and he wondered what the other man would've done if he'd told him he wasn't okay—that he still wasn't *okay* after twenty-five years. Instead, he extended the evidence bag, calling out a farewell over his shoulder.

As Azeil checked his mirrors and shifted the car into gear, his mind churned with the memory of a malignant chuckle. That distant, mocking drawl of a voice filled his mind as he reversed. *They're not real,* he reminded himself as his grip tightened around the steering wheel and his mind battled against his rational thoughts. *They're dead.*

"Because you *killed us,"* drawled that distant honeyed voice from within the caverns of his mind.

And, despite how hard Azeil tried to deny it, he couldn't.

It was the truth.

XI.

Nyx

Passers-by bumped into Nyx's shoulder, the noisy chatter of the boardwalk sashaying past her ears, and into the glittering smatter of stars above. The neon light of the carnival rides glinted off the white-capped sea as her mind wandered to memories of the fire-riddled car. It'd been two nights since she'd discovered the body inside the smoke-stained vehicle, and her fingers twisted anxiously at the belt loops of her jeans.

Her gaze darted from person to person, lingering on the patrons whose laughter and delighted grins snagged her interest. Something uneasy rankled over her skin, like a dozen ants crawling over bared flesh. The feeling tingled and stung, but still, passers-by wandered the boardwalk as if there hadn't been a murder in its parking lot only a few days prior. *Only moments ago, it seemed.* And—despite the instincts that screamed at Nyx to go home and stay within the safety of her bedroom—she continued down the boardwalk, aimlessly wandering around the rides and stalls as if she'd never seen them all before.

And maybe she hadn't.

Maybe she hadn't *seen* Celacali for what it really was. Maybe she'd only seen the surface mask of the City of the Dead. *Or maybe, you're being paranoid,* she considered, drumming her fingers on her forearm. *You stumbled across* one *body; it doesn't mean there's some greater evil.* Her eyes darted from showbag stalls to stalls with fibreglass clowns who turned from side to side, their mouths open, waiting for someone to toss a ping-pong ball in. *Clowns ... who liked clowns?* After a few minutes of careful manoeuvring through the thriving nightlife, she stopped beside the turning carousel. Haughty and yet joyous music clamoured in her ears, flitting over the wooden planks, and bouncing out across the ocean. Through the fairground music and screams drunk with adrenaline, boisterous laughter drifted and settled uneasily in her eardrums. Her stare collided with a group of Ivory Skulls, and unease drove its thick fingers into her gut, recognition skittering over her flesh. The group of men from two nights ago swaggered through the crowds, carelessly knocking into unlucky patrons, their slurred and leering conversations flitting past her ears. Nyx quickly turned her back on the men and hoped, with everything in her, that they wouldn't recognise her.

That hope was squashed beneath the meaty hand that clamped down upon her shoulder, and she reluctantly turned to face the leering smile of the dark-haired leader of the Ivory Skulls. Her stomach churned, knotting itself tightly when she shifted to leave and found herself encircled by five men eyeing her like a piece of meat. Intoxicated stares lingered on the swell of her breasts and she swallowed nervously, eyeing them back as her father's voice rang in her head, a gentle urging brimming with serious undertones. *"Resort to violence last, Nyx. If you can, get out of the situation before it goes pear-shaped, but if you can't. Make them regret ever meeting you."*

The muscles in Nyx's back tensed, poised to flee or fight when a man with green dyed hair slung his arm across her shoulders. Her instincts rankled, like the hackles along a dog's spine, when his fingertips grazed the white straps of her halter top, and she moved to retreat from his wandering hands. She suppressed the urge to snap at the men, suspecting they'd find amusement in her outburst as she bit down harshly on her tongue. And she would *not* give them that satisfaction, not even if it cost her her life.

A calloused hand wrapped around her forearm and tugged Nyx towards the group.

She swallowed her traitorous fear, batting the man's hands from her hips with narrowed eyes.

A chuckle of bemusement spilled from the swaying, alcohol-sodden man's lips, as he unsteadily stepped forward to bridge the distance between herself and him, his fingers toying with the denim belt loop of her jeans.

The pounding of her heart drowned out her subconsciousness, palms splaying across the drunken man's chest as she shoved him back.

His friends snickered and jeered, whistling tauntingly as he stumbled, then when he righted himself again, and drew nearer, fingertips digging into her forearms with a jolting sense of entitlement. "You little—"

Before he could finish speaking, Nyx stomped on his foot with as much force as she could muster, white-sneaker-clad foot colliding with his own. He released her and hissed in pain, and through the daze of adrenaline, Nyx raised her arm, curling her hand into a fist before she drew back and struck him across the jaw. Fear, adrenaline, and satisfaction churned within her chest as her knuckles throbbed and she turned to flee, instead, colliding with a solid chest that sent her stumbling backward before different hands grasped her forearms and gently righted her.

Hesitantly, Nyx lifted her eyes to familiar Atlantic-blues that peered down at her calmly. Relief washed over her as Niko dragged his gaze across every inch of her skin, the blueness lingering on her reddened knuckles and the arithmetical clenching and unclenching of her fist. Gradually, he lifted his stare to the men now shifting uneasily, suddenly wary.

"Back off, *boys*," Niko warned, lip curling into a chilling sneer when the gang members dared to step closer.

The dark-haired leader bristled with rage as Niko reached out and pulled Nyx behind him. Like the smooth ease of muscle rippling beneath the spotted pelt of a cheetah. She marvelled at the fluidity of the movement, something so simple that it shouldn't have made her heart skip, but it did, and something within her stirred like it had done on the carousel, enthralled by this newfound, protective action.

She had barely registered the movement, it had been so fast, so … natural, when the dark-haired man looked at her, leering, "Got yourself a protector, do we, *sweetheart*?" he slurred, gaze lazily dragging. "He won't always be around to save you."

Tension thickened in the air, his words hung like a dense cloud of smoke, crackling around the group like static in a storm. The gang leader scrutinised Nyx, who peered around Niko's shoulder. She started as he laughed and then dusted his palms down his T-shirt, turning to the gang members behind him. Each of the men eyed Nyx from behind Niko's shoulder beadily, sizing him up before they retreated with disgruntled scoffs and irked headshakes.

Niko waited until the last of the Ivory Skulls had melted into the crowd before he turned to Nyx, his gaze surveying her once more. Like he wanted to ensure that her fist was the only injury she'd sustained. Finally, when he was satisfied by whatever he saw, he draped his arm across her shoulders, Aerosmith tank top brushing her arm as he manoeuvred them past *Lilith's Clothes Boutique* and a group of young women browsing swivelling jewellery stands at a stall beside the archway. He steered her towards the blinding lights of the boardwalk entrance with his fluid-childlike gait, the familiar jangling of his threaded bracelets, the *chuck-tang* of his boot chains on leather, and his glinting earrings a sudden, inexplicable haven to her.

He finally spoke as they slipped between the bollards stopping cars from ploughing into the amusement sector, "You're lucky, you know?"

Nyx glanced up at him, the truth of his words reverberating within her. "I know."

"What were you planning on doing before I found you?"

"I was planning on kicking at least three of their asses before I actually *may* have needed help," Nyx quipped, shrugging his arm off her shoulders. "Thanks for your help back there, but you don't need to remind me that the male gender doesn't understand the word *no*."

He lifted his hands in surrender, a sudden glint to his eyes as he smiled down at her, a glint that *shouldn't* have sent a thrill through her but did, "Easy there, chica. Something tells me that you would've handled yourself just fine. *Especially* with the defenceless act you had going."

"You … caught that?"

He shrugged. "It's always interesting to see the moment the predator realises that their prey, isn't prey at all. It's quite … *deceptive.*"

Odd choice of words. "You make it sound easy, like breathing," she said, peering up at him, aware of the people crowding the boardwalk. "But it's not. It's *more* than that."

"It's safety, power and tact," Niko stated, listing each word with understanding.

The honking of a car horn startled Nyx as they passed beneath the red-neon archway, the blaring sound drawing her gaze from Niko to the trio that sat waiting on their bikes, the only inhabitants of the otherwise empty parking bay. Since the incident, the whole lot had been cordoned off. CRIME SCENE DO NOT CROSS. As Nyx and Niko skirted the boundary, Kade's gaze met Nyx's. She stifled a smile at his hurried approach, something within her lifting its head at the simple action as he closed the short distance between them. She saw the silver in his ears, and suddenly, he was pulling her in for a hug and she was suddenly smothered in his enthralling scent of oil-paints and pencil shavings.

His fox-like gaze, which seemed lighter, scrutinised Nyx in the same searching way that Niko's had done. And, like he was satisfied with whatever he had found, his features stretched into his customary Cheshire Cat-like grin, brimming with mirth. His hand nestled upon the small of her back before he steered her to the remaining two members of their quartet.

"Where've you been the past two nights, Nyx?" Kade breathed out in a rush, peering down at her with raised brows. "Niko and I took turns looking for you. For two nights!"

Nyx's eyes wandered from Kade to Kotori, to Orion as they sat astride their machines, eyes like weighted blankets thrust over her head before darkness plunged her senses down, down, down. With some effort, she turned away from them and refocused on Kade. "I ... thought it would be best ... to wait a few days," she explained, trailing off as her mind threw images of a charred body to the forefront of her mind. "Wait, you've been looking for me? For two nights?"

Niko and Kade nodded like it should've been obvious. A shared glance passed between them and Orion's honeyed voice drifted over, "And now you've found her," he said, drumming his leather-clad fingers on his handlebars as he started his bike. "Let's go, you three."

Niko beamed with excitement. Striding forward, he pulled Nyx gently to his bike and swung his jean-clad leg over the seat.

She grinned back at him as she followed, his delight contagious. She turned and peered over the empty black lot, seeing a five-by-five blackened patch, now cordoned off by police tape. Memory panged in her chest and flickers of a fire-riddled car danced through her mind. She *knew* it'd been there. She'd seen the wreckage with her own eyes. She'd *smelled* the barbequed skin through the shattered windows. Her mind sought to mock her, twisting the memories until she couldn't be sure she knew *anything*. It antagonised her, forcing Nyx to look away.

It was real. She reminded herself, sucking in a shaky breath as her teeth gnawed at the flesh of her bottom lip.

"Nyx?" called Kade over the low, thunderous rumble of Orion's motorcycle engine, his tone hesitant.

"Yeah?" she replied, sounding distracted.

"Are you ... okay?"

Nyx nodded automatically, barely registering Kade's question and daring a glance back to *that spot*.

Four pairs of eyes scrutinised her with interest, their awareness seeming to grow the longer she stared. Orion observed the closest of all, appearing to silently probe Nyx for answers that she didn't know she had. Together, they watched her, cataloguing every distracted gesture, noting everything the other may have missed with fine-tuned precision. Collating, sorting, storing.

"Where are we going?" Nyx breathed out softly, quelling her turmoil as she met each of their gazes.

Kade grinned, dimples embedding themselves in the flesh of his cheeks like two perfect crescent moons. "There's a party down by the beach tonight."

Niko peered at her over his shoulder, "We'll bring you back before sunrise, chica. Promise."

"C'mon, angel," Kade grinned, rubbing a palm along his jaw. "What happened to the girl who thrived in Celacali's night?"

"She found a body in the back of a fire-lashed car," Nyx stated, devoid of emotion and without faltering.

Niko's choked laugh spluttered from his lips, turning into an awkward cough when he realised, she wasn't joking. "*What?*"

Nyx raked her fingers through her hair and inhaled the narcissus-infused air into her lungs, tipping her head back before she sighed deeply and straightened. "I suppose it was about time," she mused, shaking her head to clear it. "The Fates can be cruel sometimes but, so far, they've been on my side," she turned to Orion, holding his stare, "Where's this beach party?"

"Chades Cove. It's not far from the bluff," he said, not missing a beat. Stare, cold.

"Well? What are we waiting for? Let's go!" she said.

The bikes roared to life as soon as the words left her mouth, Kotori's reluctant stare trailed over Nyx, studying her for a moment more. As though her sudden brush with death should decide her fate. "Are you *sure* you want to go, *kleintje*?" he murmured, his voice a deep and soothing rumble.

"I'm sure," Nyx assured, smiling at his use of the pet name 'shorty', and wrapping her arms around Niko's abdomen. She grasped the fabric of his shirt in her hands as he revved the engine of his bike. "Hey, Niko," she said.

"Yeah?"

"Do me a favour and don't get us killed, okay?"

Niko's laughter filled her ears as he shifted on his bike and gazed down at her. His Atlantic-blue eyes danced with mirth, eyebrows waggling teasingly as his wrist twisted and he revved the engine of his bike as if to emphasise his point. "Wouldn't dream of it."

And with that, they tore through the car park and down to the beach. Slipping through a gap in the rusted ring-lock fence barring passers-by from the crumbling ramp leading down to the shoreline. A riveted laugh cascaded from Nyx's lips, a wide grin splitting her face as her arms banded themselves tighter around Niko's waist and their hoots of elation filled the sky.

Something in her fell into place in their presence, as seamlessly as a missing piece to a puzzle. She dared to hope that the Fates *had* been on her side and, despite everything they'd put her through—beer-stained breath and unwanted caresses flitting phantom-like across her mind—that they'd led her to the City of the Dead for a reason. As she joined in with the boys' howling lust for life, and heard herself baying at the moon with them, feeling more alive than she could ever remember, two Latin words crept into her mind.

Memento Mori: Remember you must die.

* * *

A distant 80s track glided across the dense tree line shrouding Chades Cove, the light of a flickering bonfire casting long shadows over the sand as people crowded around, dancing to the music. Some, Nyx noticed, drank from squat bottles of beer, 'stubbies', whilst others passed various bottles of alcohol back and forth. A cluster of people swayed to the music that blasted from a large, well-loved boombox, stretching their hands up to the sky with beguiled smiles.

As she looked over the rag-tag beach party, the corners of her mouth pulled into a grin. It wasn't like the house parties in Malor, with their tiered and extravagant two-storey homes. This was *exhilaration* in the moonlight, outside, in the night where the scattered fold-out chairs, driftwood logs, and the occasional upturned barrel were the foundations of something greater than just a party.

The rumble of the quartet's engines ceased as they came to a stop and Orion's icy stare bore into those unlucky enough to garner his interest. A light laugh tumbled from Nyx's mouth—like water babbling down a winding riverbed—she couldn't help it. But, as easily as it had come, her heart jolted in her chest at the intensity of his sudden gaze. Kade coughed, his ever silent footfall making it impossible for Nyx to decipher *when* he had ended up beside her.

"Remember what we're here for, boys," Orion stated like he'd reiterated the same warning countless times before. His ivory complexion bathed with shadows caught the bonfire's light as he dismounted and strode off through the tree line.

Nyx tracked his path, waiting until she deemed he was out of hearing range before she angled her head to Kade. "What's the actual plan of attack, boys?"

Kotori hesitated, peering back over his shoulder at Nyx, "Be careful."

"Aw, Kade, did you hear that? Kotori's concerned about our safety," Niko drawled, snickering when Kotori rolled his eyes and disappeared after Orion.

Nyx playfully swatted Niko's side, stifling the laughter threatening to bubble past her lips, and when her gaze darted to Kade, she found only merriment. He strode forward to right her as she stumbled and her palms splayed over his chest, a slight blush dusting her cheeks when she dragged her eyes from his swirling tattoos and to his smirking face.

Kade's fingertips skittered down Nyx's arm until his fingers interlaced with hers and they walked towards the flickering flames of the bonfire. Niko traipsed beside Nyx; an arm slung over her shoulders, stooping to snatch up an unopened bottle of whiskey from someone's half-open chilly bin. His nimble fingers unscrewed the lid before he brought the mouth of the bottle up to his nose and inhaled a lungful of the sharp, malty-smelling liquor before extending the bottle to Nyx.

It was an invitation that trailed a salacious path up her spine, her mind wandering to places it didn't belong, before she took the bottle and they waited as she considered her options. *To let go, or not to let go,* she pondered as her eyes darted from one blond to the other. For a moment, she considered how they would react if she rejected the whiskey.

Nyx's gaze trailed over the partygoers, seeming to speak to herself rather than to the men by her side. "I haven't drank in several years. Not since …" she trailed off, growing distracted by her memories.

Dark eyes and grabbing hands.

Kade glanced over at Niko, something dark shifting beneath his eyes that vanished in the next breath, "Since?"

Her eyes locked on his, eclipsed by memories before she shook her head to rid herself of them. "It doesn't matter."

Shunting all thoughts aside, she brought the mouth of the bottle to her lips. Her nose screwed up with displeasure as the amber liquid burned the back of her throat, a traitorous cough spluttering from her lips. She wiped her mouth with the back of her hand and hurriedly passed the bottle to Kade.

"You know, we practically kissed just then," Niko announced after a beat of silence.

Nyx blinked up at him, "You're an idiot," she stated with playful annoyance.

Kade shook his head softly, swallowing his own mouthful before he spoke in a low, taunting jeer, "I guess we all just kissed then. Hey, Niko?" He poked Nyx's side as if it'd quell the laughter spilling from her lips.

"It's not that funny," Niko complained, pouting as Kade's laughter joined with Nyx's.

Nyx shook her head, spluttering, "It's your reaction that makes it so funny," she wheezed. "Your face dropped like someone socked you in the nuts."

"Man, you looked like a kicked puppy," said Kade, releasing Nyx's hand in favour of grasping Niko's shoulder.

Niko muttered something beneath his breath, bringing the bottle of whiskey back to his lips, tipping his head up to the sky as he swallowed the malty liquor and, *God,* did Nyx find the motion oddly attractive. *You need to get out more,* she thought to herself.

Kade's arm wrapped around Nyx's shoulder as the heat from the bonfire ghosted across her skin. The heaped coals of the fire glowed bright shades of tangerine, its flames licking viciously at the wooden pile, filling the fire-lit beach with a soft popping and snapping of wooden branches that mingled with the hits blasting from the boombox. People cheered, staggered, danced, and slurred the lyrics to the music. Men and women soaked in the sounds and the salt-riddled air, partying to their heart's content without a care. In this moment, they were content in a haze of spirits, music and firelight. And, for the first time, in a long time, Nyx wanted to join them.

Elation rippled through Nyx like waves, threatening to pull her beneath its heady tide as she tipped her face up to the sky and the seconds turned first to minutes, and then to hours of passing the bottle of whiskey, talking, laughing. Her hair cascaded down behind her and she felt the prickling weight of Niko and Kade's gazes as they danced together. As lost in the thrill of the night as she was, she couldn't help but notice how they seemed to marvel at her ease around them. Like they were still unsure, or that her comfort wasn't true.

* * *

Niko and Kade knew Orion watched them from the edge of the tree line—his frigid stare searing into the sides of their faces from across the beach—even if Nyx didn't realise it, they did. Their fox-like eyes trailed over Nyx's dark lashes; their subconscious minds noting every little thing she did like it was their holy grail.

Orion halted, eerily bright stare drifting away from Niko and Kade to Nyx. No matter how hard he tried, he couldn't help but find the bay-haired girl entrancing. He kept to the shadows, unwilling to squander his chances at an easy meal by revealing his presence. And though it irked him, he trusted Niko and Kade enough to lure them in.

He watched them as, like a well-oiled machine, the blond duo peering down at the girl between them. He knew her—had watched her for years—and he knew of the past she skirted away from, waiting to see if she'd become a wise investment. And from what he knew, she was panning out wonderfully. Kade's gaze lingered on her face whilst Niko's stare drifted from Nyx to the group of drunken people clustered around the blazing fire. The pair were familiar with the art of choosing and luring prey. Though at times, they longed for the bloodless past of their mortality. Free from their needs to feed and the slaughter they wrought … At least, *sometimes* they regretted their actions.

Their eyes met over Nyx's head and an unspoken agreement passed between them, before they seamlessly led her closer to the throng of partygoers.

* * *

Hands settled upon Nyx's shoulder, waist, and hips, sometimes lingering, sometimes ghosting across her skin as if she'd imagined it. Nyx didn't mind. Her thoughts, though fuzzy from the whiskey, were somehow still clear. Some part of her subconscious knew that if she uttered so much as a word; the pair would back off and cease their harmless caresses. And that thought comforted her as she danced beneath the stars. Niko's assorted bracelets jingled, clinking together as his fingers skittered down her arm and his hand rested upon Nyx's hip, his fingertips pressing lightly into her hip as he softly pulled her into his chest and the scent of coconuts, cigarettes and sea salt engulfed her senses with the breeze that ruffled his hair.

Kade smirked devilishly, as he stepped closer to Nyx and her heart jolted—a warmth trailing across her skin and nestling in her chest—trapping her between the two of them before his hand settled on the curve of her waist opposite to Niko's, toned chest pressing against Nyx's.

* * *

Kotori sat with his back pressed into a tree nearest the bonfire and inclined his head towards a cluster of men sitting upon a large, driftwood log. He waited for the subtle dip of Orion's head before his gaze left the men who reeked of beer and landed upon Nyx, then

Kade, then Niko. Something seemed to jumpstart in his chest then, and he knew, by default, it was like this for all of them. Every instinct of his started going haywire as the thrill of the hunt zinged through him and anticipation coated his tongue like honey; sweeter than any of their combined motives. And *much* darker.

Kotori, sensing the budding intent, pushed himself up from the soft sand and wove through the beach party before his ring-clad hand wrapped around Nyx's forearm, pulling her from Kade and Niko's grasp and into his own. Dual exclamations of protest accosted his eardrums as his arm banded around her waist, his dark eyebrows arching as if warning the blonds against reaching out and pulling her back to them. Intent in his desire to return her to the safety of her house whilst they descended on their chosen victim, keeping her and the other bystanders away from the impending hunt. A small mercy he often ensured Orion entertained. A soft giggle spluttered from Nyx, drawing the towering brunette's gaze to her. His lips twitched, fighting the grin threatening to spread across his face whilst he tightened his grasp around her and she leaned into his side.

"I think it's time to leave," Kotori murmured.

"C'mon Kotori, just a while longer won't hurt," Kade began, stepping forward as if to pull Nyx from Kotori's arms and back into his.

Niko nodded somewhat frantically. "Nyx doesn't want to leave. Right, chica?" he stated, his eyes darting to Nyx.

"He's right. I want to stay," Nyx murmured, yawning behind her hand.

Kotori just sighed. "Let's get you home, *kleintje*."

Nyx furrowed her eyebrows as Kotori began leading her back towards their bikes, "That's not fair," she muttered, peering up at him.

"What's not fair?" Kotori said.

"You telling me what I can and can't do," she huffed, raking her fingers through her hair. "I mean, that'd be like me telling you to put on a shirt since it's ... distracting. So, why should *you* decide when *I* go home?"

Niko and Kade snickered. As if in answer, Kotori's deeply timbred chuckle ghosted the shadows from the fading fire before he paused several paces away from their bikes. Then he turned, platinum blond hair capturing his attention—and theirs—as Orion sat astride his bike waiting for their return, drumming his leather-clad fingers upon his bike's handlebars.

Orion's gravelly voice drifted across to them, "How about this, sweetheart? If you can walk to here in a straight line, you and the boys can go back to partying."

Kotori, noticing Orion's stare, peered down at Nyx before adding, "But if you can't, we're taking you home. Okay?"

* * *

Nyx frowned, head tipping back to meet Kotori's gaze. Then she nodded. He stepped back from her, unwinding his arm from her waist before he gestured towards the three blonds several metres away. *Close the distance without staggering.*

As Nyx took three steady steps away from him and a triumphant grin swam over her face, she gleefully peered over her shoulder and winked. Niko chuckled, leaning his forearms onto the handlebars of his bike before Nyx squared her shoulders and stalked closer to the waiting blonds. A startled yelp spilled from her lips as she stumbled on a root jutting out from the dirt. *Damn! Where had that come from?*

Then Kotori's hands grasped her waist and she huffed in annoyance, accepting her defeat as he guided her to his bike, extending his hand out to her before her fingers wreathed in his and she clambered on behind him. Her arms banded themselves around his bare stomach as the quartet started their bikes, revving their engines until all Nyx could hear was their thunderous rumble. Niko's and Kade's hollers of delight echoed in her ears, drifting over the bike's engines when she rested her head upon Kotori's jacket-clad back and the group peeled out of the forest. Her eyelids fluttered shut as she allowed herself to be carried away.

XII.

Azeil

Sunlight glinted off the waves breaking along the boardwalk's shoreline, lapping against the pillars of the fairground sector a hundred metres from the quiet stretch of stores at its opening. Locals ducked into the quaint boutiques, acknowledging Azeil with a friendly greeting or raise of their hand as he approached the video store, pointedly ignoring other passers-by who turned to their companions and started murmuring amongst themselves, glancing or pointing at him.

As always, my reputation precedes me, he thought.

Azeil's gaze appraised the people he passed, lingering on unfamiliar faces of tourists before he strode into the video and music store he knew a certain redhead owned. Locating the young woman, who rested comfortably against the counter, he crossed the room with a determined stride, stare surveying the store and the few customers browsing the shelves.

The woman's eyes darted to him, pushing herself upright and straightening her summer dress as he halted in front of her, his elbow pressed against the countertop, and the white cotton of his dress shirt stark against the light wood countertop.

"Delilah, I assume?" he queried, retrieving his notepad from his pants pocket as his gaze held hers and he revealed his badge to her. "I'm—"

"Azeil Monroe. *Famous detective* of Celacali," she drawled, toying with the necklace at her throat. "What can I do to help?"

"I need to ask you a few questions about Eleanor Hayes. Her parents mentioned that you were close with her and Abigail before they ... passed?"

Delilah's steely irises pinned Azeil in place, her head angling. "I did—*was* their friend. We went to school together, you know? Parties, holidays and sometimes they helped around the store."

He nodded, noting her relationship to the victim's. "Can you think of anyone who might've wanted to hurt them? Any exes or jealous *friends*?"

"None that I know of," she said, brow furrowing before she added, "They used to party with the Ivory Skulls a lot, and trouble follows that gang *everywhere*."

"Ah, the *Skulls*," he confirmed, tapping his pen against the lined pages of his notepad. "Anyone else?"

She seemed to consider for a moment, lips pursed before she perked up and her eyes widened. "The bikers."

"Bikers?"

"Yeah. The Ivory Skulls *hate* them." Her words trailed off as her stare drifted from his, scanning the shop before returning to him. "I'm talking fistfights, bloodied faces and threats-*hate*."

Azeil's brows arched, jotting down the information. "Anything else?"

Delilah mulled over his words for a moment, the sweet scent of the native, blooming narcissi filling his nostrils as he waited. The floral perfume was abundant throughout the city as the plants sprouted across the landscape, adapting to the tropical lowlands and the sea salt they thrived in until they were everywhere. As Azeil recalled his years in Celacali, he couldn't remember a time in his youth or the months of studying at the local university to become a detective, if the city had ever *not* smelt of their fragrance paired with the seaweed that collected around the boardwalk's underbelly. His train of thought was cut short when Delilah gasped, snapping her fingers together.

"Eleanor messaged me the night before she died, saying something about the Skulls' rivals being at the party she was throwing," she said. Her hands darted beneath the counter as she hastily unlocked her phone, opening a message feed with Eleanor to show him.

His slack-clad thigh brushed against the stainless-steel front of the checkout, eyes skimming the messages as he pulled his phone from his pants pocket. "May I?" he asked, gesturing to his phone.

"Of course. Snap away," she said, placing her phone atop the countertop.

The soft *clicking* of his phone's camera bridged the silence that descended, Delilah's fingers drumming against the metallic surface as she watched the browsing customers wander around the aisles of movies and music. Azeil slid her phone back to her and surveyed the auburn-haired woman. "What do you know of Lilith Neaves?"

Delilah frowned. "The old lady who owns the boutique next to the comics?"

Azeil nodded, recalling the fiery woman. "Yep."

"She seems nice, keeps to herself and tries to keep her granddaughter away from the Skulls," Delilah chuckled, a smile uplifting her lips. "Mila and I used to go with Abigail and Eleanor to almost every party in the city."

He considered her words, noting the new connection before he dipped his head and tucked his notepad into his pocket. "Thank you, Delilah."

She shrugged, bashfully accepting his gratitude. "Anytime, Monroe."

As Azeil pivoted on his heel and started towards the entrance, he considered the locals' dislike of the Ivory Skulls and the new, unnamed bikers who feuded at the city's main tourist attraction. He knew, like everyone on the police force knew, that there was very little they could do about the notorious gang. Every time one of the members was arrested, they *always* got out on bail the next day—all indiscretions forgotten. It made him consider the gang's connections, and how far their reach stretched.

Did it reach Malor? Wildegulf? Or the larger cities than even Celacali? He thought, slipping around the store's shelves until the peaceful sector of the boardwalk greeted him. He supposed there was no knowing how far their connections spread because if someone didn't want something found, most would find a way to hide it. Azeil was no stranger to keeping a vast network of contacts hidden, tucking it within the shadows of his reputation so no one would see them and he could continue with his job in peace. If there was one thing people sought, it was power. And he wasn't foolish enough to assume people would be swayed by his influence, knowing someone greedy enough would seek to obtain his years-long connections.

His palm pressed into the glass door of Lilith's Store and broke his train of thought, a pleasant chime announcing his arrival as a greying woman continued to restock clothing racks. She didn't turn to him, shifting articles of clothing to place a garment onto the rack, but he knew she was aware of his presence. A chuckle rumbled from his chest as he approached her, grinning when she turned to him with warm, hazel eyes and a motherly smile.

"Here take these," she ordered, passing him coat hangers before he could protest. "How have you been, dear? I haven't seen you down here in a while."

"I'm good, all things considered," he said, following Lilith around the store as she crossed the room to another section dedicated to jackets, handing her one coat hanger at a time, as she rehung items. "I have some questions for you about Eleanor Hayes."

She turned to him, a deep crease to her aged features. "It's terrible, isn't it? Two young women murdered after such a … reprieve," she shook her head, clicking her tongue. "It's been *years* since Sophia passed."

"Thirteen to be exact but what about the constant death toll on the borders of the city? Don't those count?"

"Of course, they count," Lilith said, eyeing him with a sharpness to her gaze. "I worry, like all of us do. I *fear* for my family's lives, wondering if one day it'll be the police knocking on *my* door. So, ask your questions about the Hayes girl before I lose my nerve ... Niamh always said I had a short temper."

Azeil's eyes softened at the mention of his mother, remembering the woman who used to work with Lilith and the friendship they had shared. "Did you see Eleanor before she died at all?"

"For a moment," Lilith admitted, rolling a garment's fabric between her fingers, stare darting over his shoulder to peer through the floor-to-ceiling windows of the storefront. "Abigail and Eleanor came in and bought some clothes with Mila, my granddaughter, for a party Eleanor was hosting. I tried to warn them that associating with the Ivory Skulls was bad news." Her gaze locked upon his, heavy with regret. "They didn't listen, Azeil. I watched them walk out that door and they never came back—"

"Hey," Azeil soothed, grasping her forearm and shaking his head to dispel her guilt. "It's not your fault. You tried to stop them from going and that's what matters, most wouldn't give a damn. You're *not* to blame."

"But—"

"No, Lilith. Don't put someone else's blame on your shoulders," he said.

Lilith sucked in a shaky breath, nodding her head as she brushed a hand down her floral shirt. "What else would you like to know?"

He withdrew his notepad, quickly writing down the information she'd provided about Eleanor and Abigail prior to their deaths before his eyes darted to the sprawling calligraphy across the store's windows. "Was there anything else you remember from that night? Out of place stalls or people?"

"Two blond men were watching the Ivory Skulls from beside the antique store, you know the one that closed several months ago?" She nodded along with her own words whilst Azeil jotted down the new information. "Those two men seem to be just as much trouble as the gang, maybe more. The bikers enjoy stirring up the Ivory Skulls so, when they followed after the gang members that night and another pair joined them. I knew there was trouble brewing."

Azeil added several new scribbles to his notepad, tucking the pen and booklet away before he smiled. "Thank you, Lilith. I hope you have a nice rest of your day."

"There's no need to thank me, boy. I've always had a soft spot for Niamh's sons," she said, ushering his gratitude away with a sweep of her hand and a pointed look to the front door. "But be gone, you're scaring my preppy customers away."

He rolled his eyes, laughing at Lilith's words as he crossed the room, pausing with his foot on the door's threshold when she called out to him.

"Try Luka Ellis if you're investigating the Hayes'. He works on the force and is an old family friend to the Hayes."

Azeil tipped an imaginary hat, mentally noting to do just that.

"He'll help you get the information you need, Azeil." Her voice lowered like she didn't want anyone else to hear her. "Even if it breaks some rules."

I'm no stranger to breaking rules, Lilith, he thought, side-stepping a group of teenagers who hurtled past on skateboards.

You broke something irreparable when you killed us, the orotund voice echoed in his mind. Replaying until it clung to his skull. He couldn't shake it because it was true: Blood stained his hands. He had broken something within himself that wouldn't heal and now, he spent his days trying to atone for those crimes—or at least, to forget them.

* * *

Passers-by sidestepped Azeil, some pushing trollies filled with groceries whilst others chattered with friends, arms laden with shopping bags etched with the branding of specialty stores, heels or designer shoes clacking against the white-tiled floor of the three-storey shopping centre. Rays of light cascaded down the mall's centre from the lavish skylight, spotlighting a three-tiered fountain gushing water and a surrounding array of indoor plants. His gaze trailed across the space, people-watching as they went about their day, and he searched for Luka within the ever-moving patrons.

He spotted the umber-skinned man in his early thirties a moment later, leaning against a marble pillar with his arms folded over his black shirt, a dark satchel over his shoulder. Azeil remembered when construction had begun on the shopping centre in the months he'd been studying at Celacali University to obtain his bachelor's of policing and extended subjects related to his field. In the six months before he graduated, he had watched the construction each day he went to university and then returned home, up until the night before he graduated and left for Wildegulf to begin his traineeship. By the time he returned as a licensed and qualified detective with an abundance of connections, the building was bustling with customers and had become a popular location in the city.

"Azeil Monroe," Luka drawled, curtly acknowledging him with a gruff tone devoid of his usual light-hearted nature. "I'm honoured to be in your *mighty* presence… all things considered."

"You haven't changed at all," Azeil retorted.

Luka shrugged, inclining his head towards the sushi restaurant at his back before the pair walked, shoulder-to-shoulder and they slipped into a booth in the room's corner, sitting opposite each other. "I knuckled down enough to graduate from the police academy if that means anything to you as a detective."

"Well, shit. How did that happen?" Azeil jested, recalling the man's lively and party-filled youth when they'd met on the boardwalk years ago.

"I met a girl who encouraged me to chase my career … and then I lost her in a blink of an eye," he admitted, allowing Azeil to glean an insight into *why* Lilith had told him to contact Luka.

Privately, Azeil wondered how he was allowed to be a part of Eleanor's case. "Eleanor Hayes?" Azeil prompted, retrieving his notepad to add another bullet-point to his list, tying Eleanor to Luka.

"Eleanor was … everything to me. We'd just moved in together and she loved the parties she hosted at her parents' house, or the ones

Abigail invited her to with the Ivory Skulls. I loved her." Luka's fingers trailed across the tabletop, brown eyes lifting to Azeil. "What you asked me to bring, I shouldn't be showing you. Even *if* I loved Eleanor."

Azeil nodded, the warning sharp in Luka's tone. "I know what's at stake. Just like I know that if *this,*" he gestured between themselves, "gets back to an official. Any evidence I have will become unlawful and discarded in court."

Luka's gaze scanned the room as he pulled his leather satchel to him, unclasping its latch and retrieving the files within before he slid the sealed clip file to Azeil. "Everything is a duplicate of the original files, untraceable to the administration team in charge of the records. I mean *everything*. Photos, reports, CODs, forensics and a USB of surveillance footage to *all* the current cases' last sightings."

"Including Connor?" Azeil asked.

Luka nodded, "*Including* Connor."

"Good to hear your breaking and entering skills haven't been forgotten," he mused, tucking his notepad into his pocket before he grasped the file and tucked it beneath his arm.

"Old habits, die hard."

Azeil chuffed, nodding, "Don't they ever."

Luka straightened with the next breath he took, his eyes pinning Azeil in place. "Keep this information locked down, Azeil. I'm breaking laws and protocol by sharing it with you. Hell, I'm risking my job. I don't care if some of the police board know about the ... *lengths* you'll take to solve cases, but *nobody* finds out about this. Got it?"

"I know what's at stake, Luka," he said, rising from the chair and clasping the other man's shoulder. "Thank you."

"Thank me by finding something we can use to lock this psycho up."

"I will," he promised, releasing Luka's shoulder, and striding from the restaurant with the pounding of his heart filling his ears and a phantom burn of unease left to brand his arm—engraining the unauthorised information into his skin.

Tha-thump ... tha-thump ... tha-thump.

XIII.

Orion

Mindless chatter skirted the shell of his ears, the harsh wail of a toddler tearing through his eardrums as Orion turned towards the child and its mother out the front of a diner with an irked gleam to his eyes, annoyed that his crafted filtration of the boardwalk's noises was being shattered by the young girl. His forearms pressed against the railing at his back as he leant against it and continued his silent search for an Ivory Skull who'd forgotten his place—a place Orion would be only too happy to remind him of.

Despite the look he sent the small child, Orion didn't dislike children. He didn't understand them, but he refused to be the monster who harmed them, going so far as to ensure that the ones who became lost in the bustle were returned to their parents. Rare occasions only Kotori had been privy to, assisting Orion like he'd been doing since Leon had turned him and he'd become his trusted companion. This was followed by Niko and Kade when they joined their tightly knit circle, becoming his family, his brothers, and his pack.

Niko, Kade and Kotori's gazes swept passers-by from their scattered positions near him when he glanced over at his companions. Kotori's attention constantly switched from the people milling around to Orion, whilst the blond duo who usually caused trouble to kill time waited quietly against the barricade. The trio's senses honed upon Orion, awaiting his signal as his frigid stare settled on an ash-blond Ivory Skull beside a ramp leading to the fairground's underbelly, tucked between a stall selling novelty items and another selling plants with handmade pots. They'd returned to the boardwalk after Kotori had dropped Nyx off at her house, the moon hanging low in the sky as the build-up to their hunt began.

Orion's chin lifted; voice eerily detached as he kept the man within his sights. "Remember our plan, boys," he warned.

Niko dragged his gaze from the Ivory Skull to Orion. "The current plan or the one involving Nyx?"

"The one that's been twenty-five years in the making, Nik," Orion said, watching as the Ivory Skull turned and wandered down the ramp, pulling a cigarette from his pockets. "This is just a reminder to anyone who threatens it."

Kotori's considering hum carried like thunder through storm clouds. "Don't we already *have* Nyx?" he asked, peering down at Orion with dark eyes. "The plan was to attain what Azeil cares about most until she trusts us and then ... endanger her? Your whole plan is to make Azeil feel what we felt in 2012, ruining the comfort he finds in his daughter, but when are we going to get our *vengeance*?"

"Soon," Orion replied.

"*When?*" Kotori prompted, gesturing to Niko and Kade.

Orion awaited the frustrated vocalisation of his dark desires—those Kotori often refused to admit to having. Like he'd done so many times before in the centuries Orion had known him, Kotori had been unwilling to indulge in them because he kept his big heart tucked in the shadows of his mind.

"I understand *why* we chose Nyx but I ..." He shook his head, dark hair hurriedly raked out of his eyes when it fell in front of his face. "That's not *my* revenge, Orion. That's yours. I didn't *want* to kill those girls to entice Azeil back here ... but I did. Because it was part of *our* plan. They didn't have to die but they *needed* to ... *for our plan.*"

"He's right, Rion," Kade said, wandering away from the railing to stand before him. "You've always enjoyed a more ... mental torment. And as much as we like a little bloodshed, those girls didn't have to die. We could've killed a Skull. Except we didn't, and I don't want to kill any more innocent women. But, compared to your revenge, ours is a pretty simple, blood-stained one."

Orion arched an eyebrow, imploring Kade to continue with a flick of his wrist and half of his mind focused on the Ivory Skull who had disappeared down the ramp as he started after him. "Go on."

"We want Asher, Amir and Ryder dead, like you want Azeil dead, but *we* want to hear their screams and see their terror before we rip their throats out," Kade said, hands tucked into his jean's pockets.

Orion's head shook with mirth, a grin curling his lips as he watched his tattoo-embellished companion weave through passers-by and down the ramp leading to their prey. He had always enjoyed Kade's ambiguous nature and sadistic thought process, gravitating to the man whenever he wanted to draw out a kill because, like him, Kade enjoyed the terror they instilled in their prey. It wasn't *just* about food with him—as much as they needed blood to survive, lest they starved themselves and their bodies went into a fitful dormant phase—it was about the chase, and Orion liked that.

He also knew Kade had fled to Celacali in his early twenties after his father had destroyed his art studio when Kade had refused to become CEO and his father's right-hand man, of the Artus family business. Though, Orion wondered if Kade's love for twisted and *horrid* deaths stemmed from his own near-death experience before he had arrived in the city. Kade's father had organised a personal hit on him days after his rejection of the family business. A group of men had been paid to drag him into the ruined building of his studio, stab him to the brink of death and leave him in the debris of canvas and sculptures.

Orion could remember the look in Niko's eyes when Leon had brought Kade to the cave, something desperate in his eyes that Orion didn't understand until Niko had revealed his motives to Orion weeks later—the rockstar-like blond seeing a piece of himself in Kade. Familiarity, family.

Orion angled his head towards Niko at his side, refocusing on his surroundings as Kotori flanked his opposite shoulder. "What does that mean for Nyx then?" he asked, frowning before he rephrased his question. "Will *she* change the end goal?"

Niko eyed Orion carefully, seeming to decide on what he wanted to share with him. "You know I wouldn't mind ... keeping her alive. I like her fight, her bloody past in Malor and the spark in her eyes when she lets herself live. I like *her*." he admitted, holding Orion's gaze for several moments before he followed after Kade.

Orion recalled the day he'd found Niko bound and tossed into the ocean, beaten senseless by an Ivory Skull before Kotori and Orion had found him. Niko had been a runaway with big dreams of becoming a rockstar, walking out his front door whilst his working-class parents watched him start his motorbike and leave, his younger brothers peering through the curtains. At least, that's what Niko had told him.

From the moment Niko met Kade, the rest had been history—the pair were like two peas in a pod, inseparable and fiercely devoted to each other. He had eternally entrusted them with the task of herding their prey to slaughter.

Orion's blood brimmed with satisfaction as he glanced at his dark-haired counterpart, inclining his head towards the ramp they steadily approached whilst the blond duo stalked the lone Ivory Skull and herded him deeper into the boardwalk's underbelly, Orion and Kotori bringing up the rear. He mulled over Kade and Niko's words as the lights of the fairground gave way to dank shadows, considering before he turned to Kotori, seeking his opinion.

"What do you think?" he asked, uncharacteristically lowering his guard—something he allowed few to see.

"It depends, do you still want to cause Azeil the same pain he caused us and kill the others?" Kotori asked.

Orion dipped his head before his voice lowered, "I do."

"And Nyx? What about her? Especially since Kade and Niko have taken a liking to her. You know this has been going on for two years now."

"I know what Kade and Niko want—"

Kotori huffed, "Do you? They don't want her dead or to harm her, Orion. They want *her,* they want her *alive.* She's no longer collateral damage to them."

Orion paused before the opening of the tourist attraction's underbelly, "And what do *you* want?"

Kotori's head tipped up, jaw clenching before his dark gaze returned to Orion's. "I want revenge. I want blood to spill."

"*And?*" Orion prompted knowingly.

"I want Nyx in our world. With us," Kotori admitted, his fingers looped beneath the leather of his tribunal necklace, adjusting it. "She belongs in our world … she just doesn't know it yet."

The shadowed depths of the fairground's underbelly greeted them as they resumed their path, ducking their heads to avoid the outer beam of the walkway, straightening after a few metres when the wooden planks loomed above their heads. Pillars cemented into the sand were placed in neat rows, beams interconnecting and reinforcing the foundations as the tell-tale crashing of waves ghosted the underbelly, a crisp breeze caressing their skin as their eyes adjusted to the dimly lit area like a dozen streetlights guided their way.

Sand shifted beneath Orion's boots, a dark grin on his lips as Niko and Kade's taunting jeers met his ears and his senses honed in on the Ivory Skull's terror-driven heart. Orion paused and turned to Kotori, anticipation brimming in both their eyes.

"I suppose we have Kai to thank for Niko and Kade's interest in her but, I'll admit. I've found her interesting since that night … when she snapped and stained herself in blood. All those years of waiting paid off in that one night. It makes me wonder what she'd be like …" he trailed off as he quickly tamped down the traitorous curiosity—longing—that flayed his insides.

Kotori's deep chuckle echoed through the darkness, seeming to understand his train of thought as he finished his sentence. "It makes you wonder what she'd be like *if* she were like us, doesn't it?"

Orion shrugged, neither disputing nor agreeing with his brother's claim as he pivoted and continued deeper into the underbelly, winding around pillars, and ducking beneath low-hanging beams. Because how could he deny it when the thought had crossed his mind? More times than he'd care to admit since she'd brazenly disregarded his warning of Celacali being dangerous. Even *if* it was just to spite her and shatter everything, she *thought* she knew. The twisted shard of his being wanted him to do that, to crumble everything she knew until the only thing left standing was him but he knew he couldn't. Not yet, at least.

Something dark awoke in the depths of his chest as he wandered deeper into the shadowed underbelly, gesturing for Kotori to split off into the darkness with a flick of his wrist before the thudding heartbeat of the Ivory Skull echoed in his ears—drowning out the clamour of sounds from above. It didn't take long for the reason behind the man's terror to be revealed, Niko and Kade's eyes alight with baneful delight that matched their grins; always thrilled by the fear they instilled.

As he stepped from the darkness he favoured, the man struggled against Niko's punishing grip, who had his hand clamped around his tattooed shoulder, pushing his knees into the damp sand whilst his other hand muffled pleaded exclamations. Kade bracketed the man's shoulder, body angled towards the struggling ash-blond with his hand lifted to his face, teeth grazing the pad of his thumb as he shifted his weight excitedly, hazel gaze darting to Orion in sync with Niko.

Kotori's towering presence loomed from beside a wooden pillar in Orion's peripherals, where he glimpsed the brunette, folded arms over his chest—ever silent and poised to strike, masking his love for the suspense of a kill behind his dark eyes. Kotori had always been quiet, and reserved by nature, but he'd grown over the years, allowing himself to become unrestrained whenever he was with Niko and Kade or during a hunt. And beneath his quiet and love for literature,

Orion knew a dominant and possessive edge lay, something Kotori rarely allowed himself to indulge in, fighting his wants in favour of not scaring someone away.

Orion's gaze brimmed with something dangerous, crouching down before the Ivory Skull until his eyes held his. "What should we do with you, Ty?" he murmured, the question phrased like he had a choice.

Kade and Niko shared a look as Orion's gaze flicked up, and the pair fluidly switched their positions, Kade pinning the man in place whilst Niko bordered his shoulder. Niko's irises were dark, his lopsided grin devoid of emotion.

Kade's eyes seemed to spark like a bolt of lightning, darting between Niko and Orion as his grip tightened on the Ivory Skull. "Didn't he touch something he wasn't supposed to?" he drawled, gaze tracking to Kotori who pushed off the pillar and shadowed Orion's side.

"He did," Kotori replied, something foreboding in his tone.

Niko turned to Orion; his eyes lighter than usual. "Let's rid him of his hands," his attention shifted to the wide-eyed man. "It's not like he'll be needing them anyway ... not where he's going."

Orion considered Niko's words as Ty struggled against Kade's grasp, heart pounding within his chest. His shouts of terror were drowned out by the constant whirl of sound above as Orion's head dipped and Niko swiftly gripped one of Ty's wrists, watching as Kade pushed harder against the man's shoulders and Niko simultaneously twisted and pulled with unnatural strength until there was a sound, half *crack*, half *squelch*, followed by the man's agonised screams that Kade quickly muffled with his palm.

Blood gushed from the tattered stumps of Ty's wrists, bone protruding as Niko tossed him a wink and placed his severed hands neatly on the sand beside a pillar. Kade's head stooped beside Ty's ear and whispered a low, otherworldly command, rendering the howling silent and pliable as Ty sat against a pillar, his hands eerily beside him, blood staining his clothes.

Ty's gaze was glazed, his muscles taut with what could only be harrowing pain as Orion crouched in front of him once more. "I warned you, didn't I?" he said, lazily trailing his gaze over the ruination and sadistic length his companions went to. "The Ivory Skulls have *never* owned the boardwalk, *we* do."

Kotori chuckled hollowly. "Orion's being modest, *Ty. We* rule the city."

"It'd be wise if you remembered that for … *next time,*" Niko said, his stance widened with casual ease, hands stained with blood, a grin etched firmly in place.

Kade chortled, shaking his head banefully. "Next time? Don't be cruel, Nik, Ty here, knows there *isn't* going to be a next time."

A distressed sound rippled from the depths of Ty's chest, his eyes wide, skin pale and clammy as his body trembled with shock and terror, gaze frantically darting from one man to the next. Blood steadily squirted from his severed wrists, soaking into the sand and filling Orion's lungs with each inhale. A waste of vital fluids, but he could find someone else to sustain them. *If* Kade and Niko didn't salvage whatever blood was left gurgling in Ty's bloodstream.

"You're merely a message to anyone that touches something they *shouldn't*. A reminder of what happens when you intervene in *our city,*" Orion said pleasantly. His gaze darted to Niko and Kade, pushing himself up from his easy crouch and moving out of their way before he turned and started back through the darkness. Calling his final order over his shoulder, he laughed as a horrible chewing noise split the shadows. "Finish it."

He knew their city was stained in blood, steeped in screams and bathed in fear. But he didn't care, he couldn't when he'd spent so long ensuring its reputation upheld.

Hand-crafted and maintained throughout the years—decades—they'd stalked the coastal city, taking what they wanted whilst ensuring they left enough to keep their food supply plentiful, until they'd established a dark title for their city:

The City of the Dead.

A city fit for monsters hidden behind the masks of men.

XIV.

Azeil

Waves crashed along the shoreline along Illusion Boardwalk; a distant blend of white noise that ghosted Azeil's ears. It blended with the pounding of people's footsteps upon the wooden planks metres above his head, droning in his ears like the pulsing beat of someone's heart. And, as Azeil's silvery gaze scoured the underside of the lively boardwalk, he mulled over the squandered beauty of the night and the flapping police tape woven around its wooden pillars. Wondering how such a tranquil night could've gone so *wrong*. But, as he ducked under the yellow tape and approached the sheet-covered body, he realised nothing could explain the world's darkness.

It was a simple thought, one shrouded in a truth many chose to ignore because it terrified them, but a truth, nonetheless. Azeil noticed as he stopped beside the veiled body, that Silvia, was conversing with an umber-skinned security guard. *The unlucky man to have stumbled upon the body,* he amended solemnly.

It failed to surprise Azeil how effectively he could tell the difference between a witness and the person who had called in a dead body; his years working on homicide cases in Celacali, Malor and other cities in the Avonsano area, had proven to be a permanent fixture in his awareness. His lips twitched, recalling Nyx's puzzled voice when she'd asked him how he knew the difference between an innocent bystander and someone who *feigned* innocence. To Azeil, it was simple.

The *how* seemed to be the obvious thing people asked. Like *how* did you know? How did you find the evidence the killer didn't want found? But no one cared to ask about the *why*. Almost like it had slipped their minds that someone with such blood-stained thoughts could have a motive other than a sadistic enjoyment of agony caused. And that was where most people went wrong. A murderer *always* had a motive.

The *why* was now what bothered Azeil, bellowing as loudly as a bell tower chimed at midday. His fingertips brushed the white fabric hiding the grotesque body from view, contemplating what lay beneath before his fist grasped the sheet and he bared the cadaver to his eyes. For a moment he merely stared down at the ash-blond man as recognition flared in his stomach; an ivory skull tattooed into the right bicep identified him as a member of the notorious Celacali gang. He briefly considered the possibility of the man's death being gang-related, but dismissed the thought almost as soon as it had come.

Azeil masked his surprise at the body's trauma compared to the cases before. One thing seemed to stand out as he retrieved gloves from his pocket and slipped them on, his latex-clad fingers grasping the deceased tanned chin, turning his head to inspect a savagely torn column of throat. Like a wolf had ripped into the underbelly of an elk, hunks of flesh missing and shredded by predatorial canines. Azeil would've been lying if he said he didn't falter at the brutality of the tattered ribbons of tendons and skin dangling around the shattered bones of the man's ulna and radius. He would have been lying if he said the horror stopped there, in the blood-stained sand, as his eyes landed on the severed hands placed neatly beside the body, folded atop each other like they were politely waiting for him.

"It's not a pretty sight for the faint-hearted, is it?" Donovan mused, startling Azeil as he gestured to the brutality of the man's body.

Azeil turned to the forensic scientist, noting the formal clothing with a raised eyebrow. "Donovan … what happened to you?"

"What? You don't like it?" Donovan jested.

"No?" Azeil gestured to the black dress shirt and slacks with a deft flick of his wrist. "Just unusual."

"Dressing to impress," Donovan smirked.

"Who would you be trying to impress at a murder scene?" said Azeil. "The vic?"

Azeil rubbed his chin with a latex-clad hand. "I'm not sure this was the response you were looking for, but you killed it."

Donovan chuckled, shaking his head, "Ah, death puns at a crime scene. You *do* know the way to my heart, Azeil."

"Anyway?"

"Ty McCarthy, member of the Ivory Skulls," Donovan smiled sheepishly before he corrected himself, "*Was* an Ivory Skull, as you can tell from the tattoo on his right bicep. Thirty years old and appears to have sustained the lacerations to his throat *after* the sustained trauma to the body. Seems like the killer wanted him alive whilst they severed his hands."

"You said he was thirty years old, right?" Azeil asked, rising from a crouch to stand beside Donovan, who seemed to be recalling a well-rehearsed list. "So, maybe Ty crossed the wrong person and suffered the consequences?"

Donovan cocked his head, "It can't be *that* simple," he turned to Azeil, "can it?"

"Murder *is* simple, Donovan. We've just, as a society, complicated it. Murderers kill because they enjoy it, and it doesn't matter which part of them reigns supreme."

"So then, *detective Monroe,* what's the relevance of the severed hands?"

Azeil stared down at Ty and the discoloured tinge to his skin. At first glance, he *almost* turned to Donovan and said that nothing tied the previous murders to Ty. But, as he weighed everything he knew, he realised that each victim had been sighted on the boardwalk hours before their deaths.

Illusion Boardwalk appeared to be the grizzly death ground zero plaguing Celacali. *Or the killer's domain,* he thought with mounting clarity, retrieving his notepad to jot down his suspicion. A bustling amusement park, Azeil realised with sickening awareness, was the perfect place to select victims who would go unnoticed until it was too late to save them. Filled with screams, shouts and other deafening sounds that'd block out tormented cries of agony or screams of terror. A slaughterhouse disguised as an amusement park; its victims walking themselves into the bloodied maw of a psychopath.

"What if the murderer uses the boardwalk as a hunting ground? Hiding within the hustle and bustle so flawlessly they're hidden in plain sight?" he asked, turning to face the forensic scientist whilst he added another bullet-point. "What if the city of Celacali *suspects* who the killer is but they've convinced themselves that it's too obvious? Too easy."

"That still doesn't explain why the killer severed Ty's hands," Donovan said, folding his arms over his chest.

"But it does," Azeil countered. "Murderers *always* have obsessions—that drive them. Something feeds their tendencies, whether it's anger, jealousy, betrayal or ... lust."

Donovan's eyebrows furrowed, his gaze nestled upon Azeil's face, "And?"

"What if all these murders started driven by anger, in a pursuit of revenge, but somewhere in that pursuit they stumbled upon a known piece of their game that proved to be just as interesting? Maybe more than they anticipated?"

"Like what?"

"*Lust,* Donovan, lust." Azeil breathed out.

"But *why*? What does it matter that they're driven by lust?" Donovan pressed.

Azeil felt he was inches from the truth, mind recalling the murmured disdain from locals about a group of bikers, but that the city of Celacali didn't want him to know. He tore his gaze from the waves tumbling onto the shoreline, troubled, his palms cupping the nape of his neck. "Because it means that this unknown variable might just be what they're after, at least ... *now* it is."

"This is starting to sound like some 'final girl' shit."

"Exactly," Azeil exclaimed, ripping his hands away from his neck before he clicked his fingers together. "That's exactly the concept they're using. The killer *wants* somebody to know who they are, but they want it to be someone who'd be directly affected or tied to the deaths in some way. In some places, the punishment is deemed to fit the crime."

"So ... Ty's death wasn't coincidental, and his hands were removed for ... stealing?" Donovan murmured, the logic to Azeil's words slowly cinching into place.

"Wouldn't that," Azeil pointed to Ty's severed hands placed neatly beside his body, "be an accurate warning to not take or touch something the killer deemed as theirs?"

"I overheard the security guard the chief was questioning mention something about a disturbance on the boardwalk *before* Connor's murder," Donovan murmured almost to himself, his fingers twirling the rings on his hand as he locked eyes with Azeil. "Three blond men and one dark-haired male picked a fight on the boardwalk with the Ivory Skulls that night. Then, just last night, that same security guard said something about a blond stepping in between a young woman and the Ivory Skulls."

"I'm guessing Ty was there," Azeil stated, stifling dread at the mention of four figures who matched the locals' descriptions of the anonymous *bikers*.

"He was," Donovan confirmed, lips pursing as he frowned deeply in thought. "But it still doesn't explain what ties that person to these murders."

"It does ... it's all there. They're doing this in defence ... of someone they believe belongs to them."

Donovan's frown deepened. "How can you be so sure that it's more than one person?"

"Because *I know* who the person is—who *she* is."

"Okay … I give up. Who is it?"

Azeil tipped his head up to the wooden underbelly of the boardwalk, sighing deeply through his nose before he straightened and turned to Donovan. His mind throwing flashes of the first night he'd spent on the boardwalk and the men who'd lingered near the Ferris wheel astride their motorcycles.

"Who is it?" Donovan murmured lowly, imploring Azeil.

Azeil swallowed, turning to stare out at the ocean whilst his throat worked to rid him of the lump that clogged it. Fear cloyed in his veins like the forks of a barb-wire fence lacerating his body, tearing his skin. Flashes of a heated conversation between himself and his mother played before his eyes; she was concerned about Nyx seeing golden-eyed beasts in her pre-teens. He remembered her mocking garble like a lyrebird:

"She says she sees them, Eil. The men with golden eyes."

He remembered his own scathing reply, which now filled his skull, tightening the phantom noose around his throat:

"They're dead, *Ma. It's just a recurring nightmare she's been having."*

Those words choked him now as he forced his gaze back to Donovan, his tremor-filled voice ghosting past his lips, "Nyx."

Oh, how the past loved to catch you up.

XV.

Nyx

Flames licked at the heaped pile of wood, snapping, and popping softly. Their tangerine light flickered in the breeze, throwing shadows over the cream sand sticking to Nyx's dark plaid pants. A rock song blasted from a chipped and weathered stereo, going unnoticed by the group of Ivory Skulls clustered around the bonfire, drinking beer, or passing a joint back and forth, their boisterous laughter carrying over the music. The gang members' girlfriends perched on their laps or the vacant spots beside their respective partners, fawning over their boyfriends.

Orion, Kade, Niko and Nyx messily arranged themselves on sun-bleached logs at the edge of the clearing, in the long shadows from the trees behind them. They drank from a bottle of vodka whilst Kotori lounged in the sand, his muscular legs bent at the knees in front of him.

Niko and Kade snickered, nudging each other while Orion sat still, motionless. Nyx, decked out entirely in black—black cropped T-shirt, black jeans and her boots, dusted with sand, her favourite jacket bundled up on the log beside her, stared without focus, just happy to be where she was. With them, in the shadows.

"Are sure you don't want any? 'Cause by the time Niko's done with it, there won't be any left," Kade said, offering her the bottle.

Niko reached around Nyx and shoved Kade's shoulder so he toppled off the log and into the sand with a solid *thump*. "You were saying?" he crooned, arching his eyebrows expectantly.

"You're a dick," Kade said as he dusted sand from his jeans, "you know that, right?"

"You never complained about my dick before, Kadey," said Niko deadpanning.

"What?" he questioned, tipping his hand palm out towards Nyx. "He likes the sand."

"I doubt that," Nyx mused, eyes lingering on the sand clinging to Kade's clothes

and his muttered curses.

A deep sigh tumbled from his lips, head tipping up to the sky before his eyes fluttered shut and his tattooed hands stilled at his sides. Orion's glacier gaze trained emotionlessly upon Kade, darting towards Niko when he snickered.

Nyx froze, watching as Kade's eyelids slowly opened. Something dark shifted in his eyes that shouldn't have sent a jolt of awareness through her blood but, she couldn't ignore the way his tattooed forearms rippled above his tensed muscles—poised to strike at a moment's notice.

"You're *so* dead," Nyx mumbled, drawing Niko's gaze to her.

Niko pressed his palms into the log, peering down at Nyx, "What's the matter? Scared I hurt Kade's feelings?"

Nyx's lips twitched, gaze brimming with delight. "Nope," she gestured behind Niko; a riveted grin inching across her face, "but you *might* want to turn around."

And as Kotori downed a mouthful of vodka, Kade tackled Niko to the sand. Kotori's deep chuckle reverberated in Nyx's ears whilst Kade and Niko rolled, playfully fighting each other in a mass of jangling bracelets and flying sand. Orion's gloved fingers drummed against his thigh, a perfect cloud of smoke cloying around him. As a warning hum emitted from the back of his throat, eyebrow arched with silent annoyance, Niko and Kade whirled towards him and ceased their squabble.

Nyx silently marvelled at the obedience Orion obtained from these men. She wondered what hold he must have on them to command such a thing.

Kade and Niko brushed sand from the other's clothes, grinning in that childish way they had, before they sidled up to Nyx, bracketing her between themselves under Orion's watchful stare. Niko's arm wrapped around her shoulder, his grin growing when her heart skipped below her sternum.

Orion's head dipped and Nyx caught the movement, and the tail-end of a silent conversation between them. *What are they up to?* Niko nodded curtly, peering down at Nyx, his thumb tracing lazy circles into her shoulder—something she realised she liked a lot. It was … distracting.

She stifled a yawn behind her hand, peering up at the cloudless sky. The previous night spent with the quartet was beginning to catch up with her as she rose from the driftwood log, gauging the distance from the bonfire to the neon lights of the boardwalk.

"It's further than it looks," Orion drawled, capturing her attention as he gestured to the neon halo of the boardwalk.

"Even to walk?"

Orion's stare shifted, tracking the moonlit shoreline between the bonfire, the barrelled fire pits scattered sporadically across the beach and then the boardwalk before he turned back to her.

Something dark and foreboding lingered in his eyes and as always, she couldn't help but feel trapped. Those blue of eyes of his were like a vice.

"Don't get too close to the groups around the barrels, and you'll be fine."

Nyx dipped her head in unspoken thanks before she turned to Kade and Niko.

"Quit sulking. You'll see her tomorrow, airhead," Kade quipped, turning to Nyx with his Cheshire Cat-like grin in place. "Right?"

"Right," Nyx assured, reaching out to ruffle Niko's wild hair. "I'll see you tomorrow."

* * *

An eerie chill rolled across the Avonsano Ocean. Nyx had made it halfway through her silent trek back to the boardwalk—the dimly lit beach softly illuminated by the moon light—before she realised, she hadn't grabbed her jacket. Her realisation drew a dull, exasperated sigh from her mouth, her steps pausing as she pivoted and stared back across the shoreline to the faint orange glow behind a cresting dune.

There was nothing for it, she had to get her jacket.

She dipped her head closer to her chest and picked up her pace as a group of men leered at her from beside fire-lit barrels, the wind at her back pushing her curls into her face. Nyx suppressed a shudder, urging herself to walk faster towards the bonfire beacon, to her boys.

A foreboding of false hope flickered a warning, whispering at her to turn back, back to the lights of the boardwalk. She shoved it aside, not listening.

Nyx wouldn't hear its pleas until it was too late.

Sand shifted in her boots, rubbing irritatingly against the side of her ankles when she crested the small, sloping hill overlooking the bonfire. Her fingers darted out to grasp the branch of a low-hanging tree for strength, eyes blown wide as her gaze raked over the carnage before her.

The bonfire burned somehow brighter—almost blinding—the sickening scent of burning flesh accosting her nose and lungs, an acrid stench of singed hair and something rotten. The smell of the ocean was gone. Her heart pounded in her ears, like the beating of a terror-driven drum.

Nyx couldn't tear her gaze from the crimson-stained sand as something like an explosion of energy flooded through her. It was completely new—something foreign—and moreover, it was strange and powerful. Nyx came to know the reason for that feeling and it played across her mind in a never-ending loop. The shock travelled upwards through her toes to her fingertips, buzzing through her chest and mind like electricity, jolting her into this blood-stained reality. Her stomach twisted with nausea, coiling so tightly she was sure she'd throw up as she leant into the trunk of the tree.

She knew better than to scream.

The foolishness of the notion elicited a strong impulse to gag. The thumping of her heart played in her ears like a personal soundtrack dredged up from her darkest nightmares. Muffled rock music trickled from the blood-splattered stereo lying discarded on the sand. Her eyelids fluttered, fighting to stay open as horror clawed at her chest.

The bodies of the boisterous Ivory Skulls and their girlfriends lay scattered across the sand, throats torn open and still seeping blood. The ground was a stomach-churning red that *almost* made Nyx's legs buckle beneath her.

She swallowed thickly, cupping her mouth with shaking hands. Her gaze nestled upon the familiar outline of four bikers. Their clothes, skin and faces stained and coated with a fine, horrifying sheen of crimson. Dripping down their throats until the fabric of their clothes darkened and clung to their chests.

Turn around, Nyx. Now, while you still can.

She urged herself, fingers trembling as a spine-chilling scream punctuated the night and Nyx's head snapped towards an auburn-haired woman, who skittered away from Orion, tears streaking her cheeks. Her sobbed pleas for mercy fell on deaf ears as he stalked her, frigid eyes devoid of emotion—*of mercy*—and his gloved hands clamped around her forearms.

Something in Nyx shattered, crumbling to pieces beneath the tree where she stood, metres from the carnage. Her childhood ignorance of the world was decapitated in one blow by the scene before her. She startled when Orion's diamond-shaped face caught the flickering firelight and disconcerting shadows shifted across it. Her throat constricted, the bark of the tree branch digging into her skin. She saw as the ivory-skinned planes of his face sharpened and furrowed, the bone structure of his cheekbones and eye sockets becoming prominent, and a series of rough edges bulged that accentuated his terrifying grin.

Her gaze darted to Niko and Kade, her teeth sunk harshly into the flesh of her bottom lip to clamp down the anguish gutting her. Their nightmare appearances now obscured the playful youth they'd had before. Their teasing smiles and gleeful grins distorted in Nyx's mind, now rippling into monstrous things that cackled as Orion tore savagely into the woman's throat with elongated canines and sharpened incisors. The silent and comforting presence Kotori had nurtured vanished before her eyes as he tossed the body of a dark-skinned man into the flames, leering. His head tipped back to the star-flecked sky, crimson droplets skittering down his bared chest before they soaked into the waistband of his dark jeans.

A jarring chord struck in Nyx; the weight bearing down on her shoulders as she sucked in a shaky breath of air and forced her legs to move. Gingerly, she released the tree branch clutched in her grasp before she staggered backwards on legs that wobbled like a newborn foal. Sand shifted beneath her boot-clad feet, muffling her silent retreat until the heel of her boot pressed against the crest of the hill and a sharp *snap* sounded, tolling in her head like a bell tower. She swallowed thickly, screwing her eyes shut against the dread weaving itself around her legs. The pounding of her heart was frantic. A few seconds passed that felt like an hour before she reluctantly forced her eyes open and glared down at the traitorous stick beneath her foot.

Nyx dragged her gaze from the ground and up; a nervous stutter to her breath as she registered the chilling irises trained upon her. The angelic and deceiving masks they'd hidden behind long discarded amongst the bodies and the flames of the bonfire.

This is what they really look like.

The truth stained Nyx's mind so she'd never be able to tear it from her soul.

Her hands balled into tight fists at her sides, hiding their tremble as she watched the smooth transition of Niko and Kade's features. As they shifted back to the faces she'd known before, smoothing out like a sigh.

Her mind scrambled, halting all thought whilst it tried to put all the pieces together. She hadn't imagined it. She saw it now in the slight crookedness of Kade's nose and the Atlantic-blue of Niko's eyes as their blood-stained faces contorted into matching expressions of shock. Everything within her was poised to run, adrenaline juicing her system like a primer, but she was stuck. Stalled.

Their tentative move towards her was what set her free. Nyx started, skittering backward with her hands held out in front of her, palms turned out towards them as she stuffed the anguish that flickered in Niko's eyes to the depths of her mind.

"Stay away from me," Nyx breathed.

Niko halted, pain and ... *guilt* seeping into his eyes. His skin rippled as he seemed to fight the urge to shift on his feet, nimble fingers toying with the bracelets on his wrists.

"*Nyx*," he said, something pleading in his voice.

She shook her head frantically, stumbling further away. Panic seized her chest.

"Nyx, *hey*. It's okay. We're not going to hurt you, remember?" Kade pleaded.

The logical side of Nyx's mind laughed at her for being so foolish, reminding her of how long she'd known them and that the promise Kade had made to her wouldn't be enough. Not after she'd seen the carnage. *Their* carnage. Seen what they had done.

Fear rippled off her in waves as she saw Kotori. She shook her head reverently as if she'd be able to purge her mind of the things she saw before her. Blinking back sudden tears of frustration and shoving the niggling feeling of helplessness aside, she refused to break beneath the four pairs of eyes that now watched her every move.

"I'm going to die," Nyx whispered shakily, fingers trembling at her sides as she choked down her hysteria.

Orion smiled as her whispered words of fear brought a malignant smile to his face. Cool, baby-blue eyes sliding from Nyx to the three men who stood before her in a messy semi-circle.

"You're not going to die, chica," Niko said, voice strangled like he was trying to control his emotions.

Nyx's gaze darted to Niko, frantic and fear riddled. "*Right* ..."

Kade took two hesitant steps in Nyx's direction, using her distraction with Niko. His hands raised in a sign that he meant no harm when her head snapped in his direction.

Nyx wasn't afraid of this Kade but the one that lurked beneath his flesh. The one with razor-sharp canines that could tear through her skin like a knife through butter.

Kade threw Orion a glare, as Orion mockingly gestured to Nyx in a silent 'be my guest'. A muscle feathered along Orion's jawline, glacier gaze watching Kade with apparent annoyance.

"We're not going to kill you, Nyx," Kade reiterated. "I promised you we'd never hurt you. *Ever.*"

"You expect me to believe your promises?" Nyx said. "You've *killed* people, Kade. And I don't know what world you're living in, but nothing about that makes me want to *trust you.*"

"If we wanted you dead, you'd be dead already," Niko stated calmly.

Nyx whipped her head around, "I'm glad we cleared that up because it feels like a weight's been lifted off my shoulders. Thanks, Niko."

Kade and Kotori shared a look of disbelief as Nyx deadpanned, fear tinging her eyes whilst she hid behind her unphased mask.

"Why would you think that'd even *remotely* help?" Kotori questioned, running his fingers through his ebony hair with a deft shake of his head.

Niko turned to Kotori, shrugging, "*I don't know*. I thought it'd help."

"Leave the talking to us, Nik," Kade said.

Niko nodded, coming to Kade's side in a burst of unnatural speed. The movement was quicker than Nyx could comprehend, her eyes widening as she scrambled towards the incline of the crested hill before she collided with a solid chest. A startled scream tore from her throat as she spun around to face Orion. Nyx realised in that moment that nothing her father had taught her would save her now—no amount of punching, kicking or screaming would save her from the animalistic glint in Orion's eyes.

He lifted a gloved hand to her face, cupping her cheek with a predatory incline of his head. Nyx trembled beneath the weight of his stare, unwilling to move within the presence of the beast from her childhood stories. Of her dreams. Of her reality. Kotori, Kade and Niko's stares burned the back of her head. Nobody moved.

"Orion," Kotori began, cutting himself off when Orion's eyes collided with his.

A slow smirk curled the edges of Orion's lips into a confidently calm mask filled with sadistic intentions, a ripple of anticipation seemed to course over them.

The atmosphere was static, choking and Nyx could almost taste their anticipation, *their bloodlust*. Like an impossible itch that none of them could resist.

Orion gazed into Nyx's eyes, her head whirled to the forest beside her before she turned back to face him, doubt etched into her irises. He shook his head with malicious zeal, releasing her forearm before he nudged her towards the trees, his expression dead calm. Then a smile grew and grew across his face, nasty. A reminder of what lurked beneath, and she knew her fear fed him.

He seemed to revel in her terror, his glacier irises flickering and suddenly swallowed by the golden-white ring. His features sharpened and jutting as the bone structure made a ghoul of his face.

Nyx's heart stuttered within her chest, jolting as if someone had kick-started it into overdrive as Orion leant closer to her, so close that their noses brushed, his unnatural irises locked on hers.

The scent of cigarettes and leather stunning as his honeyed voice spoke in a heady drawl, "Run, little dove. *Run*."

XVI.

Nyx

Fear careened through Nyx as Orion's nightmarish irises held her gaze. The predatory incline to his head embedding the fear further into her bloodstream, like a nail driven into wood. But still, she hesitated, unwilling to trust him as she peered over her shoulder to the carnage around the bonfire. As her gaze trailed over Kotori, Niko, and Kade, she knew that she'd never be able to purge this bloodstained night from her mind. *If she lived.*

It was as the realisation cinched into place that she stumbled away and ran. A chilling yellow stare scalding the flesh of her back as sand flicked up behind her. She didn't need to see Orion to know he was grinning.

She ducked beneath a low-hanging branch and, despite the foolishness of running from the creatures beside the bonfire, she sprinted into the darkness of the moonlit forest as if her life depended on it. Her life *did* depend on it. Every instinct screamed, bellowing at her to run faster—to *survive*—the murderous quartet, urging her forward, screaming *not* to look back.

Moonlight dappled the forest floor, casting shadows as the stars glinted above her, watching on whilst Nyx fled the massacre of Chades Cove. *Ironic that Chades Cove translates to Death Cove,* she thought bitterly. Weak beams of moonlight provided little light for her as she ran from the night's monsters. She squinted through the dank darkness, leaves crunching beneath her boots, in tune with the erratic beating of her heart. Nyx sucked in a shaky breath of air, forcing herself to look only forward, keep going, don't lose the tiny shred of hope blossoming in her chest.

She heeded the faint warning that underlined Orion's dark urging, darting through the darkened forest, like the startled *little dove* he had mockingly called her. She ducked too late to avoid a low-hanging branch, the sharp sting of sticks cutting into her arms and cheeks burning through her nervous system. Leaves smacked against her arms as she frantically swatted the offending branches. Mother Nature seemed oblivious to the terror in her heart and, through the never-ending well, she grasped at a handle of hope, clutching onto it for dear life.

"Nyx," called a voice through the darkness of the forest, mocking her and her desperate retreat.

She stumbled as Orion's voice rang out like a ghostly whisper, taunting and yet filled with something else before his dark chuckle followed. She paused, sucking in deep breaths of air. Her eyes wide and searching the shadows for the voice's owner, turning in a slow circle. She saw nothing. Orion sought to confirm her fears, his calculated call slithering across the darkened grass like the serpent tattooed upon his right wrist.

"Nyx."

Her heart leapt in her chest. Fear flooded her bloodstream and she bolted. As his voice drew out the syllables of her name in a lazy drawl—*Nyyy-x*—exhaustion begged her to stop running. Despite all her instincts telling her she couldn't. Not if she wanted to survive. And *gods,* did she want to survive. Undiluted anguish gripped her heart, urging her legs to keep pumping. She realised—too late—that Orion was toying with her. Herding her like a sheepdog directing sheep to the slaughterhouse, and that he revelled in the terror and inner turmoil he evoked.

"Nyx."

A sob begged release from the back of her throat, clawing at the hysteria creeping in when she stumbled over one of the countless roots breaking through the earthen terrain. Defeat reared its ugly head as solace, urging her to stop running from the golden-eyed beasts lurking in the shadows. A sharp snap echoed in her ears, punctuating the silence, and she cautiously backed away from the forest behind her and smacked into something solid.

With a terrified scream that echoed across the moonlit forest, she stumbled back and whirled around to face the man shrouded in shadows. The planes of Orion's face were smattered in incandescent light as he strode forward and grasped her forearm with his gloved hand. His eyes were eerily bright as he cocked his head and dread lanced her chest. She struggled in his grasp, heart racing and, as though it annoyed him, he grasped her hands, pinning them behind her as he whirled her round, folding her back into his chest.

Her heart pounded in her ears as Orion's right hand wrapped around her throat, successfully crushing Nyx's futile hopes of escape with the subtle pressure of the leather against her skin. She stilled as Kotori, Niko and Kade appeared before them. Kade gnawed at the skin of his thumb, shifting from one foot to another before he pulled his tattoo-embellished fingers away from his face and gingerly approached. Her gaze locked on Niko, who trailed closely behind. Regret and something else in their eyes. Kotori, however, didn't move at all. His deep, umber stare focused on Orion.

"Orion," Kotori tried; a somewhat exasperated sigh spilling from his lips.

"Kotori," Orion drawled, parroting Kotori's tone.

The towering brunette eyed Nyx, tracking the panicked darting of her eyes as they flitted around in search of an escape. The steady patter of her heartbeat filled her ears, *as it must fill theirs*, she thought.

She clutched at the hope of Orion losing interest and letting her go.

"Aw, little dove. You were never going to escape," Orion cooed tauntingly; his gloved fingers caressing her throat.

Nyx's eyes widened, her gaze shifting to Kade and Niko, comforted by them despite the terror pulsing through her. She forced herself to pretend that Orion wasn't there. Mustering up enough of her courage—though misplaced and impetuous—she threw her head backward, into his. A resounding *crack* echoing as her head collided harshly with his chin.

Orion's grip wavered long enough for Nyx to rip her hands from his grasp and shove him away. Adrenaline pumped through her veins while she tried to think of some way to escape. His laugh seemed to ricochet in the night. *She amused him!* Like he was seeing her in a new—*better*—light that probed at the animalistic side of him. Her boots scuffled the sand as she took several steps back, colliding with Niko in her haste to create some distance between herself and *him*.

"Take it easy, chica," Niko chided playfully; a crooked grin splayed over his face.

Nyx peered at him in wonder. Bewildered by how he acted like he hadn't just slaughtered a bunch of people and left their bodies scattered around Chades Cove. *Did he regret it at all?*

"*Niko,*" Orion cautioned lowly, drawing the rockstar blond's gaze ever-so-slowly away from Nyx.

Faster than thought, she found herself in his grip once more.

"Cute," Orion uttered, an amused smile playing at the edges of his lips. "But you'll have to try harder than that if you want to survive."

The blue of Orion's irises swirled with a million different intentions, ways he could make this worse for Nyx. She squirmed in his grasp, knowing the others would not move to help her against him.

"Tell me, Orion. Am I right to assume that sunlight isn't your friend?" she gritted out.

"I don't know, sweetheart. Isn't it?" the smile was in his tone.

"It has to be," Nyx stated confidently. "Because why else do you show up *after* dark and not in the daylight?"

"Brave words for one whose life rests in my hands," he drawled, emphasising his words with a firm squeeze to her throat.

Nyx chortled mockingly. The grasp upon her throat tightening as Orion bristled with poorly restrained annoyance. "Are you God now?"

"Even God steers clear of Celacali, little dove."

"He steers clear of Celacali for one reason, *Orion*."

His eyebrows quirked with amusement, keeping her head angled up so she was forced to look into his eyes. "And what, pray tell, is that?"

Nyx squared her shoulders, "You. Any god would turn their back on Celacali because of the monsters that roam the boardwalk and slaughter innocents at secluded beach parties."

Orion's face hardened, a cold mask of nonchalance trickling over his features, and Nyx grimaced in his bruising hold.

"Monster?" he repeated, rolling the word on his tongue like it was foreign to him.

"Anyone with eyes could tell you enjoyed murdering that girl while she begged you to spare her," Nyx scoffed with disgust. "You're a monster."

Orion's laughter broke through the night's silence before he leant closer to Nyx; a sound conveying little amusement, "Monster, you say?" Orion waited. His leather-clad fingers brushed her curls over her shoulder and away from her throat before his gaze flickered up to hers and stuck. "I'll show you a monster."

The scream bubbling in the back of Nyx's throat died, crushed beneath the sole of Orion's boots as his fingers dug harshly into her wrists and his teeth sank into the soft flesh of her throat. Stunned, her mind became warped by panic and the sharp, tearing sensation blazing across her throat. An agonising blend that thrummed through her bloodstream like the pounding of her heart. *Tha-thump. Tha-thump. Tha-thump.* A dotting of black spots obscured her vision and her head drooped against Orion's chest. The ease with which he stripped her strength from her body terrified her, eliciting a soft sob from her lips before he adjusted his hold upon her.

Niko lunged forward, gripping the collar of Orion's obsidian T-shirt and ripping him from Nyx's throat. Snarling, his lips curled into a deathly sneer that revealed the elongated canines and incisors of his vampiric teeth. Niko's gaze strayed from Orion, darting frantically over Nyx, who clutched at the crook of her neck with wide, frightened eyes and a slight sway.

Kotori moved quickly, grabbing hold of Orion's arms, and steering him away from Nyx. The ebony-haired man's jaw clenched as he noted the animalistic hunger in Orion's eyes. Orion tugged against Kotori, his nightmare irises locked on Nyx. Kotori growled low, snapping Orion's attention to him again.

A dull chill settled in Nyx's bones, her legs begging to buckle beneath her whilst Orion turned to Kotori with slow disorientation and regret. The yellowed tinge leeched away, replaced by the Arctic blue Nyx found suddenly *some* comfort in. Orion's brows quirked, his stare trailing over her with masterfully masked guilt. Seeming to ignore the trembles raking Nyx's body and the blood-stained hand she pressed to her throat, he watched with feigned disinterest as Kade hesitantly approached her.

Nyx stared at Kade. His lifeful nature and patchwork tattoos that she'd grown to love now jarring; their intricate designs now stained with blood. Like the crimson seeping through her fingers that she pressed to her throat. She panicked when he extended a hand towards her, her palm connecting with his fingertips as she batted his hands away and sidestepped him. Then she turned and ran.

Trees darted by Nyx in a blur, the thudding of her heart echoing in her ears, lacing together with the crashing of her boot-clad feet upon the forest floor. Moonlight dappled and shifted as she raced through the forest, dodging bushes, rocks and fallen branches with adrenaline-driven accuracy. Dazed, disorientated and fear-addled, Nyx lost track of time and the distance she wedged between herself and them. Barely registering the moment her boots met the bitumen of the boardwalk's carpark and the neon lights splayed over her back.

A shaky scream tore from her throat as she collided with a solid shoulder. Blearily recognising the brown-haired twins, her eyes darted in every direction as if Orion, Kotori, Niko, and Kade would appear from the boardwalk shadows. She choked on a sob, relief and dizziness swept over her as she squinted against the fatigue creeping into her bones.

"Nyx?"

The voice seemed muffled and gravelly before she staggered and black spots darkened her vision. Her knees crumpled beneath her weight as her eyes slid shut. She caught an indistinctly uttered curse, before warmth encased her and she felt herself scooped up into someone's arms, an overwhelming feeling of safety spreading through her—she blacked out.

XVII.

Azeil

"Azeil Monroe! Can you comment on the recent murders plaguing the city of Celacali?" a blonde reporter called before shoving a blocky microphone into Azeil's face, sheepish-looking cameraman bracketing her right shoulder.

Several beats of silence punctuated by the waves crashing onto the shoreline of Chades Cove clung to Azeil's shoulders as a crease marred his forehead. With a deep sigh and a glance thrown over his shoulder to the barricaded strip of the popular cove, Azeil reached out and clamped a hand over the camera lens, throwing a pointed glare between the reporter and her cameraman. "Turn the camera off. *Now*."

"You can't—" she spluttered indignantly.

"No, I can't. So, turn it *off*," Azeil gritted out, cutting her off. His knuckles bled white as he blocked the camera lens. "Don't you have *any* respect? Multiple families have lost their loved ones and you want to parade their losses under their noses?" With a curt shove that made the cameraman stumble, he released the expensive filming device. "Go find something else to report and don't bring *my* name into your news to gain views."

"But—"

"No." Azeil cut in, shaking his head as he raised his hand and pointed towards the winding tracks within the forest, revealing the 'Authorised Personnel' tag pinned beside his detective badge. "Leave before I have an officer escort you back to your hotel."

With an irritated huff and eyes narrowed to thin slits, the reporter straightened her black pantsuit, gesturing to her cameraman with a flick of her wrist before she turned, and they marched towards the track leading back to Celacali's suburban areas. Azeil waited until he was sure they weren't coming back before ducking beneath the wooden barricades, bold text labelling this as a crime scene. His Doc Martens sunk into the soft sand, smattering them with fine cream-coloured grains that clung to his socks and the cuffs of his black jeans despite the shoe-socks, the sand found its way in, rubbing against his feet and chipping away at his irritated demeanour, his silvery gaze shifting like billowing smoke from a merciless inferno.

"Fucking vultures," he muttered, straightening the white hem of his shirt.

"Always delighted, I see, Monroe," Silvia uttered, his grey-flecked irises glinting with amusement.

"I'd hate to disappoint," Azeil jested, his gaze shifting distractedly to the activity around the smouldering bonfire and the crimson splattering the sand.

"It's worse than it looks," the chief of police assured, lips pursed grimly.

Azeil frowned, trailing his gaze over the sheet-covered bodies scattered haphazardly around Chades Cove. "*How* worse?"

"Five murders worse."

Azeil turned back to Silvia, eyebrows arched as the stench of charred flesh permeated the air. "*Five?*"

"That's what has been confirmed," Silvia stated with a shrug and an airy wave of his hand in the general direction of the bodies.

Azeil dipped his head, lingering on the forest bordering the cove. As he trailed his gaze over the shrouded bodies, he couldn't shake a niggling feeling in his chest, winding around his ribcage like a scaled serpent. It rankled across his skin, whispering his fears and suspicions. But the longer he stared at the massacre and smelled the smouldering bonfire that smelt strongly of seared flesh, he couldn't escape the thought that *they* were behind this, and that he had to tell someone.

That they hadn't died twenty-five years ago.

That he hadn't *killed them.*

His spiralling thoughts jolted to a halt when his stare caught a flash of auburn hair, his feet carrying him several paces towards a young girl in her mid-twenties yet to be covered by the forensics team. Her face had a fine dusting of freckles; blue eyes perpetually frozen in terror. The ivory tone of her skin was stained by the crusting of dark blood originating from the torn mess of her throat and the gaping ruination of her jugular. Worry prickled like tiny pinpricks across Azeil's chest, his subconsciousness reminding him of Nyx as he stared down at the young woman he'd interviewed days ago. He didn't need to be a forensic scientist or coroner to know that she'd bled to death.

"Beach party massacre anyone?" Donovan quipped, startling Azeil who whipped around to face him.

"*Don't* do that," Azeil scolded, breathing out a frazzled sigh.

The young forensic scientist raised his hands sheepishly, a lopsided grin embedding dimples into his left cheek, inky T-shirt and navy forensics jacket making him a blue blur. "Geez, what's up your ass?"

Azeil rubbed the underside of his jaw, blinking in frustration. "I'm going to pretend you didn't say that because I know you're a good kid."

"It's not my fault that you're not paying attention," Donovan stated, grinning smugly when Azeil's eyes narrowed. "*Okay*. Don't sneak up on you, got it."

"Thank you," Azeil murmured before gesturing to the corpse. "This is Delilah, isn't it?"

Donovan frowned, ring-clad hand brushing down the front of his dark jeans. "Yeah, that's Delilah Reid. I'm assuming you know she was the owner of Delilah's Video & Music store on the boardwalk?"

"I do, but how old was she?"

"Twenty-six."

"Association to the other vics?"

"She was friends with Mila Nieves," Donovan replied, pointing to a woman's body with an unnaturally angled neck propped against a driftwood log, enforcing a link Azeil already knew of. If not for the scarf of dried blood, she could have been simply sleeping. Maybe.

Azeil's gaze flitted back to the forest and its shadowed depths, wondering if anyone had fled to its canopied depths and survived the massacre around him. "I heard there was as an article of clothing found, do you think I can see it?

Donovan eyed Azeil curiously, glancing over to the other forensic scientists and then back to the dark-haired detective before he gestured to a petite woman with a moon-shaped face, part of his forensic team. "There was ... Why? What are you thinking, Azeil?"

"I think we've got *multiple* murderers and that tonight they slipped up," he said, noticing Ellis in the group of milling officers, as Moonface turned and hurried forward, flashing her forensics shirt. She extended an evidence bag to Donovan, a black denim jacket tucked safely within. Azeil politely took it from his grasp once the woman walked away, nodding to Donovan as he pulled his phone from his pocket.

Something kick-started Azeil's heart as he peered down at the dark jacket. His heart sank when Donovan extended another bag towards him, latex-clad fingers brushing against a set of keys engraved with the initials '*N.M*' through the plastic.

Nyx Monroe.

Azeil weighed the keys in his palm and his sooty irises slid uneasily to Donovan.

A lump stuck thickly in his throat, refusing to budge as he called out to Officer Ellis, and requested a search warrant for Nyx after he provided a description of his daughter.

Donovan eyed the evidence bag in Azeil's grasp, an eyebrow-raising when he noted the parental concern. "Whose jacket is that?"

Through the lump clogging Azeil's throat, he managed to answer, "Nyx's."

"Ah, shit. You know that'll label her as a suspect, right?"

"I know," Azeil sighed. "But Donovan, we *need* to find her first. Silvia mentioned it's been suspected that there's more than one killer, but has that been confirmed?"

"He didn't tell you? It was confirmed yesterday morning."

Azeil's mind tossed memories of him sorting through the information Ellis had given him as Donovan continued,

"We will find her," Donovan assured him, stepping forward to grasp his friend's forearm. He hesitated, "I think our killers just went from serial to mass murderers in zero point five seconds."

The ghostly press of gloved fingers pressed Azeil's forearms. A flash of white-blond hair flickered across his vision, marring his sight of the massacre around him. The mocking curl to the lips was etched into the depths of his mind as was the unnatural and rutted bone structure of his face. "*This* is what happens when a murder is driven by anger."

The forensic scientist-coroner scoffed, "This is *senseless.*"

Azeil shook his head; a diamond-shaped face with blood-splattered lips cloying in his mind. "This is revenge."

"Who's revenge?" Donovan questioned, eyeing his friend who barely registered his words.

Azeil gritted his teeth, a searing flash of anger blazing through his bloodstream as phantoms of his past fought their way back into his head. A resounding *thump* rang in his ears—a memory that haunted him, brought to life like a movie—followed by the sickening *squelch* of flesh being pierced. And though the past lurked in Azeil's mind, playing like a broken film forced to rerun the same scene over and over, he saw the moment a metal pole had burst through the platinum blond's chest and how his back had collided with a concrete pillar. His agonised bellow, blood staining his teeth. Then that mocking, wet-sounding chuckle that echoed in Azeil's eardrums.

But unlike all the times the blond's presence haunted his mind, the final words that usually plagued Azeil didn't follow. Instead, those glacier irises stared into his, head cocked eerily to one side as a malignant smirk stretched his face and his orotund voice rippled within the caverns of his skull.

"I couldn't get to you then, and I can't get to you now, but it seems the Fates are on my side."

Azeil knew he argued with ghosts as he snapped back at the phantom, *"The Fates have* never *been on your side. Not even now."*

"Aw, Azeil. You're still as foolish now as you once were then. Except now ... I couldn't care less whether you lived or died. Not when you've brought your daughter to our *city."*

"Leave her alone!"

"I don't think I will. She's like us."

"She's nothing *like you, or them!"* Azeil snarled.

"Isn't she?" Orion said, before a hand gently tapped Azeil's shoulder and he whirled toward Donovan.

His silvered gaze wide and panic-filled as soft pants spilled from his lips, chest heaving like he'd run a marathon. Azeil crouched down facing the shadowed tree line, his hands moved to cup the back of his head before he lowered them between his knees and screwed his eyes shut, mind fighting to shove his memories back to where they came from.

XVIII.

Nyx

The smell of freshly brewed coffee trickled into Nyx's nostrils, her eyelids fluttering open before a wince distorted her features and a throbbing ache smarted across her neck. With stark hesitancy, she lifted her hand to her neck, fingertips grazing rough gauze whilst warm, golden rays of sunlight splayed across the dusty-grey walls. Plush black leather cushions cradling her tender muscles stretched across a three-seater couch, a silky blanket shifting over her skin when she craned her neck.

The room itself was unfamiliar, but the brown-haired twin that watched her over a steaming cup of coffee wasn't. Alexander's whiskey-toned irises studied Nyx as she observed the lounge room of the twins' home above the comic store. Varying shades of black, brown, cream, and white muddled together, giving the room a dark academic feel. Dark furniture and odd trinkets nestled upon darkly stained shelves furthering this.

Her gaze trailed to a solid bookshelf lining the wall. Various books with fanciful spines jutted out from the shelves. Supernatural creatures of varying mythologies with odd, antique-looking trinkets stood in front or beside the ranging hardbacks. Nyx's brows quirked as she continued her inspection of the twin's lounge room, stare lingering on a skull that looked too real for her comfort. An antique, jar-like bottle engraved with crosses rested between a row of black-spined hardbacks, a handwritten label reading *'holy water'* in an elegant scrawl across the faded paper.

Comics lay scattered over a large mahogany table within arm's reach of the hazel-eyed boy across from her. Two brassy candelabras decorated the lounge room, placed strategically around two black leather armchairs bracketing the mahogany table. Nyx's gaze wandered to Alexander's before he leant over and shook a sleeping Tobias, jolting the coffee-eyed twin awake.

A bemused laugh rose and died in her throat at a jolt of scalding pain, a groan wheezing from her mouth instead. Tobias sobered up quickly—getting up from the armchair and disappearing into the kitchen. Alexander rounded the squared coffee table, perching atop the edge before he leant forward and grasped Nyx's wrist in his hand. His hazel gaze was dark with caution when he directed Nyx's hand away from her throat, placing his half-finished cup of coffee on the table beside him.

"Take it easy, Night," he said, softly.

Nyx tensed as his words clanged in her mind. A blue-eyed, dirty-blond man flashed before her eyes, unbidden recollections of the night before ghosting her mind. "What time is it?" she asked instead, cringing at the croakiness of her voice.

"Ten thirty."

She scrambled to get up, stopped by Tobias who pressed her left shoulder, careful to not disturb the wound as he handed her a glass of water and two painkillers.

"Your dad knows where you are. So, please *try* to take it easy."

Nyx nodded, gingerly accepting the capsules before downing them with a mouthful of water. "Thank you," she murmured, allowing Alexander to take the half-full glass from her hands and place it on the table beside his coffee cup.

Tobias grinned, "Anytime."

Despite knowing her father knew where she was, Nyx couldn't uncoil her tensed muscles or the jittery energy inside her. Her survival instincts urged her to run before Orion, Kotori, Niko or Kade could find her during the sunlit hours of the day. Even if she knew that wasn't possible, she couldn't stop picturing the front door splintering open and them standing before it.

A frown crept across Alexander's face, his irises meeting his brother's before he spoke, "Night," he began, waiting for Nyx's gaze to leave the front door and meet his. "We don't know what happened to you last night, but we want you to know that whenever you're ready to talk about it. We'll be here to listen."

She opened her mouth to speak but Tobias cut her off with a shake of his head.

"No, Nyx. *When you're ready*. Not because you feel obligated to tell us."

"Okay," Nyx breathed in gratitude. "Thank you."

"Don't mention it," Alexander assured, returning the gentle press of her fingers.

Nyx lifted the soft blankets off her legs. "Where's your bathroom? Do you mind if I take a shower?"

"Of course not. Alex can give you one of his shirts," Tobias said, "But don't get the surgical strips wet," he urged, helping her up from the couch when a wave of dizziness hit.

Nyx's ears pricked at a soft *snitching* of a door and Alexander disappearing. The whiskey-eyed twin returned moments later with a clean black T-shirt that he extended to Nyx with a gentle smile before Tobias gestured to the final door on the right and the twins left her to continue down to the bathroom.

White scalloped tiles decorated the floor and half the wall on either side of a white, clawed bathtub beneath an ornate showerhead. The sleek design of the tiles reminded her of the scales of a snake, seeming to gleam like its skin as the ceramic material leeched warmth from her feet. Sunlight filtered into the room through pearl-white curtains shrouding a medium-sized window above the bathtub, dappling the tiles with faint whirls of colour created by the frosted glass. Her gaze slunk over to the white, double basin sink along the wall opposite the door, a large rectangular mirror framed by silver swirls mounted above the sinks.

Nyx closed the bathroom door behind her, pressing her back against it, her eyes locking with the reflection that stared back from the mirror. Her hands were stained with dried blood and she grasped the fabric of her shirt before she pulled it over her head and discarded it to the cold tiles. The tanned straps of her bra were also stained a discoloured red as she began unwinding the bandage from her neck, each layer of the gauze unravelling in her trembling hand. She dropped it to her bare feet as she reached up to ghost over the bruised flesh of her throat and the perfect set of fingerprints etched into her skin.

A soft gasp of astonishment fell from Nyx's parted lips. Her hand darting away from her throat to clasp the cold basin before her, knuckles bone-white. The flesh was an angry blend of red, and purple, discolouring the column of her throat crusted with traces of blood. A hollowness crept into her chest the longer she stared at herself in the mirror. Kade's Roman features flickering before her eyes as her fingertips gripped the ceramic, like it would anchor her here and not be swept into the truth of Celacali—of the men she wished to purge from her mind.

The bruises fuelled the biting sting of betrayal and anger she felt toward them, her skin prickling with the pulsing throb of her wounds, her mind clutching onto the rage evoked by the broken promise echoing within her skull on a never-ending loop.

"I promise you that we'll never hurt you, not now or even in the future."

She laughed bitterly, Kade's voice echoing in her mind. She couldn't shake the frustration at her own naïvety and foolishness. Because, as Nyx's gaze locked with her reflection and she squared her shoulders, she couldn't deny that for a moment. Just a moment—a wane in her resolution—she'd felt a sense of righteousness in their presence. Like her past wouldn't define her.

She shook her head to banish her traitorous thoughts, gazing into the blackness of her pupils with steely resentment. "*You* are stronger than this, Nyx. You're stronger than them," she paused, worrying her bottom lip between her teeth. "You *will* survive."

* * *

The Celacalian heat seared into Nyx's back, her loose curls dancing behind her as the paint-chipped fences darted by in her peripherals and the driveway opened out to reveal the old lodge house atop the rolling hilltop. Her ears were filled with the sound of crunching gravel beneath her bike tyres and the rumbling purr of its engine. She found her gaze drawn to a beaten-up Land Cruiser parked beneath the shade of a large tree. A crease carved her brow when she pulled up beside the car, red paintwork faded from years beneath the sun before her eyes widened with realisation and a slow grin curled across her face. Killing the engine without taking her eyes off it, she pulled the key from the ignition and dismounted in a fluid motion.

Voices ghosted past her ears as she crossed the driveway and climbed the front steps of the veranda. Her father's laughter drifted from somewhere within the house, traipsing across a summery sky dotted with fluffy clouds. Her fingers wrapped around the door handle before she pulled the flyscreen door open, stepping through the doorway and inside. Nyx's boots thudded against the hardwood floor; her focus trained on the voices coming from the brightly lit kitchen when she suddenly stilled in the lounge room's centre, black boots on the border of the ornate rug as she contemplated turning around and heading up the stairs to her room. Her excitement gnawed at her insides as her mind urged her to round the wooden staircase before she shifted on the balls of her feet, and entered the kitchen.

Short, quiff-like, dirty-blond hair snatched Nyx's gaze from her father, as she stepped through the doorway with a delighted grin. The relief that burst over his features stumped her momentarily before her eyes flicked to a pair of crystalline-blues observing her from the kitchen table. Like her father's, they too were filled with relief.

"Are you okay?" Azeil blurted, his gaze darkening as it rested on the bruising peeking out from her T-shirt, palms pressing into the table as he rose. "What happened to your neck!?"

"It doesn't matter," Nyx uttered curtly, pulling her T-shirt up her neck to hide the bruise bloom from his stare.

With a huff of annoyance and a disgruntled tilt to his lips, Nyx's uncle reached over to Azeil and tugged him back into his chair. Their behaviour with one another made Nyx recall her uncle's return as he sat at their table—her illusive and beloved uncle with migrating work habits. But before she could acknowledge the eccentrically 'Bratpack' dressed man, a smile stretched over Asher's face, and he rose from his chair, crossing the room before he pulled Nyx into a hug and she returned the embrace tenfold.

His eyes danced with excitement as he stooped to meet her gaze.

"Stay right there," Asher murmured before he turned and disappeared from the kitchen.

"Where's he going?" Nyx queried, frowning with amused confusion as she peered into the lounge room after him.

Nyx's father chuckled, the previous concern slipping from his face as his eyes lit up. "You'll see."

Nyx hummed softly in acceptance; her gaze locked on the open doorway.

"Nyx." Her father began, drawing her attention. "We'll talk about the bruises on your neck later, okay?"

"Do we have to?" she murmured, her breath hitching with a terror-inducing tide of memories.

Asher walked back into the kitchen carrying a bundle of black and white fur, and Azeil's probing gaze settled on her face. Nyx's eyebrows lifted in surprise and sudden anticipation as Asher crossed the room and held the Alaskan Malamute pup out towards her, urging her to take the wriggling puppy from his arms.

She gasped as she cradled the squirming form, a happy laugh cascading from her lips when the pup's wet nose tickled the underside of her collarbone. She peered down at the Malamute, studying its open-faced markings, almond-brown irises. The charcoal-black coat and snow-white undercoat were a stark contrast, she noted. Tearing her gaze away, Nyx met her uncle's stare, confused frown firmly in place as her gaze darted between him and her father.

"What do you think?" Asher asked, grinning from ear to ear.

"It's adorable," Nyx replied, glancing down at the pup in her arms.

Asher's grin widened before he threw a satisfied wink over his shoulder to Azeil.

"Good, because *he's* all yours." Asher said, grinning. "Now, despite being two months old, he knows the basics of walking on a leash and simple commands, but you'll have to continue enforcing them, okay?"

Nyx lifted her gaze, nodding slowly as surprise plastered across her face whilst she adjusted her hold on the tail-wagging Malamute. "*Are you sure?*"

"He's yours, Nyx. It's Asher's gift to you for your nineteenth that he missed. Plus, you've been *hounding* him for years," Azeil explained, flicking Asher's forearm.

Asher turned to face Nyx with a strained smile as the excitable Malamute shifted in her arms so it could lick her chin; a soft bark of annoyance echoing across the kitchen.

"Thank you," Nyx said, as she peered back down at the Malamute.

Asher beamed with pride as Azeil muttered something along the lines of 'brown nose' under his breath. The comment earning him a swift smack upside the back of his head from Asher, who didn't miss a beat. Nyx blinked with poorly concealed amusement, stifling the growing urge to laugh.

Asher turned to his older brother. "What's the matter, *Azzy*? Someone's got to be her favourite Monroe and it's not you."

Nyx's father draped his arms across the back of his chair as his bemused chuckle filled the kitchen. "Aw *Ashy*. What's it like coming in second place?"

"What makes you think I haven't already won?"

"Maybe because Nyx will never forget the day her Uncle Asher told her terrifying stories of golden-eyed beasts."

"No fair, Eil. You know I still feel bad about that."

The two bickered as only brothers could, and her father snickered, shrugging his shoulders dismissively when Asher grimaced at the reminder of the only time Nyx had ever stayed with him for a night. Her love for the blond-haired man lasting the hours the sun filled the sky.

"And you know that I'll never let you live it down either," Azeil said.

"I hate to interrupt your brotherly bonding, but this little guy is starting to get heavy," Nyx stated, and the two brothers' gazes drew away from each other to her as she shifted the Malamute in her arms.

"What're you going to name him?" Asher asked.

Nyx peered down at the squirming pup. The adorable sled dog gnawed on her bicep with sharp, puppy teeth. Soft, playful growls rumbled from its throat as it tugged at the sleeve of her shirt. Nyx laughed softly, lifting her gaze to her uncle as she ran her fingers through the dog's silky coat.

"Maybe Ares? The gods already know how much this one will be an absolute terror," she said, smiling as he struggled to reach her chin in an attempt to lick her face.

"Ares," Azeil murmured as though testing the name on his tongue. A soft smile quirked the edges of his lips as he studied the pup within Nyx's arms. "I like it. What d'you think, Ashy?"

"God of war and battle lust," her uncle breathed as he studied the pup like he was seeing it in a new light. "I think you've named him perfectly, Night. He's *your* little warrior."

Nyx smiled, liking the sound of the small Malamute being her little warrior. Even if she knew the 'little' warrior wouldn't stay little for long. Her lips twitched with amusement; thoughts of the blood-filled night she'd barely survived pushed to the depths of her mind. Instead, a sudden lightness filled her chest as she adjusted her hold on the sled dog that'd grow to become her warrior in every sense that a dog could be.

"I like that," she admitted, stare never straying from him as he blinked up at her with doe-eyes. "Ares; my little warrior."

Asher glanced toward Nyx's father, discreetly throwing his older brother a smug thumbs up. Azeil rolled his eyes in mock disappointment, slate eyes locked on his daughter who cradled the dog to her chest as if her life depended on it. The brothers watched Nyx whilst she stroked Ares's fur, giggling indistinctively to herself when the pup licked her fingers with an excitable wagging of its tail.

"Thank you," Nyx breathed out, her gaze flickering up to her uncle.

Asher shrugged, closing the distance between them before he pulled her into a gentle side hug. "Anytime, little terror. Anytime."

"I'm going to find somewhere in my room for Ares to sleep," she chuckled, shaking her head as she mulled over her words. "Though, I have a feeling he'll spend more time on my bed than any I make for him."

Asher breathed out a soft laugh, nodding. His mind conjuring up a memory of his beloved Malamute—Leo—on his bed while he had read comics, or the way he'd protected him without hesitation. A loyalty he hoped Nyx would find with Ares that he was forever grateful for.

"I'm sure he will," said Azeil, noting Asher's quietness.

Asher turned back to Nyx, his light brows screwing together when she wasn't standing within the kitchen before, he hurried after her, calling, "What'd you say about going down to the boardwalk? It'll be like old times when you used to wreak havoc on Celacali's locals with the twins!"

Nyx clutched Ares closer to her chest and plastered a smile on her face before she turned back around to face her uncle, "How about a night in?" she asked, shifting Ares' weight in her arms. "Movies and your *famous* lasagne sound good to me!"

Her uncle beamed. Her father's riveted laughter rippled across the room from the kitchen as he nodded enthusiastically and her father's mirthful taunt carried to her ears, "You've done it now, Night."

"Ignore Azeil, he's just a little grouchy because it's past his bedtime," Asher whispered. "A night in sounds great. It'll be a nice change from takeouts, and besides, nothing beats *my* lasagne."

Nyx nodded, her voice soft as she slowly crept up the steps. "Holler when dinner's ready, okay?"

"I will. And Nyx?" Asher began, waiting until she turned back to him. "Keep him close, alright?"

"I promise. He'll never be far from me, even when he is," Nyx reassured, running her fingers through Ares's fur before she turned and climbed the rest of the stairs.

Nyx smiled as she wandered down the sunlit hallway to her bedroom, pushing the door open and closing it with her foot before she placed the energetic pup on the floor. The top of his head stopped at the middle of her thigh, making her wonder *how* she'd held him for so long. Lowering herself down beside him, Ares started to fidget, back pressing against her bed before he clambered onto her lap, licking at the skin of her neck and chin, tail wagging a million miles a minute. And, despite the lingering fear and the bruising and tenderness around the crook of her throat, she felt safe with him for company.

Maybe her uncle had been right to refer to the fluffy sled dog as her little warrior because, with him by her side, she wasn't afraid of the four vampires she'd run from or the murders they had executed. It was like—with him curled up in her lap, head resting on his paws—she could be safe and sheltered. And so, although Ares was still so young, she knew he'd grow into his name.

XIX.

Nyx

Music played softly from the speakers of a small stereo perched upon the kitchen counter, the distinct fragrances of garlic, herbs, simmering tomato sauce and browning mince on the stovetop filled her lungs. A warm Celacalian breeze ruffled the sheer curtains above the sink, brightly coloured pansies dancing in their planter boxes whilst Asher stirred the sauce in the pan.

As Asher bent down to run his fingers through Ares's fur—who was lying on the linoleum, his head propped on his paws—Nyx smiled as her gaze trailed to a silver tray beside the stovetop. Lasagne sheets from an open packet lined the tray. Azeil's fingertips drummed against the wooden tabletop in time to Bon Jovi's *'Bed of Roses,'* the wind ruffling his curls as his peppery irises strayed from Asher, who hummed along, to Nyx.

"Hey, Asher. Where'd you say you've been with Ryder and Amir for the past ..." Azeil trailed off, fingertips ceasing their drumming on the table whilst he tried to recall what his brother had told him. "What's it been? Two? Three months?"

"Three months, Eil. It's been three months since Ryder, Amir and I've been back to Celacali," Asher replied, turning the stove off before he turned to face them.

Nyx frowned, angling her head toward her uncle.

"Weren't you in Wildegulf?"

Asher grinned, pleased that at least one of them paid attention to his migrating work habits. "We were, but Ryder wanted to check up on his sons. It's been months since he left them in charge of the store."

Nyx chuckled, the dimples in her cheeks beginning to show as she tucked a strand of hair behind her ears. "The twins are fine; they take care of that store better than you'd expect from two boys. But, what's in Wildegulf?"

"Wildegulf is renowned for its rich culture of myths and legends. Ryder, Amir, and I grew fascinated with anything supernatural back in 2024. So that's what we do. We study myths and legends, deciphering the myths from reality from place to place," he explained, enthusiasm rippling off him.

"I didn't know you were a mythographer."

"Self-proclaimed mythographer, Nyx," her father pointed out. A gentle shake of his head and the diverted tone of his voice intended to goad his younger brother.

Asher narrowed his eyes, nose screwing up, his lips twitching as if he was fighting the urge to grin.

"Aw, Azzy. It beats working the shitty hours you do."

Azeil huffed out a breath, brushing a dark curl from his face with mirth dancing in his irises. "Shitty hours it might be, Ashy, but that job pays well."

"So … all I'm getting from this *enlightening* conversation is that Dad's hours are shit and you're a self-proclaimed myth buster," Nyx said, delighted by their antics.

"I'm glad you find it enlightening, Night. Because your mental enrichment means the absolute world to me," Asher jested, a playful glint in his baby-blue eyes.

As Nyx opened her mouth to retort, the stereo beside Asher abruptly cut out and plunged the kitchen into silence. The muscles in her back coiled tightly, her spine straightening when the lights of the kitchen began to flicker, bathing the room in flashes of darkness and light. Her cautious gaze glared back at her through the kitchen windowpanes as she unsteadily rose from her chair and an unforgiving gale of wind tore through the house. The sheer curtains flapped uncontrollably, whipping her curls around her face as her heart stuttered in her chest. A thunderous rumble rolled through the house, the mechanical purr of motorbike engines skittering over Nyx's senses before it disappeared in the howling wind and Ares' erratic barking.

She caught the stiffening of her father's posture, his fingers gripping the edge of the table, and Asher looking suddenly frantic. Nyx swallowed nervously at the familiar laughter ringing through the house.

"What is that?" Azeil asked, rising from the kitchen table to follow Nyx into the lounge room with Asher, Ares at his heels.

"I don't like this, Eil," Asher murmured, pivoting in a small circle as the laughter and taunting jeers grew louder.

"Neither do I, Ash."

"It's like—"

"Don't."

"But—"

"They're gone, Asher," Azeil whirled toward his brother, eyes flashing dangerously. "*We* killed them, remember?"

Nyx hesitantly tore her gaze from the flickering lights overhead, her heart racing as the unnerving sensation of being watched prickled across her skin, her voice a hoarse whisper as the jeers and laughter guttered out, plunging the room into menacing silence. "They're toying with me."

Asher and Azeil's heads snapped in her direction before her father crossed the room and grasped Nyx's forearms. "Who's messing with you, Night?" he said.

Her eyes darted up to the ceiling, to the wooden rafters as footsteps thumped ominously above their heads and along the veranda. She couldn't think coherently as she struggled against the muddled tinge of her mind and her father's grasp. Loud mumbled whispers chipped through the chaos encasing her mind, calling to her like a wolf's mournful howl.

"Nyx."

Her spine locked straight as the familiar orotund voice ghosted across the room, rippling off the walls like sunlight on a pond's surface. Azeil's grip on her forearms tightened, his head angling toward the billowing curtains as Nyx's eyes widened, and the eerie wind picked up. Asher peered over Azeil's shoulder, coaxing him to let go of her forearms.

"Eil, you're scaring her," he stated slowly, worried for his niece and brother.

"Who's toying with you, Nyx?" Azeil reiterated, shaking Nyx whilst she fought to tamp down the fear bubbling within her chest.

"I—" The whispering grew louder—deafening—as she struggled to answer, opening, and closing her mouth like a fish.

"Nyx, Nyx, Nyx."

She blinked up at her father in a fear-induced haze, begging him to understand—to *see*—the answers in her head. And he did. He staggered away from her, dropping her forearms as realisation dawned and he stumbled toward the front door. Nyx gingerly stepped forward as if to approach her father as a sharp burst of pain tore across her throat and she stumbled. The motley bruised bite mark on her neck began to throb like it sensed its maker was near.

"Nyx, Nyx, Nyx."

She scrubbed her palms down her face as her name whispered across the night, a feeling of hysteria suffocating her control. Like everything she'd known was breaking away around her and in its place was this maddening sense of spiralling unknowing. Through the twisting knots in her mind, she pressed the back of her hand to her mouth, muffling a soft whimper. Nyx opened her mouth to speak before she gasped and choked on nothing. The pain radiating from her throat amplified, burning so callously that her knees crumpled beneath her. She wondered, as Asher's shout of surprise came from far away, if this was some cruel manipulation created by the monsters of Celacali. Because, with her eyes screwed tightly shut and her hand clutching her throat, she knew this was no *gift*. At least, not to her it wasn't.

"Nyx?" Asher called, kneeling beside her before she felt his arm wrap around her shoulders.

Azeil turned in a slow circle, his footsteps echoing through the chaos filling the house. His eyes glossed over by the sudden and suffocating swell of his memories as he mutely shuffled toward the front door and his fingertips ghosted the metallic handle.

"Don't open it," Asher bellowed, an apologetic grimace darting over his face as she winced at the sudden sound, eyes refocussing.

Nyx saw her father's fear and noted his tight grip on the door handle.

"No, *don't,*" she breathed out hoarsely.

"Azeil! Let go of the door handle!" Asher pleaded as Nyx's fingers pressed against her throat like it'd ease the brandishing pain.

Azeil looked back at Nyx and Asher, gaze lingering on Nyx before he turned back to the door and pulled it open. The flickering lights, whispers, laughter, and footsteps vanished into the night as Nyx cautiously peered past her father and out into the empty front yard. The smouldering pain across her throat guttered out as suddenly as it had appeared, leaving a ghostly prickling in its wake. When a final blast of frigid air rushed into the house, a weird echoing sound left to reverberate across the sky, the howling of the wind dying as quickly as it had come, before Ares' claws clicked on the wooden floorboards and he bounded over to Nyx.

A low fog rolled in across the gravel, rattling Nyx's frayed nerves whilst Asher and her father shared a bewildered yet knowing look. Her skin prickled like a thousand insects were crawling over her and she pressed her palms flat against the floorboards, pushing herself up before the Malamute pup barrelled into her arms. She watched her father lock the front door with a quick twist of his wrist. His naturally tanned skin appeared ashen and clammy, his turbulent gaze churning with bitter memories from his past. A past she knew her father had convinced himself was gone.

Nyx observed him like she was waiting for something to snap. Her fingers twitched at her sides as she fought the urge to rub her throat. "Da—"

"Go to your room," Azeil ordered, voice frigid.

"Please let me explain myself," she tried.

Azeil was already shaking his head before she finished speaking. His fingers raking through his curls with unveiled agitation.

"Go to your room, Nyx. Because right now … I can't even *look* at you."

Nyx sucked in a sharp breath of air, not understanding Azeil's detached tone, her grasp tightening upon Ares, seeking comfort in the small sled dog. "You can't even look at me. So what? I'm as good as dead to you?"

"You might as well be," he snapped. The short leash he'd made for himself snapping along with his words. "You've been around *them* almost every night."

"Azeil!" Asher scolded, eyes narrowed.

"Don't 'Azeil' me, Asher," Azeil scoffed, gesturing vaguely to the bruising of Nyx's throat. "You can see the marks just as well as I can, and we both know where they come from. Or are you going to lie to yourself about that too?"

Nyx stooped to place Ares on the floor, chancing a glance to her uncle. "Do I get any say in this? Or are you going to cast me as the villain of this story *before* I have the chance to explain myself for … whatever I've done?"

"Explain what, Nyx? It's obvious you've gotten *quite* cosy with them," said Azeil.

"He—" Asher began before Nyx cut him off with a bitter chuckle of vexation.

She nimbly slipped around her uncle and father before she strode toward the front door and unlatched its lock, needing to escape the resentment in her father's eyes. With a disdainful glare thrown over her shoulder, she grasped the handle of the door and swung it open, ignoring her uncle's spluttered protests.

"He didn't mean it," she drawled, stepping onto the veranda. "Well … we both know that's a lie." With a dismissive shrug of her shoulders, she hurried down the steps to her bike before anyone could stop her. Nyx didn't turn around when the front door swung open,

mounting her bike, and starting its engine whilst the stars glinted in the darkness above. Her wrist flexed leisurely around the throttle, revving the engine as the crunching of gravel beneath someone's feet flitted to her ears and she turned to peer over her shoulder.

"Nyx!" Asher called out, a begging undertone to his voice.

His plea fell on deaf ears. Snuffed out beneath the thunderous rumble of her bike's engine when she twisted the throttle again. Nyx dipped her head, her lips quirking before she released the clutch and took off down the dirt driveway. Gravel stones spraying Asher in a cloud of dust as she rode into the waiting arms of the creatures of the night.

XX.

Nyx

The fragrances of the coastal fairground engulfed her senses, calming the anger from her father's words. Her hand lifted to rub against the nape of her neck, recalling the sharp burn of pain that'd plagued her whilst the buttery whiff of popcorn glided across the night sky with the tantalising caress of fairy floss, and the saline spray of the ocean's turbulent tides. A harried combination that soothed the churning anger in her chest, the tension in her shoulders beginning to ebb.

As Nyx wandered the boardwalk, her gaze skittered over a bitterly familiar man with patchwork tattoos. *Kade*. The conscious and well-thought-out side of Nyx's mind urged her to turn around and ignore the anger smouldering within her chest, to go the other way, but her rage jolted her forward and snatched at the reins of control, determined to lead her down a different path.

The blond's appraising stare rankled unpleasantly, prodding up her spine before it skittered ghostly fingers across the dark bruises along her throat. The sensation lingered while her shoulders knocked against unsuspecting tourists, her jean-clad thigh brushing against the shoulder of a small child. Nyx only had eyes for Kade. Anger drove her through the passers-by and time seemed to slow before her palms connected with his honed chest, the ringing in her ears guttering out as the swell of the boardwalk chatter cascaded in on her.

Kade's boots scuffed against the floorboards when he stumbled back into the metal railing of the boardwalk, his tattooed hand clamping around the metallic beam to steady himself. He whirled and his gaze raked over her seething form, ring-clad fingers adjusting his jacket as he straightened. Nyx's gaze trailed over the cleanliness of his white shirt and low-cut jeans, the pure-white fabric purged of the crimson stain that'd coated his skin the last time she'd seen him.

Kade's face was devoid of his usual grin. Like he could sense the churning emotions in her, eyes ablaze like burning coals. A heady tension hung in the air between them—one of anger and something else, something she refused to admit.

"What the fuck is wrong with you!?" Nyx exclaimed, shoving him again.

Kade held his ground when her palms connected, schooling his face into an unfazed mask as he angled his head and stared down at her. Nyx wondered where his companions were, an unconscious prickling of fear erupting, which she sought to smother. Just like her survival instincts that screamed at her to *not* provoke the man before her, but ... she knew it was too late for that.

"It was all a game to you, wasn't it?" she chuckled humourlessly. "Lure the naïve and unsuspecting human, get her to trust you ... just so you could all slaughter her like a pack of rabid wolves."

Kade's eyes darted to the wooden planks beneath his feet and the lively fairground around him, looking anywhere but her, as if he were ashamed of his part in Nyx's pain. He refused to meet her gaze as he shifted from one foot to the other and the truth of her words struck his chest, then hers, hurting her more than she'd admit.

"That's it, isn't it? That's *exactly* why you came up to me in the bookstore when we met?" She stepped back as if the weight of her words shunted her, a sharp pain lodging itself in her chest. Because she *had* trusted him, letting him into her life after so long of keeping her barriers up, until she felt *something* more than friendship developing between them. She blinked back the tears threatening to spill, quickly schooling her own face into an emotionless mask so Kade couldn't see.

"I should've known," she whispered, wrapping her arms around her stomach like it'd protect her from the look in his eyes. "*You* were the lure. The piece of a plan who looked angelic enough for someone ... *foolish* enough to ignore the bad omens." Her tongue pressed into the side of her cheek, hands balling into fists at her waist until her nails dug into her palms.

Kade's gaze strayed from Nyx as if it dawned on him that they weren't alone on the boardwalk beneath the stars. He noted the looks and hushed whispers thrown their way before he strode forward and grasped Nyx's forearm, steering her through the throngs to an abandoned store along the seafront's tourist attraction. Nyx's brows creased, her gaze darting around them, stumbling over her feet whilst she tried to pry his hand from around her arm. Kade led her inside the secluded building through a back door as her instincts pricked.

As Kade released her arm and disappeared from her sight, she allowed herself a moment to survey the building he'd dragged her into. Her gaze trailed the staircase Kade had disappeared up, marvelling quietly at the intricate swirls and patterns of the black railing despite herself. The building itself seemed to be in good condition regardless of its abandonment, assorted antique-looking items covered with dust lay scattered across the surfaces of tables, shelves, and floor. And based on the small assortment of antiques left forgotten here, Nyx guessed this used to be an antique store before the owner had packed up and left.

An old chandelier hung from the ceiling, askew and covered in a thick layer of dust as the floorboards beneath Nyx's feet released an unpleasant screech when she stepped further into the room. She angled her head toward Kade when he re-entered the room, eyeing him with unveiled wariness as his gaze settled upon her and he leant against the staircase. With some effort, Nyx forced herself to study the objects before her, her voice filling the quiet of the antique store whilst her fingers brushed across the metal roof of a wind-up carousel.

"I was supposed to die that night, wasn't I?"

She peered back over her shoulder at him, waiting for his response with grotesque curiosity. His face distorted into a grimace like Nyx's words left a bad taste in his mouth. She released a fed-up huff from the depths of her chest, growing tired of his refusal to meet her gaze as she bristled with anger and crossed the room, shoving at his chest again, as her voice echoed throughout the abandoned store.

"I trusted you, Kade." Nyx paused, staring up at him.

Kade's gaze nestled on her as he tore his eyes from the room to peer down at her.

"I gave you the benefit of doubt. I thought that maybe… just *maybe*, you'd be different from the arrogant assholes in Malor. Different from *him*. But you were *so* much worse, and I was stupid enough to believe your *promises* …" her breath hitched, her mind tossing flashes of beetle-black eyes and hot breath. "I was stupid enough to believe that you were different." Nyx traced the scuffed floorboards with the toe of her boots, dropping her gaze to the ground. "And you are different, but you're also *worse* than he was."

"*Who*, Nyx?" Kade said, his gaze searing her skin like he already knew the answer. "Say his name."

She shook her head, her guards raising at the glint of his eyes, unwilling to give up another piece of herself to him as the scarred flesh of her knuckles seemed to prickle—even if she wanted to purge herself of her memories by telling him. "No."

Something within Kade seemed to snap as if Nyx's words had triggered something in him that reared up, seeking to rebel against their meaning. He startled her with his speed, stealing the air from her lungs as he snatched her wrists up and spun her around, pinning her to him with his chest and hips pressing into her back. She struggled in his one-handed grasp, face pressed against the white tiles of the abandoned store's wall. The warmth of him seeped into her back, his scent of leather, copper and Chinese spices washing over her when he adjusted his hold.

"Niko was right about one thing, angel," Kade rasped lowly, lips ghosting the shell of her ear as he stooped down beside her, and his breath fanned across her throat. "If we wanted you dead, you'd be dead already."

Nyx squirmed in his hold as if she'd be able to slip away from him, as if she'd be able to ignore the bolt of attraction that careened through her chest at his rough handling and the tone of his voice. Kade's chuckle filled her eardrums, his unveiled amusement grating against her nerves as he revelled in her struggle. His hand warningly squeezed her pinned wrists, gentle enough for her to know it was a warning before he pressed himself closer to her back. She stilled, as Kade lowered his head to the crook of her throat—the silver hoop of his eyebrow piercing reflecting the dim light—and inhaled a lungful of her scent. Her mind jolted to the worst-case scenario, throwing images of yellow-eyed beasts to the forefront of her mind.

Her heart pounded in her ears, thundering like a waterfall colliding with the rocky riverbed thousands of metres below. Almost like it was trying to leap from the warm cavern of her chest. She gritted her teeth when his lips brushed the skin of her throat, opening her mouth before closing it again, anger thrumming in her bloodstream and something she wouldn't—*couldn't*—acknowledge.

"What was that?" Kade taunted, humming from the back of his throat as Nyx frantically scrambled for something to say that'd clear the haze encasing her mind.

"I hate you," she breathed out, bristling when Kade chuckled with baleful delight.

He tutted, his lips brushing against her ear. "Aw, angel. I wish I could believe you, but the racing of your heart tells me a different story."

XXI.

Nyx

Moonlight trickled in from the dust-obscured windows, spilling across the scuffed wooden floorboards as Nyx's breath choked out from her in a soft gasp. Her back collided with the wall as Kade spun her, releasing her wrists before his arms caged her in and she peered into his soulful, searing stare. His lips quirked into an impish grin, his gaze trailing across Nyx's skin in what felt like a playful, full-body kiss. She could've sworn she heard a purr-like hum resonate in her mind, caressing her subconsciousness like someone running their fingers over the plumage of a hawk.

Kade refused to remove his eyes from Nyx, his head leaned to the side whilst his eyes burned with amusement, waiting. A sudden shift crackled in the air when he stepped forward until his chest pressed against hers, the proximity making it harder for her to breathe.

Kade was enigmatic and despite everything he and his companions had done, Nyx couldn't deny that he was the picture of perfection; full devilish grin, strong Roman features, gaze mischievously burning into her soul. As she fought the prickling urge to fidget, her instincts seemed to sense a sudden change in him, the feeling coiling around her mind like a snake and its prey in its scaled grasp.

"So, *angel,*" Kade murmured, eyes searching hers. "Tell me … what is it that has your pretty pulse racing?"

Nyx barely registered his question, his enthralling scent engulfing her lungs, clouding her mind with a haze that'd unknowingly surfaced in the presence of anger. She blinked up at him and scrambled to rein in her mind. Kade's grin grew wider, and his hazel eyes darker. One of his hands slid down the tiled wall and nestled on the swell of her hip, the other palm-down on the wall beside her head, caging her without trying to. Her heart jolted in her chest, pounding in her eardrums as he hummed from the back of his throat with an air of satisfaction.

Kade trailed his fingers from her throat to her chest. Slowly. His eyes tracked the path his fingers blazed across her skin, honey-brown irises flicking up to meet hers. As if waiting for some protest to spill from her lips, for her to deny the attraction—*lust*—between them. But she couldn't, the quickened pulse of her heart an unfaltering giveaway.

"You see Nyx. I could help you with … *that* as well. If you were *mine,* I'd show you *exactly* what I thought of that little stunt you pulled on the boardwalk."

She lunged at his words, stepping away from the wall. "Stunt? You—"

"Uh-ah, none of that," Kade scolded, pushing her back. "You see, *if* you were mine. I'd show you how you're supposed to be worshipped until all you could remember is my name and the way *I* made you feel."

"I'd believe your promises, Kade, but you don't have the best track record with … *keeping them,*" she stated, angling her head up.

Kade's grin widened as though Nyx's words sparked a burning challenge. His fingers trailed lower between her breasts, his gaze dragging down with it as her breath hitched. His touch caressed her skin but she couldn't purge the mental image his words dredged up from her brain.

Him on his knees. Between her legs. Pleasing her as he peered up at her from between her thighs.

Kade dipped his head down to her neck, his lips ghosting the bared skin before his teeth nipped at the flesh of her throat. Lips trailing upwards, grazing the shell of her ear before his warm breath fanned across her throat. "What do you say, angel? Will you let me taste you?"

Her heart jolted at his whispered words as his hands gripped her hips, pressing his pelvis into her own. Nyx froze, battling with the thought that this wasn't *right,* while at the same time, falling into a swell of sinful imagery. His words cloyed in the air and her head, so much seeming to rest on his groaned plea as he lifted his head and peered into her eyes, waiting as patiently as he'd done when they'd first met.

She blinked up at him, forcing the flashes of nightmarish beasts to the depths of her mind before she dipped her head in a nod and his lips brushed against her own.

At first, his touch was hesitant, like he was afraid he'd push too far, and she'd run from him but Nyx leaned into the kiss, her lips moving against Kade's with fervent need that quashed his hesitancy. His fingertips dug into the flesh of her hips whilst he ravaged her mouth, bruising her lips. His tongue traced the seam of her mouth and Nyx parted her lips as Kade dragged her closer to him with a guttural groan.

Nothing about his kisses screamed gentle to Nyx and yet, she didn't care. A part of her pounded against her mind, seeking to remind her of who—*what*—he was. It wasn't like she'd forgotten—because how *could* she—but in this moment, she didn't care. Kade was everywhere and Nyx wanted him.

His tongue glided against hers, tasting every inch of her mouth before he grasped her hips and lifted her. Her wrists interlocked at the back of his neck, fingertips tangling in the tresses of his hair, legs instinctively wrapping around his waist. His hands moved down to cup her ass, kneading the flesh and she deepened the kiss, pressing herself closer into him as she tugged at his bottom lip, biting lightly. A low groan vibrated from Kade's chest; a noise that made Nyx feel the thing she shouldn't be feeling.

His taste clouded her mind, intoxicating and lulling her. Every one of his touches seared into her skin and thrilled her, every inch of her coming alive. She felt him grin mischievously against her lips, his fingers clawing at the fabric of her jacket before he dragged it from her shoulders. He pulled away from Nyx then, inches separating them as his blown pupils gazed into hers, his tattooed hand cupping the nape of her neck, fingers tangling in her curls.

"We shouldn't," Nyx uttered breathlessly, her lips red.

"Tell me why, angel," Kade pressed, applying the faintest of pressure to his grasp. "Tell me why we shouldn't."

"Because you're a murderer. A *vampire*, Kade. And despite how *this* feels. It's wrong." Her chest rose with every inhale she managed. It was full of him. Full of the scent of leather, copper, and something sinful she couldn't place.

"How can something so *wrong* ... feel *so right*?" He stared down at her as he gently lowered her to her feet. "Because, as far as I'm aware, *you're* in control here. Not me."

Nyx frowned, "What?"

"You don't realise, do you?" Kade cocked his head, scrutinising her.

"Realise ... w*hat*?"

"The moment you say stop, I'll do *exactly* that." He watched her silently for a moment. "I might've done horrible things, past and present, but I do understand the basics of consent."

The breath caught in her throat when he slowly sank onto his knees before her, his fuscous irises peering up at her through his golden lashes. A gasp tumbled from her lips as he unbuttoned her jeans, tugging the denim down her legs. Kade's gaze seared into Nyx like a thousand suns—blazing and brilliant.

Nyx's stare followed his, soft pants escaping her lips when he dipped his head and kissed his way up her thigh. He paused, inches away from the top of her legs, leaning back to rest his weight on his haunches. He watched her boldly as his fingers danced teasingly across her skin, eliciting delicious chills up her spine.

"You were right about one thing," he stated, leisurely caresses halting; his gaze locked on hers. "I haven't kept my promises. So, if you're not comfortable, tell me now. Because I *want* to keep this one ..."

Nyx was reminded of his easy offer to take her back to the boardwalk when they'd first met, and she had stood above the waves breaking against Elveszett Bluff. It echoed across her mind like a wolf howling at the moon, easing the swirling storm in her mind as she looked at Kade on his knees. The knowledge that, in that moment, he'd meant what he said. Even if he'd choked up before Orion's actions, something in his eyes glinted with regret. Almost like, if he could, he'd go back in time and alter the way he'd reacted. She knew he couldn't and that it hadn't been an act, but she decided it didn't matter anymore. At least, not now.

Her lips quivered; her voice laced with need, "Kade …"

It was all she had to say. He kissed the flesh of her thigh in response, his lips ghosting over the silvery webbing of stretch marks, soothing the doubts shoving against the wall in Nyx's mind. Images of Orion with nightmarish and distorted features came unbidden as Kade pulled her panties down her legs, tossing the garment over his shoulder to expose her aching core to him. His head dipped down; Nyx's hands scrambled to grab something—anything—before his tongue dragged up her labia.

A throaty moan tumbled from her lips as her head tipped back, relishing in the feeling. Her teeth sunk into the flesh of her bottom lip as Kade's tongue flicked and teased her clit, causing jolts of pleasure to course through her. Her fingers gripped his curls, pulling him closer to her cunt in the same moment Kade's tattooed arm wove around her knee and hoisted her leg over his shoulder, a deeply, satisfied grunt sending vibrations through Nyx's clitoris. She moaned.

Kade's tongue toyed with her clit, alternating between licking, and sucking the sensitive bundle of nerves and Nyx's soft pants echoed in her eardrums, encouraging him. He moved, shoving her harder against the wall, before he shifted and hiked her other leg over his shoulders, pushing her weight back and onto him.

Nyx started at the suddenness of his movements, before he tightened his grasp around her thighs. His arms coiled securely around her thighs, fingertips pressing into her skin as he delved deeper. Nyx moaned, finding herself overwhelmed by the urge to grind against his face, her building orgasm faltering as she groaned with frustration.

Nyx blinked the daze from her mind, eyes fluttering open and down into Kade's darkened irises, trained on her before he licked his lips with a smirk playing at the corners of his mouth.

"Don't worry, angel. You'll get your orgasm in a minute," he drawled, easing up from the ground, hooking Nyx's legs around his waist.

"In a minute?" she breathed out.

She instinctively reached out to clasp his shoulders as he crossed the floor and carried her up the metal staircase, seating her on the lip of a mahogany table in the centre of the room, in a motion too smooth for Nyx to comprehend. His Roman features softened, a hand nestling upon her waist whilst the other brushed her cheekbone.

"You didn't think that was it, did you?" his eyes glinted, sparkling with something sinful. "Because we're not done yet."

"Kade," she murmured, her fingers trailing up the nape of his neck.

"Yes, little minx?" he prompted, watching her with lust-filled eyes.

Nyx sucked in a sharp breath of air when she felt his fingertips brush against her clit, his movements purposeful, drawing circles until he coaxed a low moan from deep inside her chest. Her legs easily parted when Kade's hand gripped her inner thigh to make room for himself between her legs.

"Last chance, angel," he whispered.

Although the words came easy, she felt his restraint. Something in his voice sounded ... hard. He dropped his head and Nyx suddenly felt his need. Without thinking, she grabbed his chin, turning his face to hers as his eyelids lifted revealing two burning halos ringed his pupils, eyes blazing. *For her.*

"Tell me, Kade," she said. "What do you want?"

His gaze trained upon hers as he grunted, lips parted. One moment she was sitting on the edge of the table, the next they were ... down. The breath was knocked out of her as his weight pushed her down, his arms holding her to him, protecting her.

"I…" he began. His tongue wet the corner of his mouth, showing a pointed tooth.

She could feel him straining against her.

Nyx smiled, "Mmmm," shifting underneath him.

This proved to be the final straw and Kade drove himself into her arousal-slick cunt, ring-clad fingers slamming the floor.

"Oh God," Nyx uttered, back arching as her eyelids screwed shut and her head tipped back, the stab of pleasure withdrawing, only to be replaced by Kade thrusting again … and again. She couldn't speak as he moved. His hardness moving deeper, for longer, the pleasure slowly rebuilding in the pit of her stomach.

Kade's movements were rhapsodic and confident, engrossed in the way Nyx's head tipped back and bared her throat to his greedy gaze whilst pleasure coursed through her. He withdrew from her as her lips parted and a moan of displeasure slipped from her lips.

He grasped the black strap of her tank top, yanking the fabric over her head in a smooth motion, exposing her flesh. A soft hiss tore from her lips as the cold air licked at her naked chest, hardening the skin. Kade took one taut nipple into his mouth and she tightened her hold on him. His gaze snared Nyx's before he looked up at her, watching her as he moved his mouth slowly, his teeth gently grazing the nub.

"Kade … *please,*" Nyx begged softly, groaning when his fingers tauntingly trailed over her clit.

"Please what?" he murmured.

"I … need you!"

His head angled, eyes appraising. "Where?"

"Inside me."

He withdrew his hand from her cunt and purred, pulling out of her and teasing his tip along her drenched slit, collecting her arousal before he guided his cock into her once more.

Kade's pace was slow at first as he craned his neck to peer down at Nyx. She felt him gauging her reactions, noting her soft gasps and moans as he thrust deeper into her. At first, she felt like fire, burning, and consuming her from the inside before slowly turning into pleasure with each thrust of his hips. It rendered her speechless, so overwhelmed by him and the feeling of him inside her that it was all she could do to move with him, her fingers gripping his tattoo-embellished shoulder. Nyx couldn't think coherently, blinded by the feeling of being so utterly full she couldn't form a simple exclamation of his name.

Kade's thrusts quickened until she thought she was going to tip over the edge. Then, he turned her onto her stomach, her face pressing into smooth wood before he pulled her ass back and plunged himself once more into her cunt. She groaned loudly, eyes rolling into the back of her head as she felt herself clench around his cock, her hands splayed as he rode her.

"Kade," she ground out, frustrated by his grip on her hips, forcing her to stay still whilst she squirmed in his hold, desperate for the release building in her abdomen.

"So eager for me," he drawled, his lips teasing the skin of her throat before his teeth ghosted across the bared, unmarked expanse of skin.

The more she shifted her body, the more Kade preened with satisfaction, chuckling at her feverish writhing. As if he could sense the growing need coiling in her stomach, Kade's fangs nipped at the spot behind her ear, cock twitching inside her.

"Fuck!" Nyx gasped, quelling the needy whimper that threatened to spill from her lips when she tried to grind down on him.

Kade tutted; irises light with desire. "So needy."

Nyx couldn't diminish the whine that bubbled past her lips in response, relaxing into the hardness beneath her.

Kade's chest pressed into her back, his face nestled into the crook of her neck, a groan rumbled from the back of his throat. "That's it, angel, just like that," he murmured, thrusting his hips.

"Kade, please," she gasped, fingers gripping the table's edge, "I need to—"

"I know. I know," he assured softly as he affectionately nipped at her throat. One hand snuck down to her clit and rolled the sensitive bud between his fingers, eliciting a wild moan from Nyx. Kade pressed a chaste kiss to the crook of her neck when his other hand glided across her skin. Her back arched with pleasure, trying to chase the orgasm he kept just out of her reach as his fingers wrapped around her throat.

"*Please,* Kade," Nyx begged, pleading for release.

Kade's fangs embedded themselves into her throat as Nyx groaned in ecstasy and a thousand aphrodisiacs plunged into her bloodstream, dousing her mind and body with blinding pleasure. He thrust up into her, swallowing a mouthful of her sweet blood, a gratified groan vibrating from the back of his throat as she clenched down around him and bared more of her throat to his assault. The combination of Kade's fangs in her neck, drawing small mouthfuls of blood into his mouth, and the thrusting of his hips drove Nyx over the edge; her orgasm washing over her in a brilliant haze heightened by the blend of endorphins and aphrodisiacs his bite elicited.

Nyx felt when Kade withdrew his fangs, his tongue lapping at the indents left from his elongated incisors. She turned to see his eyes fluttering shut and his head tipped back, savouring the pleasure of his orgasm. His fingertips dug into her hips; lips parted as a guttural moan glided from his mouth.

As Nyx moved to push herself up, arms trembling beneath her weight, he scooped her up into his arms in a fluid motion, crossing the room to the large assortment of pillows, blankets and cushions. Nyx blinked up at him from beneath heavy eyelids as he lowered her onto the soft bed—the low of his bite-induced high leeched her of the aphrodisiacs and endorphins throughout her bloodstream, leaving her body with a faint tremble and lulling urge to sleep whilst he seemed to straighten, a liveliness to his eyes that hadn't been there before—situating himself amongst the mismatched bedding before he pulled her to his chest.

"Go to sleep, angel," Kade murmured.

Nyx blinked once. Twice, trying to rid herself of the weariness creeping into her bones from the aftereffects of his bite. "But—"

"I promise I'll be here when you wake up," he assured, staunching her inner turmoil as easily as if she'd spoken it out loud.

Despite the bellowing of her instincts, Nyx closed her eyes and allowed sleep to come, carrying her into its dark embrace whilst her head rested against Kade's chest.

The immortal tightened his hold on her, himself in Death's eternal embrace.

XXII.

Nyx

Calliope music ghosted the shell of Nyx's ears. Moonlight streamed through the glass-paned windows onto the floorboards as she shifted amongst the assortment of pillows, blankets, and cushions. Fingers grazed her arm, shoulder and head, toying with her hair. A content hum dragged from the back of her throat as she blearily blinked awake, rubbing her eyes with a soft yawn. Then, confusion as the events from earlier in the night caught up to her. She turned to peer over her shoulder at Kade, unable to mask her surprise that he hadn't vanished into the night while she slept. His honeyed stare trailed across her face, rendering her speechless.

A smile quirked the corners of Kade's mouth, his head tilting to the side, eyes dancing with a softness she'd never seen. She noticed the crookedness of his nose and momentarily forgot about *why* she'd wandered onto the boardwalk and into his arms, shunting the whispers of an argument, and that she should stay away from them, to the back of her head. Her gaze darted across the abandoned room in search of her discarded clothes. Solar-powered lights strung around the beams of the ceiling splayed soft halos onto the floor. She found them beside the makeshift bed, folded neatly and looked over at Kade.

"What'd you want to know?" he asked, shifting amongst the pillows and blankets.

She settled on a simple response, hoping he would provide her with answers. "Why didn't you do anything?"

Kade exhaled in frustration, the blankets of the makeshift bed pooling dangerously low on his hips, hiding none of his tattoo-covered body. Now it was she who waited as he considered how to explain himself.

"Do you know what a sire-bond is?" he asked as Nyx pulled her jeans up and zipped her fly.

She peered over her shoulder at him, "Only from comics. Vampires are *quite* popular in the twenty-first century, Kade."

He hummed, "Oh, I know about the twenty-first century's *enthralment* with vampires. It made life easier for us when it took off."

Nyx glanced at him. "Right," she drawled, pulling her T-shirt over her head, ignoring the dark undertone to his statement. "Well, what is it, blondie?"

"A sire-bond is a bond forged with blood. Typically, the sire's blood. For vampires, a sire-bond is the bond between the sire and his protégés. So, the *maker*, but if a sire is killed, his ties to the pack or coven fall to the first turned member. Giving them all the perks and power of the sire," Kade explained carefully, ensuring Nyx was following.

"What does this have to do with you?"

"Our head vampire or *sire*, Leon, was killed by your family in 2012. Though, we're still not sure *how* they did it," Kade whistled mockingly, rubbing a pale, square-shaped scar between his ribs. "The little shits tried killing us all too. They started with me as a distraction to snatch Niko and finished with Leon. Except our sire was too narcissistic to see it coming."

"My father—" Nyx cut herself off when Kade's bitter laughter permeated the air and he straightened, sitting upright with a resentful smile that reminded her of his ties to Orion, Kotori and Niko.

"Wouldn't do that?" he finished for her, shoving the blankets away from himself as his jean-clad legs closed the distance between them. "Well, he did. And I couldn't do a single thing to help my brothers as their screams filled my head."

"They wouldn't do that," she protested; shoulders locked with unchecked anger.

Kade arched an eyebrow, daring Nyx to disagree as his gaze skittered down her forearms. "Daddy dearest took our greeting well I see," he murmured, gesturing to the hand-shaped bruises upon Nyx's forearm with a lazy wave of his hand.

Nyx glanced down at the bruises, picking her jacket up off the floor and slipping her arms into the sleeves. "Get to the point, *Kade,*" she gritted out; hands balled into fists in the pockets of her jacket.

"With Leon gone, the sire-bond had to fall to one of us. Your father and mother were slipped Leon's blood at one of the parties we took them to … as per Leon's orders. Xander was Leon's twisted attempt to get your parents to finish the transition. But since they were halflings, when he died, they regained their mortality," said Kade, toying with the belt loops of his jeans whilst Nyx processed the information.

"You didn't drink Leon's blood?"

"In the beginning, we all did, but we realised that our bond was stronger together than it'd ever been with Leon. Eventually, we all drank from each other, forging a bond between the four of us that was stronger than any sire-bond. Despite that, one of us still inherited the sire's *perks,*" Kade said, a reminiscent gleam to his honeyed eyes.

"So, which one of you …" Nyx rubbed a hand down her face as realisation dawned on her. "*Orion.*"

"Yep," he said, popping the 'p' as his Cheshire-Cat-like grin spread across his face.

She nodded slowly. "But that doesn't explain why you didn't do anything, or why drinking Leon's blood has anything to do with it."

"There's a type of control a sire has, angel," Kade grasped her hands, thumbs rubbing soothing circles into the back of her hand. "Orion issued a command I couldn't fight through our bond. And Leon's blood—or *any* vampiric blood—is like poison once it's ingested.

It seeps into your bloodstream, starting the transition from human to vampire until every cell is tainted, on the cusp of immortality."

"You could've fought it," Nyx protested before a frown split her face and she peered up at him. "On the cusp? But—"

"It doesn't work like that. You have to take a mortal life to begin an immortal one; a life for a lifetime," Kade shook his head, licking his lips as he interlaced their fingers. "And I did fight it, Nyx. But I never stood a chance against the power behind his command. Not as the youngest of our group."

"But Niko—"

"Is about ninety years older than me and was extremely pissed off with Orion. Combine that with his naturally protective instincts and seeing you in danger ... it can override a command if it's not from the original sire," Kade explained, a soft smile across his face that did little to soothe the turmoil budding in her chest.

"Kotori?"

"Is older than Niko and me by at least half a millennium. He's mastered the art of evading Orion's commands and perfected it over the years they've spent together," Kade uttered offhandedly like he hadn't just revealed that Kotori and Niko were hundreds of years old.

Nyx blinked up at him, lips parted with wonder, mind reeling. *"Half a millennium?"*

"Immortal beings, remember?" Kade teased; a goofy grin etched across his face.

She cleared her throat, tearing her gaze from Kade's and to the room around her as she swiftly changed the subject. "What's the deal with this place?"

Kade glanced around the room. A look of pride trickling into his irises as he studied the simply furnished room above the abandoned antique store. "It's a hideaway of sorts that Niko and I found a while back." He released her hands, scratching the back of his neck with a sheepish grin across his face. "We've spent the past few nights here, away from Kotori, Orion and all the tension in the cave."

"We?" She parroted, gaze drifting to the top of the staircase when energetic footsteps echoed through the forgotten store.

There was an odd and yet even rhythm to the sound as feet bounded up the stairs with the jingling of bracelets. Boots thudded on the hardwood stairs as she craned her neck to see over Kade's shoulder.

"I'm back. Did ya miss me, Ka—" Niko's words died on his lips as his gaze locked on Nyx.

Concern flickered across his face as he discarded the paper bag on the floor and crossed the room, not stopping until he dragged Nyx into his arms and a sigh of relief ruffled her head.

"You're okay," Niko breathed out, sounding more like he was reassuring himself than speaking to her.

Niko pulled away, guitar string-calloused hands grasping her forearms before he swiftly drew her back into his embrace. The combination of weed, leather and something woodsy engulfed Nyx's senses as she gingerly returned the gesture.

She chuckled softly, her voice a low whisper. "It takes a lot more than that to break me, Niko."

He hummed softly; arms wrapped around her waist, the cool press of his rings a stark contrast to her warm skin.

She basked in the comfort and security of him, resting her head on his chest, and relaxing into his arms while he drew in a lungful of her scent. Lifting her head from his Guns 'N Roses singlet to peer up at him, her gaze traced over his cool, sand-toned features. On the right side of his face was a diagonal path of pale freckle-like scars.

A sinking realisation pooled in her gut, Kade's voice echoing in her mind as she raised her thumb, ghosting over the indistinct debits while she wondered how she could've missed them. She peered over her shoulder at Kade, who silently watched their interaction play out with a soft smile. As she lowered her hand from Niko's face, she masked her inner conflict—of what she *thought* she knew—by wrapping her arms around his waist.

Kade gnawed at the flesh of his thumb, an amused tilt to his lips, "I was wondering when you'd show that massive heart of yours, Nik," he jested.

Niko scoffed, the sound vibrating through Nyx when he rested his chin atop her head. "And I'm just going to pretend like I can't tell *exactly* what happened here," Niko quipped.

A choked laugh of mortification spilled from Nyx as she hurriedly pulled away. *"What?"*

Niko tapped his nose with a cheeky grin, "Heightened senses, chica."

She stared at him, wide-eyed, mouth opening and closing as Niko laced their fingers together and led Nyx back to the soft bed in the room's corner whilst Kade fluidly picked up the paper bag Niko had dumped beside the staircase. Her laughter came easily, dancing across the moonlit room like horses galloping over open plains, and Niko's eyes lit up in a way that made her heart skip.

As she chuckled, the dimples in her cheeks deepened, and the corners of her eyes crinkled with pure, undiluted happiness. Happiness, she clung onto as Niko pulled her into his side, wrapping his arm around her shoulders before the bed dipped and Kade nestled himself amongst the pillows, cocooning her in a blanket of warmth from both sides.

She turned toward him, "I understand why you did what you did, Kade," she said before she glanced at Niko, "What you both did." She turned back to Kade, "I don't have forever like you do, but I hope someday you'll fight against one of Orion's commands and win like Niko did."

"But—" Kade's protest was stifled as Nyx continued, grasping his hands in hers.

"You've done bad things to *survive,* Kade. Things most people would hate you for,'" gesturing airily to herself, "but who am I to judge? Who am *I* to sentence you to a life of guilt when men have done far worse, for less?"

"You've seen us *kill* people ... and we don't *regret it."* Niko said. "We've spent decades revelling in our victims' fear before we killed them, you ... know this."

Nyx knew she didn't blame them for Orion's actions, but she couldn't ignore the sliver of wariness in her mind. "I said that you were flawed, Niko. Not that I was stupid."

Kade's surprised laugh filled her ears and his fingers closed around Nyx's chin, turning her head back toward him with a delighted glimmer in his eyes. "What is it that you're trying to say, angel?" he murmured, angling his head.

"Girls don't carry pepper spray in their bags because they're afraid of you. They don't glance over their shoulders every five seconds on their way home, clutching their keys tighter in their hands because of *you*."

"You're saying—" Niko began, realisation filling his eyes.

"I'm saying that you're the monsters society tells us to fear, but men have done *far* worse than what you do," Nyx stated, conviction in her voice.

Niko threw Kade an excited glance, shifting amongst the pillows so he could peer around Nyx's shoulder to see her face and the scolding conviction in her eyes.

"Careful, angel. We wouldn't want someone to get the wrong impression now, would we?" Kade taunted, revelling in the swirling anger of Nyx's eyes.

"Aw, but Kade. I like this side of her," Niko whined, resting his chin atop her shoulder with a smile.

Kade hummed, "Niko, are you thinking what I'm thinking?"

Niko's eyes shone, his breath warming the side of Nyx's throat, arms winding themselves around her waist. "Definitely," he purred, lips ghosting her neck whilst she forced herself to hold Kade's searing gaze and ignore the mounting attraction she felt for both of them.

Kade's lips quirked into a devilish grin, raising his hand to cup her face, trailing his thumb across her bottom lip. "We're going to enjoy corrupting you, angel."

Niko planted a soft kiss on the crook of her throat, lifting his head so his lips brushed her ear when he spoke, "And we'll do it so well that you'll forget what it was like before you met us."

XXIII.

Nyx

Nyx stifled her laughter with the back of her hand, eyes dancing with delight as Kade and Niko led her through the back alleyways of the boardwalk stores. The mischievous pair shushed her, gazes swirling with amusement and Nyx huffed out a breath, worrying her lip between her teeth with a gentle shake of her head.

"Let me get this straight," she paused, sucking in a sharp breath of air whilst she fought the urge to laugh. "*Kotori* dared you to go up to a *Chinese* tourist and ask for directions, but instead he told you to say what?"

"Wǒ yǒusān gè gāowán; nǐ xiǎng kàn kàn ma?" Niko recalled, grinning.

"Which means?"

Kade chuckled, clasping her hand in his and interlacing their fingers together. A simple gesture she revelled in.

"I have three testicles; would you like to see?" he said.

Nyx chortled, slapping her hand over her mouth with wide, amused eyes. "How did you fall for that?"

Kade glanced around the empty alleyway with a conspiring glint. "Niko can be *quite* … gullible at times."

"In my defence, I thought it was a compliment to the woman," Niko stated, traipsing over to Nyx, and slinging his arm over her shoulders. "How was I supposed to know? I don't speak Chinese."

"That's *exactly* why I wouldn't have asked a native speaker," she shook her head, their footsteps echoing off the alleyway walls. "That poor girl probably thinks all men are like that now."

Niko arched his blond brows, glancing down at Nyx. "*Poor girl*? I can assure you; she was anything *but* poor."

She peered up at Niko whilst Kade led them around a corner and into the steady trickle of boardwalk-goers wandering the car park.

"Should I be concerned?" she asked.

Kade shook his head, turning to peer over his shoulder. "No. He's just tip-toeing around the story behind it."

"There's a story?" She whirled back towards Niko, a smile pulling at the corners of her mouth. "C'mon Niko, now you *have* to tell me."

Niko's gaze glittered with mischief before he removed his arm from around her shoulders and slipped between two cars with unnatural ease.

"Let's just say that said girl uttered a colourful string of Chinese profanities after she hit me with her purse … several times for good measure."

"You're joking … right?" Nyx prompted, fighting the laugh that was coming.

Kade snickered, narrowly avoiding Niko's hand and side-stepping as he let go of Nyx's hand and wandered to her bike before leaning against it.

"This is Azeil's old bike, isn't it?" he asked, lifting his gaze from the faded Honda to Nyx who was frowning.

"How do you …" Nyx paused, her eyes widening when she realised, she knew the answer—that he'd already told her. "You knew my father before he tried to kill you, didn't you?"

Niko nodded, his lips pursed as he crossed the distance to Kade, oceanic gaze locked on the faded-red bike.

"We did," he said, fingertips trailing across the leather seat before his gaze lifted to meet Nyx's. "We thought he'd make a good addition to our group since Alyvia liked him. We thought it'd entice her to complete the transition from halfling to vampire."

"Xander wasn't our finest moment either," Kade admitted, running his fingers through his hair. "But Kotori took an instant liking to him, distracting him after he'd drank the drinks we'd laced with Leon's blood, without our knowledge."

"Xander would've been seven, eternally stuck as a child," Nyx breathed out, eyeing them with disbelief; familiar warning bells beginning to toll in her eardrums.

Kade's eyes bled white-gold, and for a moment, she glimpsed the golden-eyed beast that evoked a shiver down her spine. Freezing like a deer in headlights when he lifted his gaze from the handlebars of her bike and looked at her, her heart suddenly pounding in her chest as he rubbed his jaw, thumb brushing his bottom lip. An apex predator analysing her coolly.

Nyx wondered, not for the first time, what she'd gotten herself into.

She watched him back cautiously with her mother's voice echoing in her ears, warnings and various conversations twinning together until Nyx realised her mother always offered advice with a foreboding edge. And that nothing she said could've prepared her, even if her mother seemed to know more than she wanted to disclose. Like she'd learnt it from the men in front of Nyx and couldn't shake it, instilling her knowledge into her daughter—warning her without telling her why.

"Look for their tells, Night. Everyone has something that'll give their thoughts and intentions away. You just have to find them*."*

"It's time to go, Nik," Kade bluntly stated, turning away from Nyx as he moved to slip between the cars in the parking lot.

"Kade, wa—" Nyx called out, cutting herself off when Niko shook his head with a warning gleam in his eyes.

Nyx watched helplessly as Kade slipped between cars, her gaze tracking the movement of his patchwork tattooed silhouette. Then he was gone, leaving her with a foreign emptiness that settled unpleasantly within her ribcage.

She blinked, disorientated, and confused by his sudden disappearance. "Did I say something?" she asked Niko.

Niko shook his head, a soft reassuring smile on his face. "You didn't say anything wrong, chica. Kade just . . ." he trailed off, glancing over his shoulder as if someone had called his name. "Don't worry about it too much, it's nothing personal."

"So, why'd he leave like that?"

Niko's turbulent and ever-changing irises seared into hers, trapping her, "We all have demons, and when you've been alive for as long as we have, you tend to pick up a few."

She stared after him as he walked away from her, hope bubbling in her chest when he paused and turned back to her. "Be careful, Nyx, because soon it'll be too late for you to walk away from this."

"Isn't it already too late?"

"You've only seen a shadow of the truth, and we're not about to make the same mistake with you that we made with Azeil," he said.

"So, what? If I know too much and you decide you can't trust me, you'll kill me?"

Niko held her gaze, unbothered and utterly calm. "If it comes to it, yes. But don't make us the villains of your fate if you choose wrong. The ball's in your court now, Nyx." He angled his head like a predator sizing up its prey. "Will you fight for what you want, or will you die with nothing?"

* * *

Sharp, attention-starved barking startled Nyx awake as she jolted up in her bed. She waited a moment before she rolled to the edge of the bed and peered down at the floor with her chin propped atop her hand, finding Ares, who blinked up at her, tail wagging a million miles a minute. The pup fidgeted on the floor, tongue lolling to the side of his mouth, his whiskey irises brimming with an adoration that Nyx couldn't resist any longer as she tossed her sheets aside and slipped from the bed to join him.

A content feeling filled Nyx's chest as she ran her fingers through Ares's fur, the sled dog wiggling with excitement whilst he licked the underside of her chin, tail wagging with unveiled delight. She lifted her gaze from the Malamute when the faintest creaking of floorboards drew her attention toward the doorway of her room, the door left open like it'd been when Nyx slipped through her window in the early hours of the morning, her mind churning with confusion and hurt at Kade's abrupt departure whilst Niko's soothing smile replayed before her eyes. And where there had been darkness in the waning hours before dawn, Asher now stood, leaning against the door frame with a soft smile. Ares scrambled off Nyx's lap and bounded over to him.

Nyx screwed up her nose jokingly, gesturing to the obscenely coloured shirt her uncle wore with a slight wave of her hand. "Why's it look like you just finished a shift at the dentist's?"

Asher glanced down at himself. "I'll have you know that I like this shirt, Nyx."

"Oh, I know you do," she said. "That's why you own about a million *artistically* designed shirts."

He gasped in mock horror, hand resting on his chest as if she'd truly offended him. "There's nothing wrong with my shirts."

She hummed, unconvinced before she pushed herself up off the floor. "Whatever you say, My Little Pony."

"I do *not* look like a My Little Pony."

"You sure? Because I think you'd fit in perfectly with all your shirts."

Nyx crossed the room until she stood beside her uncle, reaching up on the tips of her toes, she ruffled his hair with a cheeky grin. Asher's azure eyes danced and Nyx smiled up at her uncle with blatant adoration.

"I missed you while I was in Wildegulf," he said, pulling her into a comfortable embrace she instantly returned.

"I told you that you would."

He chuckled, "It's good to see you again. That's for sure," he paused. "I'm sorry I didn't do more last night."

She shook her head, "It's not up to you to apologise for the way Dad acts. You don't control the way he thinks or speaks."

"But—"

"But nothing. Only he can apologise for the things he said. It's not your job to clean up his messes."

Asher opened his mouth to protest, closing it quickly when Nyx levelled him with a glare. "He'll either apologise or lecture you, little terror," he pre-warned, glancing down at her as she walked past him toward the staircase.

Nyx smiled fondly at the familiar nickname and crossed the lounge room with small steps that she hoped would prolong the inevitable lecture awaiting her in the gold-plunged sunroom.

Why should she feel ashamed of something she'd known nothing about? That she hadn't been alive to see?

It wasn't her fault that her father had drank something he shouldn't have, made by people he'd barely known, that had contained Leon's blood—the infamous sire Kade had spoken of—or that he'd provoked Orion, Kotori, Niko, and Kade's immortal vengeance, essentially nurturing their grudge with his actions alone. Was it?

So, when her father turned away from the setting sun through the glass panes of the sunroom windows, she met his glower with determination. He hadn't exactly sat her down and had the 'I pissed off four vampires when I lived here twenty-five years ago' chat with her, nor had he mentioned in the many stories of the 'golden-eyed beasts' that he'd taken part in the—*attempted*—murders of said beasts.

Who was to blame? she wondered, knowing neither fraction was just.

"How long have you known about them?" Azeil asked, slate irises filled with bitter resentment. As though speaking of the four men he'd tried to kill tasted foul on his tongue.

Nyx angled her head, her brows furrowed with mock confusion. "Depends on what you mean by that, *Azeil.*"

Azeil gritted his teeth at Nyx's usage of his first name, jaw clenching when he levelled an unimpressed glare in her direction. "How long have you known?"

"Did I know they were the 'beasts' you'd told me about as a kid?" she chuckled hollowly, ignoring his question to answer one of her own. "No."

Her father opened his mouth to speak, Nyx's eyebrow arching as a brewing storm grew in her. Her eyes flashed with anger as she looked at the crumpled ash-grey shirt and denim jeans he wore, the bite marks on her neck tingling with an overwhelming urge to scratch a non-existent itch. She blinked, shunting the itchy feeling away, fingers twitching as she pushed away unfamiliar desires—to believe her father's intentions were good, or tamp the dark longing enticed by Orion, Kotori, Niko and Kade's presence.

"They're itchy, aren't they?" Azeil stated, breaking through her thoughts.

She frowned; steel-infused guard faltering as she narrowed her eyes at his knowing words. "What?"

"Aw, Nyx. You're never going to be the same after this," he murmured; his gaze laced with unwavering conviction.

"Do you really think *that* little of me?" she questioned, a disgruntled smile playing at the edges of her mouth. "That I can't decide what's best for me?"

He chuckled; the sound poisoned by his doubtful smile. Like he knew something she didn't. "But you don't know what's best for you because if you did, you would've stayed *far* away from them."

Nyx scoffed, shaking her head, "And what if I choose them?"

Her father mulled over her bitterly spat question. An easy-to-miss flash of fear came and went from his eyes. "You can't be serious? You'd choose *them*?"

"I'm not choosing anyone; this isn't some game of tug of war. You can't pull me in the direction you want me to go, and neither can they," Nyx sighed, frustrated. "But if I did choose them, what would you do?"

Azeil rose from his chair, crossing the room until he stood beside Nyx and peered down at her. "I'd tell you to not bother coming home ... because you wouldn't be welcome here as a murderer."

Her lips parted in shock when her father brushed past her shoulder. A jarring chord struck in Nyx's chest, reverberating inside her like a crack of thunder. As she turned to her father's retreating figure, she couldn't shake the feeling of something clamping down on her windpipe, choking her in a blinding daze of fear and desperation.

No one had warned her of this drowning sense of abandonment that engulfed her, threatening to pull her down relentlessly. She swallowed a bitter taste on her tongue, and laughed a dark, dangerous laugh. "Like how you murdered them?"

Azeil halted at the bottom of the stairs, one hand on the wooden railing as he turned back toward her. "They're killers, Nyx."

"I know what they are," she spat, the searing pain in her chest making it impossible to focus.

"Are you going to stand there and defend them? They're monsters."

"Monsters are made. Not born."

Something shifted in the air as her words hung thickly in the room, an understanding laced throughout her tone that she couldn't hide because she knew, on some level, what is was like to do something wrong that felt so *right.*

Azeil turned away from her and stared out the windows of the kitchen, his voice was barely above a whisper when he turned back to face her, "Just get out. I don't want you here just ... *leave.*"

"Where am I supposed to go?" she asked, lifting her hands as if emphasise the fact she didn't *have* anywhere to go.

"I don't care, Nyx. *Get out,*" Azeil snapped, pointing to the door with unrelenting resentment in his granite eyes.

Nyx blinked once. Twice as if to convince herself this was all some horrible dream she'd wake up from if she tried hard enough. But she realised her mistake when her father bent down and picked up the duffel bag she'd left beside the stairs, tossing the black bag at her feet without emotion before he inclined his head in the direction of the front door.

"Get out and don't come back."

Numbly Nyx nodded, bending down as she softly called for Ares, who came bounding over with an excitable swish to his tail. She picked him up and placed him in a black duffel bag, hoping it'd be enough to distract from the broken feeling pressing on her chest when she zipped up the bag so only his fluffy head stuck out. She swallowed the lump in her throat, hoisting the bag onto her shoulder before sparing her crumpled Guns 'N Roses t-shirt and shorts a glance. As she crossed the room and plucked her keys off the small table beside the front door, she hesitated, hand resting on the door handle when she peered over her shoulder to her father.

"Just know that I hope this moment will haunt you forever. Because if I die, you'll be to blame. *They're monsters, Nyx,"* she scoffed, pulling the door open. "Funny, because the only monster I see right now is *you*."

XXIV.

Orion

The sun slunk beneath the crashing waves of Celacali and a saline-encrusted breeze blew through the coastal town, eliciting an unusual chill over the bright and lively lowlands with growing ferocity. It carried the moisture hanging thickly in the air as if a storm loomed on the horizon, brewing above the sea with silent intent.

Leaves rustled in the gale that now whisked the breaking of a family bond to the tree line ghosting a large, lodge house. Glacier irises tracked Nyx's silhouette through the lounge and kitchen windows, predatory interest churning as relentless as the waves below.

Orion shifted his weight, adjusting his gloved grip on the branch above his head with ease. The simple, silver cross earring brushed against his face as he swung in the oak tree. Cloaked in the darkness and his black trench coat, Orion tucked the flapping lapel tightly to his charcoal-grey shirt, the dark fabric brushing against his black jean-clad legs.

"How long have you known about them?"

He angled his head, tearing his gaze from his clothes as Azeil's words drifted across the night and to his ears. As he gazed across the stretch of land before the house, bitter resentment seared his chest, reminding him of things he'd rather forget. His jaw clenched with poorly restrained anger, grip tightening on the branch above with enough force that it groaned in protest. He knew he shouldn't be here, but something drew him to the house of his nightmares, torturing him in more ways than one as agonised bellows of pain filled his mind.

An agony he'd never wash from his mind.

In some sick way, he needed those pain-filled screams to remind himself of his vow. He knew of the mistakes he'd made twenty-five years ago that had stemmed from this man in his twilight-bathed sunroom. A series of mistakes he had vowed to never make again. Maybe that's why he'd come, or maybe something within him sought satisfaction in Azeil's paranoia.

"Depends on what you mean by that, *Azeil.*"

Orion's lips twitched with faint amusement. His keen eyes watched as Azeil bristled, back tensing in Nyx's direction. He could hear that the way Nyx drawled her father's name reminded Azeil of *him,* pronouncing the syllables almost exactly like he did. Memories for memories. A simple, dark trade. Something within Orion stirred, thrilled at the effect he had on Azeil after all these years.

Azeil's voice broke his quiet, "They're itchy, aren't they?"

Orion's gaze darted from Azeil to Nyx, scrutinising her from beneath the canopy of leaves before locking on her bared throat. His eyebrows arched, puzzled by a new bite mark akin to the one he'd left on her throat except, instead of the motley bruising he'd left behind—the equivalent of a vampiric hickey—this was a paler white against her skin and had healed in the shape of two never-meeting crescent moons, four identifiable one-millimetre indents left behind from vampiric elongated incisors and canines.

He knew of only three vampires in Celacali, excluding himself. Two of whom had been MIA since he'd bitten Nyx's left shoulder. He'd known their growing curiosity for her in the years since they'd seen her in Malor. And now, Kade and Niko thriving on the life and laughter Nyx brought into their lives like sunflowers when she had moved to *their* city. Orion shook his head with mirth before diminishing his grin to the buffering wind ruffling his hair. He might have watched her for years to ensure his revenge ran smoothly—like they all had—but he'd seen glimpses of Nyx's dark side and wanted to see how far he could push her. Would she break? Or would she thrive?

Either way, who was he to find amusement in his brothers' actions when he'd done nothing but ruin their happiness in the span of a night? Crushing it beneath the sole of his boots like someone squished a bug, unflinching and undeterred by the splatter it left behind. Three men who had placed their trust in his hands—believing in him even when he didn't.

"They're killers, Nyx."

Orion staunched his thoughts as Azeil's low response met his ears, refocusing his attention on the paned windows of the sunroom. Panic careened through his chest when the emptiness of the room registered in his mind, a foolish emotion he shoved to the depths of his subconsciousness when he focused on the beating of Azeil and Nyx's hearts, following their rhythmic beats to the lounge room. The erratic, panic-driven thudding of Nyx's heart ricocheted in his eardrums, pounding in her chest in a symphony of chaos that soothed and worried his barely decipherable, human soul.

Orion leant forward—to better see this brown-haired girl whose heart called to him. Unknowingly beautiful and yet, *so* deadly—damning—to his life of bloodshed and destruction.

"Monsters are made. Not born," she said.

Orion felt the sudden shift in the air, his eyes locking on Azeil's when Nyx turned to stare out into the shadows that hid him. His resentment for her coiled tightly in his chest, like the serpent tattooed around his wrist before the snapping of a twig drew his gaze to Kotori who stood beside him.

Kotori crouched low on the sturdy branch, at ease amongst the foliage as his ebony locks danced in the wind. Orion narrowed his eyes at his companion.

"What'd you want, Kotori?" he drawled.

Kotori shook his head, breathing out a huff of frustration as he readjusted his denim jacket, raising a hand to tuck the back of his necklace beneath the collar of his jacket—always the voice of reason. Always ensuring Nyx's safety and best interests were kept in mind; a feat that had caused more arguments over the years than Orion cared to admit. "What are you doing here?"

"Does it matter?"

"Tell me, Orion," Kotori murmured, gesturing toward the lodge-like house. "What happened the last time you were near her?"

Orion clenched his jaw, disdainfully as his lip twitched into a chilling sneer. "Don't pretend to be a saint, *Kotori.* You and I both know that you ... *hesitated.*"

"That doesn't mean anything," Kotori said, shifting on the branch.

"Doesn't it?" Orion said. "So, the thought of sinking your teeth into her throat didn't cross your mind? Didn't make you wonder how her blood would taste?"

He hummed, awaiting Kotori's answer; one that wouldn't come as the Levenloos man turned his head toward the house, ring-clad hands clutching the branch in a white-knuckled grip.

"Because I can tell you that nobody's blood has tasted so *divine.*"

Kotori tore his gaze from the house as he levelled a stone-cold glare at Orion.

"Do you think blood tastes better from the better class of society, like Nyx? The ones *trying* to stay on the 'right path'," said Orion.

Kotori's lip curled, a low rumble emitting from the depths of his throat before he raked his fingers through his hair with agitation. *"Stop."*

Orion clicked his tongue, mocking his dark-haired companion, "Maybe we should keep her as a personal blood bag."

Kotori bared his teeth at Orion and snarled, when the closing of a door and the jangling of keys drifted to them.

Frustration filled Orion's mind as Nyx stepped out onto the veranda with a large, black duffel bag slung over her shoulder. He flashed an accusing glare at Kotori when he realised he'd missed a part of Azeil and Nyx's conversation.

"He kicked her out."

Orion turned to Kotori. "Azeil's a lot of things, but he wouldn't do that."

Kotori's eyebrows rose doubtfully, leaning forward so he could see Nyx better. "Look at her, Orion. She's not leaving by choice. She's leaving because she doesn't have one."

His dark eyes honed in on her as the familiar protective edge settled over him, ready to protect what was theirs if he needed to. Like he'd always done. Then, a dark chuckle rumbled from his chest. "We could use this to our advantage, you know."

Orion turned back to Nyx as Kotori's words hung thickly between them, noticing the crumpled Guns 'N Roses T-shirt, black shorts, and hastily thrown-on sneakers as she strode over to the faded, red Honda. He watched as she reached her bike and pulled the bag from her shoulder, securing it to the bike's seat with two jockey straps. He wondered if she felt an *inkling* of the pain Azeil had caused him twenty-five years ago. And if she did, a twisted shard of his being bathed in that anguish.

A soft bark drew his attention as she lifted the zippered flap of the bag to reveal an Alaskan Malamute pup wiggling excitedly. He knew he should leave her to her own devices, tempted to see how long she'd survive in Celacali, but selfishness urged him to take advantage of the opportunity. Dark whispers of revenge clawed at his mind, fusing with decades of festering rage. He knew he should've been ashamed of the thoughts swirling through his mind, but he'd long since thrown his mundane, *human* cautions to the wind.

There was an art to losing oneself in the bloodshed of the never-ending nights.

And who was he to deny himself the simplicity of accepting his vampiric instincts?

They watched as Nyx tore off down the gravelled driveway without a backwards glance. Orion turned to Kotori when she had disappeared down the driveway, a dark smile lifting the corners of his mouth, smug as he watched Azeil's distress, profanity spilling from his lips before he pulled the front door open.

"*Fuck,*" Azeil breathed out as Asher bounded down the stairs behind him.

"What? What'd you do, Eil?" Asher turned in a slow circle. "Where's Nyx?"

"She was defending them, Ash, and I just … snapped."

"What'd you do, Azeil?"

Orion and Kotori observed the brothers from the shadows.

"I told her to leave. That I didn't care where she went as long as she left," Azeil said.

"What?" Asher sighed, rubbing a hand down his face, "Azeil, we've all been through hell, but she *didn't know. You* never told her."

Orion smiled, turning to Kotori and inclining his head in the direction of the cave, silently conveying that it was time to go. And, though he knew Azeil couldn't see him, he dipped his head in gratitude, for pushing Nyx away and into the night.

Into *his* domain.

XXV.

Nyx

"Angel, wake up."

Nyx grumbled with displeasure, batting the offending hand that shook her shoulder away whilst she mumbled incoherent protests beneath her breath. She rolled over and pulled Ares closer to her chest, the Malamute oblivious to the nuisances.

"Is that?"

"Yes, Niko."

"Do you think it'll bite me?"

"Are you afraid of a puppy?" Nyx grumbled, begrudgingly opening her eyes as she eyed the two men standing at the edge of the makeshift bed.

"Of course not," Niko stated, plastering a confident smile across his face despite his gaze continuing to divert to the sled dog curled into Nyx's chest.

"You are though, aren't you?"

Kade side-eyed Niko, biting his bottom lip with unabashed amusement before he sat down on the bed and leant conspiratorially toward Nyx, his honeyed stare locked on Niko even if she wasn't sure where they stood after their last interaction. "It's one of his minor fears. Like how most people are afraid of the dark."

She frowned, peering up at Niko, who toyed with the fraying black hem of his Metallica t-shirt with childlike unease. "What happened?"

Niko slowly lifted his azure gaze from the floor, scuffing the toe of his boot across the hardwood floor as his eyes churned with unease. "It doesn't matter."

As she processed his response, cautiously turning his words over in her head, she noticed the way his eyes flickered with something deeper than the 'minor' fear he'd brushed aside. Something she noted with a gentle nod of her head, choosing to let his words fade to nothing rather than force him to feel obliged to tell her his entire life story.

"Would you like to hold him?" she asked, running her fingers through the soft fur of Ares's back before her eyes widened and she hastily spoke. "You don't have to, but it might help ease that fear."

Niko eyed Ares carefully, worrying his bottom lip between his teeth whilst his fingers absentmindedly toyed with the assortment of leather, fabric, and silver bracelets around his wrists. A moment or two passed in silence as Nyx waited for his answer, a soft hum drifting to Nyx's ears before Niko sat down, watching the puppy curled into her chest with guarded irises.

"You're sure?" Kade interjected, leaning around Nyx's shoulder to look at Niko.

"Like you said, it's one of my minor fears. Might as well get over it now," Niko stated, making a vague gesture with his hand.

"But—"

"It's okay, Kade. *I'm* okay."

Kade lifted his fingerless-gloved hand to his face, gnawing at the skin of his thumb as he scrutinised Niko. Nyx felt the unmistakable urge to drop her gaze to the sled dog in her lap, feeling as though she was intruding on a moment between them.

Kade sighed before he dipped his head slowly; like he was reassuring himself.

"Okay."

Nyx sensed there was more to his answer than Kade was willing to disclose. She scrutinised him like he was a riddle, wondering if he'd told Niko the extent of his inner turmoil from 2012 or if he allowed him to believe he was utterly unaffected by the events that had transpired. She wondered if the man with golden curls and honeyed irises had stuffed his pain so far down that he didn't know he was hiding.

She couldn't shake the thought from her head, locking her eyes with his as she peered down at him from his place beside her. "How long had you been a vampire before you met my father?"

Kade's hands stilled before he began twisting the fabric of his top mindlessly and he dropped his gaze to the creases in the material. "A decade or two."

"A decade—" She sucked in a sharp breath of air, striking realisation dawning within her mind before she glanced at Niko from over her shoulder. "You weren't tricked into drinking Leon's blood, were you?"

Niko dropped his gaze, turning away from her as he extended his hand out toward the wriggling pup in her grasp. "No," he replied, his voice hoarse with some unknown emotion.

"We didn't have a choice," Kade interjected, jaw clenching tightly as if the memories left a bitter sting in its wake. "We either drank, or we died."

Niko scoffed, lifting his hand from the makeshift mattress to rub at the flesh of his jaw. "It's the truth and yet when you say it like that. It sounds like every form of vampire media *ever*."

Kade chuckled bitterly, irises alight with avidity, tongue pressing into his cheek before he lifted the hem of his shirt to reveal his chest.

"*This* is our reality. We carry our scars and demons with us through our immortal lives, brandishing them as swords only we can wield. And we don't complain about it … what for?"

"How—" she began, blinking in shock at the scars marring his chest with pale-white scar tissue.

Scattered across the bared expanse of his chest, stomach and abdomen were three-millimetre-long lines, half an inch or two wide, pale white and never the same. Her brow furrowed with confusion, angling her head to better decipher the marks. *Knife wounds,* she thought, eyeing the scar tissue peeking through his tattoos. Carved and left as a constant reminder across his skin. Scattered like stars in the inky depths of the sky, dozens upon dozens of the scars permanently engraved into his flesh.

"We're masters of manipulation, chica. You saw what Kade wanted you to see. Nothing more, and nothing less," Niko informed her with pride.

"You haven't done that with—"

"We're many things but manipulating you into something you're uncomfortable with isn't one of them," said Niko, cutting Nyx off as he moved his hand from the assortment of bracelets around his wrist to Nyx's, dousing her with a simple gratitude as he interlaced their fingers with a soft, reassuring smile.

"What about ..." she began before trailing off uncertainly, trusting Niko to provide her with straight-forward answers.

"They come willingly. It's unnerving how easily they'll follow us down a deserted alleyway without any prompting ... sometimes I wish they didn't. Just to feel human again," Niko trailed off, frowning as he dropped his gaze to the Malamute pup that clambered excitedly into his lap.

Kade peered around Nyx, releasing the hem of his shirt as an amused chuckle spilled from his lips. "Got yourself a little friend there, Niko."

Niko blinked in slight shock, unsure of himself as his gaze flickered from the pup in his lap to Nyx. Almost like it was a default reaction to look to her for assurance. Nyx squeezed his hand softly when a panicked expression darted across his face and Kade rested his head on her shoulder.

"It's okay. He's just excited to meet new people. But if you want me to get him off you, let me know, okay?"

Niko eyed Ares doubtfully, hands held up and away from the wriggling pup that whined excitedly up at him, tail wagging. "I—what do I do?"

"When you're ready, pat him," she smiled when Ares barked playfully, trying, and failing to lick the underside of Niko's chin from his lap.

"Just like that?"

"Niko, man. You're overthinking this," Kade said, grinning from ear to ear as he reached around Nyx and ran his fingers through Ares's fur. "Let him sniff your hand and then pat him."

"Just like that?" Niko echoed his earlier words before bobbing his head in a nervous nod.

Nyx watched him closely. She wondered what could've happened that'd made him fear a small, black, and white pup in his lap so greatly. But moreover, she hoped it'd been as simple as he'd dismissed it to be. Could it have been a result of her family?

Her thoughts were interrupted as Ares licked Niko's palm. A sudden ease came to his movements whilst he hesitantly ran his fingers through the smooth pelt of fur. And like he sensed her gaze on him, Niko's gaze darted up to meet hers, undiluted happiness brimming within his cool irises as he scooped the pup into his arms and ever-so-gently sat on the hardwood floor.

She shook her head with bemusement, turning to look at Kade, who lay sprawled out across the makeshift bed with his arms folded beneath his head, grinning his signature grin.

"Comfortable?" she asked.

A cheeky glint ignited in his eyes before he moved quicker than Nyx could comprehend and pulled her down beside him amongst the stolen array of blankets and pillows. She blinked in surprise as he hummed with contentment and wrapped his arms around her.

"Now I am," he drawled. His palm splayed across the middle of her back, thumb rubbing soothing circles into her skin as she peered up at him from beneath her lashes.

"Are we … okay after last night?" she asked.

"We are, and I'm sorry," he said, smiling. "There are things that I don't enjoy talking about, not unless I have to. And I know I shouldn't push you, or anyone, away but sometimes it's harder than others to face my past. Sometimes … I just want to *escape*."

As she mulled over his words and the truth within them, she realised she'd never imagined letting someone like him into her life—someone who *knew* when they did something wrong and wasn't afraid to acknowledge it. She realised it was something she respected Kade for as she gazed at him with newfound understanding and he cinched into her life in a way she hadn't expected.

Life had a funny way of reminding you that you could never escape it, thrusting itself into your face through a series of events that tested you; both mentally and physically.

Leaving you with one choice—to fight or die trying.

* * *

Hours passed by in a blissful blur, the seconds melting into minutes and the minutes into hours. It was only as Kade propped himself up against the makeshift headboard that he noticed the duffel bag beside the bed, unzipped and scarcely filled with the crumpled and creased clothes Nyx had forgotten about, tucked into the bottom in a way that the bag appeared empty.

Kade turned to her then, his eyebrows arched with curiosity as moonlight ghosted in through the paned window. "Why're you here, angel?"

Nyx swallowed nervously beneath the scrutiny of his stare, dropping her gaze to the colourful array of blankets to hide the embarrassment bubbling in her chest.

"My dad and I got into a fight," she lifted her gaze from the blankets to peer into his eyes. "Things got heated and he told me to leave so … I came here."

Niko's head snapped in Nyx's direction, the Malamute pup forgotten in his lap while he and Kade shared a look. "How long have you been here?" he asked, turning back to Ares as he gently played with the sled dog, whose tail wagged back and forth in haphazard circles.

"Two nights."

"What would you have done if we hadn't shown up?"

She sighed, raising an eyebrow at the familiarity of Niko's words. "I would've gone to Alexander and Tobias. Asked them for a place to crash for a while, and the rest would've been history."

Niko rolled his eyes, back to Nyx. "And yet you didn't go straight there. You could've easily gone there but instead, you came here." He gestured to the hideaway above the antique store with a lazy wave of his hand, bracelets jangling upon his wrist with the movement. "To a building with no electricity, no water and no food but with the knowledge that we'd been camping out here for the past few nights."

Nyx bristled at his implication before she lifted her head and peered down him.

"You make it sound like I *need* you. I came here because my dad doesn't know where it is," she raked her fingers through her hair, "and *maybe* the spiteful side of me wanted him to worry about where I'd gone or why he couldn't find me."

Kade leant over Nyx and smacked Niko upside the back of his head.

"What Niko was *trying* to say is that we only came back tonight for some clothes we keep stashed under the stairs and if we hadn't caught your scent. We would've grabbed them and gone back to the cave."

A childlike giggle filled the soft, moonlit room as Nyx and Kade turned to see a giggling Niko being peppered with quick, playful nips to the underside of his jaw by Ares.

Nyx moved as though to pull the energetic pup from Niko's lap before a firm grip on her waist stopped her and her gaze drifted to Kade's as he shook his head.

"She could come back to the cave with us, Kade," said Niko, tipping his head back onto the mattress to look at them with dancing irises. "It's not like there wouldn't be enough room for her."

Nyx opened her mouth to protest—mind jolting to Orion. She hadn't seen him since he'd sunk his teeth into her throat. Niko pushed himself off the floor with Ares in his arms and stooped down to pick up her duffel bag on his way to the stairs.

"Kade—" she began, panicked as she whirled toward the staircase Niko had disappeared down.

"Nyx, hey. Look at me," Kade coaxed, grasping her chin in the palm of his hand, and turning her head back to him. "It's okay... okay?"

She sucked in a deep, shaky breath, willing herself to calm down before she drove herself to the brink of a panic attack. "Okay."

Kade nodded slowly, lacing his fingers with hers. "Orion won't do anything to you, okay?"

"But—"

"He *won't* do anything, angel. He'll still be his usual intimidating self, but he won't do anything." He lifted his opposite hand, cupping the flesh of her cheek as his gaze seared into hers. "I won't let him. Not this time, or ever again."

Despite how foolish a single word could seem, Nyx blinked back the panic seizing her chest, tightening her hold on Kade's hand before she spoke in a hoarse whisper, "Promise?"

Kade smiled. Two perfect crescent moons appearing in the flesh of his cheek as he gently squeezed her hands. His golden lashes and sandy curls darker in the moonlit room that cast angelic shadows across his Roman features—light and dark clashing in perfect harmony in the night's darkness.

Good and evil like the sun and the moon; never destined to meet but forever longing to meet the other, cursed to glimpse each other through the light of dawn and dusk. When Kade spoke—even the night held its breath, waiting for a collision that'd make even the moon jealous. Envious of the life it so desperately craved with the sun; two beings eternally destined to never meet, brought to life beneath their shared sky.

Kade was the darkness of the night; coming alive beneath the stars and moon. And Nyx was the lightness of the day; shining like a beacon of hope the night clung onto.

Kade kissed Nyx's forehead, chin coming to rest upon her head as his voice caressed her soul, "I promise, angel. On the sun and the moon."

XXVI.

Asher

Two days passed in a fitful haze, dredging Asher's subconsciousness with loop-like flickers of Nyx vanishing into the night, taking with her a comfort Asher hadn't known he'd needed. Asher had spent the better part of the first night restless and unable to slip into the comforting embrace of sleep, pacing the upstairs' hallway as his mind whirled with worry for his niece. And when the day came, it'd brought no reprieve from the upending spiral of anxiousness that plagued him—his worry festering and latching itself to his mind, whispering words of unease deeply into its depths that Azeil couldn't coax him from.

The second night gifted Asher with a fitful night's sleep, plagued with nightmares of beasts with golden-white irises and razor-sharp fangs. Forced to relive the torments of his past through his dreams, cloying with the unmovable tack of guilt he couldn't shake. On the second day, when light eclipsed the horizon and the sun began its ascent, Asher woke with purpose—unclouded and unrelenting purpose—his footsteps echoing down the staircase to the kitchen.

He had grown lost in his thoughts, mulling over the events of Nyx's departure whilst gnawing at the skin of his cheek when Azeil wandered down the stairs. He glanced at the clock mounted on the kitchen wall, eyes squinted as his brows furrowed with confusion when he turned and noticed the golden rays of sunlight seeping in through the open curtains. Azeil ignored Asher's gaze, crossing the room with his brother's surveying stare dragging over the disarray of his crumpled T-shirt and dirt-stained jeans left unchanged from the night before.

"How long have you been up?" Azeil asked, flicking the switch to the coffee machine with his gaze trained on Asher.

"Since dawn."

Azeil frowned, "You've been awake since sunrise?"

Asher returned to the leather-bound book in front of him. "It's been *two days,* Azeil. Two days and we haven't seen her *once.* She hasn't even come back for clothes."

Azeil eyed his younger brother warily, toying with the handle of a cup he'd chosen from the dish rack. "What're you suggesting, Ash?"

"I'm not suggesting anything. That was my way of telling you I called Ryder and Amir," Asher paused, angling his head toward the front door where the sound of footsteps echoed to the brothers' ears. "That'll be them."

"Asher," Azeil warned, his voice low as his eyes narrowed on the determined blond, who rose from the kitchen table. "You don't think that maybe she hasn't come back because ... I told her not to?"

"Did you mean it?"

Azeil frowned, irked by the question. "No."

"Then do you want to find Nyx or not?" Asher snapped, eyeing his older brother carefully.

"You know I do," Azeil said.

"Then what's your problem?"

Azeil sighed, raking his fingers through his dark curls before he dropped his gaze to the cup in his hands. "I don't trust them."

Asher blinked, mildly shocked by his brother's words. "They saved your life."

"Did they? Or did they just get lucky?"

"They're professionals."

"I've heard that before, Ash" Azeil chuckled mockingly, turning his back to Asher as he poured himself a cup of freshly brewed coffee.

"What—"

"This time it's different. We're not kids anymore, and this isn't a game of make-believe. They're not going to disappear if you close your eyes." He turned to Asher; his cup of coffee held comfortably in his grasp, steaming in the crisp morning air. "I don't trust them to keep Nyx's best wishes in mind. You know how absentee Ryder is with his sons. What makes you think he cares about what happens to Nyx?"

"They're—"

"Not like that," Azeil tutted, "Notice how everybody's been saying that lately? Because even they know what we don't. It's *always* like that."

Growing frustrated by his older brother's cool-headedness to the situation, Asher let out an exasperated breath of air, "What else can we do?"

"I'm not saying this is a bad idea but ... What if this is what Nyx wants?"

"Why would she want this?"

Azeil sighed, shaking his head, "I could understand if she did."

Asher's eyes widened at his brother's easy confession, *"What?"*

"The thrill, Ash. One you can't shake. It ignites this overwhelming urge to thrive in the night ... It's like the stars and moon welcome you, guiding your way," he paused. "At times ... I wish I'd never asked for your help back then. Because some part of me still craves that freedom, that tranquillity Orion, Kotori, Niko and Kade carried with them."

Asher gawked at his older brother, blinking his puzzlement. His gaze followed Azeil, tracking the motion of the ceramic cup of coffee as it met the bench top.

He mulled over Azeil's words, toying with the colourful collar of his shirt that brought a soft smile to his face when he remembered the playful jests Nyx threw towards his 'obscene' wardrobe. He knew Azeil worried for Nyx. Asher knew Azeil better than he knew himself, knowing his brother only drank coffee when he was stressed because, in some odd way, the caffeine soothed him and his churning mind.

Asher also knew Azeil had taken to coffee during the months that'd followed the events in 2012—when he couldn't find peace in sleep. And he knew, despite his older brother's reluctance to admit it out loud, that he'd never truly be able to understand Azeil's point of view from a parent's perspective. But he could try; he'd promise himself and Nyx that much.

His gaze lifted from the faded, parchment-like paper of the leather-bound book, drawn toward the open doorway to the left of him and the two newcomers bracketing Azeil's shoulders. The two Montes brothers beside Azeil might've matured over the years, dialling down their wardrobe that'd once given him the distinct impression of army cadets and yet, Asher fought the urge to grin as his gaze honed in on two things that'd never changed.

Ryder brushed past Azeil, muddy irises raking across the room in an almost analytical way. His mousy-brown hair was cut short, in what he'd assured Asher reflected the *hunter's way* but merely elicited a grin, reminding him of the one miserable science teacher he'd had back in Malor. A stout-faced man whose lessons had always seemed to drag on. Ryder's late forties had treated the 'vampire hunter' frigidly, gifting him with grey-flecked hair and creases across his brow.

Amir's late thirties, however, had gifted the raven-haired man with a youthful gleam to his olive skin, laugh lines etched into his face like a river winding through the earth. Amir dipped his head politely when his gaze found Asher, a surety to his soulful brown irises that his older brother lacked. Amir was the voice of reason, understanding and guidance; guiding and reasoning with Ryder whenever the mousy-haired man grew careless in his actions.

Asher wondered if the brothers would ever discard the traces of military from their wardrobe. Like the camouflage pants Ryder wore with the blood-red bandana tied around his left wrist, fastened in a neat knot since 2024 to remember his beloved Sophia. Or if Amir would ever part with his beloved dog tags, clinking softly as he crossed the room and pulled out a chair.

Azeil waited a moment before slipping into the empty seat between Amir and Asher, both younger brothers sharing a brief look of understanding.

"How the hell didn't you know, Azeil?" Ryder blurted out, drumming his fingertips across the wooden tabletop.

Azeil glared at the younger man with unveiled disdain, "How the hell didn't *you* know? *You* haven't left Celacali ... Oh, wait," Azeil leant forward; his lips curled into a sneer. "You *did* leave Celacali behind ... *and* your sons."

Ryder's jaw ticked as he ignored Azeil's goad. "Bloodsuckers can only be eradicated with fire, a stake to the heart or beheading. Everyone knows that."

Azeil scoffed, rolling his eyes. "If I remember correctly, you said the same thing about inviting vampires in. And yet, there was still Leon."

"We can't tell everyone the secrets to the trade, *Azeil,* otherwise everyone would claim to be—"

"*Professionals,*" Azeil laughed without amusement; grey eyes alight. "Yeah, I've heard that one before."

Hesitantly, as though worried to intervene, Amir cleared his throat and drew the bickering attention toward him. "How could you let her go, Az? Especially once you *did* know?" he said.

Asher watched as his older brother squirmed and his stare shifted to the tree line through the kitchen windows.

"We spoke, and I disagreed. We argued, and then I said something I didn't mean," Azeil said; regret lacing his words. "I know I shouldn't have ..." He raked his fingers through his hair, "Fuck, *I know.* But I snapped and I told her to leave. That I didn't care where she went as long as she left."

Asher studied Azeil closely, noting the turmoil and disarray of his steadfast brother; the rock that'd kept Asher bright and happy during the early days of their parent's messy divorce, almost like the divorce Azeil and Alyvia had gone through. He wondered if Azeil dared to show his vulnerability to Ryder and Amir in hopes they'd understand. That they'd feel Azeil's pain as their own and they'd help Nyx because their conscience begged them to.

Silence swept across the brightly lit kitchen, peonies swaying gently in the kitchen window planters. And after a moment, Amir nodded slowly as he turned to Ryder, eyebrows arching as if prompting the disgruntled man into asking the questions he wanted answered.

"What are her habits?" Ryder said bluntly. "Sleep all day? Hates sunlight? No reflection?"

"She's not a vampire, *Buffy*," Azeil snapped, beginning to lose his patience before Asher cut him off.

"She's not a halfling either," he said.

Asher watched as the brothers exchanged looks. Despite having spent the past six months with them in Wildegulf chasing myth after legend, and returning to Celacali sporadically to visit Azeil and Nyx between jobs that'd captured his interest, he'd been developing his ever-changing work habits and enforcing them since … well, since 2024, he supposed. Rumour of supernatural beings who thrived in the city of Wildegulf had spurred a hunt in a city that bled with stories of vampires, trickling down the cobblestoned streets, staining the crevices of the town in red—the revered kingdom of the paranormal world. So, naturally, he'd followed Amir and Ryder to the city. Like he'd done since Sophia had passed and the brothers had offered him a place in their self-proclaimed field of expertise. God knows, he'd needed the distraction.

Wildegulf was a kingdom like no other.

A kingdom a corrupted husk of a once-man had once resided over. One he'd built from the ground up like a pharaoh who had raised his pyramids in Egypt. But that'd been five millennia before *he* had turned Orion, his *eldest son*, and then three more in quick succession. Before Leon had established his home in the quaint, anaemic coastal town: popular for tourists and therefore, a formidable food supply. Leon had been many things, once; charming, polite, and friendly. But it was like the years of prowling the earth alone had chipped away at his humanity, leaving him with only a husk of a once kind-hearted nature and replacing it with a yawning, ever-hungry, never-ending cavern of loneliness.

He'd tried to fill that void with the semblance of a family. First, with Orion and then again with Kotori, then Niko and finally, Kade, desperate for something to rid himself of that eternal pit of loneliness. At least, that's what the stories had said ...

Asher shuddered at these thoughts, the depths of Leon's longing twisted into something else, warping his mind in a swirl of greed so when Alyvia and Xander had fled to Celacali, he had taken them in, promising the runaways a home on the boardwalk—a family that, like him, they had longed for. He'd spent years researching the formidable sire and learning his backstory, cross-referencing and compiling it into a journal he'd only shared with Azeil, Ryder and Amir.

Asher hated to think how long Alyvia had pretended to be oblivious to the vampires of Celacali, or what Leon had done to her mind to convince her she'd never known who he was. Xander had clutched the truth to his chest, emitting snippets of their hardships through brief, short, clipped sentences. But they'd been enough for him to glean a faint understanding of Leon's first mistake—believing that Xander was too young to comprehend the warped plan.

It'd seemed to click into place for Leon, the blissful honeymoon phase of his newest edition's arrival drawing on for months, fortifying his twisted belief that he could coerce the last few pieces of his puzzle into place. And he'd nearly succeeded, if not for Asher, Azeil, Ryder, and Amir's impromptu plan crashing—or 'vampire slaying' if the shambles of the warehouse had been anything to go by.

Amir broke Asher's spiral of thoughts, "Was she—"

"Did any of the bloodsuckers sink their teeth into her?" Ryder cut in bluntly, ignoring the glare Azeil and Amir threw him.

"Ryder, what'd we say about this?" Amir questioned, exasperated.

"We—"

"You don't *have* to know anything. You're not entitled to all the answers," Amir fired back.

"But if the bloodsuckers are back—If they ever left at all, we can't sit back and wait to find out. We *have* to know," Ryder rebutted.

Azeil sighed, "Yeah. She was. Twice."

"Twice? I thought it was only the one?" Asher probed. He turned to Ryder, eyes narrowed in unveiled disdain, burning with blue fire, "She's *not* a blood-sucking surrogate either."

Azeil barked, "Did you learn *nothing* in 2012?"

"Of course, we did," Ryder said, staring Azeil down. "Eradicate one problem, and you get rid of another. It's like killing two birds with one stone."

Azeil stood, shoving his chair back with silver-flaming irises before he swiftly rounded the table and yanked Ryder up from his seat by the collar of his T-shirt, jaw ticking with aggravation. Asher and Amir scrambled from their chairs, pulling the two away from each other. Amir rounded on Ryder, shaking his head with disapproval before he peered back over to Azeil, an apologetic smile lifting the edges of his lips.

"It's not going to be that simple, Dad," drawled a voice from the back doorway.

Their heads whipped in the direction of the voice, Asher's brow creasing with a mixture of surprise and confusion as he surveyed the twins in the doorway, the glint of silver drawing his gaze to the matching dog tags hanging from the neck of the shorter twin.

"We killed them once before, so, we can kill them again. If anything, this time should be child's play," said Ryder.

Tobias scoffed and strode into the kitchen with his brother close beside him.

"Maybe so, but Nyx wasn't a factor then. She is now. And she's somewhat of a soft spot to Kade and Niko. And they'll protect her like she's their own now," he said.

Asher watched as Alexander turned his gaze to Azeil; dark and unflinching.

"You shouldn't have told her to leave."

Tobias pursed his lips, his eyebrows furrowed with an unwavering need for Azeil to understand as his voice carried level, calm and yet laced with something foreboding. "Because now, she's in *their* domain."

XXVII.

Nyx

Stairs creaked beneath Nyx's feet, groaning out their protests with each step she, Kade and Niko took. She wondered briefly if the stairs beneath her would hold her weight or—if by some twisted fate of God—they'd snap and send her tumbling down to the sea-lashed rocks below. She winced at the thought, a cold shiver raking up her spine at the path her thoughts had taken. Her mind throwing flashes of her broken body on the rocks below, the morbid imagery of oddly bent and shattered limbs flicking through her head like an ancient film.

Wind buffeted against her back, whipping her curls around her face whilst howling above the turbulent waves crashing against the rocky cliff face. She swallowed the nervous lump at the back of her throat, watching as Niko kicked a stone down to the thundering waves below, childishly chuckling to himself before he slipped between the rock face and disappeared, his laugh whisked away by the wind.

She wondered if she should be following them, if it was worth indulging the past that called her to them, or if she should turn around and retreat up the stairs.

Kade paused, waiting for her, shoulder pressing into the coarse rock as she turned and peered out to the horizon.

Silver glinted off the waves as moonlight rippled across the ever-churning waters, reflecting the moon up at itself like a child laughing at its reflection. The stars were coming out, twinkling like a ballroom full of dancing people in lavish dresses and sparkling jewels, delighting in the candour of the night. A lighthouse towered tall and proud before the point of Elveszett Bluff, cemented in so the ocean couldn't uproot it and leave sailors led astray, to a demise amongst the reef and rocks.

That was the thing about Celacali; It provided life, adventure and new beginnings on the boardwalk or the streets that made up the coastal city, but in its wake, it always brought with it something dark and malevolent. A duo that came hand in hand, time and again. Like the sun after a devastating storm. It traipsed death, fear, and blood around like a tote bag, slung across your shoulder with little thought. A silently effective killer hidden beneath nonchalance.

Nyx tore her gaze away from the vastness of the Avonsano Ocean and to Kade who waited for her, patient in all his immortal glory, mirth glinting in his honeyed gaze. A soft smile curled the edges of his lips, sharpening his boyish features that would make the greatest artist jealous, longing to capture his Roman features on paper, parchment, or canvas.

Kade raised his eyebrows, prompting her to explain. "Is there something on my face?" he asked, lifting a hand to rub at it in a gesture so innocent Nyx couldn't help but smile, shaking her head with reassurance.

"There's nothing on your face. I was just ... thinking, that's all."

His brows screwed together, an all-knowing grin growing before he shook his head and chuckled, "What were you thinking about?"

Nyx looked out at the sea, gnawing at the flesh of her cheek. The crashing of the waves against the cliff face thundered across the sky and her eardrums, sea spray billowing into the air and ghosting her skin. "That if I stand out here any longer, Niko will steal my bloody dog."

Kade laughed, perfect crescent-shaped dimples appearing in the apples of his cheeks—a sight Nyx realised she loved seeing. His irises glittered with delight, soft and warm like honey in tea—yin and yang bundled together. Then he sobered and beckoned to the gap in the cliff face, waiting for her to take the first step into the metaphorical lion's den.

He paused, eyeing her like she held all the answers he was looking for. His joking nature pushed aside. "Are you sure about this?"

The familiarity of his words echoed through her mind but she dismissed it, closing the space between herself and him, looping her arm through his and slipping between the rocks, leading him into the dark as if she was the one with fine-tuned sight and not the enigmatic vampire.

"I'm sure, Cheshire. As sure as the sun rises above the horizon with each day, and the moon appears in the darkness of the night."

The cave engulfed her senses a moment later, sea salt filling her nostrils with each inhale, her pupils expanding to accommodate for the lack of light as a snicker echoed through the limestone tunnel from beside the custom-designed door.

"Look at you being all poetic. Kade, we have a little Shakespeare in our midst."

Kade moved swiftly in the darkness, unlooping his arm from Nyx's so he could drape his arm across her shoulders. His light, mischievous chuckle echoed through the tunnel and into the large, spaciously lit space. She didn't have to see his face to *feel* his grin; that devilish intent, twined with the innocent mask he'd mastered over the years.

"You know, Niko. I think this means we'll have to hide her from Kotori," he said.

Nyx squinted in the haziness of the tunnel, her gaze finding Niko, who leant against the rocky entrance, duffel bag slung over his shoulder, Ares in his arms as Kade led her closer.

"Oh, most definitely," Niko purred, reaching out to lace Nyx's fingers with his before he turned and led her toward the glowing light of the barrel-lit cave and down the slight staircase.

Nyx scoffed at the blue-eyed man, "How long have you been standing there?"

"Long enough," he said, knocking his shoulder into hers with a cheeky grin as Kade pulled the door closed behind them. "I promise that I won't steal *your bloody dog.*"

"For a murderous vampire, it's amusing that you're so fond of Ares," she mused aloud, scuffing her sneaker upon the sand-covered floor. "Blood, murder, fangs and all."

"Checking off a list, are we?" he said.

She shrugged as the tunnel opened out into the living space within the cave, tangerine flames dancing within the metal confines of large barrels, and the soft lighting from the hidden light fixtures illuminating the cavernous living space. Kade's embrace tightened around her shoulders, his fingertips pressing into her skin—whether he noticed it or not, Nyx didn't know. She didn't mind because it soothed the churning nerves in her stomach when her eyes met Orion's from across the cavernous room, perched intimidatingly in his ornate throne.

His steel-like irises flashed with a look she couldn't decipher, seemingly alight with a cold fire that burned hotter and yet, *colder* at the same time. Searing into her skin like a brand and pinning her in place. She felt Kade's arm slung across her shoulder and Niko's fingers interlaced with hers, and took comfort.

Swallowing the lump in her throat, her gaze locked on Orion's as she wondered if this was how a trapped mouse felt. Its tiny heart racing as its predator watched. For a moment, Nyx feared the likeness of predatory satisfaction in Orion's eyes, reflecting her fear at herself through his uncannily blue irises.

Tension crackled in the air as she held his gaze, unflinching. Movement from the corner of her eye forced her attention towards Kotori. A sharp, playful bark split the silence of the cave and Niko's childish laughter rippled off the cavernous walls as he obliviously ran his fingers through Ares's fur. The lifeful blond snickered when the pup licked his fingers before he stooped down to place the Malamute on the floor and his fingers slipped from between Nyx's as he searched for anything to barricade the darkest tunnelway from the sled dog that followed at his heels.

Orion followed Niko's movements and his lips twitched with amusement before his eyes returned to hers. "Kade?" he prompted without looking.

"Azeil kicked her out. So, we're taking her in," supplied Kade, his gaze narrowed as Orion nodded slowly, calculating gaze shifting with something unsettling.

Fear fluttered in Nyx's chest like a cluster of butterflies, pattering into her like rain. She sucked in a shaky breath of air and cursed herself for letting Kade bring her here, wondering how she could've been so *foolish* to come back to the source of her problems, like a lamb led to the slaughter.

Cigarettes and leather washed over her senses in her next inhale, an almost metallic scent marring the oddly enthralling fragrance that swirled in the air like water down a drain. Brown eyes met blue, clashing like lightning across the night sky—light and dark meshing together, unwilling, and yet unable to fight the pull. A pull neither could comprehend but both fought against the same way an antelope raced over grass plains in hopes it'd be able to outrun the lion that pursued it. Both fighting for survival, but only one would pull through the curse of Mother Nature, leaving the other to die. Succumbing to the will of the gods; beings who wouldn't be slandered by the lives of mortals whilst the victor fooled themselves into thinking they'd survived; only to be thrown back into the ring and left to battle once more.

Predator and prey. Hunter and hunted. Immortal and mortal.

Two sides to a figured eight; never-ending but eternally together.

Orion peered at her before speaking, "Welcome to the lion's den, *little dove.*"

Nyx looked to Kotori and he dipped his head, reassuring her with a soft smile, easing the fear racing through her veins as she squared her shoulders and turned her gaze back to Orion. She caught a brief, almost non-existent flickering of his eyes—darting from the blackish-blue marks on one side of her throat to the pale silver scarring on the other, before lapsing into a slow, smug smirk.

He raised a gloved hand, noticing her sharp intake of breath—from fear or the tantalising confidence he oozed, she didn't know. Some traitorous attraction slithering through her bloodstream—and cupped her cheek as softly as one would cherish a glittering jewel. "We'll see if you make it out alive."

Nyx chuckled darkly as she stepped back from his grasp. "It's not the lion the antelope fears, it's the lioness that crushes its windpipe in her jaws."

She paused, scrutinising him with an indifferent mask before Kade led her away and down a small corridor tucked behind the fountain and a large, crumbling pillar. Uneven and yet confident footsteps echoed off the rockface behind them, the jangling of bracelets paired with the soft padding of paws interlaced together with an ease only Niko carried—chaos and comfort wrapped into a seamless blend that suited the rock star blond perfectly whilst he followed them down the tunnel-like corridor, and Nyx found she appreciated his presence. Almost the same as she enjoyed Kade's.

Wonder struck Nyx's chest like a hammer, ploughing into her ribcage at the medium-sized cave that opened at the end of the tunnel. Natural ledges jutted out from the cave walls, and dozens upon dozens of candles stacked in neat clusters or alone cast soft, warm yellow candlelight and bathed the room in a whimsical glow. Sea salt-laced with something woodsy filled the candlelit cave with its soothing fragrance as seamlessly as the faint crashing of the waves ghosted throughout the cavernous hideout.

Her dark irises trailed over a Doppelgänger bed like the one in the antiques store. Pillows and blankets were scattered haphazardly over two mattresses that'd been pushed together. Sheer curtains secured into the roof above with silver screws, bent out of shape like someone had hit them too hard. A varying array of books lined the natural ledges, weathered and well-loved spines worn from years of use, the writing on some faded completely; nothing but a memory. Pencils, paint brushes and paints sat spread atop a small wooden table tucked off to the side of the cave, sketch books stacked across the wooden workspace, left open and awaiting their owner's return.

"Whose room is this?" Nyx murmured.

"Everyone's and no one's," Niko stated offhandedly, dropping her bag to the floor as he picked up an old wooden-backed painting and propped it across the entrance of the tunnel, huffing with satisfaction when the pup couldn't jump over the knee-high, makeshift barrier.

"What'd I say, angel?" Kade turned back to Nyx, gesturing to Niko with a teasing grin. "Absolute softie."

She laughed, nodding in agreement as Niko turned to face the pair with a disgruntled tut of protest.

"Until you piss me off," he finished, fiddling with a stereo perched on the rock ledge nearest to the bed. The opening chords to *'Sweet Child O' Mine'* filled the cave with the unmistakable chords of electric and bass guitars twined with the pulsing beat of drums. He turned around to face Nyx, grinning from ear to ear, his cyanic irises dancing with mirth before he grasped her hands in his and pulled her to the makeshift bed.

His deep, musical laughter echoed in her ears and the cave, his wild hair mussed around his head like a golden halo as the plush bedding pressed into their skin and Nyx propped her head up on a pillow. Kade dropped down onto the mattress beside them.

She knew she should've been afraid of the two beside her, their arms draped across her waist. Kade's fingers laced with hers as Niko's hand rested on her hip but she wasn't. A sane voice in her mind yelled at her to run away. To *live*. And yet, a louder, more spontaneous voice whispered words of solace, urging her to venture down this path of no return—this path that would bring her to life in ways the safer side never could.

"Hey, Kade?" Niko began, waiting as Kade's eyes met his over Nyx's head. "The thing with Orion ... brilliant."

"Brilliant, huh?" Kade lifted his head, "How many joints have you smoked?"

"None yet," Niko laughed.

"Yet?" Nyx prompted, swatting his shoulder playfully when he pulled a pre-rolled joint from his pocket and a lighter from another.

He lit the pre-rolled joint and propped his head against several pillows before taking a drag and humming with pleasure. Closing his eyes and exhaling a cloud of white-grey smoke before repeating the process as he opened his eyes and lazily surveyed the ceiling.

"I mean it, Kade. Reverse psychology never looked so good," he said.

"I'd hardly call *that* reverse psychology," Nyx said, toying with his bracelets.

"Oh, but it *is*," Niko protested, turning to look down at her. "He does it all the time to us, at least once a day … for decades."

"You're kidding, right?" Nyx half laughed.

"He's not. Orion's questions are never questions. His requests are never requests. And most importantly, you *never* dismiss him. *He* dismisses you," Kade interjected, his voice cut with certainty.

"But—"

Kade pursed his lips, tutting with mild distaste as he shook his head. "That wasn't Orion letting it go. That was him calculating his next move and effectively dismissing you as nothing more than a house guest. He knows you're no threat to us, otherwise, you would've found yourself dumped on your father's doorstep."

Niko leant down so his lips ghosted across Nyx's ear, breath warming the side of her neck, sending a tantalising shiver up her spine.

"He's very *protective* of us. Head vampire and all," he said.

"Protective? He sounds more controlling than anything," she muttered.

Like a switch, Niko's head tilted, ears perking up at the familiar guitar solo of *'Sweet Child O' Mine'* before he perfectly mimicked the plucking and strumming of guitar strings as if he held one in his hands.

"Do you even know how to play?" she squealed, surprise spilling from her lips when Niko shot up from the bed and hastily handed Kade his joint.

Niko clambered off the bed, almost tripping over Ares before he pushed the wooden-backed painting out of the doorway and disappeared down the dimly lit tunnel. It took a moment for Nyx to register the opening of the tunnelway, her eyes widening with worry when Ares moved to follow him, bounding around the bed and towards the cave's opening before she shot up and scrambled after the Malamute.

"No, Ares! Here boy!" she called, as her leg tangled amongst the assortment of blankets and her hand slipped at the bed's edge, face distorting into a grimace as she prepared for the inevitable impact of the cave floor.

Laughter sounded as hands latched themselves around her waist, effectively staunching her fall before it began.

"Already falling for me are we, angel?" Kade teased, pulling her back into the middle of the bed with bird-like grace.

"Absolutely," she uttered dryly as she turned to face him, patch-worked skin beneath her palms as her hands came to rest upon his shoulders. "Swept me right off the bed."

His eyes locked on hers. Dark, and light colliding time and time again like a broken record—like the sun and the moon eclipsing the sky for a few beautiful moments. Kade's grasp upon her waist tightened, his thumbs brushing against her back in soothing circles, lips curled into a grin like her own. His gaze darted from her eyes to her lips and then back again as her hand lifted from his shoulder to cup his cheek.

He leant down, connecting their lips in a feverish and all-consuming kiss. Their lips moving in perfect harmony as the chords and drumbeat of the music faded and her heart beat faster.

Kade's grasp on Nyx's waist tightened, gripping her hips as if to centre himself, her fingers curling around the fabric of his shirt for support whilst she succumbed to the descent like the sun succumbed to moon's wants amidst an eclipse. For light was always in the darkness, tucked beneath its shadows so only those who sought it out would find it and indulge in its infinite embrace.

As her fingers wove themselves through his hair, her lips moving in perfect sync with his, a soft, almost hesitant cough echoed across the room and drew their attention towards the cave entrance and away from each other. Kotori stood, leaning against the doorway with Ares in his arms, ripped black denim jeans and Cons covered in dirt, denim jacket finely dotted with the pup's pearl-white fur as bemusement danced in his dark irises.

"Sorry to … interrupt," Kotori began. "But this little guy came barrelling into the main cave behind Niko."

An embarrassed laugh escaped Nyx before she slipped from Kade's embrace and off the bed, crossing the room to retrieve the Malamute from Kotori's arms. White fur coated the black material of his T-shirt.

"Sorry about that," she uttered, gesturing to his shirt.

Kotori shrugged, brushing a large hand over the material that did nothing to hide the defined and chiselled planes of his chest. "Don't worry about it, kleintje."

Her brows furrowed with confusion, as she adjusted her hold on Ares. "Thank you." She paused, letting her words hang in the air as he dipped his head, seeming to understand her unspoken words. She glanced back over her shoulder at Kade, who lay comfortably amongst the nest of pillows with one arm tucked beneath his head, a smirk curling the edges of his lips as his eyes locked on Kotori's.

"Am I missing something?" Nyx asked.

"Only the benefits of a mind link, angel. Nothing more," Kade quipped happily, grinning.

"Mind link?" Nyx said with a doubtful tilt of her head. "So, those aren't myths?"

"Well, not in the sense that Kade means," Kotori answered, smiling as Nyx turned back to face him. "They're … complicated in a way that we can't *truly* explain."

"Right … but it works somewhat the same, doesn't it?"

"Mostly."

Her eyes narrowed on the towering brunette who grinned at her confusion. "*Right.*"

The deep timbre of his laugh rolled through the room as he gestured to the Malamute in her arms. "What's his name?"

"Ares," she said.

"Like the God of War?"

She laughed, "And Battle Lust."

Kotori smiled again and she saw the trueness of his skin, and though it was lighter than some, there was no hiding his Native genes. Not that he tried. Bearing his handmade necklace with pride, his eyes were deep and soulful, brimming with wisdom and tranquillity that soothed her. Kotori seemed to notice every little thing she did with uncanny interest built upon years of observing the lives of others.

He securitised the pup in her arms, lips twitching as he stifled the smile that wished to spread across his face like ink spilled on paper. "It suits him," he said. His gaze flickered over her shoulder to Kade, locking back on her own within seconds. "Keep him close, kleintje."

Recognition flashed through her, her uncle's voice dancing through her mind as those same three words he'd spoken rippled off her skull. "I will."

"De kleine krijger en haar voogd," Kotori said, gaze alight with unveiled mirth as she repeated his words in English:

"The little warrior and her guardian."

XXVIII.

Nyx

Candle wax dripped down the cavernous walls, trickling like dozens of tiny tree roots branching off in every direction. Nyx watched the dancing flames with rapt attention, head resting on the pillows beside Niko's shoulder whilst his nimble fingers plucked at the strings of his electric guitar.

Lavish bed sheets brushed against Nyx's legs as she nestled herself deeper into the cluster of pillows, simultaneously prompting Kade to readjust his hold on her before she resettled and peered down at the sleeping Malamute at the end of the bed. Kade nestled his head in the crook of her neck, chin resting atop her shoulder whilst her fingers toyed with his bracelets. The slow tune of the guitar chords registered in her mind, ghosting across the cave like lovers danced in the summer rain. "Are you playing what I think you're playing?"

Niko grinned, peering down at her, "What do you think I'm playing?"

"Not, I think," Nyx corrected. "I *know* what you're playing."

"Don't be shy," he said as his skilled fingers danced over the neck of the guitar.

"*With Or Without You*. U2," Nyx shook her head with amusement, forcing herself not to smile as his eyes lit up at her words. "You know?"

"Know what?"

She narrowed her eyes, "Don't play—"

"It's the perfect song for a first kiss … or second," his grin seemed to grow, "Kadey's a good kisser, isn't he?"

She blinked once, pondering the idea of the easy, almost teasing confession he'd made—turning it over in her mind whilst reminding herself that he was immortal and was bound to have tried everything the world had to offer—she wondered what Niko had seen, what he'd experienced in his decade shy of a century existence.

"Chica?" he prompted, a devious smirk playing at the edges of his lips in a way that revealed his teeth.

Nyx refocused. His scent of sea salt, weed and copper washing over her like the swell of high tide. "What's it like?" she asked.

Kade lifted his head from the assorted pillows, leaning forward, "What's it like?" He studied her face carefully, "Being immortal, you mean?"

She nodded, wonder clouding her thoughts. "I can't begin to imagine what you've seen. What you've done in the span of one of my lifespans."

Kade turned to Niko, "Why don't you tell her, Nik," he drawled, patting Niko's thigh with his lips curled into a teasing smile. "You're the old man here."

"Old man?" Niko spluttered indignantly, gesturing to the lithe definition of his body, honed from years of predatory finesse. "You're ninety-seven years younger than me and neither of us looks a day over twenty."

Kade chuckled, "*Anyway,* Niko's old enough to have seen the biggest bands in the eighties when they were just starting their musical careers."

"He means the start, chica, like when they used to play at bars and small venues." Niko stopped playing, "And now … they sell out entire stadiums."

Nyx listened, enthralled, hanging onto each of his words like they were the holy grail. Her mind reeled just thinking about it, so much time, so much information. She thought of the rehashed history books she'd been forced to study from in the lamplight of her bedroom as the moon had hung high in the sky whilst her parents argued in the next room over, laughing at the sheer misery upon her face whilst she had considered dropping out of high school altogether.

"You should take her to the concert tonight. Give her a glimpse of the lives we've lived on the boardwalk," Kade said.

Niko jolted so quickly that he roused Ares, silver earrings smacking against the side of his neck. "It's okay, little guy. Go back to sleep," he breathed out softly, stroking Ares's fur, "You don't want to come?"

"It's not the first nor the last concert I'll see," Kade said and smiled, "Go. Show her what *living* truly is."

Niko turned to Nyx, grinning from ear to ear, "What'd you say, chica? *Def Leppard*'s in town, and *nothing* beats a rock concert," he paused, considering his words. "Well, nothing beats a rock concert in Celacali."

"Nothing?" she prompted, quirking a doubtful eyebrow. "I think I'll be the judge of *that*."

Kade watched, seemingly delighted by the ease that Niko and Nyx cinched into place, coming together like two magnets. Where Niko brought forth chaos, carnage, and deceit, Nyx carried tranquillity, devotion, and loyalty. Colliding with animalistic ease neither noticed, snapping into place like two pieces of a puzzle—lost without the other.

Even if they hadn't acknowledged it.

Even if they couldn't.

"So?" Niko queried.

Nyx smiled, "Give me five, and then I'll meet you at your bike."

Niko rose from the makeshift bed, fluidly hoisting Ares into his arms before striding from the room. The candlelight cast elongated shadows over Kade's face before his gaze met Nyx's.

"You're in for one hell of a night now, angel," he said.

"Should I be worried?" Nyx asked.

He seemed to consider her words before settling on an answer that broke his bonds.

"Of Niko? No," he said, worrying the pad of his thumb between his teeth for several seconds before letting his hand drop. "Well ..."

"Well?" she prompted, arching a dark eyebrow.

"We might all be the monsters of legend, the ones you were taught to fear, but Niko is the best of us," Kade said with sobered eyes. "So no, Nyx, you have nothing to worry about. Not with Niko."

She eyed him cautiously, hearing his words and yet heeding silent whispers forcing images of a terror-driven chase to the forefront of her thoughts. "Nothing?"

"*Nothing,*" Kade repeated. "Apart from his wandering hands. He's very ... *touchy.*"

Nyx laughed, "Touchy?" she spluttered helplessly.

"Despite how it sounds, he's very *attentive* to others' needs," Kade laughed back.

"You'll see, angel. Trust me."

* * *

As she climbed the rickety steps clinging to the cliff face, Nyx wondered what she had to trust Kade with, absentmindedly dragging the coin-like charm of her necklace back and forth along the delicate chain. It couldn't have been the way he'd skilfully fastened her hair into place, taming the wild tresses with grace that confirmed her suspicions about him being the artist of the group.

She wondered about his words, brushing her hand down the silky, pearl-white front of her shirt, and noting how it complimented her body. She had chosen comfortable blue striped, wide-legged pants and sleek-black combat boots. Her gaze landed on Niko, who lounged astride his beloved motorbike, forearms lazily draped across the handlebars, the broad and yet chiselled planes of his face sent her mind scrambling as it tried to make sense of his devilish smile.

"I see now that Kade wasn't lying," Niko murmured, almost to himself as he drank her in with his gaze.

She shook her head, tearing her eyes from his as she fought the urge to smile, instead focusing on the sprawling ink of his cheetah tattoo, and jacket embellished with safety pins that glinted off his right pectoral and lapel. A coin-like sash over his left shoulder connected seamlessly with two bronze-tinged flowers, and a bronze chain hung in an arc, attached to the lapel above his left pectoral and the button above his belly button. His straight-legged jeans were ripped along the knees.

"You've got to stop dressing like that, Nik," she mused, grinning from ear to ear.

He sighed, drumming his fingers along the bike's handlebars. "Paul from The Lost Boys, right?"

She considered him and the blueness of his gaze. "It's just ... *so* uncanny. The way you seem to pull it off even though you're not trying to."

"You forget that I was *alive* during the eighties so, it might've rubbed off on me."

She nodded before gesturing to the rip along each of his knees, fighting the urge to grin. "Did you do that yourself?"

"Kade did actually," he chuckled, lifting a hand to run through his wild, eighties-imbued hair, "After I ripped one side first."

"You know, I can see that. He seems very ... artistic."

"Aw chica, Kade would put Da Vinci to shame."

"He's that good?"

He hummed, a feline-like grin stretching across his face, "Ask him about his *erotique* art."

"I thought you said you didn't speak other languages?" Nyx joked.

Niko lifted his hooded gaze to hers as he plastered a wistful expression across his face, "Nothing beats having *erotique* words whispered in your ear whilst in the throes of passion."

"I—*what?*" she spluttered.

"I said—"

"I'm good," she uttered, quickly cutting him off. "I heard you."

"It's okay, chica. There's nothing wrong with liking someone who talks *sale comme un péché.*" He grinned wickedly, "Hop on."

Nyx rested her hand upon his shoulder and swung her left leg over the seat, her thighs pressed against his, arms wrapping around his waist as the rumble of the bike thrummed through her veins. His laughter echoed in her ears as he revved the engine and they tore away from the cliff.

The rocky terrain whipped past in an adrenaline-filled haze; an elated smile on Nyx's face, like everything in her life had led her to this moment. Every mistake. Every success. Every tear. Every bolt of pain leading her to this place—this state of elysian. She wondered—as the rocky terrain gave way to the flickering light of the tree canopy—if she should feel ashamed for revelling in the night, in the feeling it evoked in her in the presence of the lifeful blond driver. The dips and jumps of the forest jolted her heart as Niko skilfully manoeuvred through the winding turns and obstacles laid out before him in the moonlit forest, wind whipping their hair.

She tipped her head back and her laughter rang out loud, her grasp tightening around Niko's abdomen as he wove them, the bike lifting from the forest floor. Breathy delight spilled from her lips as the wheels connected back with the ground and they shot out from the flickering darkness of the forest, and across the sandy beach of Celacali's shoreline.

The wooden pier loomed metres away before Niko's hand found itself on her thigh, squeezing it—her heartrate spiked as the warmth of his palm seeped through the fabric, jarring her composure with a bolt of attraction she hadn't noticed earlier—before returning back to the handlebars. He seemed to speed up before he steered the bike beneath the wooden pier with catalogued ease, weaving through the pillars in a way that showcased his decades spent living in Celacali and the well-worn track he'd grown so familiar with—that they'd all grown familiar with.

Barrelled bonfires whipped by in orange flashes, faint whisps of heat across her skin, sand flicking up behind them as the blinding lights of the boardwalk drew closer. Niko steered the bike away from the steps nearest to the Ferris wheel and tore up the ramp of the boardwalk with reckless abandon, ignoring the shouts of distress and disdain as he plunged onto the thoroughfare, through meandering passers-by.

"Niko," she began, leaning closer. "This isn't *remotely* safe."

"Chill out girl. No one's getting hurt," he said, and like they knew, tourists and locals scrambled out of his path.

"Yet."

He laughed, moving his hand so it rested upon her thigh. "*Yet.*"

"You're reckless. You know that, right?"

"And yet, here you are, in one piece," he said, pulling up beside a stairwell leading down to the beach.

She shook her head, playfully hitting his shoulder as he killed the engine and helped her off, leaving his bike where he parked it. He laced his fingers in hers, quickly leading her past the rides, food stalls and tourists toward the sound of music.

The commotion of a concert rippled over the city and under the sky, the undeniable rock song notes floating overhead, reminding her of the first night she'd spent in Celacali. She laughed as Niko slipped through the singing and dancing crowd, pulling her along behind him, at ease amongst the beating of drums and thrumming of guitar strings.

"This is your serenity, isn't it?" she said; gaze locked on his back.

He showed no signs of hearing her, continuing his relentless path through the concertgoers before coming to a stop and peering down at her so intensely, she knew he'd heard her. His turbulent irises locked on her as he swiftly manoeuvred her so his chest pressed into her back, hands coming to rest upon her waist—something so simple. Yet it sent her mind reeling, friendship forgotten—centring her in this moment like an anchor as he leant down so she could hear him over the shouting crowd.

"We all have something that comforts us in a way that nothing else can," he said, lifting his gaze to the band upon the stage, bold yellow letters lined with red accents etched out the words *Def Leppard*. "You just have to find it, and when you do. Don't *ever* let it go."

"But what if I have to?" she turned to face him, peering up at him from beneath her lashes. "What if it makes me a bad person?"

"Life isn't always dictated by 'good' and 'bad', chica. Sometimes you must do *horrible* things before you find your serenity, breaking yourself before you find it."

"But at what cost?"

"Who are you, Nyx?" He angled his head, raking his gaze over her body with burning intensity. "What is it that you want? What you *truly* want?"

"Everything," she breathed, dropping her gaze to the floor like her admission ashamed her.

Niko's fingers tilted her head back, her gaze locking upon the swirling tides of his irises. His thumb rubbed soothing patterns into her cheek before he placed a kiss on the crown of her head.

"Then that's what it'll cost you," he said, pulling away from her, trapping her with his gaze. "Nothing good ever comes without sacrifice. Some of us just find clarity in the darkness of its shadow."

* * *

The moon hung high in the sky, a million constellations smattering the inky blackness in a pattern few would recognise, bridging light and life with darkness and death. Nyx wondered if the night always felt this long—this eternal—amid the laughter, screams and shouts of the fairground. Or if she'd grown so lost in the music engulfing her senses that time felt as if it'd come to a stop, halted in the heart of Celacali's siren call.

She observed the concertgoers, forcing herself to look away from the stage and focus her attention elsewhere, her eyes flitting from person to person. Curiosity rushed through her about the locals and tourists who crowded the stage and stands, wondering what drew them to the coastal city's thrumming nightlife. If they knew themselves.

Salacious words whispered in her mind; a part of her being she shoved back against like a drowning man fought for survival—desperate and unflinching. Because she couldn't—*wouldn't*—allow herself to grow entangled in its thorn-like barbs. Not again. Not now. Not when she'd purged her hands of the stains that'd once marred her skin, for the world to see her sins. Her father's playful jests danced in her head, twisted, and warped but filled with a truth she refused to admit. Despite the startling conviction behind them and the truth they held.

Because she *had* taken to learning how to throw a punch, to fight, with uncharacteristic interest. An interest deviating from the darkness of society's social norms. From the violence and pain swept beneath the rug, blaming *these* for the actions of unsavoury men. For the sins they committed and brushed aside with the same rehashed phrase: *She was asking for it.* And Nyx supposed there was some irony to it when her knuckles were stained with blood, her flesh torn and bruised by the time her father dragged her away from the bleeding man.

She shook her head to rid her mind of the images of the once leering man reduced to nothing more than a bloodied, whimpering mess. Reminding herself it'd been two years since that day, and she couldn't live in the past. In the turmoil it evoked; left to fester and burn deep in the caverns of her chest. She knew she'd lost a piece of herself that day, or gained a newer, *darker* shard that had carved itself into her being—almost like it had belonged there all along.

And maybe that's why she felt at ease with Niko—with them all—because she knew, despite the darkness coiled around her heart, that they'd revel in the demons of her past. The quartet at home amongst the blood-stained skin of her past, like Kade and Niko told her, time and time again, boasting it with baneful smiles.

She wondered, as Niko's hand clasped hers, leading her deeper into the crowd, if she was any better than them. Or if she was destined to become as monstrous.

She glimpsed Alexander and Tobias from her peripherals, turning her head, feet continuing to carry her, whilst she craned her neck. They'd gone, lost in the crowds. She puffed her cheeks out in irritation, lifting a hand to the coin-like charm around her throat, tugging it back and forth along the chain absentmindedly before she turned back to Niko and let him lead her.

"What's the rush, rockstar? The concert's not finished yet."

He grinned. Glancing down at her as he led her around a series of rides and stalls to his bike. His delight rolled off him in waves, infecting her. He lifted her then, situating her on the leather seat of his bike with feline-like grace. A shocked laugh tumbled from her mouth as he swiftly stepped between her legs, irises blazing with something intense.

Nyx sucked in a shaky breath of air, her gaze tracking his whilst he studied her, seeming to engrave every inch of her into his mind with fine-tuned precision. His tongue darted out to wet his bottom lip, gaze lifting from her lips to her eyes. The sensual drumbeat and guitar riffs of *'Love Bites'* drifted across the sky when he spoke, his voice raspy with poorly restrained need. His thumb ghosted her lip for a moment before he tore his fingers away and balled his hand into a tight fist that unfurled and rubbed at the crook of his throat.

"I would *very* much like to kiss you right now," he said.

Nyx peered up at him from beneath her lashes, inviting him to close the distance between the two of them. "What's stopping you?"

The blue of his irises clashed with hers as his gaze tore from her lips and his hand moved to grip her waist whilst the other slid from her face and to her neck, cupping the back of her head with his palm as he stepped impossibly closer.

"Nothing."

His lips descended upon hers with a need that rivalled the passion of Patroclus and Achilles, coming together like the gods had foretold; two beings driven together like two pieces of a puzzle left forgotten and waiting for someone to fit them together; to complete it in the way it was made.

In the way, *she* was made.

Nyx let herself fall into his embrace, Joe Elliot's voice the soundtrack to their languid, inexorable movements. Her fingers gripped the lapel of his jacket as his lips moved in perfect accord with hers, finding pieces of themselves in each other.

XXIX.

Nyx

Noise seemed quieter—muffled—like her head was beneath a ripple-free pool of water. Oblivious to the world around them as Niko's fingers clutched the silky material of her shirt, crumpling the fabric in his fist as he drew her closer to himself and her hands trailed to the back of his neck.

The life of the boardwalk bustled around them, continuing like they were specks in its eternal thrall. Passers-by threw them envious looks, while most screwed their noses up at the public display of affection. Nyx and Niko ignored it all, their lips dancing to a song only they could hear, breaking only as the rumble of approaching engines turned deafening. They pulled reluctantly apart.

Her gaze darted to the stripped-down motorbike to her left, umber irises finding hers in the neon lights of the boardwalk. Kotori's ebony locks cascaded over his leather jacket as his presence registered in her mind over the noise of his idling bike. His chest bared as he planted his boot-clad feet on the floor. Nyx's gaze lingered on the wolf tattoo peeking out from the waistband of his black jeans, slit along the knee like Niko's.

Kade rode a second motorbike to the right of her, and she wondered what she'd done in a past life to garner his devious smile. His forearms draped across the silver handlebars, bike idling.

Deeply rooted dread curled in her stomach when Niko's hand skittered down the back of her head to her waist, shifting his body so he could peer over his shoulder and back at Orion, the third rider. His platinum blond hair was tousled and yet, impeccably styled into a starkly, spiked mullet.

"Forgetting something are we, Niko?" Orion drawled, cigarette tucked snugly behind his right ear.

Nyx frowned, ignoring the way Kade's gaze darted to Kotori and Niko with a knowing glint, like he knew more than he was willing to let on. No one answered.

"Let's go, boys," Orion said, his gaze tunnelling on her, "Little dove."

She stared back at him, unwavering in the face of his intimidating aura before straddling the seat behind Niko, blocking Orion's view of her.

"What do you think, chica?" Niko murmured, peering back at her from over his shoulder.

Her lips pursed, considering his question for a moment. "I think Orion has something up his sleeve. Something I doubt I'll like."

"You'd be right to assume that," Niko said and paused, turning his head away from her as he revved his bike's engine. "But I don't think we have any other choice but to follow him."

His words hung in the air as they took off after his brothers, an unwavering conviction echoing in her mind—warning her of the danger lurking in the night's shadows. The darkness stirred in her chest, shoving against the confines she'd made for it with reckless abandon, unrelenting as it fought to free itself.

As it fought to free her.

* * *

Trees passed by in a blur before the stone-littered trail opened into a clearing in the darkened forest and they pulled up in a messy semi-circle. Nyx's gaze settled on a weather-beaten warehouse bracketed by towering trees and spindly brambles, thorns itching to tear across unclothed skin. Her grasp tightened around Niko's waist; the soothing rumble of the motorcycle engines gone—nothing but unsettling silence left to fill the night sky and add to her unease.

"Aw, don't tell me you're scared of a little warehouse," Orion crooned, startling Nyx, who whipped her head towards him.

He smoothly dismounted from his bike, kicking the stand into place before he began toward the rust-stained building, pausing beside the ajar door hanging unsteadily from its hinges, a gloved hand braced upon the doorway as he turned his head to peer back over his shoulder.

"Don't worry. There's nothing to be afraid of in Celacali, little dove," he taunted, throwing Nyx's words back at her before slipping into the warehouse door.

If only that were true, she thought bitterly.

Nyx loosened her hold upon Niko, turning her head away from the dark doorway and to the three men who remained. She worried her bottom lip between her teeth, fumbling for answers or clues in the depths of her mind that'd prepare her for whatever lay beyond it, her gaze darting to each of the men in search of the faintest foothold of reassurance. Her instincts raged, urging her to run—to forget this desire to find somewhere she fit—and simultaneously begged her to stay, and see what their lives of darkness could offer her.

Kotori angled his head, his gaze boring into her soul before he rose from the stripped-down motorbike and strode towards her, stopping so close to Niko's bike that she had to tilt her head back to see into his knowledgeable gaze. "Forget what you *think* you know, *kleintje*. It won't do you any good in there," he said.

"What *is* in there, Kotori?" Nyx asked.

He turned toward the warehouse, a look she couldn't decipher slashing through his irises, "I don't know," he admitted softly. "We're as blind as you are, Nyx ... but something tells me that whatever he has planned, it's for you, and you alone."

"What—"

"It's a test," Kade interjected, swinging his leg over his bike, and coming to stand beside Kotori. "If he can deem you unworthy, he can get rid of you."

"Get rid of me?" she parroted with mounting dread.

Kotori knocked his shoulder into Kade's, eyebrow arched in exasperation. "And you said Niko was bad for unhelpful information."

"He's right though, and you know it," Niko stated, knocking his stand into place before dismounting and helping Nyx. "All bets are off in there, chica. You have to fight, or you'll die."

"We can't hide our true natures, nor will we deny them," Kotori said, lifting his hand to run through his hair. "You'll find out who you *truly* are in there, one way or another."

She sucked in a shaky breath of air, forcing herself to be calm as she nodded her head slowly, processing their warnings. "Let's get this over with then," she said. Then, laughing without humour, she added, "I wouldn't want to *disappoint* him."

Kade grinned—his Cheshire grin—before he grabbed her hand, twinning their fingers together as they started toward the warehouse, with Niko and Kotori at their side. Her heart raced despite the calming breaths she took, a dredging sense of familiarity ghosting her mind, breathing in through her nose and out through her mouth, dank darkness engulfing her senses when Kade led her over the threshold of the warehouse and into the belly of the snake.

Mould fused the air, permeating the crumbling walls with greenish-black patches, an almost earthy undertone masking a rancid stench. Concrete scattered the floor around an enormous hunk of pole-entangled wreckage that'd been pushed away from the gaping hole in the ceiling, rotting crates stacked against the walls, their footsteps echoing—an eerily ominous song that rattled her nerves.

Nyx paused several paces from the halo of moonlight illuminating a hunched and bloodied figure bound to a chair. The man's clothes and skin were stained crimson as Kade stumbled, unprepared for her abrupt halt. She gazed at the man, wary in her appraisal of the blood-stained floor. Crimson collected around the chair in dark puddles, red dripping from the arms of the dishevelled man, whose dark hair was matted and hanging in his face.

Nyx cast a terse look at the three beside her, ready to run—to fight—at a moment's notice. The halo of light the man was bathed beneath displayed the sadistic theatrics Orion so loved before he spoke.

"Fascinating, isn't it?" he drawled, voice carrying like it'd done in the forest. He stepped into the halo of moonlight and rested a gloved hand atop the slumped man's shoulder, jerking the man's head back to reveal his bruised and swollen face. "The naïvety of man and his *foolish* delusions."

Orion's head cocked to the side. His icy gaze scrutinised her and the easy postures of Kotori, Kade, and Niko beside her. Like they'd known all along and their words of reassurance had been perfected lies. A slow, lazy grin curled his lips into a malignant smile at the flicker of surprise in her eyes. "Didn't you say that you wanted everything?" He chuckled darkly, "Your everything starts here, right now, little dove. Amid the *monsters,* you were warned about. Told to fear."

"And if I refuse?" she prompted, lifting her chin, and squaring her shoulders. Her irises darkened; ridding herself of everything she *thought* she knew.

"Oh?" Orion grinned, eyes ablaze with the challenge. "I'm afraid you don't have a choice. It's now … or never."

Growls of warning rumbled from Kade and Niko's chests, a possessive sound that sought to discourage Orion and remind him of their claim. Their lips curled into chilling sneers as they unconsciously adjusted their stances, so they partially blocked Nyx from sight. Nyx frowned like Kotori did, his lip twitching as he fought to suppress the leer itching to grow across his face, determined to portray the mute indifference Orion loathed. Orion's bemused chuckle ghosted the moonlit room as his gaze flickered from his companions to Nyx.

"Cut the knight in shining armour façade, *boys*. We all know that you've been waiting for this moment." Orion snapped. *"Eagerly."*

Nyx turned to face them then, studying the trio as if it'd rid her mind of her confusion. Her eyebrows furrowed as she forced herself to focus on the melodic rise and fall of the bloodied man's chest and not the games Orion played, twisting his words into something worse than the blood staining the floor.

"You're quite the actress, sweetheart." Orion mused, clicking his tongue, and drawing her attention away from the bleeding man. A malevolent grin etched firmly into his ungodly and yet angelic features. "You have everyone fooled … even yourself. It's impressive really, how easily you've deluded yourself into believing that you're … *good.*"

"I—"

"You can't lie to me, Nyx. Not when your blood's been in my veins. Not when I've seen," he paused, lips pursed. "No. *Felt* the darkness of your soul … After so many years, you've turned out *perfectly*. A wise investment that was … eager to stain itself in blood."

"You know *nothing* about me," Nyx bristled, spine straightening at his choice of words. "Don't for one second *delude yourself* into believing that you do."

"So poor Kai here was collateral damage?" Orion said, tutting mockingly, pleased by the recognition that flickered in her eyes.

"What?" she cut herself off, shaking her head vehemently. "That was an a*ccident*. I didn't—"

"I don't believe in accidents, little dove," he purred. He peered down at the bloodied and bruised face of the man, *Kai*. "*He* certainly doesn't."

"What do you want from me?" Nyx said.

"Isn't it obvious? I want you to finish what you started two years ago," Orion said, grinning wickedly. "It's his life … or yours."

DO NOT CROSS POLICE

CRIME SCENE DO NOT CROSS

CRIME

CRIME SCENE

CRIME SCENE DO NOT CROSS

DO NOT CROSS

POLICE LINE

PART TWO

"Remember, darkness does not always equate to evil, just as light does not always bring good."

—P. C. Cast

LINE DO NOT CROSS POLICE LINE DO

CRIME SCENE DO NOT CROSS

CRIME SCENE DO NOT CROSS

CRIME SCENE DO NOT CROSS

CRIME SCENE DO NOT CROSS

ICE LINE DO

XXX.

Nyx

Orion's words hung in the air, echoing off the mould-smattered walls like they clouded her mind—deafening and absolute in their calamity. Clattering to the floor with a distinct *clink* like a dagger slipped from his hand and connected blade first with the floor, she knew with jarring certainty that she hadn't misheard him—despite wishing she had—the starkness of his stare left no room for uncertainty.

She wondered, despite the coolness of his blue-eyed stare, how much of the ridged-faced beast with golden-white eyes stared back at her, watching her every move from behind whatever barricade Orion built for it. *If* he'd bothered to build one at all. Maybe he'd embraced the violent bloodshed others shied away from.

"You—" she cut herself off as she tried to quiet the resounding roar in her eardrums.

Nyx shook her head. Fighting to purge her mind of the memories of the golden eyes that'd watched her for *years*. She didn't *want* to die. She wanted to live. She thought of the price she'd pay as she dropped her gaze to the rubble-littered floor, thought of the blood that'd stain her hands and rid her of her clutched at hopes of being *good*. Like being forced to watch as her past unravelled before her. Forcing her to choose between her life and Kai's.

Her lip twitched, and her onyx stare met Orion's, uncharacteristic indifference in her eyes. A dark grin spread over his face, knowingly watching as she fought for control.

Come on, girl. Relax.

Nyx gasped, shaking her head vehemently as she staggered back, unbidden memories and voices surfacing suddenly, dredged up by an unseen force. Her hands trembled as the stagnant scent of beer and thumping music dug its past talons into her chest.

I can show you a good time.

"Stop fighting it, Nyx," Orion urged, calling her attention to him and away from the brewing memories she kept tucked in the darkest corners of her mind. A feat she was mildly grateful for, despite everything *he* had done to her.

"Let it *go*."

Phantom hands gripped at her clothes, tugging, and pulling in their desperate attempt to rid her of the oversized band T-shirt. Tying her to the bitter reality of her darkened past whilst her mind begged to slip away and refocus on the world around her.

No. Stop!

Her face twisted as her voice echoed in her head, eerie and distorted.

Get off me.

Her hands ached and her gaze darted to the scarred flesh of her knuckles.

Her vision warped and twisted. Brown, almost black eyes flashed before her. Dun-brown curls darkened by blood. Blue-metal stones beneath her knees spattered with crimson, like her hands, soaking into the blue of her jeans. A heart-shaped face bloodied and bruised beneath a waxing full moon.

Nyx! What have you done?

She couldn't remember that—but, when she'd turned toward her father with torn knuckles and blood-splattered jeans, she remembered she had laughed; a cruel jagged sound. And she'd known then, like she knew now, that whatever she'd done couldn't be purged from her father's mind when she turned back toward the bleeding man weakly whimpering in pain, unmoving as he trembled beneath her stare and her voice had filled the night. As eerie and disconnected as the memory itself.

Guess he should've kept his hands to himself, shouldn't he?

Horror had struck her father's face when she'd pushed herself up off the floor and turned toward him.

Oh, don't look so ... disgusted. He was asking for it.

Nyx shook her head, blinking the swell of memories from her mind long enough to recentre herself in the present. "How?" she said.

Orion cocked his head, shadows dancing across his face where the moonlight couldn't reach.

"Aw, little dove. I like to keep tabs on my 'would-be' murderers," he said.

"You *knew,*" she whispered, mind reeling with a thousand memories of golden eyes throughout her life before she cleared her throat. "You knew who I was when you sent Kade after me."

He tutted mockingly, gesturing to the three men beside her.

"*We* knew," he corrected, shaking his head with bemusement. "You were supposed to join the missing person's board that first night. But I suppose you have Kade to thank for the change of plans two years ago ... or was it, Niko?"

"Do you always talk this much? Or do you just like the sound of your voice?" Nyx interjected, suddenly angry.

"Would you look at that? You *can* bite back," Orion said.

She opened her mouth to utter a thinly veiled insult before he moved, disappearing into the shadows as if he were one himself. The muscles in her body coiled in preparation for whatever came next. The distinct feeling of being circled by a pack of wolves crept in as she registered the empty space beside her where Kotori, Kade and Niko had been.

A startled yelp spilled from her lips as she nimbly jumped back into the halo of moonlight to avoid being crushed by the wooden crates that tumbled down onto the spot she'd been standing. Her nerves thoroughly rattled whilst she pivoted in the ghostly light, searching the shadows. Watching. Waiting.

"Scared to face me, Orion?" she taunted into the darkness.

His dark chuckle drifted across the room, "It's ironic that your father said the same thing twenty-five years ago. Except … he's everything you're not."

"He was too … *righteous.* Wasn't he, Kade?" Kotori said. The deep timbre of his voice followed by his footsteps echoing up to the ceiling and the night sky.

"Righteous?" Kade's baneful snicker caressed her cheek with the faintest jingle of Niko's bracelets. "He was *afraid* of what he'd become."

"Not like you, chica," Niko stated proudly from the shadows, his laughter rippling off the walls. "You *revelled* in the bloodshed you caused two years ago."

"She did. Didn't she, Niko?' Kade questioned in a sing-song tone of voice.

Nyx stopped turning in her slow circle, focusing intently on what they were saying. Cigarettes, leather, and something metallic washed over her senses before a gloved hand wrapped itself around her waist and pulled her into a solid chest, the metallic press of a blade ghosting dangerously over her throat. An amused hum filled her ears as she froze, warning her of the danger in the theatrics of the knife.

"It's you or him, Nyx," Orion stated calmly, his honeyed voice laced with a hand-crafted softness intended to soothe her. "His fate lies in your hands … it's your choice. Don't hide from your decision. Not when we all know what it'll be."

"If you know the answer. Then why are you doing this?" she gasped. "I can't *do* what you want me to. I just—I"

"*Easy,* little dove," he breathed out softly. Calmly. His lips descended to her throat and placed the faintest of kisses on the crook of her neck, stunning her with the simplicity of his act.

Orion turned her toward the bloodied man, his blue eyes ablaze before the press of the knife to her throat and his arm around her waist vanished into the darkness of the shadows. Nyx's breath hitched in her throat when Kade stepped out of the shadows and stopped before her, his honeyed stare scolding as he rested a hand upon her hip and cupped her cheek with the other, his fingerless gloves warm against her skin. A weight settled itself on her shoulder before Niko wrapped his arms around her waist and pulled her flush against his chest, resting his face in the crook of her neck with a leisurely hum of contentment.

"Don't make me do this," Nyx pleaded softly, fighting everything in her that urged her to do something irreversible—to save herself.

"We're not making you do anything, angel," Kade murmured, thumb caressing the flesh of her cheek.

Niko hummed in agreement, "It's just, we've tried everything … *good*. And you missed every one of our hints. You didn't even recognise Kade when you've seen him before."

"I haven't seen …" Her eyes widened with realisation as she shook her head, recalling the moment she'd collided with Kade beneath strobe lights two years ago. "Your hints and the familiarity when I first saw Kade, those were instinctual warnings. *Those* were the hints?"

Niko chuckled with dark amusement. "I knew Kade was right when he suggested you'd respond better to the 'bad' in us. It was only a matter of *how* we'd get you to see the truth, and Kade planned that down to the last fault."

"So now, we're taking a page out of *our* book. Not *yours,*" Kade finished, leaning down to kiss her lips. "All you have to do is decide whether you'll kill him … or we do."

Nyx blinked up at him as he smiled down at her before her gaze darted to the shadows, searching for Kotori. Her mind clinging onto the fragile belief that the ever silent one, who radiated unbridled serenity, would centre her. Ridding her of her traitorous thoughts. Panic gripped her heart when she couldn't find him and her gaze returned to immutable Orion.

Kade and Niko shifted with excitement beside her, their irises ablaze whilst their gazes flicked from her to the space behind her, calming her mind that raced with the weight of their hands upon her hips and the knowledge Kotori towered above her. The wolfishly silent man's scent of freshly fallen rain, copper, and something earthy encased her senses when he stepped forward. His bared chest pressing into her back before his ring-clad hands settled upon her waist above Kade and Niko's, splaying over her shirt.

"Those urges in your head won't fade with time," Kotori said, leaning down so his deep and soothingly timbred voice filled her ears. His lips brushed against her ear, "Heed them. *Act* on them."

"But you said—" She spluttered in confusion.

"I said that you'd find out who *you* truly were. Not that we didn't already know."

"I don't—"

"Yes, you do," he assured firmly. "Don't run from it, *kleintje.*"

"Embrace it, angel." Kade urged, stepping forward to ghost his fingers across her cheek as Kotori released her chin.

"Give into its thrall, chica," Niko coaxed. "There's an art to getting lost in the darkness. He's just the key."

"Come with us, Nyx," Orion drawled, glancing down at Kai as he stirred in the metal chair. His uncanny irises lifting from the bound man and back to hers. "Become who you're *meant* to be. You'll never have to be ashamed of those urges with us. Not now. Not ever."

Nyx knew she should've fought it and shoved her desire for revenge to the back of her mind. She *should've* ignored it. The pull that called to the darkest depths of her soul, swirling in her mind with anticipation. Waiting. Desperate for her to act on the impulse searing through her bloodstream. Her dark gaze locked on the blearily, blood-matted face that blinked up at her, Kai's brows furrowed with confusion as he shifted in the metal chair, tugging at the restraints around his arms and legs with unfiltered fear.

She supposed there was an irony to the way Kai now pleaded for his life, her gaze dropping to the bound man with a dangerous glint in her eyes. The begging man before her, fighting against the bindings on his wrists and ankles. She remembered the boasted taunts he'd sneered into her ear two years ago after his kind-hearted mask ruptured.

Aren't you going to beg like the others did?

Her lips pursed with disdain, rage stirring in her chest. Kotori's raven-coloured hair brushed against her shoulder as he lowered his head to her ear.

"Acknowledge those blood-stained urges, *kleintje. Act* upon them," he said.

Something dark stirred in every atom of Nyx's being when she lifted her gaze from Kai and met Orion's stare. It rippled through her body like a tidal wave, gaining momentum and laying waste to anything in its path. Orion arched his brow as he offered her the knife he'd held to her throat, the snake-encrusted handle glinting in the moonlight. She cautiously grasped the cool hilt in her hand and weighed it.

Kai's pleas grew frantic, desperately tugging at the rope around his wrists. His beetle-like gaze imploring her to let him go.

"Please! I'll do anything—just ... don't kill me."

Her breathing slowed, "Haven't we lost enough because of you?"

Kai's eyebrows furrowed with confusion. His incessant tugging at the restraints around his wrists faltering before Nyx's bitter laughter danced through the warehouse with the slow shake of her head.

"Don't tell me you forgot," she crooned dangerously, lips curling into a deadly smile.

Orion's gaze blazed with delight, irises locked on Nyx's when he crouched down beside Kai. His gloved hand rested upon the blood-splattered fabric of Kai's T-shirt as he filled in the blanks for the bloodied man. "The other girls?"

Niko and Kade snickered as Kai's eyes widened with realisation and fearful tremors racked his body.

Simmering rage bristled in Nyx's eyes as she artfully twirled the polished steel in her hand. "I was feeling merciful ..." she trailed off, watching the light dance off the blade. "*Until* you showed no recollection of your various *conquests*, as you liked to call them, if I recall correctly."

"Please—"

"I want you to remember this fear," she interjected, moving swiftly as she grasped the handle of the dagger in her hand and plunged the knife into his thigh with a sickening *squelch*. Her head cocked to the side; onyx gaze tunnelling in on his face. "Do I have your attention now?"

Screaming in agony, Kai nodded. His face had distorted into a pained grimace as Orion grinned delightedly from beside him, attention focused solely on Nyx as she hummed with dangerous satisfaction.

"Good, because this is for all the girls you touched *without* their consent."

She yanked the dagger from his thigh with little remorse. Pausing long enough to survey the gushing wound before she drove the knife apathetically into his right hand, metal hitting metal with a resolute *clang* as the blade collided with the chair. Kai's harrowed scream echoed through the room as his blood gushed from his thigh and ran to the rubble-flecked floor. Red rivulets trickling down the arm of the chipped chair from his hand whilst he thrashed against his bindings. Feebly attempting to escape the pain.

Niko and Kade stepped forward and pressed down on Kai's shoulders, pinning the man to the chair as they looked on at Nyx with rapt attention.

She tore the dagger from Kai's hand, sick delight twisting in her gut as she watched him struggle. Her fingers gripped his hair, eyes dark as the ocean's depths before she tipped his head back with a firm tug and leant down to his face, lips ghosting across his. *"Dii te acriter."*

Silence settled deafeningly as Nyx's words hung in the air. She tightened her grasp amongst the blood-matted tresses of Kai's curls, ignoring his agonised pleas. She didn't think as she moved fluidly, dragging the blood-slicked blade across his throat in one quick motion. Like a knife through butter, staining her shirt crimson as Kai's throat gushed and spewed blood, a sickening gurgle spilling from his lips.

A jarring clarity struck Nyx's chest as she clutched the dagger's hilt tighter, the encrusted handle digging into her palm. Kai's eyes stared up at her, unblinking and glazing over, frozen in eternal terror as the calamity of his death registered in his own eyes.

There's no going back now, she thought.

Death greeted Kai like an old friend beneath Nyx's stare, whisking him away as quickly as the obscene amounts of blood spurting from his carotid artery.

Orion's gleeful voice slunk across the room, tearing her attention away from Kai's lifeless body.

"Welcome to the club, little dove."

XXXI.

Nyx

The thunderous rumble of the cliffside ghosted the cave walls, rippling through the barrel-lit living space within. Tangerine flames danced in their aluminium prison, itching for a freedom that would never come. The flames blustered in one direction and the other by the breeze slinking in through the tunnels and interconnecting caves with a ghostly sigh. A sound of beating wings snared Nyx's attention, dragging it away from the dancing flames to the uppermost ledges carved into the ceiling, where two doves nestled beside each other.

There was an irony in the way the birds sought refuge in the cave. Making a home for themselves in the presence of apex predators who roamed the night. Like they knew something she didn't. With her head tipped up to the limestone ceiling, she saw it. The safety they relished in. Thrived in. Unbothered by the footsteps echoing off the ceiling because they'd established a greater form of protection than teeth and claws could provide. Hiding in plain sight with the golden-eyed men as their unwitting protectors.

The skittering of rocks drew her gaze from the cooing doves and to Orion, who leant against the cavernous wall beside the makeshift bookshelf, his arms folded across his chest, a complacent smirk playing at the corners of his mouth. Kotori's dark stare caught hers. The brunette's head cocking to the side before a wolfish grin crept across his face and he tossed a glance in Orion's direction. Kotori eyed her for a moment before shaking his head with mirth, and disappearing amongst the shadows of the cave's entrance. Her eyebrows quirked, wondering why they seemed so *smug*. Their actions were embedded with a predatory zeal like they'd gained everything, and she'd won nothing. Orion surveyed her for a moment longer before turning and disappearing into the darkness of the cave's entrance.

As he disappeared, Nyx exhaled a drawn-out sigh, lifting a blood-stained hand to the claw clip in her hair before freeing the tresses from their confines, sending her curls tumbling down her back. She spared the living space a measured once over before she crossed the room, winding around the ornate throne and beaten couches to the chipped pillar supporting the candlelit tunnel's entrance, determined to forget the night's events. Her footsteps echoed off the walls and back to her ears as she followed the tunnel to the flickering candlelight of the smaller cave; her bedroom. If she could even call it that.

She stooped down and moved the wooden-backed painting from the entrance, delighted and comforted by the excitable barking that greeted her. Ares spun in small, excited circles, tail wagging as he jumped up at her legs, tugging on the stained material of her pants with a playful growl. She chuckled as she bent down and picked him up, ruffling the fur atop his head whilst the pup licked the underside of her chin. Ares wriggled in her grasp as she crossed the room and placed him in the makeshift pen tucked into the corner of the room, ruffling his fur one last time before she turned to the black, clothes-filled bag beside the bed.

Nyx sifted through its contents in search of something comfortable, something clean and blood-free, humming in satisfaction when her fingers brushed the black fabric of an oversized tee, and she plucked a pair of grey shorts from the bottom of the bag. She tossed the articles upon the mismatched bedding and, with crimson-stained hands, lifted the blood-smattered shirt over her head before tossing it to the floor, eyeing the red splotches.

A startled gasp spilled from her lips when arms wound themselves around her waist, threaded and metallic bracelets brushing against her stomach as their owner nestled their face in the crook of her throat and inhaled. Their warm breath fanning the bared expanse of her left shoulder and neck. Blond hair ghosted her skin as weed, copper, and an undertone of something woodsy curled around her senses. Guitar string calloused fingers drew small circles into the flesh of her hips. "Niko …"

He hummed in acknowledgement; the vibration rippling across her skin before his grip tightened around her waist and he pulled her closer to his chest.

"I'm covered in blood," she murmured distractedly as he leisurely caressed his thumb over her hips, mulling over whether his advances could distract her—if she'd forget what she'd done for a moment … or two.

He raised his head from the crook of her throat with a drawn-out groan, his voice deeper by a few octaves as he squeezed her hips. "Fuck. I *know,*" he said as he lowered his head back to her shoulder, trailing soft, hungry kisses along her throat and the underside of her chin. "You look hot covered in it, though."

"She looks *ravishing,*" Kade stated, stepping around to her right before he came to stand in front of her, his gaze alight as he stepped closer and rested a hand on her hip whilst the other cupped her cheek. She stared back as he smiled devilishly, closing the remaining space between them, and kissed her.

He moved closer as he deepened the kiss and she grew enthralled by her desire, his chest pressing into hers. Lust-driven and ravenous, his fingers tangled in her hair, pulling her impossibly close whilst Niko shifted behind her, and the ruffling of fabric tickled her ears.

Nyx's eyes glazed with unbridled lust when Kade pulled away, grinning from ear to ear as he angled his head, honeyed eyes gauging her reaction before he leant back in to kiss her with *starved* urgency.

She couldn't think straight as Kade's tongue traced the seam of her lips. Parting of their own accord, the taste of him in her mind, embedding itself into her being. She sighed into the kiss as Niko's lips trailed down her throat, nipping at the skin with his teeth. Lust clouded her mind as she trailed her fingers up Kade's chest, now almost frantic in her tangent of want. Desperate for more as her hands slipped from his hair and grasped the fabric of his T-shirt, tugging the material in a daze intensified by Niko's ministrations to her neck.

As Kade grinned into the kiss and then pulled away, Niko's fingers curled around her chin, turning her head toward him. She saw the cyanic-blue of his irises that seemed to burn so fiercely, his pupils dilated with hunger—for *her*—that couldn't be purged. Niko's lips descended upon hers with a searing passion, his tongue scouring the depths of her mouth with feverish grace. His grasp upon her chin lessened as his opposing hand kneaded the flesh of her waist possessively. Like he was claiming her in the tempest of his lust-driven haze.

Nyx's mind reeled, twirling in circles at the feelings evoked in her. Trying, and failing, to find her footing amidst the company of killers. She paused, grasping Niko's shoulder as Kade shifted behind her and she turned to him. His lips were bruised like hers, his eyes heavy with a look she couldn't decipher. She knew it wasn't love—the notion alone sounded foolish—but something primal. It seemed like something dangerous rippled off his chest, his brown-eyed stare blazed across her skin with twin emotion to Niko's. And she knew, as her gaze lowered to his scar-littered chest and the intricate tattoos sprawling across his skin, that she should've been ashamed, considering she'd just killed a man. But as his hands groped at the fabric of her pants, she found she *didn't* care. Niko's nimble fingers skittered down her body, replacing Kade's whilst he unfastened the button of her blood-stained pants, tugging them down her legs. Her lips moved with Kade's leisurely, her fingertips digging into his bicep, and a soft gasp spilled from her lips when Niko pulled her into his chest and pressed firm, wanting kisses to her throat.

Kade shook his head with delight. His hand lifted to his face as he deviously gnawed at the pad of his thumb. "It's getting to you. Isn't it, Nik?"

"Shut it, *Kade,*" Niko warned in a low voice, lifting his head from Nyx's throat.

"I didn't say anything," Kade crooned tauntingly, grinning as he brushed his thumb along Nyx's bottom lip, "I didn't *have* to."

Niko's lip curled into a warning snarl, an animalistic edge to his movements as Nyx turned and peered up at him before she pushed herself up onto the tips of her toes and pressed a lingering kiss to his lips. She rolled her eyes with a soft chuckle before she pulled away and turned back to Kade. "Aw, Kade. Play nice," she said.

Kade shook his head, "Aw, angel," he parroted, rolling the words over his tongue with malevolent ease. "There's nothing *nice* about us. Appealing, yes. But nice?" He laughed, the sound honeyed and dark as it echoed off the candlelit walls. "Niko's growing antsy because he *always* gets possessive when he's turned on."

"And Kade *always* gets territorial," Niko answered, batting his lashes as his gaze locked on his blond-haired companion. "Especially if he's already had a taste of the *forbidden fruit.*"

Kade shrugged, neither agreeing nor disagreeing as Niko brushed his lips against Nyx's in a tentative kiss. He grasped her hips and turned her to face him, Kade's lips now following the curve of her neck.

"Are you sure, chica?" Niko questioned, lifting his hand to cup her cheek whilst he waited for her answer.

She turned toward Kade, her nose brushing his as he leant back to accommodate her, hazel irises simmering.

"I am," Nyx said firmly.

"Are you? Because there's no going back after this," Kade warned, leaning around her shoulder so he could see her face.

Nyx chuckled, brows furrowing as she tried to find the right words to describe her certainty. Even if the question required a simple, yes or no. "I am. Something tells me that if I don't act on whatever my subconsciousness is trying to tell me. Then I won't feel so ... *alive*."

Kade raised his eyebrows, "Niko. I think we're rubbing off on her."

Niko smirked, "I think you're right, Kade ... but I don't think we should stop now." He leaned in to kiss her deeply and they made their way towards the makeshift bed.

"Fuck, you're hot," Niko whispered, stepping between her legs once he'd situated her on the bed, a calloused finger tracing her clothed clit.

She sucked in a sharp breath of air when he leant down to her, his hand gripping her jaw, thumb gliding over her lips.

"So, fucking wet and we've barely touched you."

Kade made quick work of the rest of her clothing before he teasingly dragged her panties down her legs, leaving her bare and quivering in anticipation underneath the weight of Niko's gaze as Kade stepped aside, content to observe her and his companion whilst Niko's other hand travelled up and down her inner thighs, caressing her skin with the gentlest of touches. All the while, pressing kisses to her lips.

"Please," Nyx breathed, thighs squeezing together. She gasped when Niko harshly pushed her legs apart, taking away the, albeit small, amount of friction.

"Such a good girl for using her manners," Niko cooed, pausing in the ministration of his thumb pressing circles into her thigh, "Don't ya think, Kade?"

"I think she knows what she wants, Nik," Kade said, eyeing Nyx whilst Niko began stripping what was left of his clothes. "You're just making her wait for it. Isn't that right, angel?"

"Yes! Fuck just ... please," Nyx pleaded, squirming, hoping to ease the dull throbbing between her legs as she reached up and grasped Kade's shoulder, pulling him toward her until their lips met in a lust-filled kiss.

Nyx ignored the huff of laughter and gleam of Kade's eyes when he pulled away, taking his time to kick off the rest of his clothes, tossing the garments carelessly to the floor as he held her entrapped with his gaze in nothing but his boxers. Excitement and adrenaline thrumming through every inch of her. As he watched her, a pang of arousal infiltrated her mind.

She couldn't understand why she felt so d*esperate* for their touch, but as Niko stepped closer to her and ghosted his fingertips along her thigh almost leisurely, she fought the urge to beg. There was something heady about the way she skittered along the precipice of danger, carefree above a greying black line of boundary that enticed her. Thrilled her. She sucked in a sharp breath when Niko trailed his fingers up her inner thigh, languidly grinning down at her as his eyes darkened with mounting lust.

His thumb pressed down on her clit, drawing slow, purposeful circles upon the sensitive bundle of nerves in a sinful blend of skill and pleasure. Her gaze darted to Kade—who watched her carefully, his lips parted—fighting the urge to close her eyes and immerse herself in the pleasure coursing through her body, forcing herself to look away from his honeyed stare and to Niko.

A mistake as Niko's grin grew feline and he pushed a finger into her cunt. She moaned softly, shakily, as he pumped his finger inside her. His head tipped to the side as if he'd be able to see her better from another angle. Pleasure clouded her mind as he moved, her eyelids fluttering shut and her head tipping back, her lips parting with soft indecipherable pants. She couldn't think as her hands gripped the mismatched bedding and Niko added another finger, curling them inside her with unaltered ease. A throaty moan tore from the depths of her throat as she dug her fingers into the mattress, her eyes fluttering open as the bed dipped behind her and Kade's lips brushed against her throat.

Kade's teeth grazed the bared skin purposefully, grinning against her neck as his hands trailed over her waist and stomach, to the underside of her breast. He kissed her throat and cupped her breast in his hand, rolling her nipple between his thumb and forefinger, toying with the taut flesh as Niko abruptly pulled his fingers from her cunt.

She groaned in protest, her eyelids fluttering open to peer up at him. She saw how he fisted his cock, his hungry gaze locked on her as he teased her entrance with his tip.

"God, you have *no* idea how long I've waited for this," Niko rasped, his wrist brushing against her waist as he gripped her hip, pushing the head of his dick into her slick wetness with a guttural groan.

"Fuck, Niko," Nyx moaned harshly.

Kade's amused chuckle rippled over her skin. His lips trailed down her throat and to her shoulder, smattering butterfly kisses over the bared skin in between soft nips designed to leave marks.

"Oh, angel," he whispered. "This is *nothing*. Niko plans to absolutely *ruin* you. It's all in his head," Kade chuckled. "It's all he can think about."

"You're so wet, chica." Niko ground out, his fingertips digging into her hips as his gaze raked across her body. "Does the thought of me ruining you turn you on?"

Kade hummed with delight as Nyx released a sharp, needy whine, his words rattling around in her mind, arresting as he thrust into her then, plunging every glorious inch of himself into her. She gasped and tipped her head back into Kade's shoulder, baring her throat. Niko began a slow roll of his hips—a fluid motion—before he adjusted her legs, each thrust making her pussy clench down on him after how he'd teased her.

Kade's hand wrapped tight around her throat when Niko pushed one of her legs back, turning her face toward his as the sound of skin against skin rasped in the cavernous room. She could hear the obscene wet sounds from her arousal, and she saw the way Kade's lips curled into a sinful smirk.

"Can you hear that, Nik? She's fucking *drenched,*" Kade crooned into her ear. His gaze locked on the rhythmic thrust of Niko's hips, whilst the room became punctuated with the noises tumbling from Nyx and Niko's lips.

Niko lifted Nyx's leg over his shoulder before letting himself fall forward, using his hand to brace himself on the mattress, caging her in. She ignored the burn from the stretch, opening her eyes as Niko's fingers curled around her chin and turned her head to him. He seemed to be ensuring her vision was full of his chiselled face, his azure gaze gleaming in the candlelight before he grinned wickedly, "Maybe I should fuck you more often. Obviously, Kadey didn't do a good enough job."

"No, Niko—Ah! Niko ..." she trailed off, unable to finish her sentence as Niko's thumb caressed her cheek, and he pressed himself deeper into her.

Her head tipped back and her eyes met Kade's, his boxers were down and he had his hand wrapped firmly around his cock, stroking himself to the rhythm Niko set with his thrusts. She watched with heavy-lidded eyes as Kade tilted his head back into the headboard, letting out a moan as he visibly fought the urge to close his eyes.

Nyx could hear the pants spilling from his parted lips, watching as his head tipped back down and his hazel gaze locked on hers. Niko's teeth grazed the skin of her throat and she forced herself to speak, "Kade's more than capable of *pleasing* me."

Niko hummed into the juncture of her neck whilst he placed open-mouthed kisses there. The groan of agreeance from Kade stole Niko and Nyx's attention, enticing their mounting orgasms. Kade's hair looked like a tousled mess from where he'd raked his fingers through it, and his lips were nearly bitten raw. He had little patience, and yet, there he sat on the sidelines, gripping his thigh harshly as if it'd keep him in place. He looked pent-up, ready to implode or cry. It was like every ounce of his strength had gone into forcing himself to remain in place and not intervene. But his stare told another story, blazing and itching to pounce.

Nyx's hands reached up in surprise as Niko's thrusts sped up, his grasp tightening around her waist, the head of his cock brushing against a spot inside her that made her toes curl and a wanton moan escape her lips. Her hands gripped the corded muscles of his biceps. It only lasted a moment, like Niko was teasing her, determined to prolong her hastening orgasm, which grew with each deep and measured thrust of his hips. She felt it as her inner walls clenched his dick and Kade's quiet moan and hitch of breath flitted to her ears.

Niko pulled away from her throat, peering at Kade with a grin. "And that's why he's not going to cum, *right*?" he said with a threatening edge.

Kade let out a strangled whine, his hand slowing as Niko's eyebrows lifted, daring him to disobey. "Fuck, Nik. Please—"

Niko tutted, glancing down at Nyx with dark finality, "No." His gaze met Kade's for a moment. "You cum when she does."

When Niko looked back down at Nyx, he looked downright lethal. The wildness in his eyes grew as he held her jaw, squeezing it until it ached. Niko tilted his head whilst he studied her face, soft pants mutely spilling from his lips. It seemed like a split-second decision, but then he was leaning down. Pressing his lips hard against hers in a heated kiss, his fingertips digging into the flesh of her hip as the hand around her jaw loosened and nimbly tilted her head upwards, deepening the kiss before his tongue glided across hers. "Fuck. Kade can have my sloppy seconds. You want that, huh? Do you want me to cum inside you? Fuck my cum into you, so you'll be good and wet for him?" Niko rasped against her lips.

Nyx's response was breathy and needy as she agreed, practically begging for him to do it. He moved with lithe grace, grasping onto one of her shoulders as his mouth pressed kisses wherever he could reach. Down her cheek, across her jaw, to the pulse point at her neck. His pace altered in her next breath, thrusting so hard the only thing keeping her from inching up the bed was the hand holding her shoulder.

His pace was star-inducing, consuming her thoughts in a blinding daze of pleasure as she felt his blunt teeth sharpen, feeling them grazing her throat. But, despite the palpable danger, she tugged the long, blond strands of his hair, her other hand dragging welts down his back as each drive of his hips slammed against the sweet spot inside her. Nyx closed her eyes, arching her back as Niko's hand supported her head. Her thighs trembled as her release came closer and closer, agonising in its mind-dazing pleasure.

Niko lifted his head to stare into her eyes. His face changed; all sharp edges and long fangs, his blue irises a chilling golden-white. She almost didn't notice how his other hand snaked between their bodies to rub and press into her clit. Her gaze locked on the golden eyes staring down at her as her heart jolted. Fleeting fear carved a jagged path through her chest, tearing itself from her sternum as a loud throaty moan slipped past her lips and an intense wave of pleasure washed over her in a blinding daze.

"Fucking cum for me, chica," Niko urged softly, leaning down to press a soft, reassuring kiss to her lips.

As Niko's rasped order clamoured in Nyx's ears, she felt her resolve slip, swirling away as she screwed her eyes shut and came with a pleasure-riddled shout. Niko's thrust didn't slow as he fucked Nyx through her orgasm, her body trembling beneath him as he pushed himself towards his release. She heard Kade as he groaned.

Niko continued to thrust deeper into her pleasure-slick cunt as her insides squeezed down around him and he continued to roll his hips into her. His head dropped to the crook of her throat before his fangs embedded themselves into her neck and he drew a few mouthfuls of her blood into his mouth.

A gratified moan jolted past her lips as endorphins coursed through her bloodstream and she clenched down upon his cock, fingers digging into his back.

He cried out a guttural exclamation of her name, pulling away from her throat as she felt the first spurt of his cum and, like he'd done with her, he fucked her through his orgasm until he was twitching.

"Fuck, *that* was hot." Kade breathed out after a beat of silence; his voice thick with lust as he watched with post-orgasmic eyes.

Niko's tongue lathed over the weeping bite mark on Nyx's neck, to ensure its closure before he lifted his head and studied her closely, ensuring she was okay before he leant down and pressed a kiss to her forehead. "Thanks, Kade."

Niko fussed with the bedding momentarily before he pulled several silken blankets over Nyx's naked body, adjusting the pillows around her as he laid down beside her and pulled her flush against his chest, face burying into the crook of her throat possessively.

"No. Thank *you*," Kade corrected, raking his fingers through his sand-coloured curls, pulling his boxers up his navel before he skittered down the bed and nestled himself against Nyx's other shoulder. He pressed an affectionate kiss to her collarbone, leaning over her to press a gentle kiss to Niko's jawline. "You covered in blood was one thing, angel, but *that* was fucking *hot*."

She laughed lightly, lifting a hand to leisurely run through his curls as Niko's lips brushed gentle kisses to her throat.

"Vampires," she muttered, rolling her eyes jokingly whilst she sidestepped the bloodied events prior in the night, pretending they hadn't happened for a few misguided seconds until she couldn't. "I *murdered* someone tonight."

Nyx straightened whilst her words hung in the air between them, pushing herself onto her elbows as a plunging sensation filled her stomach. Every moment she'd spent as a child terrified of those golden-yellow eyes that watched her, now flitted before her eyes. Those eerie footfalls echoing through their Malor house whenever she was alone in their home, or the vivid dreams—nightmares—of a dozen kills she'd experienced in her pre-teens. Of the countless times she'd pleaded with her family that something—somebody—was watching her and they'd brushed them all aside as dreams. Of the nights she'd left the local library alone and something had lightly grazed her arms, neck or spine. All those times she had pushed what she knew aside. And then had come … Those months after she had stained herself in Kai's blood.

It was them ... all along, she thought.

Had everything been their careful orchestration intended to set her onto a path of no return? Her parent's divorce and Azeil's determination to move to Celacali? Was everything she'd ever done a part of their plan? Every milestone, or happy memory? Was her terror and restless nights of their making? To keep her on edge and aware of their presence. Had they constructed the day she met Kai so they could test her? To see how far she'd go to protect herself—to see if she was like them at all?

She blinked back the tears pricking her eyes, fisting the sheets as rage and helplessness warred inside her. Because now, she was stuck. Bound to them irrevocably with Kai's death pressing down upon her shoulders. A very dead weight. She couldn't go back to what she'd once had, once been, and she realised they would never let her.

Not now. Not ever.

"Breathe, angel," Niko cajoled, shunting her from her thoughts and clouding her reason with déjà vu.

He'd said that to her before. At a spring-laced park on the same day she'd first met Kai, when he'd saved her after she'd almost been kidnapped by a masked man. *Kotori,* she realised. Her nose scrunching with distaste when another piece clicked into place. They'd orchestrated that terrifying day in her life to spend a fraction of time with her, to see if their asset was becoming the person they wanted her to be. And she'd fallen for it, even after all her family's warnings and the necklace Grandma Niamh had given her for protection.

She was a fool; a perfect tool for their decades-long revenge.

"I killed someone," she repeated, voice trembling. "You *made* me kill someone."

"You did," Kade confirmed without pause, ignoring her accusing words. "And stressing about it won't change that."

"But—"

"If you hadn't killed him. We would've," Niko said, cutting her off before she could utter her protest.

"Orion said—"

"That it was his life or yours," Kade interjected, propping himself up onto his elbow so he could look at her. "He *wanted* to test you. *We* wanted to test you."

She opened her mouth to speak, mind reeling as she blinked at him exhaustedly. "What?"

"You were never going to die. That's not what Orion wanted—what *we* wanted," Niko explained, effectively sending her mind into a muddled haze as she tried to centre herself against the growing allure of sleep.

"I—" she began, brows furrowing with confusion and distress as she turned to the cave's entrance.

Her eyes widened, her heart pounding obnoxiously in her chest, beating against her ribcage like fists upon wood as her irises clashed with the unearthly blue of Orion's. His footsteps echoed off the cavernous tunnel walls as he strode closer, each calculated step imbued with predatory finesse. Her palms dampened with sweat, her skittered retreat toward the headboard stifled by Niko and Kade, who grasped her hip and thigh, pinning her between them as they lazily turned to Orion.

"You," she started, tugging against the hands latched around her hip and thigh, irises ablaze.

Orion folded his arms across his chest, "Now, now, little dove. There's no need to get so worked up."

"*You* made me *kill* someone," Nyx snapped furiously, her struggle against Niko and Kade's grasps futile.

"I didn't *make* you do anything," Orion said.

"Bullshit! You told me that it was my life or his."

"He also told you to let go and embrace the darkest parts of yourself," Kotori interjected, stepping out from behind Orion and into the cave like a wolf. His dark irises locked on her. "He never told you to kill him. *You* chose that yourself."

Orion chuckled darkly, stepping further into the room. "*You wouldn't be welcomed here as a murderer.*"

Her eyes widened, bitter realisation weighting her chest as she tugged at the hands holding her in place, itching to wrap her fingers around Orion's throat. "You—"

He stood at the foot of the makeshift bed and smiled at her malevolently. "I did what had to be done. It's not my fault that dearest *Azeil* is blinded by his anger."

Her lips curled into a sneer as she stared into his eyes, "You're *despicable.*"

He hummed, grinning as if her words pleased him. "I prefer driven, but despicable works."

"I'm going to *kill* you. I promise you that," Nyx hissed, colour high in her cheeks.

"I look forward to it," Orion said and spun on his heel. "But for now. *Sleep,* little dove."

A whine of protest tumbled from her lips as she fought the haze suddenly clouding her mind, pushing down on her relentlessly before she sagged in Kade and Niko's grasps. Her eyelids fluttered shut against the violation, plunging her into darkness as lips brushed against her temple and the coolness of leather ghosted across her cheek, eerily comforting the swirling turmoil in her mind, begging her body to obey. Her mind fought against the glass-like prison sealing her in, leaving her reeling as she fell into darkness, her *hate* for him spiralling around her. She vowed to kill him.

If it was the last thing she ever did.

XXXII.

Tobias

Children's delighted screams echoed across the sky, tangling with the boardwalk's nightlife and the heavily populated tourist attraction. Tobias shuffled a stack of comics beside him and arranged a select few in the metal comic holder secured to the front of the paint-chipped counter, his fingertips drumming against the wood absentmindedly.

An old rock song played softly from a beaten stereo propped against a stack of unopened boxes filled with new orders—punctuating the silence interrupted by the commotion of the boardwalk. Alexander glared half-heartedly at him from around the stone pillars bordering the tiered display tables, flipping him off now and then with a playful grin across his face. Tobias rolled his eyes at his older brother's antics.

Tobias watched with vague interest as the cardboard box Alexander rested on his hip tumbled to the floor, the comics scattering across the floor in a colourful heap. Alexander cursed softly, staring down at the mess as if he were contemplating leaving them there; a colourful blot of glossy paper amongst the dull grey concrete.

"You can't leave the comics on the floor, Alex," Tobias scolded as he rested his chin in his hand.

"I think they look good there," Alexander sighed. He paused, peering over his shoulder at Tobias. "I say we leave them there."

"Alex," Tobias warned.

"All right, yeah, yeah," Alexander said. "I'll move them." His eyes narrowed into a playful glare. "But I'm not moving them because you told me to."

"Right," Tobias said, thoughts already elsewhere.

Alexander huffed out an exaggerated breath of air, stooping down to pick up the fallen comics before he turned to Tobias with several Spiderman comics clutched in his hands. "This," he gestured to the room around them, a comical scowl on his face, "is why neither of us have girlfriends."

"Huh? I never would've noticed," Tobias drawled, deadpanning his older brother.

"Smart-ass," came the reply.

"Oh, c'mon. You walked into that one."

Alexander nodded fatalistically, "At least we got one thing out of this."

Tobias rounded the ancient-looking cash register, "And what's that?"

"We managed to piss Dad off," Alexander peered up at him with a devious grin. His gaze flickered around the empty store and then to the comics scattered at his feet. "He told us to run the store, didn't he? To keep it in business. But when we did *exactly* that—and better—might I add, he got all moody."

"Only *you* would find satisfaction in pissing our father off," Tobias mused. He frowned as his thoughts drifted to Nyx and the conviction their father held towards her.

"Hey, Alex," Tobias said.

Alexander hummed in acknowledgement, not bothering to lift his gaze from the last few comics he scooped up and placed carefully into the box, brushing the dust of the floor from his black skinny jeans. He frowned as he picked up the cardboard box and placed it beside the beaten stereo, surveying his younger brother carefully. "Tobias?"

Tobias lifted his coffee-like stare from the dull concrete. His fingers absentmindedly toyed with the chequered pastel-yellow rolled sleeves of his dress shirt. He shook his head, hoping to rid himself of the niggling worry festering in his gut as he ceased his anxious fidgeting—for only a moment—before his hands rubbed uneasily down his jean-clad thighs.

"Tobias?" Alexander repeated, worry in his words. "What's wrong?"

"I think Dad's going to do something *incredibly* stupid."

Alexander shook his head bitterly. "When is he *not* doing something stupid?"

Tobias shook his head vehemently, imploring his older brother to understand him. "No. I'm worried about Nyx, Alex. You know what he's like just as well as I do."

Alexander's grin slipped, "What're you saying?"

"I'm saying we need to find out what he's planning, because he will be planning something, and we *need* to warn Nyx," Tobias said.

"You want to warn her?" Alexander uttered slowly, confusion marring his voice whilst surveying Tobias cautiously. "She looked fine to me, Bias."

"*Alex,*" Tobias said.

"What? She did," Alexander defended, raising his palms. "How much trouble can she *really* be in if she's swapping spit with a *bloodsucker?*"

"Alexander," Tobias warned lowly, levelling an unimpressed glower in his brother's direction.

"She's traipsing around with *vampires,* Tobias. If anyone will be okay, it'll be her," Alexander said.

"It's *Nyx*. We can't just *watch* from the sidelines."

Alexander arched a dark eyebrow, "Why can't we? She has *four* vampires at her disposal."

Tobias rubbed a hand down his face, groaning frustratedly from the depths of his throat as he turned towards the tourist display filled with an array of tokens with 'Celacali' painted across every surface in blood-red letters. He spared his brother a withering glare before he picked up a spongey stress ball and threw it at his brother's chest.

"What the hell, Tobias?" Alexander exclaimed, his eyes narrowed and all traces of amusement shoved aside.

"You're a dick, Alex," Tobias snapped, toying with a stainless-steel bracelet.

"And you're gullible," Alexander quipped, sighing as he bent down to retrieve the yellow, smiley-face-imbued ball. Tossing it into the air, "How're we going to ruin *Daddy Dearest's* plans, little brother?"

"By whatever means necessary. Starting with warning Nyx," Tobias said.

"And from there?"

"He'll already be coming up with some ... *unthought-out* plan," Tobias said, trying to quell the rattling nerves in his chest. "I say we stick around and play the dutiful sons he *raised,* learn his plan and then we'll go from there."

Alexander nodded his head slowly. His hazel irises swirled with his thoughts, lips pursing as if they'd left an uncomfortable itch at the back of his throat. "There's a giant hole in that plan."

Tobias sighed, pressing his tongue into the flesh of his cheek to calm rising anger, "Which is?"

He impatiently followed the purposeful drumming of Alexander's fingers against his chin, gritting his teeth in hopes it'd quell his bubbling annoyance.

Alexander dropped his hand from his face, clicking his fingers together as he shook his head with unbridled satisfaction. "The four *vampires,*" he murmured, lifting his gaze from the floor with a taunting smirk. "You know, like the one we saw her with earlier tonight?"

Tobias cursed, raking his fingers through his hair, his head tipping up to the ceiling as if he were praying to the Gods above. "Damn it!" He paused, turning to face Alexander as an uncanny calm swept through his chest. "That's fine. We'll wait for her to come to us."

Alexander opened his mouth to speak but thought better of it as Tobias's eyes narrowed.

"In the meantime, we'll focus on learning Dad's plan."

"Don't forget about ruining it," Alexander interjected, grinning from ear to ear.

Tobias sighed, levelling his older brother with a playfully, frustrated glare. "We can't ruin his plan if we don't know what it is."

"Huh ... good point," Alexander said, pivoting in a slow circle as he surveyed the empty store around them, humming the lyrics of the rock song playing through the beaten stereo speakers before he turned back toward his brother. "We don't even know *if* she'll come to us."

Nyx's onyx eyes danced through Tobias's mind, crinkled with undiluted happiness as she laughed at something they'd said. He shook his head to rid himself of the memories. "She will," he assured with steel-infused certainty.

"You—"

"She always has, Alex. Since we were kids," Tobias said. He glanced over his shoulder to the bustling nightlife of the boardwalk passing by beneath the star-filled sky. "She's always come to us when she needs someone."

He turned back to his older brother who watched the people pass by the comic bookstore. Tobias wondered if he'd heard Alexander wrong when he spoke—voice unwavering and sure—his eyes locked on the bustling boardwalk that thrived after the closure of the murder investigation and Azeil's client's, the Hayes, closed his case.

Tobias followed Alexander's gaze to the blinding lights of the Ferris wheel, where people parted like the Red Sea for Moses around two stripped-down motorbikes. He knew, without truly trying, who sat astride those bikes, down to the last bracelet. He also knew who sat beside the ebony-haired biker *Kotori,* who looked like he belonged in a romance novel. Tobias watched as Orion shook his head, a charming tilt to his lips when he glanced at his dark-haired companion and revved his bike before taking off down the wooden boardwalk.

He turned back to Alexander as the two notorious bikers sped down the boardwalk and past the comic bookstore, their howlers of delight rippling off the waves lapping at the fairground.

"I hope she knows what she's doing, Bias," Alexander mused, following their silhouettes until they disappeared from his sight.

"I hope so too, Alex," Tobias said. He peered down the boardwalk like his brother, his hands rubbing down his thighs anxiously. "Do you think…"

"She'll turn?" Alexander threw him a quick look before turning back to the boardwalk and its nightlife. "I think that's up to her, she'll be the one who'll have to live with it."

"But—"

"Bias. Darkness does not always equate to *evil,* just as light does not always mean *good.*"

"What're you saying?" Tobias said.

Alexander turned to him then, focusing his entire attention on his younger brother. "There is no such thing as good and bad. Just as there is no such thing as black and white. The lines are blurred in Celacali, brother."

The pair turned back to the boardwalk and its inhabitants.

"The City of the Dead *is* the city for the lost," Alexander said.

XXXIII.

Nyx

Sunlight warmed the flesh of Nyx's arms as she wandered the boardwalk in the early hours of dusk, the sky a colourful blend of pinks, purples, and oranges. Waves lapped against the wooden pier, filling her eardrums with their soothing rhythm, calming her frayed nerves and throbbing head. Ares walked beside her whining softly as his almond irises jumped from person to person who milled about in the afternoon light whilst Nyx searched for the nearest phone booth.

To call *who*, she didn't know.

She cursed herself softly, wondering how she could've been so foolish. So stupid and naïve. But worrying about the what-ifs wouldn't help her now. Not with blood staining her hands. She forced herself to search the boardwalk calmly, her gaze darting to and from stores in search of one of the few phonebooths she knew she'd passed, quelling churning unease in her gut.

She tried not to think of the events which had led her here—or back to it—forcing the dark and joyous laughter from her mind. But moreover, she longed to forget the glacier-like eyes that flashed before her mind and that harmful satisfaction in their depths. She longed for the day before she'd stumbled upon the boardwalk and the murderous beings who revelled in the bloodshed of the night. Wishing with every fibre in her being that she could go back to the time when life had been simpler. Less blood-stained. For she couldn't understand the comfort and security of this darkly, blood-stained descent, or she didn't want to.

And maybe that's why some foolish sliver of her soul whispered its desires, riddled with the belief that if she could rid herself of Orion; she'd be free from the darkness she longed to embrace. *It'll take more than luck to rid yourself of him,* she mused bitterly, humouring thoughts of Orion's demise and the re-establishment of her mundane life free of the quartet. Her mind clung to the notion, turning it over until determination rose—a human-like naïvety lashing her thoughts when her instincts rioted, urging her to submerge herself in the life Kade, Niko, Kotori and Orion lived.

Even if she knew she shouldn't have found comfort in the knowledge that Kai was dead. *Murdered* at her hands. But she *couldn't* shake the deep-seated comfort it elicited. And that's what scared her the most, that she didn't regret what she'd done … or the things she would do. Nyx knew with unwavering finality that she'd do it again, if she had to.

If that's what it would take to rid the world of another vile, self-entitled man.

She shook her head, hoping it'd purge her mind of the malicious thoughts. Refocusing herself in the present and the task at hand, her gaze finding a weather-worn phone booth tucked beside a closed video and music store, several outdoor settings tucked beneath an awning, delicate fairy lights twinned around the framing as families with small children escaped the bustle. To her immense relief, she noted the emptiness of the booth and the lack of patrons awaiting beside it with a relieved, albeit breathless laugh. Throwing a glance over her shoulder before cinching the door shut behind her.

The air was fetid inside the tiny booth and Nyx turned to the phone, grasping the metal handset in her hand and pressing it to her ear, her fingers hovering over the dial pad as she paused, hopelessly unsure in herself as she stared at the metallic numbers.

Her hand dropped from above the numbers she longed to press, sifting through her jean pockets instead as she pulled out a cluster of silver coins. There was more than enough for a phone call, for countless calls if she needed it. She needed supplies for Ares. For herself. And those seemed more important in that moment, as she slotted the coins into the fee slot, pressing a number she'd remember with her eyes closed into the dial pad and waited anxiously as the dial tone sounded in her ears.

A cautiously gruff voice filled her ears. A wave of longing infused her chest as her lips pulled into a grin at the sound of his voice.

"Hello?"

"Xander," she breathed out with a light laugh, clutching the phone as her adopted brother's features flickered behind her eyes. His tawny-brown hair brushing his shoulders. The dark brown of his irises, flecked with hazel. His broad face, stubble-speckled jawline and full lips. She chuckled, shaking her head as her grip tightened on the phone pressed to her ear. "I know better than to be insulted by the silence, Xan. You never were good with voices."

"Nyx?"

"Surprised?" she taunted playfully.

His laughter drifted through the speaker followed by a faint shuffling as he mumbled something beneath his breath to whoever was with him. "That you know what a phone is? Definitely."

"Don't let him fool you, Nyx. He's missed you," came Alyvia's voice moments later, and Nyx could practically imagine the way she leant over her brother's shoulder and how Xander would've angled the phone in her direction.

"Thanks," Xander said.

"No worries."

Xander huffed out an exaggerated breath of air, eliciting a chuckle from Nyx.

"It's good to hear your voice, Night, but we both know who you called for." Slight shuffling filled her ears as Xander passed the phone to their mother with a mumbled, "Don't say anything I wouldn't."

"Hello, my little shadow," her mother's silvery voice filled her ears, trickling through the phone's speaker like water down a riverbed.

"Mum," she murmured shakily, her unphased demur slipping as longing panged in her chest and her mind conjured up flawless flickers of her mother. The warm, chocolate-brown depths of her eyes, alight and framed by her thick lashes. Her loving smile and nurturing guidance. Defined beach wave curls tumbling down just past her shoulders in a thick mass of hair that framed her diamond-shaped face.

"How's Celacali been treating you?" Alyvia asked, curious and concerned.

Nyx hummed, mulling over her mother's question for a moment, "It could be better."

"What's the matter? Are you alright?"

"I'm okay," she replied. Because what else could she say? Bitten by three of the very vampires her mother so feared? That she was living with them because her father had kicked her out? "It's just ..." she frowned, not knowing how to explain herself without sounding delusional.

"It's *different* there, isn't it?" her mother prompted knowingly, filling in the blanks without Nyx having to speak. Like she'd always done throughout Nyx's life, a constant beacon of assurance and understanding.

"That's one word to describe it," Nyx admitted, raking her fingers through her curls, leaning against the hard plastic of the phone booth as she glanced down at Ares, who waited dutifully beside her feet. "But that's not why I called you."

"What's wrong?"

Nyx heaved a deep breath of air from her lungs, toying with the metallic cord attached to the phone nervously. "Dad and I got into a fight a few days back. He got angsty and I got defensive," she sighed. "Push led to shove, and Dad snapped."

"Nyx ..."

She shook her head vehemently, breathing in sharply to calm her fraying emotions. "He told me to leave. That he didn't care where I went just as long as I left."

"Oh, my little shadow," Alyvia exclaimed, sounding pained by Nyx's gritted out words. "You can always come here, back to Malor. I can get Xander to pick you up."

Nyx sucked in a shaky breath of air, tipping her head back into the metal framing of the phone booth as she blinked back tears, growing overwhelmed by the attentiveness and concern in her mother's voice even if she was thousands of miles away. She chuckled wetly, clearing her throat of the emotion that constricted her vocal cords. "You know I can't do that."

"I know, sweetie. But I'm always here for when you can," Alyvia paused, mulling over her words before she continued, and plunged Nyx's heart with dread. "You're stronger than *Orion.* Don't *ever* forget that."

"But what if I'm not? What if I'm just like him? Or worse."

"They found me a long time ago. Lost in the lights of the boardwalk," she sighed into the speaker. "They're not all bad, but I'm sure you already know that. They're merely … lost."

"They're *monsters*. Nothing more."

Her mother's laughter filled her ears. A warm, delighted sound that confused Nyx, "We're all *monsters,* Nyx. In our own sense," she said.

"But … you said—" Nyx spluttered.

"I know, my little shadow. I know."

"Then what *are* you saying?" Nyx demanded.

"*Be careful.* My past with them will not cloud your future. My … fear won't cloud it. It's just …" Alyvia paused before continuing in a softer-toned voice. "You were always meant for so much more. And if … you find that with them, with the darkness of their life. Do what you must."

"But what if I forget who I *am*? What if the only way to find out who I am, was through killing someone from my past? What then?" Nyx asked, begging her mother to provide her with the answers she so desperately sought.

"Nothing good ever comes without sacrifice, Nyx," came the reply.

Nyx sucked in a sharp breath of air. Her gaze darting to the dial pad of the phone booth like she'd be able to see her mother through it. She shook her head vehemently as dread latched a hold of her stomach at those eerily familiar words her mother had spoken. Flashes of a dirty-blond biker with cyanic-blue irises appeared before her eyes in a thunderous swell of confusion, the feeling of having her feet knocked out from beneath her embedding its talons into her flesh.

"W-what did you say?" she uttered, clutching the phone tightly in her grasp until her knuckles turned white, a dull beep warning her of the impending end of the connection.

"Don't be afraid, my little shadow," Alyvia said.

Nyx straightened, voice terse with unease, "I know you knew them. But, *how* did you know them before Dad did?"

"I was a runaway looking for a home amongst the nightlife when Leon found me and brought me back to the Bluff. And at the start, it felt like I'd found what I was looking for. But then your father came, and I realised they were more like brothers to me."

"But you *drank* Leon's blood?" Nyx pressed.

"I know, my shadow, and I did it willingly," Alyvia paused as if mulling over her next choice of words. "Unlike your father. But I couldn't tell him ... not when he looked so content."

"Does he know that?"

A troubled sigh trembled down the phone line. "Why do you think he divorced me, Nyx?"

"W-what?"

"Don't be afraid. Embrace it," she said as the final warning beep resounded before her final words were cut off. "Some of us find clarity in the darkness of the world."

* * *

The boardwalk bustled with people in the heat of the afternoon, grinning and laughing as they slunk from one ride to another. Nyx's shoulders coiled with a tension that hadn't eased in the saline-encrusted breeze. It had never occurred to her that her mother had been lying, feigning the oblivious mask she'd worn so well. Nor that she'd once lived a life in the shadows with the same men Nyx now sought to … to what? Avoid? Embrace? Something like betrayal wove itself around her ribcage when she thought of Niko and Kade.

For how long she'd be able to hide—or how successful she'd be—she didn't know. A shudder raked up her spine when she thought about what would happen when they found her, because she knew it was only a matter of time, and no amount of wishing or pleading would change that fact. But she also knew something they didn't. That Orion didn't know or wouldn't let himself acknowledge. She wouldn't lie to herself. Not again. Not like she'd done before. She was afraid. That much she knew, but festering inside the terror was something stronger. Something infused with her will that couldn't be broken—*wouldn't* be broken.

It built in her chest like a hurricane, drawing the blistering anger and determination coiling in her chest up amongst the frigid reminders of the vampires who sought to pull her into their blood-stained and malevolent thrall. Her lips curled into a chilling sneer, her irises dark and brimming with something steel-infused. Something clawed at her chest, itching to be freed from its confines as it whispered sickly-sweet promises imbued and stained in blood. She wondered if this dark turn to her thoughts could be faulted to the golden-eyed beasts she'd entangled herself with, or if this was who she truly was.

Lost.

She shook her head with finely veiled resentment, budding like roses in a sped-up summer. Nyx would yield to its siren-like call, but it would be *her choice*. Not theirs. The darkness sang to her, filling her mind with its alluring song until it was all she could hear. A place—if she chose to walk its path—she'd never return from. Never the same anyway, instead vastly changed. Honed in the darkness of the world like a blade, crafted for destruction or great ruin if she wished it. She knew she shouldn't have found satisfaction in the knowledge, that someday *she'd* be as revered as the books of old.

Not by the mortality that seemed to be falling behind her, could she blend back into it, even now? But by the monsters in the form of men.

Gods stained in the crimson-red blood of men. Baneful smiles carved into their faces like the unearthly beings they were, their eyes ablaze with white fire, eclipsed by the unnerving gold that accentuated the colour of their irises. Unnatural ridges twisting their angelic features into something darker, malignant grins split with something bordering good and evil.

The chaos of the boardwalk bled into her ears a moment later when Ares tugged harshly at the leash in her hand, and his erratic barking rushed into her eardrums. She shoved her thoughts away and pulled lightly on the leash, a quick and yet firm tug. His almond eyes were lighter in the sunlight as his tail wagged excitedly and he stared up at her with unwavering adoration.

Neon-green light cast a faint halo around the sled dog and the wooden planks beneath her feet, the faintest trickle of music ghosting her ears before she lifted her gaze to the store in front of her. As she stepped into the familiar comic store, her gaze raking across the shelves of comics, she noted the quietness of the store; empty besides the twins who leant against the paint-chipped counter.

Alexander lifted his head from the paper in front of Tobias, nudging his brother with his elbow as his hazel eyes found hers and a lazy grin stretched across his lips. His hands toyed with the cuffs of his multicoloured striped dress shirt left unbuttoned over a white T-shirt.

"You look like shit," Alexander stated bluntly, grinning from ear to ear.

"Thank you, Alex," Nyx quipped, chuckling lightly as Ares squirmed excitedly.

Tobias shook his head, his eyes brimming with brotherly disappointment. "Seriously?"

"It's fine, Bias," Nyx assured, cutting the younger twin off as her fingers found the hem of her shirt. "I need to ask you something."

Tobias leaned his elbows on the chipped countertop before he urged her to continue with a slight wave of his hand. The stainless-steel bracelet on his left wrist captured her attention for a moment.

"How would someone, hypothetically, kill a vampire?" Nyx grimaced, unsatisfied with herself as she continued, correcting what she truly wanted to know. "That isn't a myth."

Alexander and Tobias shared a look before Alexander rubbed his hands together delightedly, "We know vampires are real, Night," he said in a rush, nudging his younger brother as he rocked on the heels of his feet.

Tobias turned to Nyx with a thoughtful expression, "And we're not the only ones. Our father, for one, thinks you're a creature of the night."

"Your *Dad* thinks I'm a vampire?" Nyx said, almost to herself as she turned his words over in her head.

"Pretty much," Tobias gestured to Alexander with a lazy flick of his wrist, "*We* think he's going to do something stupid with that hunch."

Alexander sobered, ceasing his fidgeting as he glanced down at his brother and then at Nyx, "So please, be careful. Because we both have a feeling that whatever ends up happening won't be good," he urged, imploring her to understand how serious he was.

She hummed softly in acknowledgement, shaking her head with disbelief as a light laugh tumbled from her lips. "This is crazy. You know that right?"

Tobias sighed with frustration, a faintly amused smile itching to grow across his face, "We know. But seriously, Nyx. Be careful."

"I will," she said, turning away from the twins and to the open doorway with Ares at her heels.

She managed a single step before Tobias called out her name and she turned back to face the brothers, "Yes?"

Tobias grinned, throwing a mischievous look towards his brother for a moment. "If you want to get rid of a vampire, Night,"

Alexander smiled crookedly, finishing his brother's sentence without missing a beat, "Drive a s*harp* wooden stake through its heart."

"Just make sure you don't miss," Tobias said.

Nyx nodded once and strode for the exit of the store with an apparent lightness to her stride. Her dark eyes alight with ferocity.

Just make sure you don't miss.

Just make sure you don't miss.

Alexander called after her, "What do you say about a movie day? Like old times."

"When?" she called back.

"Today?" Alexander glanced around the quiet store, pausing on Tobias who shrugged dismissively. "Now?"

"You have a store to run," Nyx said.

Tobias chortled, shaking his head with amusement. "We're our own bosses, Nyx. We can close the store whenever we please. So, what do you say?"

Nyx smiled softly, glancing between the twins she saw as her siblings. "I'd like that … a lot."

She shook her head then—as the twins moved around the store closing up—peering at the sky through a window and watching as the sun hung halfway above the ocean in its descent. Taunting her and the plan forming in her mind whilst effectively reminding her that her time was running out. And that soon, the four men she'd left behind in their cavernous home would come searching for her amongst the blinding lights. That anything good she saw in them wouldn't save her. Not Niko's kind-hearted nature and the protectiveness of his gaze, not Kade's attentiveness and understanding words, not Kotori's silent comfort, guidance and willingness to go up against Orion. Not even Orion's air of authority and his unwavering loyalty to his companions.

Glacier irises flickered before her eyes as she stopped beside the storefront, resting her hip against the brick wall and staring out across the ocean upon the horizon, watching the waves form and collide with the shoreline with a calmness that challenged the churning nerves in her stomach.

Though Orion saw her as nothing more than a *little dove,* she hadn't been lying when she'd fought against Niko and Kade's hands, her fingers itching to wrap themselves around the platinum blond's throat. Because she *would* kill him if it was the last thing she ever did.

And she w*ouldn't* miss.

XXXIV.

Nyx

An artificially-crafted voice crackled through the speakers of the twins' flatscreen, the familiar bone-white slasher mask perpetually stretched into a horrified scream playing across the screen as the opening scene to *Scream* punctuated the silence of the lounge and the second kill of the movie, Casey Becker, darted through her lavish house.

Although Alexander and Tobias's main living space was bathed in the dim afternoon light, it did little to hide the glances they cast toward Nyx, who pretended not to notice. She waited for the moment the duo would falter, quashing their silence beneath the soles of their feet in favour of asking her everything they wanted to know. It amused her—as it'd always amused her—as they fought to uphold their unbothered masks whilst their fingers twitched or brushed the fabric of their pants, giving away their desires to know more than they let on.

Content to let their itch for answers grow, she reappraised the room she lounged in, ingraining the varying tones of browns, blacks, and creams into her skull like the one residing upon the large bookshelf. As odd as the room's setup was, with a black leather couch on one side of the coffee table to a pair of matching armchairs, it suited the twins she'd grown up with. She remembered working with them as they'd painstakingly angled the chairs so they could see the TV from any vantage point. They'd mounted it upon the moderate wall dividing a proportion of the kitchen cabinets from the lounge room.

And, like the first time she'd been in their house above the comic bookstore, her instincts shifted anxiously, gaze darting to the windows and front door as if she expected Orion, Kotori, Niko and Kade to break it down in their pursuit of her. But with a soft sigh, Nyx cast the unbidden anxiety to the depths of her mind before she turned to Alexander without jostling Ares, whose head rested upon her thigh.

"Do you remember when we first watched this?" she said, grinning, chuckling with deeply rooted nostalgia as she turned to Tobias, "He was *terrified* of the opening scene."

"And the way he used to shout at the screen when she answered wrong," Tobias added, rubbing his palms down his thighs with mirth to his dark irises.

Alexander scoffed as he rolled his eyes, "I didn't *yell* at the TV."

"So, what did you call the: 'It was his mother, *she's* the original killer,' profanities? Encouragement?" Nyx goaded, snickering when Alexander opened and closed his mouth like he was trying to respond but his brain wouldn't compute.

"At least I wasn't terrified of mythical 'golden-eyed beasts' after Asher told us *that* story," Alexander quipped, a satisfied glint to his hazel irises.

As unbidden as the knife plunging into Casey Becker's sternum, Nyx stiffened against the memories of blood-stained sand and the sickening stench of burning flesh. The muscles of her shoulders and along her spine locking up as glacier-blue irises with white-gold rings flashed before her eyes, a razor-sharp agony in her throat as the slowly healing wound blistered.

A solid *thump* resonated in her eardrums when Tobias smacked Alexander's shoulder, followed by Tobias's gruff scolding before Alexander whirled toward her and grasped her hands in his.

"I'm sorry, Night. I—I didn't mean it like … *that,*" he said.

Nyx sucked in a deep breath, shaking her head hurriedly like it'd rid her of the memories etched in her mind. "It's fine, Alex," she said. "They're just stories."

Tobias hummed, unconvinced. His dark eyebrows arched whilst he feigned interest in his stainless-steel bracelet.

"We both know *that's* a lie. Don't we?" he said.

"Do we?" Nyx challenged, eyeing him with an eerie tilt of her head.

"How'd you get that wound when you ran into us in the parking lot that night?" Tobias said as he gestured to the silvery marks on the opposite side of the dark, garish scarring, "Or that pale-white scarring?"

"Tobias," Alexander warned, glancing between his younger brother and Nyx. Poised to put himself between them if they decided words weren't enough. They could all recall how the pair as children used to tussle until one accepted defeat.

Nyx's onyx gaze surveyed Tobias frigidly, waiting for a fissure to puncture the dark-eyed twins' façade before she could strike. But, when it didn't falter, like he'd honed his walls, she huffed. *The lion finally found its claws,* she silently mused, finding a brief sense of pride swell within her heart as Tobias's lips tugged into a crooked grin and he reclined into the couch's cushions. Because she remembered the boy he'd once been, the one she'd spent hours comforting whenever Amir would mention their father and how he couldn't make it to whatever event they'd invited him to.

She remembered the boy who had been crushed by the crumbling hopes he'd clutched onto—as she knew he had—it smarted across her skin like a jolt of electricity. She glanced between the twins she called her brothers, weighing up her options and the questions she wanted answered, knowing they'd give her the truth even if she didn't want to hear it.

Almost unsurely, Nyx worried her bottom lip between her teeth, "What *do* you know about vampires? Besides how to kill them," she said.

"Depends on what you want to know," Tobias replied coolly, his eyes narrowing when Alexander blurted:

"Everything!"

Nyx chuckled, shaking her head as she stroked Ares. "Besides stakes, what other weaknesses do they possess?" she asked.

Alexander straightened, grabbing the TV remote before abruptly turning it off. "See, here's the cool part. Stakes kill them, *but* … anything that isn't wooden, or without the intention of killing them like an umbrella, doesn't harm them. If you're looking to weaken or paralyse them, *pure* silver is your friend."

"But of course, you've always got fire or decapitation as a backup. Then again, that'd harm anyone," Tobias added, grinning at Alexander's giddy excitement. Like all the years he had put into researching had finally paid off.

"And the myths?" Nyx prompted, itching to know more about the beings she was entangled with.

"Garlic; they can eat. Like any human food, except it doesn't sustain them for long—" Tobias scoffed when Alexander cut in, fidgeting until he sat on the couch's edge.

"Reflections like mirrors, photos etcetera will appear. They're like us but not. With more strengths than weaknesses. True predators," Alexander said.

"Alex," Nyx urged, reaching out and grasping his hands before he started rambling. "What else are myths?"

"Holy water, crosses and anything religious doesn't have any effect on them," he said. "They don't sleep in coffins or turn into bats, those are just stories vampires created to fool humans."

"Anything else I need to know?" she said.

Alexander appraised her carefully, his eyes lingering on the bite marks on her throat. "*Matebonds,*" he murmured before clearing his throat and speaking more clearly. "Matebonds don't exist. Everything about vampirism is honed upon conscious and untapped desires. *Nothing* is without consent, even if it's a shard of your being that you refuse to accept."

"So, subconsciously you could want that lifestyle …" Nyx began.

"And if you happened to ingest their blood, it'd begin the transition from human to vampire," Tobias supplied, finishing Nyx's sentence.

"But—"

"That's all it takes, Nyx," Tobias stated with steel-cut precision. "It doesn't matter whether you know it or not, if some part of you wants it, all bets are off."

Alexander's fingers ghosted the pale scarring along her throat, startling Nyx before she whirled toward him, and he peered down at her with brotherly concern. His eyes held something she couldn't place, something between anger and understanding. Like he knew something she didn't.

"One more thing, Night," Alexander said, waiting until Nyx impatiently gestured for him to continue. "Their bite can kill you. Not because there's venom or anything, but because one minute you'll survive from the blood loss. And the next, they'll manipulate your blood into thinning without lifting a finger. Altering the thrombopoietin levels until your blood is *extremely* thinned and to the degree of a class four haemorrhage."

Nyx blinked at Alexander, turning his words over in her mind with mute shock. "W-what?" she said.

"You'd be dead in under a minute," Tobias uttered bluntly, toying with the threading of his pants.

"Under a minute?" she echoed.

Tobias hummed, lifting his gaze from his clothes to meet hers. "You're lucky, you know that right?"

For the first time since she had stumbled into the world Orion, Kotori, Niko and Kade traipsed with ease, Nyx couldn't shake the truth of Tobias's words, or the underlying knowledge that she could've been dead. Another face upon the Missing Persons Board. But was it luck that her heart pounded inside her chest? Or the twisted manipulations of men with monstrous natures and blood-stained pasts intent on their pursuit of revenge?

She wished she didn't know, but some sliver of her consciousness did. Crooning the bitter answer within her skull in an orotund-toned voice,

"Welcome to the club, little dove."

Until all she could hear was its honeyed voice and the weight of her actions pressed upon her shoulders. There was no going back now. Not even if she tried. There was only a forward. A path she couldn't stray from, lest she grew lost within the saccharine allure of Orion, Kotori, Niko and Kade's lives. An allure she *couldn't* grow lost in, *couldn't* linger amongst in case she became stranded.

Cursed to forever wander a path with no end, stranded in their darkness with nothing but their bonfires for guidance.

Lost, but never alone.

XXXV.

Nyx

The bookstore's bell chimed pleasantly behind Nyx when she stepped out onto the quieter, slower-paced stretch of the boardwalk. The creased spine of a faded black paperback peeked out from beneath her arm, Ares trotting dutifully along beside her. Neon light plastered the wooden planks with an array of colours. Reds, blues, greens, yellows, and pinks of various shades dancing upon the weather-beaten bookstore in the impending twilight darkening the cloudless sky. She cursed when the darkness registered in her mind, tipping her head back up at the glittering sky with an unending tremor of fear, pulsing through her veins like the beating of a drum.

Her head whipped towards the dankly lit alleyway illuminated by a flickering lamp post, her grasp tightening on Ares's leash as unease curled within her chest. As she turned toward the blinding lights of the bustling boardwalk, she cursed herself and the traitorous sun before she ever-so-slowly turned back to the unnerving darkness that stared back at her like the giant maw of a great beast.

She scoffed, shaking her head and the feeling of being watched away before she urged Ares to follow her back to the welcoming glow of the fairground's lights. "Not tonight," she breathed out, glancing back over her shoulder and to the darkness that seemed to shift under her scrutiny.

Delighted laughter traipsed the night sky as she marvelled at the never-ending life of Celacali's tourist attraction. Her gaze followed a grinning boy and girl who giggled at the Twirling Teacups, their youthful features contorted into matching smiles as they excitedly chattered, before a flash of patchworked skin shifted in her peripherals. She sucked in a sharp breath, her heart jolting in her chest when she whirled to the ever-moving patrons, rising onto the tips of her toes to peer over people's heads. Hoping, and dreading, to find the sandy blond her subconsciousness *knew* slinked amongst the nightlife.

It felt like her nerves crackled in her veins, skittering anxiously through her chest like a swarm of butterflies. Her fingertips dug into the flesh of her palms when she gently led Ares away from the fairground crockery and further into the masses of boardwalk-goers. Seeking safety in the swirling tourists like a sheep sought comfort in its flock. Nyx scolded herself for her flighty behaviour, loathing the *defenceless* demeanour as another *closer* clinking of chains ghosted her forearm with the brush of something metallic.

Wild blond hair wove between the stalls, cyanic irises glinting as Niko peered back over his shoulder at Nyx, winking devilishly at the same moment that gloved hands brushed against the back of her neck and she spun around. Coming face to face with nothing but the life of the boardwalk. Her heart pounded in her ears, betraying her to the men toying with her. Predators toying with their prey.

She turned her head in search of Niko, leading Ares along beside her whilst she wove through people and the neon-lit rides, unnerved when she couldn't find him.

"Nyx."

She startled at the voice whispered in her ear, eyes widening as she twirled. Ares whined uncomfortably beside her, hackles raising before he stared off toward the turning Ferris wheel. Nyx refused to follow his gaze, knowing exactly what she'd find if she did.

Maybe that's why she turned her back on the four sets of eyes searing the flesh of her skin. Or maybe her instincts knew something she didn't. Whatever it was, Nyx didn't contemplate *why* she sidestepped giggling children or wove around elderly couples meandering along the fairground's bustling stretch with Ares. Her heart careened in her chest as if it wished to tear from the dark cavern of her sternum. For the third time that day, Nyx regretted being on the boardwalk and wondered if her time spent bartering with the bookstore's owner had been worth this mind-gripping terror. But she knew she would've regretted walking away from the tome now tucked snuggly beneath her arm, even as terror gripped her—a priceless movie script that she'd been waiting to add to her collection.

"Where are you going, angel?"

Nyx turned towards the playful voice, her gaze searching the patrons passing by obliviously as she came face to face with the same nothingness she'd been gifted with before. Her temper flared, irritated by the unending cycle of torment as her heart pounded in her ears, deafening in all its fear-riddled might. She inhaled deeply, slowly, hoping it'd calm her rattled nerves. Cigarette smoke hung in the air, where before there had been only salt, spiking her nerves and eliciting an unchecked jolt of fear as she turned her head.

As the presence now behind her registered in her mind, Nyx forced herself to continue walking. To mask the galling unease he evoked in her. She wove through the passers-by in a daze before she slipped down the shadowed depths of an alleyway, tossing a glance over her shoulder, her gaze raking the boardwalk-goers. Her back collided with the dankly lit alleyway wall, as she leant heavily upon the cold bricks, trying to calm down. Ares whined. She jumped as purposeful footsteps echoed in her ears, head turning towards the darker depths of the alleyway.

"You know, you should be more careful, *kleintje,*" Kotori drawled when he stepped into the faint light trickling in from the boardwalk.

Her spine straightened subconsciously, remembering the darkness that swirled in his eyes like a storm upon the ocean. Kotori surveyed her closely and Nyx knew she shouldn't waver in the face of a true predator—but she couldn't calm the erratic *tha-thump, tha-thump* of her heart if she tried—and she saw how it captured Kotori's interest.

His head cocked to the side, eyebrows raising as a wolfish grin crept across his face and he stalked closer, his footsteps concise and self-assured. "You never know what's lurking in the shadows," he said.

Nyx scoffed, pushing herself away from the wall and the grinning brunette as she turned her back to him and hurried from the darkness, manoeuvring around a stall selling abstract sculptures, the artist conversing passionately with a young man. Thoughts of the true nature of the dark-haired man shoved to the depths of her mind, rolling like the fabric of a fortune teller's tent as incenses filled her lungs. Her eyes rolled with deft annoyance when his footsteps echoed off the wooden planks and to her ears, his jacket sleeve brushing against her arm as if to remind her of who—or *what*—she'd turned her back on.

"I think I can take a wild guess, Kotori," she said, then paused, angling her head toward him, side-stepping giggling children and glaring teenagers. "And it's not *what* lurks in the shadows. It's *who*."

Annoyance rippled through her chest like a rock colliding with the still surface of a lake before she slipped between stalls and food carts, weaving and side-stepping patrons upon the boardwalk with unveiled determination. Hoping she'd be able to lose the dark-eyed man—and his companions—in the bustling throng of nightlife. She choked back a startled scream when he stepped out from beside the lengthening line of a fairy floss cart, his dark eyebrows arched tauntingly as he perfectly matched his stride to hers.

A smirk played at the edges of his lips as he peered down at her. His umber irises impossibly dark and swirling with unfiltered mirth.

"You're not running away from me, are you?" he said.

"No," Nyx replied hotly.

"No? Then what's the rush?" he said. He paused, stride never faltering as he studied her, grin growing and teeth glinting in the neon lights as he shook his head with taunting amusement, "You're not afraid of me, are you?" he said.

She side-eyed him, her gaze holding his for a moment before flitting back to the ever-changing boardwalk. "I'm not afraid of you," she said.

"Then what's making your heart race?" Kotori asked.

Gravel stones crunched beneath the soles of her shoes as she let Kotori's question hang in the air, passing beneath the neon arch of the boardwalk and into the car park with little thought to the man who walked confidently beside her. The yellow glow of the salt-weathered lights cast eerie shadows across the gravel-flecked pavement bordering the concrete ramp to the beach.

As Ares nipped at her heels, Nyx angled her head toward Kotori, "It races because I don't like being in the presence of murderers," she said.

A darkly malicious chuckle emanated across the star-flecked sky, and she knew, without having to look, whose laugh met her ears. With exaggerated reluctance, Nyx turned towards four familiar stripped-down motorbikes parked in a messy line. Her gaze fell first on Orion, who sat astride his bike with regal ease. His gloved hands rested upon the handlebars as smoke curled up and around him in soft grey wisps. Niko and Kade leant against the concrete railing of the night-plunged beach entrance, passing a joint back and forth as a jolt of uncertainty darted through Nyx's chest—unsure on where she stood with the men after the new information Orion dredged forth and what their relationship was. Were they friends with benefits? Was she somebody to pass between themselves? A pawn on their chess board?

Kade's grin grew impossibly large when he lifted a fingerless-gloved hand and waggled his fingers in a taunting wave, his hazel irises burning with something dark she couldn't place. Niko arched his blond brows, a smile playing at his lips as he brought the joint to his lips. His blue eyes flickered to Ares before he abruptly snuffed the glowing joint upon the railing. Orion raised a perfectly gloved hand as he pulled a creased newspaper from the inner pocket of his jacket and tossed the article to the dirty floor with a smug smirk.

"Now that's hardly fair, little dove," Orion said as he gestured to the bold text splayed across the creased newspaper with a dangerous glint in his eyes. The words *'Body found in an abandoned warehouse South-West of Celacali'* jumping out of the page as she stared down at the article and the familiar blood-stained floor amid the front page's grotesque headline. He waited, allowing the bold letters etched across the front page to register in her mind before he continued with self-satisfaction.

"Considering your hands are just as stained as ours," he said.

Nyx lifted her gaze from the newspaper, eyes narrowed on his grinning face as she tightened her grip on Ares's leash and squared her shoulders. "I'm *nothing* like you," she said.

"When will you stop lying to yourself and *let go*?" Orion said, tutting, lazily gesturing to the others leaning against the railing and to Kotori at her side before he leant forward onto his handlebars. "Join us, Nyx."

"Over my dead body," Nyx said.

Orion cocked his head to the side, eyebrows lifting with the barest annoyance whilst he seemed to contemplate her words. And, for a moment, she panicked. Afraid he'd take them seriously and dispose of her like she'd done with Kai, but she knew he would want to draw out her death. Content with hearing her screams ring out across the night as her blood stained his skin and she begged for it to end. For him to kill her. Almost like he knew, Orion shook his head slowly, ensuring she saw it before Kade seamlessly pushed himself off the railing and crossed the gravel-flecked pavement.

An arm wrapped around her shoulder as Niko appeared, easily slipping behind her and resting his chin upon her shoulder before drawing in a deep lungful of her scent. With exaggerated reluctance, he lifted his head from the crook of her throat, lips ghosting her ear.

"Aw, chica. You don't mean that. Does she, Kade?" Niko said.

"Not in the slightest," Kade responded; his face stretched in a grin so wide it was unnerving. "I would *kill* to see her covered in blood again though. Wouldn't you, Kotori?" he crooned mischievously, lifting his hand to his mouth to hide his dark smile.

Nyx lifted her head to peer up at Kotori, watching as Kotori's lips pulled into an almost wistful smile. He tipped his head up to the sky and angled his head away, jaw ticking like it took all his strength to right himself and the steadfast demeanour he possessed. Nyx didn't know what to think as he closed his eyes and breathed in deeply, shaking his head before he opened his eyes and turned back towards her.

Kotori's soulful gaze shifted from Nyx to Kade as that wolfish grin etched itself into his dark skin. His earring swung deftly in his left ear, the deep timbre of his voice eliciting a delightful shiver down her spine.

"It would be a fucking sight to see," he said.

"I'm not killing anyone else just to quell your *twisted* fantasies," Nyx stated firmly, eyeing each biker in turn.

"C'mon angel. It'll be fun," Kade purred, stepping forward and effectively trapping her between himself and Niko.

"I'm not going *anywhere* with a*ny* of you," Nyx said. She paused, arching her eyebrow as Kade opened his mouth to protest, standing her ground amid her uncertainty of their dynamic.

Orion's lips twisted into a smirk radiating an immense swell of satisfaction as he laughed with cold delight, "There's no going back now, *little dove,* and there's certainly *nowhere* you can hide where we won't find you," he said.

All emotion leeched from her eyes when she peered over Kade's shoulder and levelled a simmering glare in his direction. "Fuck you, Orion," she said.

Kade's honeyed irises met hers as his eyes widened and he quickly stepped aside with a swift, warning shake of his head. Niko's arm fell away from her shoulder before he slipped around her and strode towards her red Honda. The sight of her bike jolted Nyx, as she warily looked to Kotori for some sort of guidance—her sole beacon of light as she grappled at the distorted ones she associated with Kade and Niko, hoping to find *something* to make sense of her turmoil.

But, as the muscle in Kotori's jaw ticked, she knew none would come. In some way, she'd somehow pissed them all off with her sharply snapped words. But she wouldn't allow herself to regret them. Not even if everything inside her screamed at her in both warning and disapproval. Two never-ending pieces of a puzzle that fought against the other, desperate to come out victorious while the other faded and crumbled.

Left with the consequences of her actions, Nyx lifted her chin in the only act of defiance she could think of. Tensing her back as she squared her shoulders, she forced her hands to quell their faint tremoring, refusing to lower her gaze as Orion's fingertips drummed the metal of his handlebar. A tense silence hung thickly in the air as he studied her without emotion, the barest twitch of his lips the only indication he found her defiance amusing.

"Get on," he finally ordered, his voice oozing an unnatural power-filled command.

A garbled whine spilled from Nyx's lips before she screwed her eyes shut and forced herself to fight the ethereal power urging her—*forcing her*—to move against her wishes. Her conscious mind reared up, thumping its enraged fists upon the glass-like dome staunching its control over the rest of her body. Pounding against the clear prison it had become trapped behind until its fists bled, staining the divide with the blood of itself before it rested in defeat. But Nyx fought on as the *good* half of her soul gave up, thrashing against the chilling confines burrowing its claws into her flesh and tearing at the skin as it painfully warned her to comply, to surrender to its unearthly command.

She forced her eyes open, irises brimming with a pain that matched the throbbing in her temples whilst she fought his command. Horror bled into her eyes when her legs moved, carrying her towards Orion and his deep, dark smile, enthralled by the fight she possessed as her feet stopped mere inches from his bike. A pained gasp spilled from her lips when she forced herself to stop, to fight. Orion watched as Nyx bared her teeth in a sneer, tightening her grasp on Ares' leash, shaking her head like it'd rid her of his presence in her mind—of the control he had over her.

"Fighting it only makes it worse," Orion crooned, twisting a key in his bike's ignition, and plunging her ears with the deft roar of its engine.

Nyx's poorly constructed control slipped as her body moved of its own accord and Ares followed her obliviously, bringing her closer to Orion and his idling bike. His charismatic smirk grew when she swung her leg over the back of his bike, her hand clutching his shoulder as she situated herself numbly behind him and the leather seat seeped through her jean-clad thigh with the rumbling engine. Nyx's forehead creased when her gaze followed the swift movement of Kade and Niko—coupled with the burning sting of betrayal as Niko pushed away from her bike and came to stand beside her—unlooping Ares's leash from around her wrist, picking Ares up from beside Orion's bike before carrying the Malamute towards *his* bike.

It shouldn't have hurt as much as it did, watching as he tucked Ares safely into the black duffel back strapped onto the back of his bike, but it did. It ripped down her chest, slicing through bone and muscle whilst she struggled in the dome-like prison hand-crafted by Orion. *He won't do anything, angel,* a voice said in her mind. Her eyes screwed shut as if it'd block out the memories plaguing her mind and the promises she'd believed. Again. She blinked them back, lifting her gaze as she searched for Kade. A Doppelgänger pain lodging itself in her chest as it twisted like a knife, slicing a jagged path beside the marks Niko left behind.

Kade moved as swiftly as Niko, grasping the worn handle grips of her bike before he pushed it toward the dense tree line bordering the rusted fence of the beach. She wondered what she'd done in a past life to deserve this upending spiral of pain as he disappeared between two cars and into the shadowed depths of the forest. Returning moments later, she watched as he joined Niko on his own bike, fingerless-gloved hands tapping anxiously against his handlebars.

I won't let him. Not this time, or ever again.

She wanted to laugh at the bitter sting of Kade's words, but she couldn't. Forced to watch as they took pieces of her and hid them away, one left in the shadowed depths of the woods, the other shifting with naïve wonder in a slightly unzipped bag behind Niko.

Niko, Kade, and Kotori brought their bikes to life, twisting the throttles with little thought as baneful smiles spread across their faces and their howls of delight rang out across the sky.

As if Orion could sense her thoughts, he turned and peered over his shoulder at her, a long slow smile carved sinfully amid his stubble-dusted jawline that *shouldn't* have been as attractive as it was.

"I *hate* you," she spat through gritted teeth.

Orion chuckled darkly, his gloved fingers cradling her chin as he tipped her head back so the only thing she could see, smell, hear or think was clouded by his charismatically dangerous presence. "Your illusion of control is merely that. An *illusion*," he said.

She opened her mouth to speak, the protest on the tip of her tongue fizzling out as he leant impossibly close. His unnaturally pleasant breath warmed her face before his lips brushed hers and his gaze carved straight through her steel-infused guards, reducing them to nothing but rubble as he sifted through the various emotions like someone turning the pages of a book.

"You can't win this, Nyx, but I'll enjoy every second of breaking your *fragile* beliefs until there's nothing left but darkness," he said, with unwavering conviction.

He pressed his lips to hers then, a possessiveness entangled in his actions, his grasp tightening the barest fraction upon her chin as she unknowingly succumbed to his touch and grew lost in the feel of *him*. The grounding pressure of his fingertips on her chin as his teeth tugged at her bottom lip, his tongue licking the slight sting seconds later. A niggling feeling warned her she didn't want this, but it fell away as her hands moved to steady herself on the black lapels of his jacket.

Orion pulled away from her several seconds later, his gloved thumb trailing along the flesh of her bruised bottom lip as he surveyed her with churning irises.

He leant down to press a final, lingering kiss to her bruised lips before his thumb caressed her cheek. Something dangerous shone in the depths of his eyes. He observed her silently, watching her scramble for footing with terrible delight.

"There's no one left to save you but yourself, little dove," he whispered, mocking her and the shambles she called her life. "You're *ours*. And we'll continue to remind you. Until there's nothing left but us … and the blood that w*ill* stain your perfect skin."

XXXVI.

Nyx

Seagulls cawed in the distance, their cries rippling off the cavernous walls and through the silent cave, a salt-gilded breeze blowing through the natural tunnelways, a soft sigh that brushed Nyx's skin, reminding her of Ares as he dozed somewhere within the cave. She worried for the Malamute whom she hadn't seen in days, his playful barks and lonely whines drifting through the cave like a restless spirit. A painful reminder of the figurative knife lodged in her chest, or back, that sustained a festering rage.

She'd been foolish—*naïve*—in her pursuit of belonging. Of finding herself in the blinding and ever-changing lights of the boardwalk filled with the unending and enthralling laughter and calliope music. She berated herself and her decisions whilst she tried to centre herself and the crashing swell of her mind, wondering how she could've missed the tangled vines that had woven around her legs, slicing her skin with their razor-sharp thorns until they became impossible to remove. Her mind was overcome with a flight-like urge to bolt if Orion reappeared from the tunnelway he'd disappeared down, terrified of the unearthly power he possessed.

But where the sunlight now eased her churning thoughts, it also served as a bitter reminder that once its comforting rays of light disappeared below the horizon, she'd be at the mercy of monsters in the guises of men. Those men with beast-like natures who blended in amongst the bustling nightlife of Celacali, but she supposed that was part of their appeal. She scoffed bitterly at the thought, the sound echoing off the walls and back to her ears, unable to shake the hurt Niko and Kade's actions had elicited—or lack thereof—or the lashing sting their part in Ares's absence caused to smart across her skin. The Malamute was tucked somewhere in the labyrinth tunnels she'd never reach.

Nyx understood the charismatic and enigmatic way they carried themselves, like they feared nothing and nobody. And it had not surprised her when Niko had breezily admitted to the ease with which their victims followed them to their demises—walking themselves into the slaughterhouse—because she could understand the level of physical attraction. She knew better than most. What would be the point in denying it? The two pale-white bite marks on her throat would contradict her anyway. But she couldn't pinpoint *what exactly* made them so … addictive and alluring. And a part of her didn't want to know, content to stay safely tucked away in the darkness of the unknown, if only she could *stop* thinking about it.

They invaded her mind like a virus, infecting every healthy cell in her body whilst her white cells sought to attack the intruder, effectively attacking her red blood cells in their pursuit to protect her from the harmful virus embedding itself into her bloodstream. Nyx wondered why it bothered to save her if it would destroy itself in the process. Wouldn't it be easier to just let her succumb to whatever sickness had latched itself onto her than to fight an already lost battle? She knew that was what this was. A battle she'd already lost two years ago beneath a full waxing moon with torn and bloodied knuckles.

As her thoughts hung heavy in her mind, she shoved herself up from the beaten couch and crossed the unusually decorated living space to the tunnel entrance, guiding herself down the tunnel with her hand running along the uneven walls before she slipped pass the oddly shaped door. The shrill call of seagulls grew stronger the closer she shuffled to the entrance, the thunderous crashing of the waves brushing past her tracksuit-clad legs and into the cavernous hideaway. She climbed a single flight of stairs with white knuckles, gripping the swaying staircase's handrail and quickly scampering up the groaning steps.

Despite her better judgement, she peered down to the crashing waves below, breathing in a harsh gasp of breath before gingerly sitting down with her back pressed against the cliff face, tipping her head up to the cloud-flecked sky. She regretted leaving the cave when the staircase swayed uneasily in the buffering winds, whipping her hair around her face, sea spray plastering her skin. Her dark lashes kissed her cheeks when she closed her eyes, the crashing of waves roaring in her ears, a welcome white noise.

A part of her knew she shouldn't find comfort in the fading rays of sunlight. The same part of her being that urged her to run and hide, to *forget* the pain dripping down her chest like blood collecting on the floor of an abandoned warehouse deep in the grasp of a shadow-blanketed forest. But she couldn't purge herself of the immense feeling of a surety she felt when she opened her eyes and smiled.

The sky above bled pink, purple, yellow, and orange in a startingly and yet mesmerising smear of colour whilst the sun sank beneath the horizon. Nyx had always loved sunsets, finding the ethereal colours crafted by the gods as beautiful as she found the night. She supposed it made sense, that she loved the sunset before the night's darkness.

For there was never one without the other.

Her mind lurched in a jagged spiral of thought, pushing, and pulling her in every direction as the past weeks she'd lived in Celacali caught up with her, snatching her from one flash of memory to another; ethereal whispers of her name in a dark forest, her father's slate irises ablaze with decades-old memories, a crimson-stained hilt of a snake embellished dagger, delighted howls beneath a star-flecked sky, and the rumble of motorbikes. Two pairs of hands ghosting across her bonfire-warmed skin, leather gloves cupping her chin. The bitter sting of betrayal, a darkly immovable promise of bloodshed, and concerned brown eyes warning of a plan that could go wrong.

As the sun steadily descended beneath the white-capped sea and the vibrant colours staining the clouds trickled away, the sound of footsteps carried to her on the breeze. She turned toward the cave's entrance, peering down the first flight of stairs with guarded irises. Dark, ebony hair danced in the wind, whipping around Kotori's back in a way that reminded Nyx of the fierce warriors depicted in the legends of old. Against her better judgement, her instincts grasped the reins of control, sending her heartbeat into a frenzy of panic-stricken *tha-thump, tha-thump*'s.

She turned her gaze away from the dark wisdom-filled brown of his irises, staring down at the waves as they formed and rolled into the beaten cliff face with a deafening rumble. Water vapour cascaded upward like the glittering of a million minuscule diamonds tossed into the wind. The weather-beaten stairs creaked out their protests as Kotori climbed each step with wolfish confidence, sparing the dangerous drop a fleeting glance before he sat down on the swaying platform, dangling his legs carelessly over the ledge, as if the prospect of falling didn't terrify him.

Kotori's gaze burrowed into the side of her face for several moments before he turned his head and stared out to the greying horizon.

"What's on your mind, *kleintje*?" he said. A beat of silence followed when he turned back to her, a sad smile flickering over his face, "You've been avoiding us."

I'm planning on murdering your bleached-blond buddy, Nyx thought, staring down at the relentless waves. But, instead of voicing her thoughts aloud, she rolled her eyes. Her gaze narrowed on the darkening skyline with a disgruntled shake of her head and a feigned smile quirking the edges of her lips. "Are you surprised? Is it so hard to see that what you're doing is wrong?"

"Is it wrong because you *think* it is, or because society *told* you it was?" Kotori pressed, surveying her carefully like he was studying the components of a science experiment before he turned back to the soft beginnings of stars in the greying hours of twilight. "We've all done horrible things to survive. Some of us have just found comfort in its ruination of right and wrong," he said.

Nyx pursed her lips, mulling over his philosophical words with unveiled curiosity. She studied him in the softening light, everything about him marred by something dark—something *appealing*. For a moment, she wondered if she could trust this man beside her and then cursed her own foolishness. She'd trusted Kade and Niko, and both had—knowingly or not—driven a jagged blade into her back. So now, her gaze wavered as she fought the urge to shove herself up from the decaying wood and climb the stairs to the steady surface above. Should she confide in him or should she put as much distance between them as possible?

"How'd you know?" she allowed herself to whisper, dropping her gaze to the unruly waters as Kotori turned to her.

"How'd I know what?" he said.

She sighed, rubbing her face with her hands before she inched closer to the edge of the platform and swung her legs over the ledge. "How'd you know this life was for you?"

"I didn't," he replied. "I just knew that if I didn't join Orion ... I would die."

Nyx frowned, lifting her gaze from her lap and to Kotori, patiently waiting for him to continue. And, with a deep chuckle, he did.

"Like Kade and Niko, I was ... dying when Orion found me in 1502. I had been left beaten to within an inch of my life for the wolves to finish off," he said humourlessly as he licked his lips, lifting a ring-clad hand to finger his tribunal necklace. His Adam's apple bobbed in his throat as he swallowed. "A fate worse than death in my culture, but the men who left me for dead found it ironic."

"Ironic how?" Nyx asked cautiously as she prepared for an ugly response. If he gave her one at all.

Kotori turned to peer down at her, his dark gaze clashing with hers, "Wolves are sacred in some cultures. Mine was no different," he said as he rubbed at the nape of his neck with a large hand, gnawing at the inside of his cheek as he tried to find a way to explain his backstory. "My tribe saw wolves as gods in animal form. Protectors and bringers of life or death ... but the ultimate legend told from generation to generation was what became of a Levenloos man or woman in the presence of a lone grey wolf."

"A lone wolf? Wouldn't a pack be ... deadlier?" Nyx asked.

He shook his head, mirth dancing in his eyes. "Traditionally, yes. But this lone wolf wasn't revered for its *normalcy.* This wolf was my tribe's equivalent of the Grim Reaper, but it was something different altogether. *Levenloos,* we called it," he said. His gaze darkened with the deep, unwavering timbre of his voice, "Lifeless."

"You—"

Kotori dipped his head in a curt nod, confirming her unspoken question.

"*Levenloos* was an omen of death, and we chose to adhere to its simplicity by keeping its name as unremarkable as my tribe believed death to be." He turned his gaze to the white-capped sea with a faint, pained smile, the black of his lip ring glinting in the soft light, "I was twenty-seven at the time when the world we knew fractured and brought with it a tide of death we *never* could've prepared for."

Nyx swallowed the lump in her throat, afraid to urge him to continue, "What happened?" she asked.

"The same as what always happens, *kleintje*. Dozens ... upon *dozens* of innocents were slaughtered; butchered because some men could, and we were different," he said. His words were final.

"I'm *so* sorry, Kotori," Nyx said as she breathed out, reaching forward, and clasping his large hand in her much smaller one.

He smiled softly down at her, the corners of his eyes crinkling. The gesture was so unlike him that it reminded her of Kade before she could dismiss it.

"Don't be," he said, smiling. "It's not your fault. It's something that happened hundreds of years ago." His thumb traced intricate circles into the back of her hand before his gaze dropped to their interlaced fingers. "I appreciate the ... empathy and curiosity. It says more about who *you are* than what the world wants you to be."

Nyx nodded slowly as Kotori's words rippled through her, growing conflicted by the past events that stained her soul in more ways than one. Her gaze dropped to her lap before she pulled her hands from his, a troubled crease in her forehead as she worried her bottom lip between her teeth. Kotori's curious stare pierced the side of her face as she wrung her hands anxiously in her lap, mind swirling with thoughts quicker and more intense than she could comprehend.

Uncertainly, she lifted her gaze to the imploring and yet reassuring brown of Kotori's eyes. The subtleness of his woodsy scent calmed her mind when she breathed in a steadying breath of air, "What if I'm not any better than those men?" she finally said.

"You are *not* those men," Kotori assured firmly, leaning down so his gaze was levelled with hers. "The things they did are their faults alone. Never yours."

"But—"

"You can't fix the past, Nyx, but you can learn from it," he said.

"If I'd learnt from my past, I wouldn't be in this situation with my best friends' father *thinking* I'm a vampire," Nyx muttered.

"What?" Kotori said, sharply.

Nyx chuckled, "Oh yeah," she drawled, kicking her feet over the ledge like she would on a swing. "My childhood friends warned me that their father would do something stupid based on his suspicions that I was like you; a vampire."

Something dark flashed in Kotori's eyes before he masterfully masked it.

"Your *friends'* father being …?"

"They only warned me to be careful," she answered, avoiding the question. She lifted her gaze from the ocean to the Levenloos man with an easy grin, "… and how to properly kill a vampire, if the need should arise."

"Huh?" Kotori said. He nodded his head slowly, a wolfish grin growing across his face as he matched her energy with predatory ease. "Their father wouldn't happen to be a *Montes,* would he?"

Nyx's expression faltered, "He is …" she confirmed, eyeing him warily.

Kotori loosed a dark laugh before slowly nodding. Perfectly portraying the mask of a man's contempt at the answers he'd been given, he turned his gaze to the horizon. Her instincts screamed at her then, warning of the eerie calm, urging her to run as far and fast as her legs could carry her. But, like so many times before, she stayed them and refocused her attention on his apologetic smile. She froze as his dark gaze locked upon her, her heart thumping obnoxiously.

Before it fully registered in her mind, Nyx's palms pressed into the wooden staircase, and she jolted upright. Whirling onto the balls of her feet in a movement as fluid as water before she scrambled toward the first few steps, clutching the railing as it swayed in the wind. A terror-stricken scream tore from her throat as her shoes scraped the first stair, and large hands grasped her forearms in a movement faster than light.

Kotori hauled her back toward the spot in which she'd sat, swiftly tugging her onto his jean-clad lap in an iron-infused grasp. She sucked in a harsh breath of air bordering on a whimper as her struggles grew with the lightening of his irises. Now they bled white-gold and his features sharpened into those ridged vampiric planes that haunted her fitful dreams. She couldn't move.

Kotori held her terrified gaze, solid, still, unwavering.

"Please forgive me, *kleintje,*" he said, his words terrible in their meaning.

Nyx's eyes widened in horror as his gaze seemed to soften with wolfish determination, his fingertips brushing her curls over her shoulder with a gentle sweep of his hand—rivalling his intentions—so he could bare her throat to his unnatural gaze. He held her gaze for a moment that seemed to stretch forever.

Nyx shook her head vehemently, straining against the easy manner Kotori trapped her to his chest. "No, Kotori. Please … don't."

His face twisted into a mask of reassurance as he bent to press a kiss to the crown of her head, speaking in a whisper laced with something unnervingly soothing.

"Don't fight it, Nyx. It makes it worse than it has to be," he said.

Her heartbeat filled her ears, the frantic pulse echoing in the depths of her eardrums so all she could hear was the mounting terror in her chest, she screwed her eyes shut, gasping air into her lungs as a fear-riddled sheen of sweat covered her skin.

Then Kotori did a strange thing. He placed his palm on her chest, over her heart, to calm its panicked beating. She saw him close his eyes and breathe in deep.

"Calm, Nyx. Be calm," he said.

And suddenly, the fight went out of her as instead, she forced herself to calm. Quieting her racing heart and churning thoughts with each breath of oxygen in her lungs. Her breath caught when Kotori's lips tenderly brushed against the curve of her bared throat, pressing a chaste kiss to the pulsing vein of her jugular, the brush of his lip ring against her skin sending a shiver down her spine. His ebony locks brushed teasingly against her skin in the saline-encrusted wind. The smell of him enveloped her senses, the scent of freshly fallen rain, copper, and something earthy. How carefully he moved, like every motion was calculated and measured as his fingers tangled in her curls and he gently angled her head further back. Nyx felt herself letting go, and her gaze locked on the glittering stars above.

"I'm not going to bite you here," he assured, tracing her jugular with his fingers before he trailed them four or five inches away from her pulsing artery and to a spot in line with her earlobe, applying the slightest pressure to the spot with a self-satisfied hum. "But here, your blood will still flow but it won't *kill you*."

"But Orion—"

Kotori tutted playfully, tracing the darkened outline of Orion's still-healing bite mark with his fingertips. "If he wanted to kill you, he would've torn into your jugular. But he didn't. And neither do I," he said.

"Why?" Nyx said. It was the best she could come up with, all things considered.

"I don't want to kill you, Nyx," Kotori said as he kissed the place beneath Orion's dark bite—the first man whose mark she couldn't forget—seemingly marking where he planned to sink his teeth into her skin. "And neither do they … despite what Orion w*ants* you to believe."

As Nyx opened her mouth to speak, Kotori's elongated fangs sank into her neck. A strangled gasp of surprise wrenched from her lips, mind reeling at the sensation of his elongated incisors and canines in her throat. His grasp tightened in her hair whilst the hand he'd traced her throat with skittered to her waist.

Nyx's thoughts flew. At first, flung far and then boomeranging back as she found herself wondering how she'd never noticed this ethereal blend of pain and pleasure with Kade and Niko. She supposed it made sense, why everything felt so intense. So *divine.* But now—when she wasn't blinded by lust-filled kisses and the pleasures of skin on skin—she scrambled for purchase in her endorphin-filled mind. Lost in the blinding euphoria carried in her bloodstream and filling her mind, clouding it with something so *tantalising* she couldn't stop herself from bowing into Kotori's firm grasp and baring more of her throat to him.

The quickening *tha-thump* of her heartbeat filled her eardrums with each mouthful of blood he sucked into his mouth. Nyx knew she should've been terrified that he wouldn't stop, but something assured her he would. Even if it was to ensure his investment lived. And, despite the naïvety of her thoughts, she latched onto their surety and batted away the creeping dread. It took everything in her to suppress a needy whine as spots danced across her eyelids, and she felt herself being drawn out. It was a true paradox, she thought in a detached way, the faint chill creeping into her bones and the comforting warmth from Kotori's chest. To be embraced by death and to embrace it back.

Her grasp loosened and tightened sporadically on Kotori's jacket-clad shoulders and, though Nyx knew she shouldn't have, she couldn't stop the soft and albeit needy moan that escaped her parted lips as Kotori retracted his fangs from her throat and his tongue dragged across the weeping bite marks left behind. As he lifted his head from her throat, he peered down at her with dark searching irises, surveying every inch of her oblong features with ridged-less features.

Nyx blinked blearily up at him, fighting to stay alert as the spots in her vision became clouds, and the blinding endorphins fled her bloodstream, leaving her with nothing but the overwhelming urge to succumb to sleep.

He kissed her lips then, and she blinked sluggishly as she tasted herself. Her eyelids fluttered shut and plunged her into a swirling darkness between consciousness and unconsciousness. The sea-salt-infused breeze filled her nostrils as Kotori readjusted her in his arms, one hooked beneath her knees as they rose.

She was only dimly aware of him cradling her bridal-style to his bared chest before the deep, wistful timbre of his voice filled her ears,

"I *can't* feel that pain again, kleintje. Because I wouldn't make it through the pain of losing them ... or you," he said.

His words seemed to come from very far away as the bleak darkness of sleep pulled her into its abyss.

* * *

Voices drifted in and out of focus, the noises growing and fading in Nyx's ears as the plush cushions of a couch cradled her and she scrambled to push her fatigue away so she could open her eyes. A futile effort as exhaustion embedded itself into the marrow of her bones, her strength stripped from her in the aftermath of Kotori's actions.

"You *can't* do that," came Kotori's frustrated voice, capturing her shifting focus beneath the darkness of her eyelids.

"Why not?" came Kade's response, sounding closer to her than Kotori.

A drawn-out sigh echoed across the room and Nyx could picture the look Kotori sent his companion, etched with exasperation.

"Because the twins have nothing to do with this *or* our revenge. You can't do that to her," he said.

"Think about it, Kotori. If we get rid of them, as well as her family, she'll *need* us," Kade said.

Niko's snicker traipsed past her ears, the couch dipping as he sat beside her. "No, Kade. She'll hate you. And all of this will be for nothing."

"But—" Kade protested, cut off by his two companions.

"*No,*" Kotori and Niko said in unison.

A huff sounded from the patchworked blond as though the aversion to his ideas annoyed him, and Nyx found she was grateful for their defiance. Grateful that they were willing to put Alexander and Tobias' lives above their bloodied revenge scheme. It seemed that a fraction of humanity existed within them, despite the darkness they favoured.

Niko almost sounded disappointed as he spoke, his fingers ghosting her forearm. "Sometimes ... you and Orion are *too much* alike. We don't need senseless bloodshed."

"We need blood to survive, sure, but we don't *need* to kill innocents," Kotori said. "Hell, we could survive off every *corrupt* person and never need to harm an innocent ... That's what we *should* be doing."

Kade's baneful laughter clamoured in her eardrums. "There's only so much bad in the world, Kotori. How long would it sustain us?"

"What Kotori means—" Niko began before Kade cut him off.

"I know what he means—what you both mean. I'm just saying what we're all thinking," Kade said.

"No, you're not," Niko said with a certainty Nyx felt in her chest. "If we give up all our humanity, then we're no better than the 'corrupt' mortals we kill. If we give it up, we're monsters. And I don't *want* to be a monster."

Before Nyx could hear Kade and Kotori's response, the dark abyss of unconsciousness wrenched her back into its embrace.

XXXVII.

ALEXANDER

A ghostly breeze howled through the bricked apartment complex, racing through the gaps in the foundations as Alexander angled his head, straining to hear movement behind the door his fist hovered above. Tobias leant against the opposing wall, chipped red bricks pressing into the bared flesh of his shoulder, his boot-clad foot tapping impatiently upon the scuffed hardwood floor outside their father's front door, disdain-leeched glances thrown to the darkly stained door from across the hall.

"Wait," Alexander began, cocking his head further to the side as he plastered a hopeful expression across his face and shoved the urge to laugh aside.

"What? What do you hear?" Tobias urged, subconsciously leaning away from the wall and closer to his brother.

Alexander's lips curled into a lopsided grin, turning his head away from the door and to Tobias with a mischievous glint in his eyes, "I think, that if you glare hard enough at the door. It *might* open," he said.

Tobias's eyebrows slanted before he rolled his eyes—reminding Alexander of their father. "You're an idiot."

"But you love me regardless," Alexander said.

"Stuck with you, you mean," came his brother's reply.

Alexander's eyes widened with mock surprise, his hand on his heart as he jokingly stumbled away from the door, "Your words wound me, brother," he said.

"Your presence wounds me," Tobias grumbled, fighting a losing battle not to laugh.

"Just admit it, you'd be lost without me, Bias," Alexander said, fist hovering above the closed door with the rusted numbers screwed into it.

"We *have* to do this, Alex. For Nyx," Tobias gently urged from behind him, sensing the waning determination in his older brother like only he could.

And for that, Alexander was grateful. "I know," he murmured, rapping his knuckles upon the wooden door.

Tobias offered him a reassuring smile, knocking his shoulder against Alexander's in a gesture that reminded Alexander of when they were children. A time so much simpler than the one they manoeuvred through without the stability of their father. Though he supposed their father had never truly been a 'father'. Not in the traditional sense at least. That title had fallen to Amir—their uncle—who'd spent more time with them than Ryder ever had, ensuring they both had some form of stability growing up. He supposed that was why this would be so easy, because their father didn't *know* them.

He shared a knowing look with Tobias, when the wooden door swung open, and they met Ryder's deeply engrained scowl. Alexander bit down on his bottom lip, dropping his gaze to the scuffed floorboards to hide the upward tilt of his lips as his mind registered the disarray of their father's appearance. Undoubtedly from the sleepless nights resulting from the first plan to dance across his mind.

"Boys," Ryder Montes half-grumbled in acknowledgement, dipping his head in a curt nod before he stiffly stepped aside to let them in.

Alexander nudged Tobias, urging his younger brother to feign nonchalance.

Ryder had the decency to grimace, following his youngest son's swift retreat into the industrial-styled one-bedroom, one-bathroom home.

"He's still mad at me, I see," Ryder said to Alexander.

"What'd you expect? You've barely been a part of our lives," Alexander cut his father off when Ryder opened his mouth to rebut his eldest son's words. "You've missed more birthdays than I can count, and your *brother* practically raised us. We're here for one reason and one reason alone, *Dad,*" he stated, waltzing past his father and down the hallway to the open-planned apartment.

The front door closed with a soft click behind him before Ryder followed his sons to the large living space that masterfully made the apartment seem larger and less quaint. A large arched window filled the room with natural light, basking the ceiling and walls in a welcoming hue that glided across the hardwood floors. The raw, brushed bricks continued into the living space, meeting the arched windows on either side.

Tobias sprawled out over a leather, three-seater couch, TV remote in hand with his boot-clad feet propped up on an antique trunk-coffee-table, as if he were a fixture.

Alexander took in the lavishly designed apartment, turning to his father with a displeased quirk to his eyebrows, "Myth busting's going well, I see," he said.

Ryder shrugged as he crossed the room and sat in an ash-coloured armchair beside an ironwood box, "Well, enough."

"Enough that you can't be bothered to call?" Tobias quipped, levelling a dangerous glare at their father. "It takes about a minute to dial a number and wait for it to ring, but then again, I wouldn't have been surprised if we never bothered to *pick up*."

"Tobias," Alexander warned, his back to his father and brother as his fingertips trailed over the glossy covers of assorted magazines spread across the oak four-seater, dining table.

"He's—"

"The only reason we're here, Tobias, is for Nyx, remember?" Alexander said.

Tobias folded his arms across his chest, "I know," he said.

Alexander nodded, "You've seen those guys she's been hanging around for the past few days, right?" he said to their father.

"The bikers on the boardwalk?" Ryder said.

Alexander clicked his fingers, a delightfully feigned smile of attainment flickering across his face when Tobias dropped his gaze to his lap. He artfully contorted his features into a disgusted scowl. "Yeah, those *wannabe punks,*" he said.

The faintest fissure appeared in Ryder's expression of nonchalance, head angling as a frown spread across his aged features, "Three blonds and a brunette, right?"

Tobias turned to their father; both boys playing the confused children they knew their father thought them to be.

Alexander forced himself to be calm, to hide any budding satisfaction under his father's muddy gaze as suspicion gave way to something sweeter that tolled in his head like a bell tower. It rang so fiercely in his mind that he was sure, if not for the silence plunged across the apartment, the sound would've reverberated through the coastal city of Celacali.

"Everyone's shit-scared of them," Tobias supplied with feigned disdain, his fingers toying with the stainless-steel bracelet around his right wrist.

"It's like they're the kings of Celacali," Alexander added.

"*Kings?*" Ryder chuckled without amusement, his fingertips drumming the armrest of his chair. "Those bikers—*bloodsuckers*—are only kings because they've killed anyone who crosses them," he said.

"You think they're bloodsuckers?" Alexander questioned, layering doubt thickly into his voice. "I thought they were just stories you told us as kids?"

"They can't be real, right, Dad?" Tobias said.

"You're further from the truth than I'd like you to be, boys. Because while you've been running the comic store, bloodsuckers have been stalking the boardwalk," Ryder stated, eyeing his sons with a fierceness that pleased Alexander more than he'd care to admit.

"So that leaves us with one choice then, doesn't it?" Alexander prompted, playing into their father's newly established trust.

"We've got to get rid of them ..." Tobias said, frowning and blowing out an exaggerated breath of air before he rubbed the balls of his hands into his face. "But how? How do you get rid of *vampires*?"

Ryder smiled. The truest smile Alexander had ever seen from their father before he pushed himself up and out of his chair, rubbing his hands together with blatant glee.

"I have a plan for that," Ryder said.

As their father's words hung thickly in the air, Alexander couldn't shake a feeling of pure delight. The mischievous spark in his irises crackled into something else. Something that burned like a wildfire through forest, burning through his bloodstream, searing him from the inside out. He shared a knowing look with Tobias and they both turned to their father, who had begun pacing the floor.

Alexander knew, like Tobias did, that they'd fooled their father without truly trying to. Using nothing but mediocre acting and their father's resentment of the beasts from his past. Falling for the same manipulations the notorious monsters of mankind used—leading Ryder astray with nothing but his own beliefs.

Tobias—the voice of reason—masked his satisfaction, "Is there anything we can do to help?" he said.

Ryder nodded curtly, his brown eyes dropping to the watch around his wrist before a string of colourful profanities tumbled from his lips and he rushed about the living space in search of his car keys. His gaze flitted between his sons like he was weighing up the odds of telling them something. With a deep sigh of resignation, he said,

"Be at Elveszett Bluff in three days around noon, and we'll see if you can be of any help."

Alexander nodded eagerly, pinching Tobias's thigh between his fingers, and effectively prompting his brother to speak with a stifled yelp of surprise.

"Count us in," Tobias squeaked.

Ryder nodded, a pleased expression on his face before he turned away and strode towards the front door, pulling it open in one moment and disappearing through it in the next.

Silence hung in the apartment as Alexander leant forward, straining to hear Ryder's retreating footsteps whilst Tobias flicked through the TV channels with mild interest.

"So …" Tobias began, his gaze periodically darting between Alexander and the TV.

"He's gone," Alexander finished, leaning back into the couch with a feline-like grin, his arms tucked beneath his head as his shirt rode up over the waistline of his navy cargo pants. "But he's in for one *hell* of a surprise in three days, that's for sure."

Tobias chuckled, "Let's just hope he doesn't kill us when he finds out."

Alexander snickered at his brother's words, allowing himself a moment of amusement before he sobered enough to quell the blaze searing through his chest.

"He's out for blood, Bias, but it won't be ours. It'll be *theirs*," he said.

XXXVIII.

Nyx

Flickering light flecked her closed eyelids, dancing to a silent waltz she wasn't privileged to know. As her eyes adjusted to the soft candlelight of the unfamiliar cave and the metallic press of cuffs around her wrists grew in her consciousness, Nyx strained to hear anything over her thoughts, to recall the memories of a conversation she'd overheard before she'd succumbed—once again—to the darkness of sleep. Her gaze trailed analytically across the cave as she shifted in the steel bindings and her brows knitted in confusion, her arms screaming their protests with each movement.

Candles scattered the floor and ledges that jutted from the cavernous walls, filling the room with an unsettling edge, hiding something in the shifting shadows that she couldn't place. Panic begged to be let in and her frayed instincts grew more terrified with every flicker of the candles, but she wouldn't let it take hold, not now. She pulled at the cuffs around her wrists, tipping her head back and peering up at the chains that clattered through an eyelet bolt secured in the limestone ceiling.

She followed the straight-link chain over her shoulder to the jagged rock face behind her, where a beaten but well-loved stereo was propped up beside the bolt the chain was d-shackled to. Nyx pulled at the restraints around her wrists, watching the excess chain of about fifty centimetres shift and clink through the secondary eyelet bolt. She angrily tugged again, the clinking of metal-on-metal echoing in her ears and throughout the cave, feeding the budding anger licking at her insides.

She dropped her gaze to the grainy, stone-like sand under her feet and saw it shift. She froze, fingertips ghosting the cold chains above her head as Nyx groaned internally at the disarray of her mind, scolding its foolishness with a swift clattering of metal-on-metal that echoed through the cave and into the labyrinthine tunnelways.

"Having fun, I see," Orion drawled as he stepped out of the cave's dark entrance and into the candlelit area.

Nyx turned towards him, her gaze narrowed and ablaze with an inferno of unchecked rage as he strode confidently into the cave—jail cell—with an unlit cigarette tucked behind his right ear. He stopped in front of her, mere centimetres beyond her grasp in a dark reminder of who *truly* held the power. With that bitter realisation came a burning itch of the sinister fate she planned to bestow upon him—*a life for a life*. Where he sought to pull her into a darkness she wished she didn't long for, Nyx plotted Orion's demise with a steely focus. She would revert her life to the mundaneness of morality with the silenced *tha-thump* of his heart.

"The time of my life," she quipped lightly, pulling on the bindings around her wrists for emphasis.

"That pleases me greatly," he said, matching her tone.

She scoffed, "Would you like to know what would please me?"

"I would *love* to know," Orion said.

"A stake through your heart would please me … *immensely,"* Nyx said.

A dangerous grin quirked Orion's lips. The baby-blue of his irises blazed with a searing fire as he folded his arms across his thundercloud-grey shirt. "I'd like to see you *try*. *That* would please me," he said.

“Of course, dying would please you,” Nyx muttered.

“You underestimate me, little dove,” he said, gesturing to her chains with a placating chuckle. “But that’s okay.”

She glanced around the cave, raking her gaze across the room for the rest of her captors before she reluctantly turned back towards Orion. “Where are the rest of you?”

Why am I chained up when ... hours earlier I was free? Unconscious and weak but free.

“Oh, they’re on their way,” Orion said, “Don’t you worry.”

“I wasn’t worried,” Nyx replied.

“No?” he drawled, cocking his head to the side as footsteps echoed through the labyrinth of cavernous tunnels. “Good, because *I* have a question I want answered ... so they won’t be joining us until I have my answer.”

Her gaze weighed heavily on him as she eyed him wearily, “And if I refuse?”

“It would only be fair, I suppose,” Orion said. He shook his head, chuckling, “But would the consequences be worth it?”

“What’re you going to do? Bite me?” she chortled back, scuffing her bare feet in the gritty sand. “Because we’ve already done that and the whole *mind control* thing.”

He nodded in silent agreement, the coolness of his gaze skittering across her flesh whilst he silently studied her, “We have, haven’t we?” He paused, shrugging his shoulders before he uncrossed his arms and rubbed his gloved hands together, “But you’ll find that the mind is far more *persuasive* than you think. And that, with the slightest application of pain, it crumbles,” he said.

His words resonated in her mind. A snide comment on the tip of her tongue snuffled out like a flame doused with water as she shoved the niggling whispers of panic back, to the depths of her mind. She knew Orion continued to scrutinise her face, waiting for the most minuscule of fissures to slice through her indifferent guise of bravado. And it did, she couldn’t hide it, seeping in like blood staining the pristine white fabric of a T-shirt.

Still, her pride bellowed its protests, cementing its feet in the grainy sand like a statue, "Do your worst, Orion, because it won't do you any good," she said defiantly.

"Just remember that I warned you," Orion stated firmly. His gaze burned brighter as he stepped forward, "Do you know what it's like to be burned alive?" Orion asked softly, watching with delight as Nyx faltered. "No? Well, neither do I ... *but* I've heard it can be *quite* painful. Shall we find out?"

"I'd rather not," she said.

He tutted, pursing his lips in a show of disappointment. His gaze flickered to the floor and then back to her before a sadistic tone bled into his voice, "It's a good thing that you don't have a say in this then, isn't it?" he said.

"When I get out of these," she said, rattling the chains around her wrists with dark, frenzied irises, "you're a *deader man*."

"Well. We'll see about that," Orion said.

Something foreign itched across Nyx's skin as hesitant flames danced before her eyes, flickering anxiously in the backseats of a grey-panelled car beneath a cloud-obscured sky. Rain poured onto the bitumen of a familiar car park before her eyes widened in horror-filled realisation and she fought to shove Orion's memories from her mind with gritted teeth.

The flames grew under four bikers' gazes, swallowing the car and the corpse in seconds—a tangerine inferno that burned without restraint in the pouring rain.

"Get out of my head!" she ground out through clenched teeth, wincing as a dull throbbing pulsed in her temples.

"What do they have planned, Nyx?" Orion asked, ignoring her angrily snapped words as the flames swallowed the grey-panelled car and the smell of burning flesh filled her nose.

"Who?" Nyx grated.

"Your father and those *wannabe* vampire hunters," Orion said, his words smooth as glass.

Nyx frowned, fighting to shove him out of her mind, "How would I know? He kicked me out, remember?" she said.

"Come on, little dove. Don't make it worse for yourself," he cajoled.

"Make what worse? *I don't know anything!*" Nyx insisted.

An agonised shriek loosed from her throat as a searing pain blossomed over her, and the dancing of flames flashed before her tightly clenched eyelids. It was as if she were the car, as if she were on fire. Nyx tugged at the cuffs around her wrist with reckless abandon, knuckles turning white as she gripped the chain above her head and willed the pure agony of Orion's flame-imbued torture to cease. Painful rasps of breath spilled from her lips because even though her mind couldn't fathom the difference between what was real and what was fake, some part of Nyx knew, that this wasn't real.

Instead, the feeling of her flesh being burned by the apathetic flames didn't waver or show signs of relenting. *It grew.* Burning through her flesh and bones with a steady fierceness that terrified her whilst she pulled at the bindings and whimpered in pain. She felt her bones begin to char. Traitorous tears escaped her clenched eyelids.

Oh God, the pain.

Nyx gritted her teeth against the harrowing fire, knowing she couldn't allow the screams that bubbled in the back of her throat to fill the air. Knowing it'd grant Orion far too much satisfaction than he deserved. So, she gripped the straight-link chain holding her upright with every ounce of strength she possessed, squaring her shoulders against the pain as her knees begged to give out beneath her. A garbled groan filled the cave as she dropped her head to her chest, her chin shaking above her sweat-slicked flesh.

"All you've got to do is tell me their plans and this will all stop," Orion urged soothingly.

His request was so simple. His honeyed voice filled the cave with his promises, and she wished she knew the plan he spoke of, just so she could tell him and be free of this agony. But she knew no such reprieve would find her, wincing as a stronger—*harsher*—bolt of pain tore over her flesh and into her marrow.

"I don't know any plan," she rasped, forcing her eyes open so she could meet Orion's steely gaze. "I was only w*arned* about it."

"Why would they warn you of a plan you know *nothing about?*" he said.

"I *don't know,*" Nyx moaned, tugging at the restraints around her wrists with rage and pain, her face tear-streaked.

Orion seemed to contemplate her words as she watched him watch her, and for a moment, the agony retreated.

Hope blossomed in her chest as silence swept the cave. She flinched then, as he moved toward her, those truly immortal irises searing into her face when he lifted her chin. She remembered his kiss in the hours earlier, now a faint memory in the wake of her agony.

"I don't believe you," he breathed out in the same moment the maddening blaze of fire returned tenfold, and her unrestrained scream of agony hit the cavernous walls.

* * *

Silence, punctuated by her ragged and shaky pants hung heavily across the cavernous room as Nyx's fingers curled around the chain shackling her wrists, legs trembling beneath her weight. Her gaze tunnelled in on Orion whilst she soaked in the absence of his mental torment, free from the searing agony that had lashed her insides, even *if* it was only for a moment.

She watched Orion watch her, glaring at his desolate expression; not a trace of empathy. She knew, on an instinctual level, that she wouldn't find regret because he wasn't remorseful. Some part of her knew he'd never regret what he did to her in the hours that'd passed, but the larger part wondered *why* he'd so fiercely tormented her with a fire-lashed car and the scalding agony of blistering skin. Did he enjoy hearing her scream until her voice was hoarse? Or was the way she struggled to free herself from the bindings at her wrists until her skin was red-raw and dotted by blisters what he enjoyed? Or, could this be his warped sense of loyalty to his companions? Could it be the protectiveness Kade had mentioned Orion possessed toward them? Was he hurting her to protect them? Or was he doing it to find answers so he could ensure their past never repeated?

Whatever the reason, a part of her didn't want to know. Didn't want to consider why he'd been so persistent and unwavering in his repeated question. She supposed recklessly, in a perfect world where she wasn't being held captive by murderous men, that it was admirable. That his bond with Kotori, Niko and Kade pushed him to these dark lengths, never faltering in his desire to quash anything—*anyone*—who endangered them. She knew he'd find the answers he sought to protect them, even if the lengths he went to were horrid, she suspected he'd do it for them.

The muscles in Nyx's arms bellowed their protests, strained and tired of being held above her head like her legs ached from standing for so long. A drawn-out sigh tumbled from her lips as she tried to roll her shoulders and the clattering of metal-on-metal bounced off the walls. Orion's head angled at the sound, his arms folding over his chest as he swept his gaze over her, seeming to catalogue whatever he found.

Nyx's heart jolted when he stepped forward, forcing herself to stand still, lifting her chin. She waited, eyes locked on him. Waiting. Watching. Desperately hoping he wouldn't continue, doubting she had the strength to remain conscious if she was forced to relive another death.

Orion paused in front of her, centimetres dividing them, peering down at her even as Nyx angled her head to hold his stare. And found, to her horror, that she couldn't help but look at him … Her eyes darted to the dark fabric of his broad shoulders before she could stop herself. Then dragged their way up the line of his neck. She cursed herself and her traitorous thoughts. *What are you doing!?* Up his neck and to across his chin, to his mouth. *Stop!* She *shouldn't have* found him attractive. After what he'd done, after what he'd been doing. To her. As hard as she tried, she couldn't shake the memories of his lips against hers. Of how she'd *let* him kiss her. Of how she'd *enjoyed it*. Even when she shouldn't have.

Something so simple yet damning, and it had left her in turmoil. One part of her reasoned that she *shouldn't* want him, that she should put as much distance between him, between *them* as possible. But the other part filled her with a dark, unfurling elation because … as much as she *should have* been disgusted, she wasn't.

Nyx could admit that much to herself as she waited for Orion to do something, anything. And, like he sensed her budding frustration at his silence, his lips upturned into a dangerous grin, sending her heart toppling as his voice filled her ears, orotund and laced with a feigned tone of reassurance; like she was *safe.*

"What's their plan, Nyx?" he asked like a dying mantra.

Nyx's eyes narrowed. "We've been over this a hundred times already, but I guess you couldn't hear it over my screams so, I'll say it again. *I don't fucking know.*"

A low hum emitted from the depths of his chest, glacier irises trailing across the plains of her face. "I still don't believe you."

"Shocker," she uttered dryly, shaking her head.

"It's good to see that you're not afraid to bite back … all things considered."

Nyx's eyebrows rose, surprise dappling her eyes. *"All things considered?* Because *torture* isn't a big deal."

His hand raised to rub along the underside of his jaw, an irritated glint to his eyes as a sigh caressed the shell of her ear. *"Nyx—"*

"Don't," she snapped, cutting him off with the thinly veiled anger throughout her tone. "Don't you *dare."* The resentment she felt for Orion darkened the hue of her eyes, reinforced by her frustration because she didn't understand *why* he was doing this and why her emotions were so out of control. She couldn't put her thoughts together fast enough, scrambling for pieces she didn't have—that he hadn't given her—whilst others eluded her. She was strung up in chains and he was teasing her. It was all wrong.

She tried to focus. She knew so little of his past with her family and even less of her family with the quartet. "Why are you doing this?" she murmured as Orion's gaze trapped her.

"This?" he asked, gesturing lazily between themselves with unvoiced meaning as he waited until she nodded, recalling his silent torment. "Because I *have to."*

She frowned. "You don't *have to* do anything, you *choose to.*"

"That's not true."

"Isn't it?" she prompted, leaning closer to him with a taunting edge to her tone. "Then tell me, who else are you doing this for if it isn't yourself?"

"I do it for *them,*" he spat, pointing to the shadowed depths of the tunnel's entrance and the men she knew lurked somewhere within the cave, stepping closer until his chest pressed against hers. "If I have to be the monster in everyone's story to protect them ... then so *fucking be it.*"

"But *why,* Orion? *Why* go to these lengths?" Nyx asked, unwavering in the face of his emotionless stare and the eerie cock of his head.

Orion tore his eyes from hers, a muscle along the underside of his jaw twitching as he clenched his teeth. A shuddered breath passed from between his teeth, and Nyx's heart pounded anxiously in her chest as he slowly turned back to face her with something unnerving in his irises. Tension crackled in the air like a taut wire stretched to its breaking point, cloying in her lungs as slick as oil across skin.

"I almost lost them twenty-five years ago," he said, voice barely above a whisper. "Azeil wanted to be free of the transition from human to vampire after he found out what we'd done—what Alyvia had kept from him. But when Asher, Amir and Ryder told him how he could free himself ... he acted rashly." His gaze pinned hers. "They drugged Niko, torturing him whilst they left Kade for dead, luring Kotori ... and me to a warehouse. Niko almost died ..."

Nyx shook her head frantically, trying to shunt his words and the imagery they dredged up to the back of her mind. "My family—they wouldn't do that."

Orion tutted, a sound etched with mockery. "Believe whatever you want, little dove, but I have the *scars* to prove it. We all do. Their stories aren't mine to tell but I can tell you what *Azeil* did to me."

Nyx swallowed, shifting nervously beneath Orion's gaze. She didn't want to know. "What ... what did he do?"

"*What did he do,*" Orion repeated with a harsh laugh, taking a single step back from her. "Azeil wasn't *entirely* in the wrong, that much I'll admit. He watched Niko 'die' before I knocked him off the raised walkway he stood on. I think he broke a bone … or two when he hit the floor. And he fought like I've never seen a man fight for their life, desperate to not die in the vat of *boiling* water sunk into the floor. He pushed me onto a metal pole. Onto *two* metal poles. He *skewered* me."

Nyx sucked in a sharp breath when his chest pressed against hers. Orion stooped his head until his lips were inches from her own, voice a dangerous drawl, "Azeil has spent twenty-five years believing I was dead—that we all were—because I *let* him. He's been haunted by *me,* by the memories of twin poles piercing my back until they ripped through the skin of my chest because I *wanted* him to suffer. Like we did."

"You're a *monster,*" Nyx said as the weight of his words pressed down on her.

The dawning realisation that her torment had been for a twenty-five-year-old grievance she hadn't even been alive for—that she was being punished for her father's crimes—cleaved her chest like a dagger, dragging an agonising path from her sternum to the base of her ribcage.

His voice was muffled in her eardrums as she held his gaze and he stepped back, wandering to a ledge at the other side of the room before he sat down, forearms perched on his thighs. "You say 'monster', I say 'vengeance'. It's all about perspective, little dove," Orion paused, lounging against the rocks like it were a throne.

"Go on," Nyx urged, equal parts exhausted and enraged. "Ask the *same question* so I can give you the *same answer*. It won't change no matter what you do because I don't know anything."

Orion mulled over her words, pursing his lips before he straightened and retrieved the cigarette tucked behind his ear. "And I still *don't* believe you."

And then came Kade.

He strode confidently into the cave and stopped mere metres away from her. His presence was like a knife to her heart.

Nyx's lips curled into a sneer, betrayal settling in her stomach like a dead weight.

She didn't know where she stood with him, one minute there was friendship, then there was something more and lust-filled kisses … now this. A frigid cold settled in her chest, hurt she wished didn't exist.

"Kade," Orion greeted in a low voice, his gaze never straying from Nyx as she gripped the chains around her wrists, trying to blink away the exhaustion pressing down on her shoulders.

Despite the weariness thundering in her eardrums, her mind greedily drank in the sight of Kade's ochre linen pants and the silvery-white smattering of scar tissue that peeked out from beneath the cropped hem of his signature white shirt. Like a woman starved of water in the Sahara Desert. She forced herself to look away as someone whistled.

Niko.

"You're brave, chica," Niko said, sidling up to her. He ran a finger down the length of her screaming arm, from wrist to pit.

She almost couldn't feel it.

"And, paired with Orion's manipulations of your mind, I'm impressed. Not many have that strength."

"You're *impressed* by my strength after *none* of you tried to intervene," she said, scoffing with a shake of her head. "You're unbelievable."

"So I've been told," he quipped.

Kade's impish grin grew as he rubbed his hands together, grinning. He closed the distance between them, trapping her between himself and Niko. A dynamic that jolted her heart like a bolt of electricity through her bloodstream, betraying her like it'd done so many times before, tainted by fear and her exhaustion.

Kade's fingers brushed her cheekbone as he pressed closer to her, his chest flush with hers. "So, you're sure you don't know anything? Because I'd hate for Orion to continue his … questioning, angel. I don't like hearing you scream, unless it's my name."

She met his stare head-on, resolute certainty simmering inside her. "I don't."

Kade stepped aside with a doubtful nod; lips pursed as if he was fighting the urge to grin whilst his fingers twitched beside his legs. She hadn't forgotten what she'd overheard, couldn't forget his suggestion to kill off her loved ones. The hawk-like blond's irises glittered with mischief, angling his head toward Orion in a silent prompt.

"I say we make this a little more … *interesting,*" came the one voice that had been missing. Kotori, appearing from the cave's shadows with wolfish ease.

His umber gaze locked on her, startling Nyx with their intensity. A knowing grin tugged at the corners of his mouth, ebony hair rivalling a raven's plumage. Like his companions, his boot-clad feet echoed indistinctively across the cave as he stopped behind Orion's right shoulder.

The stark whiteness of Orion's hair jolted a bolt of prey-like fear through Nyx's chest. Orion's glacier irises were now aflame with a blue fire that unsettled her further.

"What do you suggest?" Orion asked, turning his entire attention to Kotori.

Kotori's dark irises flickered to Nyx for the barest of moments before his teeth sank into the flesh of his bottom lip. Like he was struggling to shake the vivid imagery in his mind from his head.

"Bite her," he said, "and if her heart rate doesn't spike with the endorphins, she's free to go, regardless of what she knows."

Kade spluttered indignantly. His head snapping towards Kotori, eyes narrowed as his gaze darted from Kotori to Orion and back again, "What? No way—"

Orion's gloved hand rose. His chilling irises locked on Kade as his eyebrows rose, daring him to continue. A silent but effective order that silenced the shorter man's protests, her heartrate spiking as Orion dipped his head in a curt nod that dripped with satisfaction before he turned back to Kotori with a lazy wave of his hand.

"*But,* if her heart rate *does* spike," Kotori said as his dark irises peered over Orion's shoulder and down at Nyx, directing his next words to her, "she *willingly* stays with us. Even *if* she knows more than she's letting on."

Niko pressed an excited kiss to the base of her throat and despite the absurdness, her heart skipped a traitorous beat, his bracelet-covered wrists jangling as he wrapped his arms around her waist.

"What'd you say, chica? Fancy a wager?" he said.

Four pairs of eyes locked on Nyx, awaiting her answer with bated breath. She knew which pair mattered as they turned to peer down at her, knowing he held the power. So, Nyx met Orion's eyes, determination seeping into her bloodstream.

"If I win, I go free and you'll leave me alone?" she said.

"As free as a bird, angel," Kade supplied from beside Orion's left shoulder.

Nyx nodded but refused to tear her gaze from Orion, "And if I ... lose?"

Orion grinned his charismatically sinister smile, his smouldering gaze trailing over her like a weeping veil. "If you lose, you stay here, *willingly*, as ours," he said.

"Yours?" Nyx said.

He nodded in agreement, "As ours. *Forever.*"

"But—"

"Are you game, Nyx?" Niko interjected, his lips brushing against the shell of her ear as she gazed up at Orion.

"Do I have a choice?" Nyx asked.

"You've *always* had a choice, you just always pick the *harder* one," Kade said, peering at her deeply, reminding her of every interaction she'd ever shared with him, with the quartet.

"Those—"

"Count, kleintje," said Kotori, cutting her off before she could rebut Kade's words. "You knew we weren't saints, but you *chose* to ignore it. We didn't force you to do that."

Nyx closed her eyes as the truth of his words slammed into her chest like bricks, piling themselves atop her chest like a Jenga before she forced herself to open them and face the golden-eyed beasts surrounding her. "I'll do it," she said, her voice barely above a whisper.

Now that she had answered them, she toyed with the idea of formulating and finalising her plan under their noses until she could strike, taking Orion down with the crudely sharpened edge of a stake, and recentring her life as she thought it should be. Even if, in the depths of her mind, a warped shard of her being found comfort in the knowledge that they'd always been there throughout her life. Her guardians with blood-stained appetites and twisted wants.

"Sure?" Kade asked, his gaze alight with poorly restrained excitement.

"I either do it or I spend the rest of my life—" she rattled the chains above her head, "—like this."

The frigidity of Orion's gaze blazed across her skin, pure and undiluted triumph radiating from his entire being as his lips pulled up into a dangerous smirk filled with something dark and vast. His gaze darted to Niko, who shifted from one foot to another with excitement. "Niko, would you care to do the honours?" His uncanny irises drifted back to hers as he gestured to the chains around her wrists with an easy wave of his hand.

Niko skittered his fingertips over her bare arms, his breath warming the crook of her throat whilst his nimble fingers unclasped the steel cuff from around her left wrist. Feeling surged back into the limb, pain igniting her muscles. He wrapped his fingers around her red-rubbed skin, blistered and on the cusp of breaking, before he purposefully extended her arm towards Orion.

With a swift inclination of his head, he grasped her wrist in his gloved hand and dropped his gaze to the bared expanse of her forearm. The chill of leather seeped into Nyx's flesh as he cradled her wrist in his hand and traced a calculated path across the veins in her forearm. He paused several inches below her wrist, thumbing the bluey-purple vein in her arm before his glacier gaze flicked up to meet hers, and the breath in her lungs tangled in her throat.

"These," Orion murmured, tracing the springy cords, "are your tendons and, unless you don't want to move your hand or fingers again, I won't be tapping into this vein here." His fingers traced a dark vein cocooned by two tendons, dancing his fingertips across her forearm and to the soft flesh several millimetres away from her inner arm, "But this one, poses no threat to you … unless of course, you fight. And then you'll successfully tear open your forearm."

Nyx's thoughts clouded her mind, swirling with uncertainty the longer she stared into the depths of Orion's chilling irises. As he angled his head ever-so-slightly, almost owl-like, his unearthly irises bleeding white-gold.

She panicked.

Her heart beat in her chest, pounding against her ribcage as fear crackled through her bloodstream and she pulled at her entrapped wrists. She swore internally, loathing the skittish and terror-driven instincts that bellowed admissions of defeat, enforced by her earlier torment. It *angered her*—like a persistent sandfly biting the flank of a horse. And, with aggravating determination, she forced herself to calm down and ignore the mocking arch to Orion's eyebrows.

She sucked in a shaky breath as she watched him change. The impossibly monstrous and yet … angelic quality to his vampiric features rendered her mute and stole her air. But, despite herself, she stared at him and into the nightmarish whites of his irises. She watched his elongated incisors and canines sink into the soft flesh of her forearm before a grimace distorted her face and her brows came together, a low hiss of pain tumbling from her lips and through the candlelit cave, enticing four pairs of animalistic brimming gazes to her.

As the sharp burn of pain trickled away and she appraised Orion—who held her gaze as securely as he clasped her between his leather-encased hands, supporting her wrist with one hand and her elbow with the other—she felt the unmistakable surge of endorphins in her bloodstream, infecting her with an aphrodisiac that gravitated through her as easily as honey seeped from the shattered honeycomb of a beehive. She shook her head, hoping it'd rid her of the traitorous thrall invading her bloodstream and mind. She fought to keep her heartbeat steady, unwilling to lose so easily despite the endorphins racing through her blood like the rapids before a waterfall. It was maddening to fight the ecstasy that came for her, clouding her mind and dilating her pupils beneath her closed eyelids, sweeping the fraying edges of her control into a wide open chasm.

Without her truly noticing, Nyx leant into the warmth and steadiness of Niko's embrace. Her head tipped back and rested upon him as the aphrodisiacs running rampant through her latched themselves onto every crevice of her being, drowning out any semblance of sanity left in her mind. Her heart rate spiked and a blinding daze of pleasure coiled around her, cocooning her in a blanket of dark warmth others would shy away from but Nyx couldn't.

Instead, she found herself yearning for that lulling embrace fragranced with sea salt and weed. Her chained hand grazed the steel links above her as if it might centre her before she forced her eyelids open and her pupil-eclipsed gaze met Kade's. Darkened by his emotions—hope, longing and … guilt swirled within their depths—silent in his appraisal half-hidden behind his clenched fist, the pad of his thumb trapped beneath his teeth. Like it'd be enough to hide his enigmatic hope for her to be in their lives—to be in *his* life.

The metallic tang of blood pierced the air when Orion withdrew his fangs from her forearm and the jutted planes of his face smoothed like he'd been given relief, an analgesic. She watched as he slowly resembled the steel-blue-eyed man her mind found comfort in, and she wondered if some critical part of her had just shattered somewhere in the darkness of Celacali; lost to the crashing waves against Elveszett Bluff.

An odd thrill trickled up her spine when Orion held her gaze and dragged his tongue across the crimson-weeping wound, supporting her wrist and elbow as carefully as one would a priceless jewel. His tongue darted out to lick his lips, purging the pink flesh of her blood.

Nyx blinked up at him with widely blown pupils, fighting to recentre herself. Niko's grasp tightened on her waist as he pulled her closer to his chest with a deep chuckle. His nimble fingers deftly freed her right wrist from the steel cuffs supporting her weight, pressing the gentlest of kisses to her temple as metal-on-metal clattered throughout the cave and she leaned into him for support. She almost didn't register the dull aching pinch of the released limb.

Kade stepped forward.

Kade. Kade who had been her first. Kade who had hurt her. So much.

His eyes burned like the embers of a fire and his fingertips brushed her cheek. But he looked down before stepping away like he refused to let himself find true satisfaction, guilt dappling his eyes as they darted to her before he moved away.

Then there was Kotori. The darkness of the Levenloos man's gaze bored into her soul as his warm, ring-clad fingers tilted her face to his and he leant down to press a lingering kiss to her lips. She remembered what he'd said earlier and as she peered up at him, she saw him in a new light. A better light. As he pulled away, he peered down at her, a genuine smile gracing the planes of his darkly handsome features before he trailed the pad of his thumb along her bottom lip, tracking the movement with longing.

Niko's lips peppered butterfly kisses to the column of her neck, his fingertips pressing deliciously into her hips when Kotori wandered to Kade's side, the pair watching as he pulled away slowly, the reluctance of the action reverberating along her back as a low growl of displeasure tumbled from his lips and his breath warmed the skin of her throat.

Then came Orion. He grasped her chin and tipped her head back, baring her throat to his smouldering irises. Orion pressed himself closer to Nyx until his chest was against hers and his scent of cigarettes, copper and leather engulfed her senses. He kept her head firmly tipped back as he dipped his head and his stubble brushed against the smooth expanse of her throat. The warm press of his lips seared into the centre of her neck as he pressed a single possessive kiss to the bared skin. Then he reconnected his lips with hers. The same fiery intensity that blazed in his uncanny irises was conveyed in his kiss. Nyx felt herself falling as she blindly reciprocated, her mind lost in a dark comfort she didn't understand. Orion's gloved fingers released her chin in favour of cupping her cheek and angling her head back so he could deepen the kiss—entrapping her in his darkly divine presence with an ease that terrified and yet aroused her.

Nyx's mind stumbled at the lingering warmth of the group's kisses, the consequences of her blood loss tugged at her. Desperate to send her tumbling to her knees before the four pairs of eyes that scrutinised her closely, watching as she took from them, just as they had taken from her.

"You're *ours* now, little dove," Orion crooned, leaning down to look at her, "Forever."

XXXIX.

Nyx

Lips brushed against hers in a shadowed alcove of the cave, gentle at first as Nyx's fingers tangled in the white-blond hair at the base of Orion's head, her thighs straddling his waist, his grasp tightening on her hip before he angled his head back and Nyx deepened the kiss, a low groan reverberating from the depths of his chest when her teeth grazed his bottom lip.

Nyx smiled into the kiss, a smugness etched into the cavern of her chest as Orion's fingers trailed up her spine and his hand wrapped in her curls, abruptly breaking the kiss. His lips were a hairbreadth away, warm breath fanning the bruised flesh of her mouth, glacier irises alight with blue fire—with a blazing passion and want.

"Why are we doing this?" she breathed out, soft pants tumbling from her mouth as she shifted on his lap, the coarse rock face of the natural ledge pressing into his back as he leant forward and he dragged his tongue up the centre of her throat.

His lips twisted with a smirk as he lifted his head, peering up at her, something heady in his tone. "You tell me, little dove. What is it that *you* want?"

Nyx's gaze darted across his face, pupils dilated as her lips brushed his and the darkened shard of her soul answered before she could stop it. "*You.* I want you."

And before the truth in Nyx's words could register themselves in her mind, she vanquished the space between their mouths, pressing her lips against his with scalding and pent-up need. Orion swiftly returned the bruising and almost desperate nature of her kiss, the hold on her hair tightening whilst his opposing hand trailed from her waist to her thigh, fingertips sinking into her jean-clad flesh, dragging her closer to him.

His teeth grazed the flesh of her bottom lip like she'd done to his, the hand woven in her hair tipping her head back as his teeth nipped at the underside of her jaw before his lips pressed a soothing kiss to the spot seconds later.

Orion's breath warmed the column of her throat as a thrill—part fear, part lust—careened through her bloodstream, heart pounding against her ribcage.

"I'll be the villain in your story, Nyx," he said against her skin, sending a shiver down her spine at the sensually murmured words. "I'll be the thing you refuse to have. The person you crave and loathe all at once. For you, and you alone …"

A panicked gasp left her lips as her eyes snapped open, drifting out and across the cavernous living space plunged in sunlight. Like a whisper of a ghost retreating through the abandoned wreck of a once prestigious manor, she shook away the dream. As she tugged at the chains wrapped around her wrists, the clattering of metal-on-metal rippled throughout the cave.

Absolutely not, she thought, blinking the haze of sleep from her mind. Of the tantalising promise whispered into her skin, of the phantom press of his lips against her skin, of the words she'd spoken that she refused to accept.

It was just a dream. It didn't *mean* anything.

"You. I want you."

"I'll be the thing you refuse to have. The person you crave and loathe all at once. For you, and you *alone."*

The words replayed in her mind as she shifted in the metal chair trapping her, and she noted the golden rays of light cascading down from the eroded ceiling, smattering the coastal hideaway with the golden-yellow light of dawn. Nyx forced herself to study the cave in the lightness of the day, noting the way the white lights were tucked artfully into crevices so they wouldn't be seen, as though it would be enough to keep her mind from the darkness brushing its taloned hand against her subconsciousness, slipping flashes of her blood-stained hands to the forefront of her mind. Fragmented shards sliced through her wavering guards despite the determination she clutched to her chest, yelling at her to fight the alluring call to the world's darkness—and her soul's.

But she *couldn't* fight it, this warped shard of her being begging to be accepted. It knew it could be accepted and would thrive if she let go of the morals society deemed acceptable and instead, followed the enigmatic foursome down this path of no return. Their grins stretched widely across their faces in her mind, their hands extended out toward her, palms turned up at the sky and their irises ablaze with malignant delight.

Despite the thoughts swirling in her head, Nyx found comfort in the sunlight illuminating the cave from the varying glass-patched holes and cracks in the limestone ceiling. She didn't know enough about the vampires who called this cavernous hideaway their home, but something in her chest deflated in the natural lighting, the crashing waves and cries of seagulls smoothing over her skin like a cool balm intended to soothe her racing heart.

The metal chair dug uncomfortably into her spine, a firm but constant reminder of the glorified illusion of *freedom* she had whilst simultaneously reminding her of the crimes she'd committed. The murder of a dark-haired man bound to a metal chair like the very same she sat on, the memory indelible.

"Welcome back to the land of the living," a voice said.

Nyx's heart raced in her chest when Orion stepped into view. Like he'd always been there, just out of sight. She mulled over the fact that he spent *far* too much time reappearing and disappearing within the darkness before his head cocked to the side and his uncanny irises pinned her to the chair.

"Or the dead," he added, belatedly.

"Lucky me," she rattled the chains around her wrists. Her gaze straying to Kotori, Kade, and Niko as they manoeuvred through the cave's shadows before she forced herself to meet Orion's sinister stare, "The captive thing is starting to get old, Orion. Don't you think?"

The skittering of rocks echoed off the uneven walls when Niko jumped down from the jutting ledge beside an overflowing bookshelf, his boots toeing the sun-imbued living space. An electric grin stretched across his face, his hands fluttering beside himself as he traipsed the fine border between light and the shadows, his oddly energetic stance, testing boundaries.

"But you look so … *ravishing* all chained up," Niko drawled, inching closer to her in the grey hue of the shadows.

Kade jumped down beside Niko with bird-like grace, grinning from ear to ear. His fingertips ghosting the softly billowing curtains of the forgotten nook, his artistically carved voice laced with a darker undertone as he spoke, "It's the perfect blend of good and bad … all chained up and at our mercy."

Nyx's gaze darted to Kotori as the Levenloos man stepped from the depths of the blackened shadows, slinking through the darkness that shadowed his face with the grace of a wolf. His dark irises locked on hers as he spoke in that deep and yet melodic timbre.

"She's agathokakological," he said. "Something composed of both good and bad."

"Agathokakological," Orion said, rolling the word over his tongue as if he was tasting the comparison before he pursed his lips and nodded with satisfaction. "I like that. It suits her."

"So …" Nyx began. Orion's eyebrows arched as she paused, prompting her to continue from the shadows he favoured. "What now?"

"Now you uphold your end of the deal, and we'll uphold ours," he said simply.

Nyx frowned at his words, confused as she sifted through her memories. "But you don't *have* an end to the bargain," she said.

That smirk again, except now the steeliness of his irises seemed somehow brighter in the shadows.

"Oh, we know. Don't you worry," he said.

Orion stepped purposefully into the beams of sunlight cascading from the crumbling roof. And as he did, her mind scrambled, toppling over itself like dominos, ricocheting off her skull like a ping-pong ball. Everything inside her screamed—it didn't make sense to her how he didn't burst into flames with the first brush of sunlight.

She realised with another clattering epiphany that she was naïve—a mortal thrust into the world of beasts and monsters alike. Expected to prosper in the darkness of their world, as if she belonged there.

Kade, Niko and Kotori shared dark bemused grins before they too stepped out into the golden rays and crossed the room to the beaten couches staggered around her chained body. Nyx longed to tear her gaze from the lifeful blonds bathed in sunlight, and the happiness brushing against her panicked heart as Niko and Kade tussled beside the Cerberus statue.

The thought of navigating their world terrified her, and she wouldn't have been surprised if she did prosper. A part of her longed for the bitter abyss of death it'd provide, but the jagged shard infecting her bloodstream whispered darkly in her mind; bitter and undying in its path of corruption that eroded her just and acceptable morals.

Orion dragged a weathered chair toward her, his gaze holding firm as the jarring screech of rust-imbued metal filled her ears. She keenly noted the theatrical ease of his darkly clothed form and the directness of his chair in front of hers. Every inch of him was as calculated as his ultra-violet halo. This was all a game to him.

Every foolish grain of comfort she'd clutched at in the warmth of the sun's caress was a lie—a manipulation—the four men had cradled and nurtured in her presence, unconcerned by the variables she'd *believed* to be true. Like a lamb being led dutifully to the slaughterhouse.

A distressed whimper of pain tumbled from her lips before she could prevent it—a desperate girl trapped amid monsters who revelled in her shattering beliefs—because the darkness in her chest called to theirs like a distant siren song.

The concept of their invulnerability choked her.

"But—how?" Nyx blurted out after a confused beat of silence, her eyes darting to each of the men in turn before she held Orion's unwavering gaze.

Orion shook his head with dark amusement, pulling an unlit cigarette out from behind his ear and into the gloved confines of his fingers.

"Modern media and some strands of folklore call us *daywalkers;* vampires with all their strengths and none of their weaknesses," he said. "But the exact *how* isn't important right now. Not until we've cleaned up a few *loose ends.*"

Nyx straightened in her chair, banishing the feeling of hopelessness in favour of gaining something that would help her. "What *loose ends*?" she said.

Kade's head snapped up from over Niko's shoulders. His fingerless-gloved hands shoving his taller companion away before he swiftly crossed the room and dropped down into the nearest couch. He propped his chin upon the heel of his palm, honeyed irises shifting with sinister mischief and dark affection for her, and her alone.

"Just a few wannabe vampire hunters we should've killed a *long* time ago," he said.

"You can't kill them," she exclaimed, tugging at the chains around her wrists.

Kotori silently stepped around her. A bundle of black and white fur clutched carefully to his chest as he crouched down beside her and placed Ares on the sandy floor. His dark gaze searched hers as he spoke, "Why *can't* we?" he said. "They tried killing us twenty-five years ago."

She scoffed; her heart aching to run her fingers through the tresses of Ares's fur. "So what? Two wrongs make a right?"

Niko snickered, crossing the room in a few quick, bountiful strides before he carelessly dropped down into the plush couch beside Kade, "It doesn't. But the chase is *always* fun," he said.

"It makes the kill *so* much better, angel," Kade drawled, leaning forward so his impish grin appeared shadowed in the light, imploring her to believe him. He sighed almost wistfully, eyelashes brushing against his cheeks, seeming to reminisce his blood-stained frenzies before he forced his eyes to hers. "To know that they're terrified of us and their inevitable death … is unlike anything you'll ever experience," he said, staring at her wistfully.

Nyx hardened her stare, narrowing her eyes at them. "You're not *killing* them. I won't let you," she said.

Orion tutted, inhaling a lungful of nicotine-infused smoke, "It's a shame that you're the bait then, isn't it?" he said, exhaling a grey-white cloud.

She blinked once. Twice. Her eyes darting across his stubble-shadowed jaw, searching his eyes for something that would reveal his ulterior motives and the truth she wished to discard. "What?" she stammered.

"You're the shiny lure leading the gullible humans to their deaths," he said sweetly, cigarette ash cascading to the ground with a precise flick of his wrist whilst his tongue traced his teeth. Like he could taste the cloying darkness of his words. "Because, while you were unconscious and restrained, Kade and Niko were at your house … collecting the details of the plan you didn't know anything about."

"You're *dead*," Nyx said, the straight-link chain dug into her wrists when she tugged at the bindings, fury rising.

"I think it's the other way around," Kotori said as he shook his head with contempt. "Your father and his rag-tag group of vampire hunters are *dead*."

Nyx furiously blinked back anger-driven tears, shunting the flicker of betrayal she felt to the back of her mind, "You can't do this!" she wailed.

"We're *technically* not doing anything," Niko said. "They're the ones walking to their deaths." His arms draped comfortably along the top of the couch as he watched her sympathetically.

"You're monsters," seemed the only logical reply.

"We never said we weren't, little dove. And if we have to use you to get to them, we will," Orion uttered in a measured tone; the promise laced in his words was impossible to miss.

"Don't do this ... please," Nyx implored him.

"It's too late for begging now, especially when they're already on their way," Kade answered.

"Now?" She glanced at each of them, confused. "But that's suicide!"

"It's life, angel," Kade supplied, as something demonic rose in his fuscous irises.

"And we're just the predators at the top of the food chain, doing what we must to obtain our revenge" said Kotori, chiming in with his pack.

"You're at the top of the food chain because you're *murderers,*" Nyx stated, fighting the righteous whispers that plagued her mind—reminding her of the indecipherable differences between herself and the vampiric men.

"Murderers, predators, monsters, vampires," Niko sing-songed like he was checking off a shopping list. "It's all the same but with different names, chica."

Orion rose from the paint-chipped chair, taking a final drag from his cigarette before he tossed the butt to the floor, grinding it out with the heel of his boot. Smoke swirled around his face like a nicotine-infused mass of snakes, curling around and against his jaw as he artfully exhaled.

"You can't do this, Orion," Nyx said, trying again. Her eyes flickered to Kotori, Kade, and Niko in turn before she turned back to Orion. "This is wrong."

Kade and Niko shared a look from over Kotori's leather-clad shoulders, shifting upon the beaten couch so they could—seemingly—watch Orion and Nyx in action.

"Why *can't* we, kleintje?" Kotori breathed out, the deep timbre of his voice tingling over her skin like a pleasant caress of lightning.

"Because you shouldn't be the ones to decide who lives and who dies," Nyx said, her eyes flickering up and away from him, meeting Orion's gaze as he stared down at her. "You're not gods."

"We might not be gods, but why should we deny ourselves what we want? When we're the monsters mortals fear?" Orion said as he lifted his eyebrows, prompting her to question his century-garnered logic as he leant down and his breath warmed the column of her throat.

Orion's lips brushed her skin, faint and indistinctive, like the brush of a butterfly's wings. Her breath caught in her throat as she fought the longing in her chest. Because she *couldn't* succumb to the wants of him, of them. Even *if* some part of her longed to. Even *if* some part of her understood the men on some level. That darkly twisted shard of her being whispered in her mind, longing for the security they possessed, as if she needed it to survive when Niko crossed the room, trailing his fingers across her collarbone.

Niko's lips pressed into her skin—firmer—as he stooped down, and despite her physical protest on a truly molecular level, the rushing of blood pulsing in her eardrums and through her body took over. It was like everything she'd endured over the years that'd led her to Celacali had festered, waiting for this moment. Like her soul longed for them. Even *if* her mind urged her that she couldn't let herself venture any further into the darkness of their world, even *if* she needed it to survive—to thrive. It would cost her *everything* she was, and she wasn't sure she could endure the blood-stained world they wished to show her.

It occurred to her that she should've fought against their touches or been disgusted by them, but that warped side of her revelled in Niko's touches to her throat, alternating between nipping, and sucking the bare expanse of flesh in a possessive and claiming tangent. A soft sigh tumbled from her lips when he sucked harder at the centre of her throat just above her windpipe, a groaned profanity dancing over the shell of her ear from the couch.

Her eyes opened as Niko pulled away and Kotori replaced him, continuing his claiming kisses to her throat whilst Orion rounded her shoulder and peered down into her lust-stricken irises. A salacious smile brightened and yet, *darkened* his eyes like a storm cloud plunging the world into darkness as the sun fought to break through the grey-black clouds.

Nyx's mind relaxed, absurdly comfortable despite the lingering recollection of the danger they possessed, allowing herself this moment. Devilish shadows danced across Orion's face, lightening his eyes until his gaze appeared to burn with blue fire. But Nyx could barely focus on him as Kotori's teeth grazed her skin—softer than Niko—marking her skin leisurely.

"Don't believe *everything* written in the legends, little dove," Orion warned, as Kade appeared by her side and his lips descended upon hers from behind her head, with animalistic need.

His tongue glided over the seam of her lips in a silent request she accepted, parting her lips. He pulled away—and she told herself it'd be the last descent she would allow herself into their world—before his lips brushed against hers.

"Because we're *worse* than mortals' myths," he whispered.

Kotori pulled away from her throat, at the same moment that Kade's lips left her mouth, and he rose to his full height.

Kotori grinned wolfishly with the easy descent of his lips upon hers. Sandalwood, and copper cloying on her tongue before his large palm cupped her throat and his thumbs brushed circles into her skin. It drove her mad, blinded by their euphoric prowess as the chilled caress of Kotori's rings against her skin tingled until he pulled away.

The soothing timbre of his silvery voice rippled over and throughout the cavernous home, embedding itself into her skin like the marks blooming over her throat.

"And we'll revel in corrupting you, kleintje. Until all you know is the darkest parts of our world," he said.

XL.

Alexander

Wind pawed across the rock-littered cliffside, tugging at Alexander's hair as Tobias cursed softly and his head *thumped* against the window. As he turned to glare at his older brother, Alexander stifled riveted laughter, fingers drumming leisurely upon the steering wheel.

"Wipe that grin off your face before I do it for you," Tobias grumbled, arms folded over his chest like a disgruntled toddler.

Alexander chuckled when another particularly harsh bump jolted Tobias in his seat and his jean-clad knee collided with the glovebox. "Someone's a little *testy,*" he said.

"*Testy*?" Tobias parroted indignantly, swivelling his head towards Alexander. "You've been driving over every bloody rock for the past half hour, and every time, some part of *me* hits your car."

"I *have not* been driving over *every* rock," Alexander said.

"Tell that to my bruises," Tobias retorted.

"Want me to kiss them better, baby brother?" Alexander snarked.

"I w*ill* hit you," his brother said.

"And then we'll go off the cliff," affirmed Alexander.

Tobias groaned, turning his head away from the white-capped ocean and the jagged cliff ledge, one of his hands clutching the door handle whilst the other's fingertips dug into the leather seats. "Don't remind me."

"I forgot that you're scared of heights," Alexander mused, easing his foot onto the brakes.

"I can't stop thinking about the cliff edge," Tobias said plaintively.

Alexander hummed in acknowledgement, focused upon the rolling waves stretching out until they met the pristine blue of the horizon whilst he parked the car and pulled the key from the ignition.

Silence descended as the twins stared out at the horizon. He was unsure about the events that'd led them to the rock-littered terrain of Elveszett Bluff—where, up until now, they'd been prohibited from venturing out to.

There wasn't much to look at upon the Bluff, and he supposed that's why it made for such an 'in plain sight' hideout. A forest loomed metres away, tree branches and oceanic shrubbery swaying in the buffeting winds that plagued the coastal city and plunged the summer's day into a chill. Alexander squinted, trying to gauge the expanse of forest to the strip of land bordering Celacali's beach before undoubtedly concluding that this was the same forest that bordered the beach of the boardwalk. He marvelled at the oddity of Elveszett Bluff and the history of its crumbling cliff face. A thought he knew Tobias didn't share as his younger brother unclipped his seatbelt and flung open the car door, climbing out of the car like his moss-green hoodie was on fire.

Alexander glanced at Tobias, following his brother out the car, folding his arms over his chest whilst he toed the sand, tracing odd patterns into the gritty soil with his boots. He knew Tobias was troubled—worried—about the path ahead and the actions that would follow, just like he also worried for the brown-haired girl they'd set out to save, or at least, ensure she remained safe. So, Alexander couldn't fault his brother for his concern, not when he shared the same sentiment as Tobias when Nyx was involved—their sister in everything but blood.

Tobias spoke, his voice almost carried away by the wind, "*This* is the vampire's lair?" he said.

"He said Elveszett Bluff," Alexander replied, turning his head to peer at the wind-buffeted landscape, "… and this *is* Elveszett Bluff."

"I don't have a good feeling about this, Alex," Tobias said.

Alexander held his brother's searching gaze with as much confidence as he could muster, "Neither do I, Bias. But it's for Nyx," he said.

Tobias' Converse-clad foot tapped nervously, palms rubbing anxiously against his thighs, "How the hell are we supposed to pull this off? It's two against four," he said.

Alexander gripped his brother's forearms, "We're not fighting them, remember? We get in and out of there with Nyx and then leave. Dad can do whatever the hell he wants, but she's *not* getting hurt because of him," he said.

"So that's it?" Tobias prompted, rolling his shoulders to ease his pent-up nerves. "We get in and out?"

"That's the plan," Alexander said.

"But—"

"Dad, Amir and the Monroe's *are* the distraction," Alexander said.

"But—"

Alexander sighed as his twin clutched at every worst-case scenario he could think of. "Trust me, Bias … please," he said.

Tobias's gaze darted over his shoulder, staring at something for a tense moment before he turned back to Alexander, a sudden calm to his eyes. "I trust you," he said, his dark irises locked on him, "With my life."

The crunching of rocks beneath tyres drew Alexander's attention from Tobias to a beaten-up red Land Cruiser that stopped closer to the cliff's ledge than their car. The thud of four doors and the four men now approaching them made him wonder as he squinted in the harsh light. He tried to remember if his father had changed clothes since they'd last seen him.

Ryder, crease-clothed as ever, approached with their Uncle Amir at his heels. It occurred to him, as Amir murmured firm warnings to Ryder, that he'd blindly jumped head-first into some unknown disaster and like a fool, he'd dragged his brother into it.

Unlike their father, Amir's clothes screamed 'army cadet' from his black T-shirt and silver dog tags around his neck, to his camouflage pants and the tan boots on his feet. His gaze trailed from his raven-haired uncle to a blond man with sky-blue eyes, quiff-like hair ruffled in the wind, a mixture of amusement and disgust etched on his face as his nose crinkled and he turned in a slow circle on the Bluff.

Asher Monroe, Alexander's mind whispered, reminding him of the brightly dressed man's name, his patterned shirt burned a hole in his eyeballs.

As Alexander's gaze left Asher, they landed on the fourth man: *Azeil Monroe.* Nyx's father. Something about the dark-haired man had always unsettled him, rattling his nerves. He supposed it was the prestigious pedestal Nyx put him on—a man he knew she'd never spoken ill of or could ever stop loving.

Like Asher, Azeil's jean-clad legs complemented his ribbed, black singlet, red flannel jacket, and beaten-up Cons. His appraisal of the dark-haired patriarch of the Monroe's was broken by his father speaking:

"Are we ready, boys?" Ryder said.

Tobias dubiously turned to his older brother. His dark eyebrows arched as he inclined his head in a silent go-ahead, letting Alexander answer rather than himself.

"To do what exactly?" Alexander said.

Asher whipped around to Ryder in confusion, "You didn't tell them?"

"Of course, he hasn't," Azeil snarked with a disdainful shake of his head. "He's the *professional.*"

"Azeil," Asher warned, narrowing his gaze upon the dark-haired man.

Azeil scoffed, kicking a stray pebble away in anger. His arms folded over his chest, hand gesturing mockingly to Tobias and Alexander. "Go ahead, *Buffy*. Enlighten them," he said.

Alexander eyed Azeil carefully, his gaze darting from the oldest Monroe to his father, urging Ryder to speak with a deft wave of his hand. "Well?"

Ryder eyed them, as though he wasn't sure he could trust them.

"It's more of a get in, get out type of plan," Ryder explained slowly, watching his sons as the air caught in Alexander's throat, "Azeil and Asher get Nyx out whilst Amir and I find the vampires and kill them all. One of you will stay with Azeil and Asher, whilst the other scopes out the cave and disposes of the bloodsuckers with us," he said.

Tobias's eyebrow arched, "Can't we be the lookouts? Because I don't think separating us would be in anyone's best interest," he said.

"I agree with, Bias," Alexander said unhelpfully.

"We don't *need* lookouts," Ryder said, glaring; voice eerily calm.

Silence except for the howling winds filled his ears as their father's plan settled.

"That's it?" Tobias questioned, breaking Alexander's observations as he turned toward Ryder, who scratched the back of his neck anxiously.

"It's simple but I think that's why it'll work. A complicated plan would only end in ruin," Ryder said as he glanced at Amir for support, "So, what'd you think?"

This is the worst plan I've ever heard; Alexander thought as his tongue darted out to wet his bottom lip. Despite the simplicity of their and their father's plans, the difference was that he and Tobias didn't plan on killing anyone. In the end, however, Ryder's plan was so simple it *could* work. By some miracle, it could. But neither Alexander nor Tobias were about to tell him that. So instead, Alexander mirrored the emotionlessly bored expression he'd mastered over the years, fixating on their father with something he *hoped* resembled single-minded anger derived from foolish and moulded upbringings. "It's brilliant," he breathed out with as much vehement enthusiasm as he could muster.

Tobias copied his falsely determined tone with a darker edge, "Let's kill those bloodsuckers, once and for all," he said.

Azeil rolled his eyes, shaking his head in disappointment, as though he'd hoped they wouldn't follow wholeheartedly. Asher and Amir shared a look, like they knew something he didn't, before their gazes of blue and brown collided with his.

Truthfully, Alexander and Tobias couldn't have predicted their father's reaction, and the genuine grin that brightened the sharp age lines over Ryder's face startled them both. Ryder approached his sons and clapped them both over the shoulders with delight. Then he spun on his heel and strode towards the Land Cruiser, stooping into the open back window and pulling out a series of utility-like belts, each decked out with vials of assorted liquids and wooden stakes sharpened to dangerous points.

Alexander could *feel* Tobias's gaze upon the side of his face, but he refused to turn towards his brother, instead, keeping his eyes locked on Ryder as he gestured to a slight raise in the rock-scattered terrain, Amir and Asher turned to follow him.

Alexander turned, catching Azeil who seemed to be studying them all with an intensity Alexander had previously thought he'd lacked.

In the next moment, the dark-haired man turned away and followed his brother and band of odd friends over the rise of the slight hill. Tobias groaned and Alexander was suddenly doused in a startling clarity that this could be the last time he saw his brother—if their plan did not work.

If they died in there at the hands of the men with the golden eyes. Men who were content to live in the darkness of humanity's shadow—thriving in a world that had otherwise forgotten about them. Monsters.

"Are you *sure* about this?" Tobias asked, picking at the seam of his jeans.

"I'm not sure of *anything*, but what other choice do we have?" Alexander answered.

Tobias sighed, forcing himself to stop pulling at his pants before he raked his fingers through his hair. "I just wish there was another way, Alex," he said.

"So do I, Bias. So do I," Alexander said.

Alexander realized it was now or never. The thought terrified him as he pushed himself off the hood of his car and into the path of the four men before him. Each footstep sounding like a nail in his coffin.

He paused at the crest of the small hill, peering down at the crashing waves below and the rickety staircase clinging to the cliff face.

He knew absolutely one thing as he stared down at the white-capped ocean and the unrelenting waves colliding against the cliff face. He knew, like Tobias knew, that *nothing* could prepare them for whatever lay in the cavernous lair below.

Or for the bloodshed that would follow.

XLI.

Nyx

Attainment fluttered in her chest like a swarm of butterflies over a field of blooming flowers, kissing her ribcage as she smiled and her bare feet padded silently over the sand-littered floor, using the little time she had to escape the cavernous home. Something whispered that this *shouldn't* have been so easy. And she supposed it was—despite everything in her that screamed she was wrong—because why else had they unchained her like she was nothing more than a nuisance? Nyx turned to peer over her shoulder, seeing the sunbathed living space and the surrounding darkened tunnel entrances, searching for the blond duo tasked with watching her.

As if they knew, Kade and Niko stood leaning against the limestone tunnel's entrance, grinning wickedly when she turned away and her gaze found theirs. Blocking her chance of escape, she bristled at their grins. Some sliver of herself still found them enthralling despite the hurt they'd caused her. Her palms connected with Kade's chest as she shoved him back a couple of paces before he righted himself, gaze brimming with mirth as he peered down at her. Niko's laughter echoed in the room, a dark undertone to the lyrical sound as his hands wrapped around her waist, and he ushered her away from the entrance.

"Your *Twisted Sister-looking* ass better get out of the way. Right now," Nyx exclaimed, eyes narrowed as she batted his hands away.

Niko ignored her, glancing to Kade over his shoulder.

"I don't look like someone from *Twisted Sister*," he protested, his cyanic gaze searching Kade's, "... right, Kade?"

"Well," Kade began, scuffing the toe of his boot sheepishly upon the floor.

Niko half-gasped indignantly.

"I don't want to say, I told you so but—" he began before cutting himself off.

Niko's eyes narrowed in playful disdain; blond brows arched as he dared her to continue where Kade left off with a sweep of his hand.

"You were saying?" he said.

Her gaze darted to Kade, who grinned like the Cheshire cat, as she raised her chin and tucked her traitorous feelings for the pair aside, "... I told you so," she said.

Niko hummed, tapping his chin thoughtfully; devoid of his usual lifeful energy. "I *thought* that's what you would say, chica," he said.

Kade's boyish features became suddenly alight with something ungodly, like a lion before it sank its teeth into a wildebeest's throat. His gaze met hers and his lips moved as he mouthed a single word, thrilling her with heady anticipation:

"Run."

The lone word jolted her heart as she dragged her eyes from Kade to Niko, who leered at her with darkened irises. He stepped forward and she stepped back. Just enough to start the ball rolling, and for his gaze to spark with something animalistic and for her blood to thrum with malignant excitement.

Nyx belatedly realised the name of this game she'd unknowingly stumbled head-first into. Cat and mouse.

She ran.

Feigning left before she skilfully changed her footing and darted right, side-stepping Niko's hands as she rounded his shoulder. Her gaze locked on Kade—whose irises blazed dangerously, *excitedly*.

Niko's presence loomed in the back of her mind as she whirled towards him and her heart skipped a beat when she couldn't find him. Kade lunged as Nyx moved. Teetering out of his grasp and into Niko's as sea salt and weed ensnared her senses.

Nyx didn't think as she threw her head back into Niko's chin, ignoring the bolt of pain as his grasp loosened and she drove her elbow into his stomach. Relief flooded her system like a soothing balm as Niko's cry of pain echoed off the walls and she shoved him back and darted past him. She barely registered the gloved hand clamping around her forearm, until it brought her frantic movement to an abrupt halt.

"*Sit down,*" Orion gritted out from between clenched teeth.

Anger seemed to be coiled around him tightly as he pointed towards the couches and an otherworldly undertone coated his words.

Nyx bristled at the command, forcing her to obey as she dutifully crossed the cavernous room. She sat beside Kotori, who turned to peer down at her with his usual dark, open inquisition. Orion dismissed Kade and Niko with a flick of his wrist as he sat on his throne, before the pair moved swiftly to the opposing two-seater couch. Niko's gaze locked on her as he rubbed the red-tinged splotch over his chin, and Kade refused to look at her as they dropped unceremoniously onto the faded couch, disgruntled as their fun was cut short.

"I *hope* they stake you," Nyx spat at Orion.

"That's not very nice," Orion chuckled with a dark smile, "But I'm sure you do, little dove, and I'm sure *you* want to be the one to do it," he said.

Freshly fallen rain and sandalwood engulfed her senses with each inhale as Kotori leant forward, his lips brushing against her ear. "Make sure you don't miss, kleintje," he said.

Nyx turned to him, determined, "I won't," she said.

"Well … I look forward to it," Orion angled his head, "But you're going to *stay here* and not *say anything* that'll give us away, okay?" he said.

Nyx ground her teeth together as she screwed her eyes shut, hoping it'd purge her of his command with a shake of her head. It did little—but she couldn't fight it as they waited. They watched whilst she tried to shove the glass dome from her mind, her head dipping in a barely decipherable nod. A simple confirmation that rippled over them like sunlight upon the sea.

Satisfaction blazed like a blue fire in Orion's eyes when he straightened in his chair, *"Good girl."* He waited until his companions had filtered from the room before he rose purposely from his chair and paused. As if he couldn't find it in himself to walk away, despite the differences between them.

Because there were many.

He was everything she was not. And she, Nyx thought, was everything he *would not* allow himself to have. He released a breath of air as he pulled further away, his gaze boring into her; heavy with something she couldn't understand.

"Don't do anything stupid, little dove. I'd hate to have to kill you."

She wouldn't succumb to his wishes, or his softly uttered words. Not now. Not ever. He would learn that the hard way.

* * *

A skittering noise sounded throughout the cave, like someone had stumbled and their feet had sent the rocks rolling, lifting Nyx's attention.

She wondered why the quartet hadn't revealed themselves or stalked the labyrinth tunnel system to snatch whoever entered into the darkness and dispose of them. And as the thought traipsed across her mind, Nyx suddenly knew why they hadn't, knowing they sought to draw the suspense to an all-time high before they struck. She could imagine how easy it would be for them—to stride into the light and snatch her family from her—even if they chose to lurk within the shadows until they deemed the moment right. If that moment arose at all, because she knew Orion would pull the plug if he didn't see a downward spiral of events in his favour.

Nyx startled when pebbles tumbled down the marble staircase, her gaze darting from the shadows to the cave's entrance when footsteps echoed off the tunnel walls and she leant forward, straining to see whoever had been foolish enough to stumble into the carefully laid trap. Her eyes rolled with unveiled disdain when Ryder Montes' eternal scowl burst into the sunlit living space. His lips curled as she eyed him, noting the creased shirt and the scuffs over his black army boots.

Ryder's gaze met hers—dark and judging—sunlight glinting off the face of his watch, the red bandana around his opposing wrist blazing a burning red. He seemed to size her up from the tunnel's opening, cautious as his eyes flickered over her body and his eyebrows screwed together when he couldn't find any restraints.

If only he knew, she thought bitterly.

Ryder stepped into the cavernous home with Amir following close at his heels, raking his serene gaze across the cave with finer, less obvious scrutiny. Amir's dark eyes softened, masking his suspicions as he cautiously approached her and she surveyed his army-like wardrobe: silver dog tags, black T-shirt, camouflage pants and tan boots. Oddly ironic as she lifted her chin and searched the tunnel for her uncle's familiar face.

Asher's voice carried across the cave, waxing and waning before his eyes collided with hers and his face split into a relief-fuelled grin. Nyx mirrored Asher's smile, happiness bubbling in her chest as she fought against Orion's commands, longing to run towards her uncle and wrap her arms around his waist.

She couldn't. Forced instead to relish in his brightly patterned shirt that she had so often teased him for—the grip over her mind tightened almost painfully before her smile slipped. Forcing herself to focus on the crisp blueness of his jeans and the darkness of his age-worn shoes instead of the jarring sting of longing in her chest.

Asher's voice carried to her like a whisper of reverence, ignoring Ryder and Amir's protests as he shooed their hands away, "Nyx. You're okay," he said.

Nyx winced, thrashing against the domed prison around her mind, swallowing the ugly lump forming in her throat as her gaze darted to the dark-haired man behind Asher. And in that second, she wished she could free herself from the reinforced hold over her mind. She didn't care that the last time she'd seen her father had been amid the heated words of an argument. None of it mattered as she saw the blinding relief in his face and he shoved Ryder's hand away. Her eyes found the plaited leather bracelet around his wrist—a gift from her mother all those years ago.

Warm hands cupped her face, engulfing her in her father's presence whilst his eyes traced every inch of her face with true concern.

"Nyx …" his voice wavered, struggling to formulate a sentence that'd convey his relief, "We're going to take you *home*."

Nyx choked on the sob forming in the depths of her throat, because how could she tell him she wasn't going home? That she'd bargained her life away to the four men who lurked in the shadows, their gazes boring into her even now, from their positions in the darkness. Or how could she *possibly* tell him she felt whole in their presence? That every moment after her hands had first been stained with Kai's blood had felt *wrong*. Like she'd only been half alive until she met Orion, Kotori, Niko and Kade. And what would he think of her when he found out that she'd *killed* someone? That she'd revelled in the terror-stricken hue of Kai's irises like the warped shard of her being had always longed for.

The simple answer was that she couldn't.

No matter how much she craved to purge herself of the malignant darkness, it wouldn't let go. And a growing part of her didn't want it to.

She *wanted* to succumb to its safety.

She felt the satisfaction of Orion's allure in the depths of her mind like it was her own, sensing her gradual acceptance beneath the roaring flames of her anger. Everything in her screamed, begging her to do something—*anything*—to save her family and the twins who walked into the cave with guarded eyes. Her brothers in everything but blood.

Nyx pushed every ounce of her desperation into her eyes, hoping they'd see her warning as she purposefully darted her gaze towards the darkened alcoves that hid Orion, Kotori, Kade, and Niko.

Tobias paused beside the tunnel's entrance, catching her looks, and angling his head before he subtly tapped Alexander's arm and both boys watched her carefully. Nyx flickered her gaze to the men in the shadows, relief guttering in her stomach when Alexander nodded, and Tobias ambled over to her.

His hands were tucked into the pocket of his hoodie like he was forcing himself *not* to pick at his black jeans before he causally rested his hand upon Azeil's shoulder. Her father's head whipped to Tobias, eyes narrowed before he noted the boy's calm.

Nyx fought for purchase in her mind, raining her fists upon the mental prison with fierce desperation when Alexander stepped toward the nearest tunnel tucked beside the leaning bookshelf. His gaze darted to her—apologetic and determined—and suddenly, all she could hear was a distant roar in her eardrums. Asher's soothing assurances bled away to white noise, like her mind and its glass-like prison. Her harrowed scream tore through her head, echoing off her skull as she thrashed at the bindings woven around her.

Don't be stupid, Alex, she begged, clawing at the glass-like dome housing her mind. *Walk away*.

Alexander stepped closer to the darkness and the ebony-haired man lurking in the shadows. Kotori, Nyx thought, screwing her eyes shut, desperately engraving Alexander's black pants and grey band T-shirt into her mind so she'd never forget the dun-eyed boy with soft, brown curls.

It was as he took another step closer to the shadows and Tobias, Asher and her father moved to follow him that Nyx spoke, gritting her words out through clenched teeth, "Don't."

Her teeth ground together against the sharp, slicing pain that ripped through her head, splintering her skull. Orion's gaze seared into her brain, the tell-tale sound of skittering rocks accompanying his purposeful movement. And, despite the one desperate word, her father, Asher, Tobias, and Alexander all strode towards a darkened tunnel.

Azeil and Asher shared an odd look between themselves, their eyes glancing purposely back to her. It sickened Nyx when the shadows played across their skin, suffocating her whilst she mentally fought the vice-like grasp over her mind.

A glass cage for a *little dove.*

Nyx lifted her gaze from the four men determined to walk into a trap and turned to Ryder, imploring the self-proclaimed vampire hunter to do something—to stop them—before it was too late. Ryder's brow furrowed, the creases over his forehead deepening as he hesitated, turning to Amir with rare uncertainty.

Ryder crossed the sunlit cave, his gaze darting uneasily around the mismatched furniture and odd trinkets until he towered above her, casting a stony glare down at her. "Don't?" he asked, crooking a dark eyebrow as he awaited an answer she couldn't give before he continued, ignoring Amir's scolding whisper. "What'd you know, *vampire lover?*"

Nyx blinked up at him, mind scrambling before she started, whipping her head towards the small cluster of doves that scattered towards the gaping holes in the ceiling. Their beating wings echoed off the uneven walls as Asher and Azeil shared an anxious look, backing away from the pitch-black of the tunnels and into the sunlight.

Dread curled in her stomach, dragging its razor-sharp claws down her chest until it held her racing heart. She *knew* the varying shades of white, cream, and brown coloured doves hadn't taken flight by coincidence. Her nerves felt frayed in her body, like they were attached by sheer threads as Ryder moved swiftly amidst the distraction.

He crouched down in front of her, his glare boring into her before he leant closer, "I know what you are, *halfling,*" he snarled. His hands moved at his side before he made a sudden lunging motion towards her.

As an equally sharp and dull pain lanced her chest, Orion's vice-like grip seemed to shatter. Freeing her from his bindings as a stunned scream tumbled from her lips. Her eyes widened when she dropped her gaze to the crudely sharpened stake jutting out from beneath her ribcage. And through the blinding pain, she supposed she should've been grateful that his aim was horrible, lest it have been accurate, and she be dead with a wooden stake protruding from her chest. But her optimistic thoughts did nothing to mask the agonising burn of pain stemming from her ribcage. Her fingers dug into the cushions of the beaten couch; her eyes screwing shut against the maddening anguish. With every deep inhalation of oxygen into her chest, she winced against the pulling sensation of the stake in her midsection. A metallic stench of blood engulfed her senses, filling her nostrils as effectively as her blood stained the hands she pressed firmly around the wooden intruder.

She knew the moment Ryder revealed the stake that Orion had halted his plans, putting himself and his companions' safety first. Like he always did and always would. Her revelation rankled. Would she be forced to wander this path of pain alone because Orion wouldn't risk Niko, Kade or Kotori's life for hers—not like he'd done twenty-five years ago?

Through the ringing in her ears and the sharp, tearing sensation below her ribcage, she heard the tell-tale sound of rocks purposefully tumbling down a shadow-blanketed tunnel. Nyx forced herself to lift her head away from the steady trickle of blood weeping from her wound and to her father over Ryder's shoulder. Her eyes imploring him to understand—to run—and not look back as words failed her amid her pain. Despite everything in him that would protest, she hoped they would get out of this alive.

Alexander and Tobias seized Azeil's forearms. His head turned from one twin to the other before he realised what they were doing.

"No! Let me go," Azeil exclaimed, tugging against them. "We can't leave her here!"

Nyx loved her father then, in that moment, a burst of emotion seized her, flooding her body as the twins seized him. She met Asher's gaze, knowing him as well as he knew her.

"Go", she gargled.

Her face was void of any emotion, Asher hesitated, seeming to fight within himself. Her father's desperate cries danced off the cavernous walls, deafening as he bellowed his protests and the scuffing of shoes along the floor filled her ears. It amused her through the blur of pain swarming her mind, how quickly Ryder rose from in front of her and seized the collar of Asher's T-shirt with Amir at his heels.

"We're *not* going to abandon her here," Asher stated, pushing at Ryder's arm with narrowed eyes, "We're not *leaving*!"

"Yes, we are," Alexander interjected, teeth gritted as Tobias, and he dragged Azeil closer to the tunnelled entrance.

"She knows that better than we do," Tobias pointed out, apologetic as he readjusted his grasp.

"She doesn't know what she wants," Azeil snapped, starting towards Ryder with an aggravated sneer, "And you're *dead*."

"We'll all be dead if we don't get out of here," Amir stated, oddly calm.

Tobias and Asher scoffed, Asher moving to help them drag Azeil kicking and shouting from the cave.

"Let go of me!" Azeil bellowed, his gaze softening as he turned to his younger brother, voice soft as he continued, "We can't leave her, Ash."

"You have to," Nyx ground out, gasping as she unknowingly jostled the blood-stained stake.

"We *have to* leave her," Asher tried, angling his head away from his brother, jaw ticking as blue and grey eyes alike met hers.

"We *can't*," Azeil said, pleading now.

"We *can*, Eil," Asher murmured, refusing to meet her gaze as Ryder and Amir slipped past them and disappeared down the tunnelled entrance.

"*They* can leave. To hell with them. Let me go!" Azeil snapped, swivelling within Alexander and Tobias's grasp as though he'd hoped it'd catch them off guard.

"Go," she urged again, "Please," pushing herself up onto the edge of the couch despite the jagged pain. A garbled groan spilled from her lips as she leant too far forward and tumbled to the floor. Her bloodied palms wound around her waist as she angled her body and her side connected.

Asher shifted, his eyes pained as he moved toward her and she lifted a bloodied hand, staunching his movement.

Nyx shook her head, her gaze locked on the ceiling and the sunlight cascading down upon her blood-stained clothes and hands. She closed her eyes and the cold of the floor soaked into her skin. Black spots danced across her eyelids, pulsing and twinkling. Nyx concentrated on the dull crashing of waves and scuffling ghosting the shell of her ear as she swallowed thickly. Her rasped warning echoed off the walls and to her ears like a bell tolling on midday—deafening and brimming with a jarring warning, “It’s a trap.”

Silence followed, and for a moment, she mistook it for comfort before a flurry of movement ensued and her senses darkened. The barest glimmer of satisfaction breached the numbness plaguing her before she succumbed to the true silence of unconsciousness. She *had* done something stupid, and now it *would* kill her.

But *he* wouldn’t be the one to deliver the final blow, and that filled her with relief. This little dove had broken from its glass-like cage and Orion could do nothing as it shattered in his hands, beaded with her blood, staining his pristinely fused glass.

Life and death eternally at war. Battle after hard-won battle, ravaging the coastal city of Celacali. His cage was death, and her blood was life. All she had to do was *give in* to the world’s darkness; for she had to accept the darkest parts of herself before she could live.

XLII.

Orion

The scent of blood descended on the darkened tunnelways before it engulfed Orion's senses with a tangent sting of metal. It stained Nyx's shirt a dark *bloody* red and ensured chaos careened through Kade and Niko's chests. Kotori's calm but worried disposition was unable to reach the pair, though Orion knew Kotori fretted for Nyx like the others, and he felt their desperation.

At first, Orion didn't understand their sense of frenzy, his chilling gaze surveying the scene before him with biting indifference. It didn't compute why Niko's energetic personality flipped like a switch, plunging him into a sombre light. Nor could he understand the tremble of Kade's fingers when the golden-curled vampire traced his fingertips across Nyx's skin.

Orion thought for a moment, unsure for the first time in a long time, in his immortal life. Something about the fear playing at the edges of Niko and Kade's eyes unsettled him, poking at the protective instincts hidden away in his chest. He watched Kotori, who had reappeared from the darkness of a tunnel with an array of bandages and a first-aid kit, gaze locked on Nyx.

He saw as Niko's jean-clad knee sank to the stone floor and he pulled Nyx carefully into his lap, cradling her to his chest whilst Kade rounded his shoulder and dropped to his knees before her, anxiously interlacing their fingers. Somewhere in Orion's chest, it aggravated him. It was stamped in their eyes—their concern and … adoration—and he wanted to crush it like a bug beneath the sole of his boots.

Because he *couldn't* understand the desperation for the girl in their midst. She was just a human. A fleeting being who would disappear in the blink of one of their lifespans, forgotten by them in years to come. At least, that's what he *tried* to rationalise the faint prickling sensation beneath his sternum.

Orion's gaze stayed locked on the trio clustered around Nyx, watching them as he pulled a lighter from his pocket and lit his cigarette, dropping into his ornate chair with wisps of smoke curling around his face. But as he inhaled a lungful of smoke, and Kotori reached for Nyx—Niko's eyes bled a dangerous white-gold. The broad and yet chiselled plains of his face contorted and sharpened, shifting beneath his skin until the bone structure of his features balanced something from nightmares and dreams alike. Niko's lips curled into a deathly sneer, elongated fangs bared at Kotori. A sound mirrored by Kade and the lightening of his eyes as his fangs peeked out from beneath his lips, Niko pulling Nyx closer to his chest whilst Kade adjusted his position so she was protected from every angle. A warning snarl reverberated from the pair, daring Kotori to try and touch her.

Orion blew out a cloud of white-grey smoke, his fingers drumming upon the armrest of the ornate chair when he leant forward, "Take it easy, boys," he said.

Niko whirled to face him, Kade's displeased growl paired with the unrestrained rage rippling across the room, "*Take it easy*? She could die!" Niko hissed.

"She *won't*," Orion said.

"You don't know—" Niko began.

Orion's irises brightened, flickering between blue and gold as he cut Niko off and his voice lowered to a frigid murmur, "*Listen*," he said quietly.

Niko exhaled, eyeing Kotori and Kade's tense back as he quirked his head and listened.

Orion leant back into his chair, lifting his cigarette back to his lips and taking a drag as the quick but persistent thumping of Nyx's heart drummed in his ears. It pleased him when Niko's eyes with their bone-white hue, returned to cyanic-blue. Like Kade's did a moment later, the muscles of his back uncoiling as his features returned. "If you don't back up and let Kotori stop the bleeding, she *will* die," he drawled, steeling his gaze as Kade turned and subtly pried Niko's fingers away from Nyx.

Niko murmured something between an insult and a protest before allowing Kotori to pull Nyx onto his lap and tend to her wounds. Something flickered in their gazes—there one moment and gone the next—that Orion barely caught, almost missing it.

If he hadn't recognised the emotion they tried to hide; the *exact* emotion he wished to purge from his bloodstream, that he longed to rip from his veins like he tore into people's throats, ridding himself of something he *couldn't* allow himself to feel. A face Doppelgänger to his, thrown to the forefront of his mind, their lips twisted with a sneer as the ghost's voice filled his ears.

You're destined to be forgotten and betrayed by those who you care about, brother. Maledictus.

"She'll be okay, Niko," Kotori murmured; his dark eyes troubled.

Orion quirked his eyebrows, a mocking smile dancing along his lips as he shoved his ghosts to the back of his mind and he noted the glances his companions spared him, "You're blaming *me*?" he said before he chuckled lowly, shaking his head with cold amusement. "She's just a human, Niko. They come and they go. Give it a couple of decades and you'll get over her," he said.

"Of course, *you'd* say that." Niko sneered, a muscle ticking in his jaw when his arms folded over his chest.

"What's that supposed to mean?" Orion asked lightly.

"You couldn't give a shit whether she lives or dies," Niko said, his eyes flaring. "She's *just a human* to you."

Orion breathed out a soft, disdainful laugh, "Don't tell me you caught feelings for her, Nik? After all, weren't you the one who said she'd make *one hell of a meal?*"

"Things changed, Orion," Niko said.

"I guess you and Kade have that in common then," Orion turned to Kade, "Isn't that right, Kade?"

Kade tensed beneath the weight of Orion's gaze, his shoulders locking before he clicked his fingers softly at Ares. The black and white Malamute had tucked himself behind the gauzy curtains and now came bounding out.

Orion bristled at Kade's disregard, at the conflicting interests in his companions—in his brothers he'd spent centuries roaming Celacali with. He *knew* he shouldn't abuse the power given to him as their leader but, as Kade swaddled Ares in his arms and peered down at the almond-eyed pup from Nyx's side, something rattled inside Orion. He was enraged by the shifted loyalties, that their concern for a mortal had changed everything they'd built together.

And he *knew* he was wrong—in every sense—but he couldn't quell the blue fire licking at his insides like the forked tongue of a serpent. It ravaged his bloodstream without remorse. Taking what it wanted, when it wanted. And despite his best efforts, the twisted and selfish side of him urged him to let go. To fracture his steely exterior and unflinching prowess that kept him rooted in the ornate chair plunged in sunlight. But he wouldn't let it fool him, not like it used to. He *couldn't* let it as his cold irises refocused on the cave around him and a grimace contorted Kotori's face, the man's fingertips slicked deep crimson.

"What is it?" Orion asked, his voice splitting the air like a clap of thunder.

Kotori's eyes flickered up to him and then back to the blood-stained stake protruding from Nyx's midsection, "She *could* die—" he said.

Niko and Kade's heads snapped to Kotori, Niko's hands clenching and unclenching at his sides as he stepped forward, "*What?*"

"I have to remove the stake before I can *attempt* to stem the bleeding," Kotori said; he looked uncharacteristically stressed as his eyes traced the stained flesh of Nyx's abdomen.

Something twisted painfully in Orion's gut. *Almost* like a knife plunged into the top of his sternum and dragged to its base, spilling his innards into his lap.

"Do what you must, but do it quickly," Orion said, listening to the slowing *tha-thump, tha-thump* of Nyx's heart, "She *is* fading."

"What'd you care if she lives or dies?" Kade snapped, "You're the one who said we should keep her around as a blood bag. Not us."

Some sadistic side of Orion still did think that, but he wasn't going to admit that to Kade as he put Ares down. Instead, devoid of all emotion, he pushed every ounce of primal power from the sire-bond onto Kade. He watched with unmoved interest, waiting for the first fissure to appear.

Kade's eyes widened with betrayal and recognition, before a pained groan tumbled from his lips and he pressed a hand to his chest, glaring at Orion.

Niko rounded on Orion then, yanking him up and out of his chair by the collar, rage contorting his features. And Orion knew, as Niko's eyes darted between his eyes and jawline, what he longed to do. What he *wished* he could do.

"Let it go, Niko. He *wants* your reaction, and you know it," Kade urged, dropping his gaze back to Nyx. "There are more important things to worry about."

And in the next moment, Kotori swiftly pulled the stake from Nyx's mid-section and tore open a sachet of medical-grade glue with his teeth, pouring a liberal amount of the powdery substance over the gushing wound before Niko released Orion.

Kotori waited for the bleeding to slow as he prepped a needle and stolen surgical thread with steady hands; his years spent as a volunteer nurse in the 1700's engrained into his memory.

Criss-cross, criss-cross, criss-cross.

But he *knew,* deep down, that it wasn't sudden—his companions' fondness for Nyx—despite what he wished to fool himself into believing. He'd known, like they had. But still, he hadn't expected the surprise that flickered in his chest. It almost comforted him. *Almost.* But instead, he swatted the wayward warmth from the darkest depths of his soul, determined to remain unchanged as Kotori's skilled fingers stitched up the square-shaped wound below Nyx's ribcage and he cleaned the blood from her stomach with antibacterial wipes. *All good on the outside. But what about the internal damage?* he wondered, intensely eyeing Kotori.

Some warped side of Orion *couldn't* let her go, despite how fiercely he shoved those traitorous thoughts away. They consumed him, egged on by his selfish side that crooned in his ear. That he couldn't make sense of. He *wouldn't* allow himself to have her like he craved, but maybe he could settle for being hated by her—if only to be within her presence and for the siren's call of her heartbeat to fill his ears.

He wasn't saying he was perfect, because he knew he was the furthest thing from perfection. But he hoped it would be worth it when he rose from the ornately designed chair, crossing the room, and crouching down beside his brothers, who eyed him warily.

His teeth elongated in his mouth, pushing his jacket's sleeve up his arm before his fangs sank into his own flesh and the coppery tang of his blood filled his tastebuds. Orion's gaze burned like a blue fire, uncanny and immortal in every sense as his eyes met each of theirs in turn, finding nothing but resolute understanding. His opposing hand slipped beneath Nyx's head, angling her head back as he brought his bleeding wrist to her lips, allowing his blood to drip into her mouth.

He waited—like they all waited—his breath lodged in his throat as he pulled his wrist away, lathing his tongue over the weeping indents until he felt the skin stitch itself back together.

Nyx swallowed. Her throat worked as her unconscious body sealed her fate and plunged her into the darkness of another world.

Our world, Orion thought.

He knew she'd thrive in it, even if she couldn't see it herself. Because where some found comfort in good and justness, he knew she'd find comfort in his darkness. A place into which few were brave enough to delve and where fewer thrived.

A world ruled by the night.

XLIII.

Nyx

A gasped breath burned up Nyx's throat and past her lips, her heart seeming to explode. Her gaze darted, searching the dancing light for someone—anyone—to quell her unease. She shifted in an assortment of bedding—legs tangling in what felt like cotton sheets. Then, propping herself up on the mattress with her elbows, she groaned as a ripping pain seared through her midsection, and she rushed to press her hands to the agonised ache. Her teeth gritted, she looked down at her bandaged mid-section as a gloved hand grasped her shoulder, pushing her gently back.

Nyx startled, whipping her head towards him. His gaze, as cold and crisp as ever, his clothes as black as night. She tried but failed to ignore the attraction she felt toward him, there was no denying his uncanny beauty. His blond hair as white as snow and an aura as otherworldly as all the lives he'd lived; an immortal who walked the mortal world.

"Easy, little dove," Orion drawled, his teeth in shadow.

Nyx glared at him as she shoved his hand from her shoulder and turned toward the end of her bed, feeling the subtle rise and fall of Ares by her calf. Her unease waned at the presence of the familiar

Malamute. Her little warrior. But her peace didn't last long as she turned back to Orion, wondering where the others were.

"They're sleeping," Orion said. He placed a cigarette between his lips as he watched her, lighting it. Wisps of smoke coiled around his face like a snake as he exhaled, "I had to make them go. They wouldn't leave your side."

Nyx nodded, watching him closely. "How long have I been out?" she said.

"A couple of hours," Orion said. He gestured to the bandages woven around her mid-section with a measured sweep of his hand, "You took *quite* a blow."

The mismatched sheets ruffled, shifting with her as she pushed herself up and her back pressed into the finely carved headboard.

"Yeah, no thanks to *you*. He thought I was a halfling," Nyx said bitterly.

She swallowed the lump that swelled in her throat, following the tresses of smoke as they brushed over the stubbled flesh of Orion's jaw like it'd calm the racing of her heart. As she looked at him, something built in her chest, growing, and expanding like the building chords of a song before the final verses. If it was a symphony, it sang to her like a dozen bows upon violin strings, pulsing in her ears like drumbeats, guitar riffs and a pianist coupled with the agonised vocalist whose voice carried far and true, never faltering in its mournful and tragic song.

Nyx paused, it suddenly seemed to her that Orion looked ... guilty. The look in his eyes unnerved her in a very different way from before. Her palms felt slick with nervous sweat and she fisted the sheets in her hands, ignoring the blaze of pain in her midsection when she swung her legs over the edge of the bed and waved away Orion's disapproving frown.

"What did you do?" she asked.

His eyes darted from her face to his wrist, flicking the ash from the cigarette to the floor before lifting his eyes back to her, "What had to be done," he said.

"Had to?" she asked, a growing unease filling her. *What did that mean?* "You didn't *have to* do anything."

"So, you *wanted* to die?" he asked, his voice cold.

"That wasn't the question. *What did you do,* Orion?"

"I saved your life unless, of course, you'd rather have bled out in Niko's lap," he said. Orion cocked his head, a dark undertone lacing his blue irises, "But that's not what you really want to know, is it?"

Nyx shook her head, her voice wavering in a way she loathed, "No,"

"You want to know *what* you are, right?" Orion asked.

She nodded, her eyes dropping as Orion came closer. His fingers slipped beneath her chin and tilted her head back, so her ochre gaze collided with his frigid blue. His enigmatic presence registered fully in her mind along with his proximity, the breath in her lungs caught and the tide of her thoughts swelled. His lips hovered over hers, close enough to kiss if she wished it. And some part of her did—as his gaze darted between her lips and her eyes—that piece of her that fit so perfectly inside her chest like it had belonged there all along. Like *she* belonged in the darkest parts of the world.

Cigarettes and leather trickled into the crevices of her senses, engulfing her with an ease Nyx hated but that seemed to please Orion.

"Use your voice, Nyx," Orion urged, his honeyed voice soft and yet laced with something dominated by centuries upon the earth.

"Yes," she breathed out shakily, her eyelashes brushing against her cheeks.

"Yes, what?"

Her eyes rolled, "*Please,*" she whispered.

He hummed, tracing his gaze over her face before he stepped back, and his fingers left the underside of her chin, "You're like us now but not," he said.

Dread pooled in Nyx's stomach, dousing her like a bucket of ice-cold water. The white of her shirt was stained red with her blood. Nyx forced every ounce of emotionless malice into her voice, unwavering, "*What?*"

"You're a halfling. Not quite human, not quite a vampire. You're in between darkness and light," Orion said.

She chortled without amusement, "Between life and death you mean."

"Call it what you want. But I *saved* your life," he said.

Nyx's eyebrow arched, daring the platinum blond as she stepped closer to him, art supplies scattered around her. Orion grinned and she grinned as she reached behind him, her fingertips brushing against the wooden handle of a paintbrush. Nyx leant in, her lips ghosting across his, fingers curling around the forgotten brush before she pulled it into her palm and clasped it tightly in her grip. Her hand returned to her side as the other skittered up his arm, grasping the fabric of his jacket in her fist.

"You *killed* me," she spat, her lips brushing against his as she moved quickly, plunging the dull-ended paintbrush into his chest without flinching.

Orion stumbled back, colliding with the makeshift workspace, and sending art supplies tumbling to the floor. Surprise flickered through his gaze when he righted himself and his icy gaze dropped to the paintbrush protruding crudely from his chest. His lips stretched into a crooked grin as pure, undiluted terror crashed into her. The pain in her mid-section quickly shoved to the back of her mind as she spun on her heel toward the beckoning darkness of the cave's exit. Orion's arms wound around her waist—careful to not jostle her wound—and he pressed her back flush against the limestone walls. His hips pressed into her stomach, leather-clad hands snatching her wrists up and pinning them above her head whilst she struggled.

"I thought we went over this, sweetheart," Orion crooned, a predatory glint in his eyes as he peered down at her. "You only had one shot to kill me, and I told you not to miss."

"Please—" Nyx started.

"So, you're going to beg now? For what?" he said and paused, hand moving to cup her jaw, so his gaze seared into hers. "Mercy?"

"I—just ... *please*. Let me go."

"Shh, I'm not going to hurt you," Orion said. The lie was sweet and deadly.

Her gaze darted anxiously over his face, searching for something to reassure her. Not that it helped, for his gaze was as still as an undisturbed pond and revealed nothing.

Orion clicked his tongue, "I'm *not* going to hurt you," he breathed against her lips.

"I don't believe you," Nyx said.

"You don't have to believe me," he said as his lips brushed against hers, gentle and possessive. "And I don't expect you to, but you *shouldn't* have done that, little dove."

"I thought you said you'd look forward to the day I tried to kill you?" Nyx said.

He chuckled, a lightness to his eyes as he leant down and his lips brushed against the underside of her jaw. "It's *because* of that," he moved his hips, grinding himself into her crotch in a way that made her gasp, "Can't you *feel* what you're doing to me?"

A deep timbred cough echoed from the opening of the tunnel, followed by unceremonious groans as Nyx's head turned towards the commotion. Niko, Kotori and Kade. Orion chuckled, pressing a firm but possessive kiss to the underside of her chin before he released her and stepped aside, leaning his shoulder into the coarse rock, and crossing one foot over the other.

"See what you did, Kotori," Niko whined, swatting his dark-haired companion's shoulder before he traipsed over to Nyx and his lips pressed into hers. His fingers tangled in her curls before she parted her lips to his ministrations and he deepened the kiss, pulling away moments later with a playful nip to her throat. "I was enjoying the show."

"We know," Kade taunted, his eyes skittering over his scattered art supplies when he strode into the cave with bird-like grace.

"Aw c'mon, Kade. You're going to try and tell me that *you* can't feel the tension between them?" Niko said.

Kade arched his sandy eyebrows as his dimples appeared. Nyx peered up at him when he stopped in front of her and pulled her into his arms, winding them around her waist and resting his chin upon her shoulder with a steading inhalation of her scent, a comforting warmth settling in her bones despite everything he'd done.

"It'd be hard to *miss,*" he said.

"Niko, even Ares can sense the tension between them," Kotori stated, crossing the room, and pulling Nyx out from Kade's arms, who groaned in protest, and into his own.

"There's *no* tension between us," Nyx protested, bristling at the unconvinced hum that rumbled in Kotori's chest and into her back, his ring-clad hands splayed over her hips whilst his chin rested atop her head.

"*Sure,*" Niko mocked, drawing out the word with a soft snicker. "You hate him, he hates you," he clapped his hands together, startling her and Ares, who lifted his head sleepily, ears flicking back against his head, "tension."

Kade rubbed his hands together, grinning, "And don't get us started on angry sex."

Orion chuckled, pushing himself off the rock wall as their gazes swivelled to him.

"As much as I'd like to indulge you all, we have more important things to worry about," he said.

Nyx's heart stuttered in her chest, drawing the steeliness of Orion's gaze to her as she swallowed the unease gripping at her throat, "Like what?"

Orion's lips curled, "We have humans to terrify, people to torment … *blood* to spill."

She knew it wasn't just anyone's blood they sought to spill. That would be too easy. Too painless and unsatisfying. It wouldn't satisfy them at all, nor would it quell the vengeance they wished to reap. It had to be someone they loathed, someone's blood they wished had stained their skin twenty-five years ago. She knew whose blood would spill, and she wasn't sure she'd be able to stop them when the time came.

Or if she'd have the strength to try.

XLIV.

Tobias

Tension crackled like a taut wire, humming in the air to a silent song. Tobias's gaze followed Azeil, who paced the hardwood floor, his footfalls echoing. Tobias recognised Azeil's stifled anger, fighting to uphold his own mask of indifference when all he wanted to do was punch something.

Azeil turned suddenly to Ryder, eyes ablaze with silver fire. Asher and Amir leapt forward, snatching Azeil's arms before his curled fist collided with Ryder's face. "How can you stand there and pretend this isn't *your* fault!?" Azeil spat, shrugging Asher and Amir off with a forceful roll of his shoulders.

Tobias watched the interaction raptly as his father remained silent, sullen brown eyes darting anywhere but the fuming Monroe. With an irked scoff, Azeil stepped forward, before Alexander pushed himself off the wall and into Azeil's path, laying a firm hand upon the older man's chest.

Ryder opened and closed his mouth, resembling a fish out of water whilst he scrambled to find any words to explain himself, "I didn't mean to … I just thought—"

Alexander pinned their father beneath the weight of his stare, "It doesn't matter if you meant it or not. You *assumed* you knew, and you did something unforgivable," he said.

"And that pain is real," Tobias stated, his voice dangerously low and measured. "No matter how you'd like to fool yourself into believing that it's not." His gaze hardened with disdain as he dragged his eyes up and down his father. "You *know* there'll be consequences," he finished.

Asher sighed, raking his fingers through his hair as he resumed Azeil's pacing, glancing sidelong at Ryder with stark anger, "You just had to provoke them again, didn't you? Once wasn't enough? And what? Nyx is your collateral damage?" he said.

"You've learnt *nothing* in twenty-five years, Ryder," Azeil snapped, chest heaving as though it took everything in him to speak in level tones. "You're still the same *boy* clutching at straws. And, if I lose my daughter because of you—" his lips curled into a sneer, his voice lowering several octaves, "—*they*'ll be the least of your worries." Azeil stared Ryder down, silence hanging palpably in the lounge room as they waited before Azeil climbed the wooden staircase and disappeared down the shadowed hallway.

Asher hesitated, chewing the inside of his cheek, as if their situation reminded him of the past.

But Tobias knew, as Asher blew out a heavy sigh and his head shook, that whatever had brought that look to Asher Monroe's eyes would remain a memory privy only to him. The colourful patterns of Asher's shirt brushed Ryder's forearm as he slipped past and up the staircase, following his older brother.

Tobias observed silently, watching the ensuring puzzle pieces scatter to different corners of the house as Alexander turned too, footsteps echoing off the hardwood floors as he disappeared out into the sunbathed front yard. Tobias knew his brother needed time to rein in his anger and re-establish some sense of calm. Their father was at the top of Alexander's hit list. Among others.

"Why do you do it?" Tobias asked abruptly, slicing through the tense silence when Amir left the room to give him space to vocalise his thoughts.

Ryder blinked, confused, "What?"

"Why do you *hunt* vampires?" Tobias pressed.

"To protect people," Ryder said as he stepped forward, the confusion shoved aside and replaced by unwavering certainty. "It's always been about protecting innocents!"

Tobias angled his head, arching an unimpressed eyebrow, "So, what was Nyx?" Ryder opened his mouth to speak, the rebuttal dying on his tongue when Tobias's head shook with measured anger. "Because she certainly wasn't evil."

"I didn't—" he began.

"*Think*?" Tobias finished for him as he chuckled bitterly, pushing himself off the doorway and approaching his father, "Oh, I know you didn't. Because if you had, we wouldn't all be waiting for our inevitable deaths."

"We're *not* going to die, Bias," Ryder said.

Tobias's eyes closed with the soft utterance of his name. The muscles in his jaw ticked, teeth grinding together before he forced himself to speak through the mirage of punches the nickname evoked coming from his father's mouth.

"*Don't* call me that. *You* don't get to call me that," he said.

Ryder released a drawn-out sigh, dragging his hand across his face as he levelled Tobias with an almost pleading look. "I keep trying to be a better father … even when everything I do seems to backfire," he said.

"Because it does!" Tobias said as he shook his head, shoving balled fists into the pockets of his hoodie. "I just *wish* you'd stop trying."

"How can you say that?" Ryder asked.

"Because I'm *tired* of waiting around for *my father* who's afraid of his own shadow," Tobias said, breathing in a steadying breath and pulling his unfurled hands from his pockets. "I can't keep waiting around for a dad that doesn't appear. And neither can Alex. So, stop trying … *please*."

It hurt more than Tobias cared to admit as he said the words, and he watched a multitude of emotions flicker over his father's face. The truth stung. Biting at the open flesh of his chest like some beast had raked its taloned paw from his bicep to his opposing hip, and then someone had poured salt into the open wound. He supposed it'd been a long time coming. And he was glad he'd finally said it so calmly—so unwaveringly—face to face.

He thought of Nyx and her voice dancing off his mind, the memory of her urging him to tell his father the truth playing like his own personal broken record—he turned and stepped towards the kitchen doorway, and the awaiting back door.

Ryder's hand shot out, clamping down around his wrist before Tobias turned.

"I'm *not* afraid of my own shadow like some child afraid of the dark," Ryder said.

Tobias chortled, "Oh? Well, I guess you better fight for *your* life ..." He shrugged the hand from his wrist with a disdainful twitch of his upper lip. "Since *you* condemned all of *us* to death," he said.

Tobias's gaze trailed over the homely kitchen, rounding the table before his hand closed around the metallic handle and something collided with the back of his head. Tobias staggered forward, forehead knocking into the glass portion of the door, his hand pressed into the pulsing pain at the base of his skull before he saw his father. Bitterness was etched into Ryder's face and the crude metallic glint of a gun disappeared beneath the waistband of his pants. As Tobias fought the uneasy sway accompanying the dancing spots in his vision, his free hand reached out to grip the edge of the nearest benchtop.

Ryder closed the space between them, his steps calculated and light.

Tobias knew with upending dread that whatever substance filled the syringe his father now pulled from his back pocket would hinder his already failing consciousness. It didn't stop him from trying as he staggered back, his palm clammy and slicked with sweat. Tobias shook his head, hand curling around the door handle and twisting before Ryder moved swiftly. Unsheathing the silver needle and digging his forearm into Tobias's chest, he slammed the door shut with enough force to rattle the glass. Tobias's hands grasped Ryder's forearm and he shoved, teeth grinding together, eyes wide with a frantic need to escape. To run. To fight.

The dancing black spots were now a fog creeping over his vision, growing darker the more he struggled, and the needle of the syringe flashed in the sunlight. Betrayal blew through Tobias's chest like a knife straight to the heart, slicing through the open wounds of an acceptance garnered from the vacancy left behind in the shape of his father. His nails drew blood and Ryder hissed in pain before plunging the needle into Tobias's neck, thumb sinking on the plunger.

Tobias stared at his father in shock, breathing heavily when Ryder withdrew, hooking his hands beneath his underarms as he lowered Tobias gingerly to the floor. Tobias blinked once. Twice, trying to purge himself of the blanket thrown over his senses, his hands clenching and unclenching on the floor beside him. Now Ryder towered above him with a look he couldn't fathom and, as Tobias turned his head to the side, refusing to look at his father, his vision shuttered. Blurring, and sharpening as Ryder crouched down in front of him, a dark shadow plastered across his features.

"You might not agree with the things I do, Tobias," his father's fingers grasped his chin, turning his son's head toward him. "But I *won't* let you ruin what I've waited thirteen years for."

Tobias swallowed thickly, vision plunging in and out of focus, "I *hope* they rip you to pieces, and your blood stains these walls," he said.

"Oh, blood *will* stain these walls," Ryder said, eyes alight with blinding conviction. "But it won't be mine. It's a shame you'll miss it, and that you won't see Nyx again."

"Leave her out of this," Tobias mumbled.

"I wish I could. But, like you said, she's somewhat of a soft spot for them," Ryder said, his words growing faint. "And … after all, where do you aim to kill?"

Dread curled in Tobias's stomach, keeping him hanging on. His voice trembled, struggling with the effort it cost him to speak, laced with anguish before he squeezed his eyes shut and he whispered a final response.

"At the soft spots."

PART THREE

Life is the art of dying.

—Atticus.

LINE DO NOT CROSS POLICE LINE DO

CRIME SCENE DO NOT CROSS

IME SCENE DO NOT CROSS

CRIME SCENE DO NOT CROSS

CRIME SCENE DO NOT CROSS

LICE LINE DO

XLV.

Nyx

Sunlight warmed Nyx's skin against a chill creeping in across the ocean, trickling in from the tunnelways and the glass ceiling lights, bathing the couch beneath her in a golden-yellow hue. She listened to the shifting of doves in the steel rafters echoing off the walls, and the soft crackling of fire licking the confines of the rusted barrels.

Through the speakers of Niko's well-loved boombox something indistinctively rocky played, soft and almost swept away by the natural sigh of wind winding through the labyrinthine tunnelways. Her focus shifted from the white noise to the murmur of the foursome's voices, and she found herself lost in the ever-changing tide of her mind, forgetting about the arms wrapped around her waist.

The warmth emanating from Kotori seeped into Nyx's body, briefly registering in her mind as her back pressed into his chest and his thighs rested against her hips. It was a silent reminder to not run. That she couldn't run. Not even if she tried. So she quietly simmered, harbouring her anger, and honing it into something dangerous, something deadly. Her gaze found Orion, who paced back and forth in front of the formidable map sprawled across the wall behind his throne-like chair, his frigid irises blazing like blue embers.

She sensed his intent laced with a knife-like craving for bloodshed built upon years of festering anger. Honed with the intent to kill, brandished with the apathy of resolute men—content with the blood staining their hands.

"So … what's the ultimate goal again?" Niko asked, a lazy grin curling the edges of his lips as soft wisps of smoke snaked off the joint perched between his fingers.

Kade snickered beside him, knocking the dirty-blond's shoulder with a mischievous shake of his head. Both blonds found amusement in the withering glare Orion levelled them with. Their responding snickers and playful grins seemed to annoy Orion further as Nyx observed their carefree nature.

"Are we going to kill them or … pace until they die of old age, Rion?" Kade taunted.

A muscle in Orion's jaw ticked as he stopped pacing, "That would be a death too kind for them. And I would *hate* to disappoint with something so … *mundane,*" he said.

"So, what's the plan?" Kade asked, sobering up like a flick of a switch as the promise of bloodshed dappled his eyes.

"We use dearest Nyx as an incentive," Orion said, pausing when Nyx scoffed.

"Something amusing you, Nyx? Or do you have something stuck in the back of your throat?" he asked sweetly.

"You want to use *me* as an incentive, again? Because that worked *so well* the first time," Nyx said; her onyx irises darkened by her anger.

"The only difference this time, *little dove,* is that we're willing to do whatever it takes, however blood-stained that might be," Orion answered.

"Right," Nyx said.

"There are some flaws to that logic, Orion," Kotori warned.

"Oh?" Orion prompted, eyebrows furrowed.

"The *incentive* will only work for Azeil and Asher. Not for Ryder or Amir," Kotori said, and she wondered if—hoped—he'd purposely chosen not to mention the twins. His ring-clad fingers caressed

Nyx's hip in a motion too calculated to be subconscious. "We'll need to distract them, or at least throw them off enough to slip inside. But that shouldn't be too hard ... considering our arsenal."

Orion's lips twitched with a slow but pleased nod of his head, "We turn their minds against them. Moving around the house until they can't pinpoint our exact location, but so they *know* we're there," he said, agreeing.

"That leaves us with two options," Niko pointed out, straightening up and leaning forward so his forearms rested upon his thighs. "We can either slip in *undetected,* or we make our presence known and manipulate them further. Toying with their amygdala so their actions are rushed and driven by fear, controlled by it," he added gleefully.

Kade nodded in agreement, "From there, it's a simple divide and conquer. Niko and I do this all the time with our kills," he shifted beneath Orion's gaze when the platinum blond turned away from Nyx and Kotori, sobering with the promise of bloodshed.

"You split them up and pick them off, one by one," he continued. "Or you can choose the one you want to go after and focus only on them, making their lives a constant whirlwind of terror before you act. Like you always do."

Nyx hoped they'd fail as they plotted murder as easily as rain fell from the sky. She hoped their plan would shatter and splinter into a million pieces wrecked beyond repair. And, if she had to nudge it downhill and off the cliff, shattering as it collided with the ocean-lashed rocks, she would. She'd do it to save the ones she cared about.

"And what do you suggest we do once we've 'captured' them?" Orion drawled, phrasing his question as an open suggestion to fill in the remaining pieces to the dark puzzle.

"We bring them back to the cave ... and kill them," Kotori stated with calm indifference.

"And if Azeil and Asher don't want to comply, we use Nyx as a leverage of sorts," Niko finished, grinning as if he'd just won the lottery.

"Or we could use a *little* force," Kade suggested; his Cheshire-like grin now so tainted.

Orion turned to Nyx, pinning her beneath his stare as the weight of their plan settled in her mind. She should've known the dark lengths they'd go to and the satisfaction they'd find in her loved one's demises—for their desire for revenge ran deeper than the clandestine cavern in the ocean.

"What do you think, Nyx? Dark enough for you?" Orion crooned; a crooked grin imbued with sinister intent etched over his face, lightening his irises in a way that sent a shiver up her spine.

Nyx turned her head away in response, ignoring him despite the raging anger that burned through her veins and spread through her body with the intensity of a wildfire. Her mind threw flashes of every way she'd like to kill him to the forefront of her mind, plaguing her with rage-driven desires. Kotori's arms tightened around her waist, his fingers pressing firm but light enough into her hips, reminding her of his presence. Her heart jumped in her chest; kick-started by the graze of his fangs over the flesh of her neck. An effective reminder and push to get her to answer.

"Answer him, kleintje. What thoughts are running through your head," he said.

"Are you sure you want to know?" Nyx asked.

Niko nodded, shifting on the couch so he could pick Ares up, "C'mon chica. *Enlighten* us," he urged, cradling the Malamute to his chest, and running his long fingers through Ares' fur whilst the pup sleepily blinked up at him.

Kade's leather-clad hand caressed Ares' black and white pelt, as his hazel gaze sparked with mischief. "What's the worst you can do?" he said.

"I might say this a lot *but* … I'm thinking up all the different ways that I'd like to kill you all," she said.

Orion's eyebrows arched, "So, what do you call earlier?" he said.

"Practice?" Nyx stated, drawing out the word so it sounded more like a question than a real answer.

Orion smiled, his gaze flickering to the dark stain upon his chest. A silent reminder of his doubt, "For the real thing?" he asked.

"Exactly," Nyx said.

Kade chortled, his fingers toying with the bird-like charm hanging from his earring, "Practice makes perfect, right?" he whooped.

Nyx deadpanned with disdain as Kade and Niko joked amongst themselves, using her as their punchline.

"I'm sure *we'll* all look forward to it. Won't we, boys?" Orion drawled, eyeing each of his companions before his attention returned to her. "Let's go, boys," he said, his gaze locked on Nyx's, directing the next part of his sentence to her. "We wouldn't want to keep our *hunters* waiting."

Nyx cursed her traitorous heart when it stuttered in her chest and Orion's gloved palm stretched toward her. With exaggerated reluctance, she grasped his hand and allowed him to pull her up from the couch, letting him lead her out of the cave and up the rickety staircase with Kotori following close behind. The chilled press of rings against her forearm halted her, steering her away from Kade and Niko when she started in their direction, and toward Orion.

"Not so fast. You're riding with Orion," Kotori murmured, gently ushering her toward the smirking ivory-skinned biker.

"Why can't I ride with Kade or Niko?" Nyx said, frowning.

"Because leaving you with those two worked out *so well* before," Orion drawled; his voice carrying over the crashing waves and buffering wind. "Now get on," he said.

His blue irises seared into her before he condescendingly waggled his fingers. Daring her to take his hand and climb on behind him. With a scowl, she grabbed his hand and swung her leg over the bike, her thighs pressing against his. Orion twisted his hand upon the throttle in the next moment, revving the engine as her arms wrapped around his waist and the salt-laced air caressed her face.

The place below her ribcage no longer ached, the wound almost fully healed. She shoved the thought aside when her mind reminded her of Orion's dark confession. The newfound knowledge of the half-life thrust upon her with his blood in her veins beckoned her to places unknown.

She would at least *try* to save her loved ones from a fate worse than death. A fate now in the hands of four men who revelled in the promise of blood.

Bringers of death with the ease and swiftness of shadows—monsters hidden behind the masks of men.

XLVI.

Nyx

Celacali was not the serene coastal city portrayed in travel advertisements, postcards, or the stories her father and uncle told her about. Instead, it was everything between a dream and a nightmare, something Nyx couldn't fathom as the wind whipped her curls around her back and her arms tensed around Orion's waist. If she were a fool, she'd convince herself that it felt like a personally crafted euphoria, but she wasn't—at least, not in this situation—and she knew that warped, shattered, and twisted piece of her soul had found comfort in the city's darkness. A city with a formidable and blood-stained title honed through years—*centuries*—of unexplained murders and disappearances. She frowned, conflicted by her desires because she *knew* she should've been disgusted or terrified of the men who hollered and cheered beneath the crisp blueness of the afternoon sky.

But she wasn't.

And that terrified her more than their golden-eyed natures—more than the blood staining her hands.

Nyx wished the thunderous rumble of the motorbike engines would drown out her thoughts, and that she could focus on something other than the lodge house at the end of the gravel driveway.

But she couldn't untangle the knot of roots drawing terror, anger, and apprehension into her bloodstream. As Orion, Kotori, Kade, and Niko tore up the driveway, their hollers of malicious delight echoing in her ears, Nyx remained silent. Watching the house approach from over Orion's shoulder with mounting anger and a bristling sense of determination, her onyx irises skittered over the two stories and the slanting roof shrouding the sunroom, searching for any signs of movement within the house. Orion smoothly brought his bike to a stop beside her uncle's Landcruiser, sending small gravel stones flying with a darkly satisfied chuckle.

The silence of the large, veranda-wrapped house unnerved her, unsettling something deep in her chest when she craned her neck to see over Orion's shoulder. The eerie prickling of goosebumps over her bared skin was like a silent deterrent, warning her of something she couldn't see. She searched the windows of the house, growing antsy the longer she stayed seated, and Orion, Kotori, Kade, and Niko appraised it. Something was wrong, that much she knew—wronged before the quartet had arrived—and no amount of analysing the wooden beams, swaying potted plants or roof tiles would change that.

Orion shifted in front of her, killing the engine of his bike and nudging the kickstand into place with a mechanical *thwack*. It startled her and she sucked in a shaky breath of air, unwinding her arms from around his waist. Despite her anger at him, she couldn't let him walk into something that sent her instincts reeling as he swung his leg over his bike and dismounted. She didn't let herself think, to convince herself *not* to warn him. He managed a single step forward before her hand shot out, grasping the inky fabric of his jacket, her fingers digging into the material as he halted, and three pairs of eyes zeroed in upon her.

"Something's *wrong*," Nyx warned, refusing to waver beneath his frigid gaze when he eerily pivoted around to face her. His glacier-like irises flickered to her hand grasping his jacket and then back to her face with an inscrutable arch of his eyebrows.

"I don't know *what*... but something's wrong. I—just... I can *feel* it," she said.

"You can *feel* it?" Orion said, his lips curled into a dangerous smile, his irises alight with zeal. "We appreciate your *concern*, little dove, but I think we'll be fine."

She huffed, rubbing the heel of her palms into her eyes before she shook her head and her hands dropped into her lap, Kotori's silent presence bracketing her back. "Did you say something that stupid to Niko when you found him after he'd been left to drown?"

Orion's mouth opened to respond when Niko cut him off, "Chill out, chica. Nobody's going to get hurt," he said.

"Well apart from those wannabe hunters," Kade mused, unmounting his bike, and coming to stand beside Niko with a darkness to his smile.

"You're not *hearing* me," Nyx whispered, sighing before her gaze dropped to her lap and her blood-stained clothes—*her* blood.

The three men peered at her, varying emotions etched across each of their faces, but one remained the same when her head lifted, and she surveyed them. It smarted across her flesh, because they *didn't* understand the unease and jittery fear plaguing her, having grown accustomed to being uncaring beasts of legends for too long. Nyx wondered what a life without fear, without uncertainty, without the worry of being shunned by society would be like. And that splintered shard of her panged in the depths of her chest, answering a call she couldn't—*wouldn't*—let herself understand.

If she was supposed to live in the world millions endured every day without pause, why did she feel so *wrong*?

Why did she long so immensely for the life they lived? Like without it, she'd cease to exist.

Why?

No answer. No gods. No inner consciousness. *Nothing*. And neither of the trio thought to shake her from the confines of her mind and the swirling tide of her thoughts. They turned away and prowled towards the lodge-like house, blue and brown eyes devoid of emotion besides their combined lust for bloodshed. Of revenge laced with her loved ones' demise. It was like a switch flipped in their minds. One minute they were men and the next, they were monsters who could focus only on closing the distance between themselves and their prey.

Kade disappeared around the left side of the house with a nasty grin and Niko followed, his shout of delight echoing across the clear sky, vanishing with bountiful strides around the right expanse of the veranda, his footsteps echoing off the wooden flooring. Orion turned, his icy gaze landing on Kotori behind her.

Kotori towered over her when she turned her head toward him. As Nyx shifted upon the bike, swinging her right leg over the seat so both her legs rested against the left side of Orion's bike, Kotori's umber gaze lowered, focusing upon her with a soothing calmness. His dark irises softened, lightening before he lifted a ring-clad hand and cupped her cheek in his palm. He stepped between her legs, situating himself between her thighs as she stared up at him and his opposing hand splayed across her hip—anchoring himself to her. With the prowess of the *Levenloos* wolf, Kotori's voice filled her ears and distracted her from the anger and unease tangling in her chest. "Remember what I said, kleintje?"

We can't hide our true natures, nor will we deny them.

Nyx nodded, remembering his warnings with clarity found in the understanding that blossomed within her.

Kotori's lips pursed and a low prompting hum emitted from his bared chest. She looked down, above the defined muscle of his v-line, and saw raised silvery-white scar tissue. Her eyes darted back up to his before returning to his scars. Her eyes traced the raised and crudely shaped debits on his browned skin as his hand upon her waist moved to push aside his jacket and her gaze landed upon the unmistakable scarring of teeth.

Canines honed for predatory finesse like his own, embedded in his flesh for the rest of his life. And, as her eyes darted up to the wolf tooth earring in his ear and back to the scarring along his hip, she knew what creature had torn into his skin. The knowledge lodged itself in her chest like a knife, twisted further into her flesh when she lifted her gaze and his lips pulled into a soft, almost embarrassed, smile.

In that moment, Nyx truly understood the anger and ease these men had garnered over the years they'd prowled Celacali. She understood the vengeful hollers echoing through the sky and to her ears as Orion, Kade, and Niko tormented their intended prey—stalking and circling the house like a pack of wolves. Because, as Kotori caressed her cheek and she lifted her gaze back to his, she realised they had not been born monsters. That the world and its inhabitants had created them, forcing them to become something they hadn't started out being.

"Don't do that," Nyx softly scolded, sympathetic to the Levenloos man and the embarrassed smile across his face.

"Do what?" he said.

"Don't blame yourself, Kotori."

"But—"

Her irises hardened, enraged at his sense of blame. "It wasn't your fault. *You* didn't choose to be left for dead," she peered around his arm, gaze lingering on the house before she looked back to Kotori, "And neither did they."

His smile changed, shifting into something genuine. Something *real*.

Orion, Kade, and Niko's hollers and taunts turned to white noise when Kotori pulled away, his thumb stroking her cheek with a softness unaccustomed to the natures he'd warned her so vehemently about. He seemed to study her for several moments but, with the faintest tick in his jaw, pulled away from her completely, turning and striding off toward his companions.

"Kotori," she called, drawing his attention back to her. Nyx worried her bottom lip between her teeth, fighting within herself. "Be careful and please … make sure they don't do anything stupid," she said.

"I promise, kleintje," he said, walking backwards before turning.

Nyx watched as he disappeared around the left side of the house, waiting for several tense minutes before she jumped off the back of Orion's bike and crept across the gravelled driveway. She climbed the front steps of the veranda, grimacing when a floorboard groaned beneath her foot, heart pounding in her chest. With light steps, she slunk around the right side of the house, hoping with everything in her that Niko had moved on to the other side of the house when she rounded the corner. A sigh of relief tumbled from her lips when neither of the quartet lingered upon the veranda. Their taunts rippled off the crispness of the afternoon's breeze, carrying over her skin and rankling her nerves with every step she took.

The back door loomed mere metres away, taunting her with its closeness to the sunbathed kitchen she could glimpse through the windows. Her hand closed around the metallic handle and twisted. Opening the door slowly and slipping inside with a soft sigh of relief, Nyx's back pressed against the glass proportion of the door as Orion, Kotori, Kade, and Niko's foreboding taunts sounded through the unusually shadowed house like lightning webbing through clouds.

Though she understood that neither one of them chose this path stained in blood, it didn't mean she'd let them satisfy their decades-long revenge with the death of her loved ones. The thought itched like poison ivy, prickling over her skin, and daring her to scratch. But her decision had been made hours ago when Orion had revealed exactly what lengths he'd gone to, to keep her alive. And she wouldn't let them kill her father, Asher, Tobias, or Alexander.

Her gaze trailed across the room as she searched her mind for an appropriate distraction before a smile began. *It didn't need to be something,* she thought with a deadly resolution, *it could be* someone.

The fridge hummed lowly in the background, the fan whirring loudly when she pushed off the door and precariously stepped forward—feeling like she was stepping into enemy territory in her kitchen. It unsettled her and something in the back of her mind urged her to be careful, to take each step around the kitchen table and to the lounge room warily. Always alert.

She paused with one foot on the threshold to the living room, contemplating her next move. The raw wooden walls left unpainted contrasted with the softness of the sunlight trickling in through the windowpanes to the right. Nyx's gaze scrutinised the staircase with furrowed brows, the same unease she'd felt on the back of Orion's bike returning tenfold. And, though she wanted to turn around and disappear through the kitchen door, she couldn't.

She *wouldn't,* and though that might have made her foolish. Naïve. Suicidal. She *couldn't* let herself flee at the first glimpse of danger. Not when the people she cared about most were inside.

Nyx forced herself to take several steps into the lounge room. Her instincts screamed like sirens tangled together in a mass of ear-splitting sounds, urging her to run. To survive. And she froze, coming to a complete standstill, ears straining to hear whatever jostled her conscience in the light bathed sunroom.

A floorboard creaked obnoxiously and a hand clamped over her mouth, a broad arm wrapping around her stomach. Her heart raced as she struggled, fingernails digging into the hand over her face with wide, panicked irises. Whoever pinned her to their chest sighed as if her constant struggling annoyed them—aggravated them. Their hand over her mouth was unrelenting, fingertips pressing into the soft flesh of her cheeks to stop her from biting their hand.

"If you scream or make any noise, you'll die. Right here. Right now, okay?" warned a gruff, angry male voice that sent realisation careening through her chest.

He paused, awaiting her response, and when she faltered amid the recognition spiralling through her mind. He nudged her with little care, "*Got it?*"

With some reluctance and a swirling grasp on the world around her, Nyx nodded. Stumbling over her feet when he began to drag her through the lounge room, her shoes snagging on the edge of the three-seater couch as he led her to a darkened part of the house she'd never thought to re-enter. Not seeing the point of such a lavishly and elaborate dining room in a house better suited for the life and excitement she'd been brought up in.

She should have known. She *should have* seen it coming. But she hadn't. He seemed satisfied with her compliance as he pulled her toward the dining room—if only he knew it was a guise and the way her mind shifted. He pulled her to a rough stop in the doorway of the formal dining room as either Niko or Kade's eerily drawled taunts glided past the kitchen, and their footsteps echoed somewhere in the house.

The grip on her chin tightened, digging further into the soft flesh of her cheeks until the pair of footsteps faded to nothing. "I'm going to remove my hand now, and you're not going to make a sound, okay?" he said.

The hand dropped from her face, both hands wrapping around her forearms in a bruising grasp before he harshly turned her toward him.

Nyx's eyes narrowed.

Ryder Montes stared back at her, all harsh age lines, and grey-flecked hair, as stoic and disdainful as she remembered him. The older man tutted disapprovingly, pursing his lips with exaggerated disappointment that poorly masked his resentment toward her; even if his hands were still stained with her blood and his gaze darted to where he had staked her. The white gauze of her bandages peeked out through the crudely shaped square; a jagged 'X' torn into her shirt. Dully aching but not forgotten as Ryder's stare hardened and his fingernails pressed into her skin.

"Now remember what we talked about, Nyx," he warned, lifting a hand to her face, and using his fingertips to turn her head toward the poorly lit dining room. "Because we wouldn't want them to get hurt now, would we?"

Nyx's anger roared to life inside her, echoing like a river in her eardrums whilst simultaneously stifling and blistering her insides like an uncontrolled wildfire when her gaze zeroed in on her father and Asher.

Bound to two of the finely carved dining chairs, coarse, fraying rope digging into their arms. Their faces, contorted with relief and fear, were marred by darkening bruises dotting their faces, blood dripping from her father's nose, and a split in Asher's lip. Nyx's stomach dropped, plunging her beneath an icy torrent of water as her anger guttered and then reinforced itself with the imagery her conscience refused to acknowledge. At first, her gaze darted between her father and her uncle, and then dropped to the mousy-haired twins at their feet, sprawled as if an afterthought. Ryder had done this. To his own sons. Her brothers in everything but blood.

Nyx vowed she'd make him regret this day, for loyalty was a two-way street.

And she was determined to remind him of the mistake he'd made.

XLVII.

Nyx

Nyx's gaze raked across the room, darting from the shadow-blanketed furniture to the flickering light globes of the hanging fixtures above the seven-seater table, to her father and Asher before halting upon Alexander and Tobias. Two sides of the same coin battled in Nyx's head, where one numbly took in the scene before her. The other raged, angered by the betrayal her mind homed in on. She couldn't comprehend *how* Ryder could have done this. Or why he'd done it. It didn't add up in her mind, though it shone as brightly as a spotlight. How he could've done this to her family? His lifelong friends of over twenty-five years. It didn't make sense as her anger rose, amplified by the knowledge that he'd been the one to drive the crudely sharpened stake through *her* mid-section those hours prior.

Those hours ago felt like decades now, in the grey-light trickling into the dining room from the squared windowpanes of the lounge room with Ryder's hand tightly wrapped around her forearm and her gaze locked on his sons discarded on the hardwood floor. She'd always known relationships were difficult to maintain, even the bonds forged through blood were tricky to navigate, but she hadn't thought the tense relationship between Alexander, Tobias, and Ryder had been this bad. Though she supposed no one truly understood the lengths people would take when pushed too far. Or when someone would reach their breaking point and snap. Or when they'd find comfort in something they shouldn't—*someone* they shouldn't.

As Nyx tore her gaze from the twins, she wondered what had been Ryder's breaking point. Or if he'd simply broken long ago but hid it well, waiting for the day he could act on the anger and resentment in cold storage. Her eyes met her father's and then Asher's, searching their faces for any injuries she could've missed. Nyx stepped toward them, fighting her anger. She forced herself to breathe, to calm the surface of her rippling temper, and while she wanted to scream—to punch something—she knew it would do nothing.

Azeil pulled at the rope around his wrists, struggling with the fraying bindings strapping him to the chair. Nyx stumbled back into Ryder when his grip upon her arm tightened, and he tugged her roughly to the threshold of the dining room.

"I wouldn't do that," Ryder warned, his fingertips digging into her bicep.

Her gaze fell instead upon his sons—and the slight bruising decorating their necks from whatever Ryder had done to them. Though, if their constant state of unconsciousness was anything to go by, she knew it had to be a kind of drug. Intended to keep them unconscious for however long Ryder wished. Her eyebrows furrowed, gaze lifting from the twins to scan the dimly lit room for Amir, his lack of presence in the room gaping like a sinkhole. A small piece of her hoped he was okay and that he'd avoided his brother's warped plan, but an even smaller piece dreaded what Ryder might have done to his brother if he'd drugged his sons and bound his friends.

She turned and stared up into his eyes—into the darkest depths of his irises, shadowed by something twisted.

"My sons *betrayed* me for you," he said. "They were so caught up in saving you," he paused, brows coming together before he corrected himself, "*protecting* you. That they were going to ruin everything."

Nyx stared up at him, unflinching, "Let go of me, Ryder," she said.

And like a switch, the echoing hollers and taunts that once drifted through the house like white noise ceased, plunging the room into an eerie silence that comforted her rather than unsettled her.

Ryder's Adam's apple bobbed in his throat, the only indication he was unnerved.

Nyx's lips twitched, fighting the urge to smile, refusing to meet her father's and Asher's gazes before a familiar voice broke the silence.

"Of course, she couldn't stay on the damn bike," Orion muttered, his honeyed voice drifting past the windows of the lounge room.

Niko's responding snicker amused her, "Are you really surprised?"

"No," came Orion's reply before four pairs of feet echoed off the wooden veranda, circling the house like the pack of wolves they were.

Nyx refused to waver when Ryder's expression turned deadly, and his grasp tightened like a vice. A definite sneer curling his lips, teeth bared like a rabid animal.

"Call them off," he hissed.

It amused her that he thought she had any control over the quartet prowling around the house. Like they obeyed her every beck and call. "No," she replied simply.

Ryder huffed, scowling as his gaze held hers and his left hand disappeared behind his back and he pulled a matte black gun from the waistband of his pants, expertly flipping the safety off, cocking the gun directly at her racing heart. And, like her heart had stuttered when he trained the gun upon her, the prowling footsteps paused. As if Orion, Kotori, Kade, and Niko froze with the metallic *click* of the gun.

A darkly smug smile upturned Ryder's lips, his tawny hair brushing across his forehead as his head angled patronisingly.

"*Call them off,*" he repeated.

A cold chill swept over Nyx's skin, latching itself into her bloodstream when she lifted her chin and squared her shoulders, straightening her spine under the weight of his stare. Staring up the barrel of a loaded gun aimed at her heart without faltering, despite her instincts screaming and the jackhammering of her heart, she ignored the frantic rustling of rope being tugged and her father's protests.

Asher's protests came softer—more methodically—like he knew something her father didn't, who continued to relentlessly struggle against the rope from her peripherals.

So, when she spoke and her voice refused to waver, it rang out louder and more ominous than the rumble of thunder amid a storm. "I said *no.*"

Ryder abruptly readjusted his hold on her, pulling her to him and pinning her to his chest. Her onyx irises flecked with grey locked on her father and Asher's terrified faces. She forced herself to remain devoid of emotion and unflinching, the harsh barrel of the gun pressed against her temple. She'd been down this road before, she could do it again. The crude metal was cold against her warm skin, solid and dangerous. With the simple press of his finger upon the trigger, he could end her, end all that she was.

She loathed him for possessing this weight and power as his breath fanned over her neck. Unwelcomed, and disgusting as she turned her head away and further into the barrel of the gun. Flickers of beer-stained breath, grabbing hands and unwanted attention played through her mind—longing to pull her beneath the tide of her thoughts—like a broken tape forced to replay the same scenes over and over.

"Stop!" Hands gripped at her clothes, tugging, and pulling on the denim of her jeans as she blearily shoved wandering hands away, the blood in her eardrums roaring like a river as he wouldn't listen. "I said no."

Nyx blinked the suffocating memory from her mind.

Her eyelashes fluttered and the biting sting of her nails in her palms recentred her in the present moment whilst her mind swirled and sought to turn against her. The firm press of the gun against her temple shouldn't have soothed her, shouldn't have reminded her that Kai couldn't hurt her anymore, that nobody could. Not now. Not when the broken shard in her chest finally felt at home—at peace—in Celacali. With them.

Ryder's gruff voice cut through her thoughts, jolting her back into reality as he roughly nudged her temple with the barrel of the gun.

"This can kill you just as well as a human, *halfling*," he said.

Nyx's voice carried like the calm before the storm; a calamity waiting to happen. "So can they," she said.

With little thought, Nyx threw her head back into Ryder's face. The back of her skull connected harshly with Ryder's nose. A sickening *crunch* reverberated in her ears followed by a hiss of pain and the waver of his grasp before she whirled, shoving his arms away from her. Her palms connected with his chest, and she pushed, shunting him backwards whilst his right hand rushed to cup his nose, his blood gushing through his fingers when she turned and hurried toward Azeil, the echoing clatter of the gun colliding with the floor filling her eardrums.

Crouching down behind the ornately carved chair, her eyes darting frantically from Ryder and to the rope around her father's wrists, her hands delved into her boot before she gripped the hilt of the snake-encrusted dagger and pulled it out. Her lips twitched with the barest smile as she marvelled at the blade of the dagger and how Orion hadn't noticed its disappearance.

Without hesitating, she drew the pristine blade through the coarse rope around her father's wrists and deftly unravelled the bindings before she pressed the dagger into her father's palm and rounded the chair. Her stare locked on his and then Asher's, holding each of their gazes for several seconds before she offered them a reassuring smile and ran past Ryder. Her footsteps pounded against the hardwood floors, her feet stumbling beneath her as she narrowly avoided running into the rounded coffee table.

Nyx stumbled, fumbling for the door handle before she flung the flyscreen door open, and it slammed into the wooden wall with a loud *bang*. She sucked in a ragged breath, willing her hands to stop shaking, for her heart to stop racing, as the flyscreen swung back into her, and her hand gripped the steel handle of the front door. It turned easily in her grasp as though sensing her desperation—her need to escape—and swung open with the force of her hand pushing into the wood. Her gaze collided with Niko's, like the front door collided with the stone pot beside it, rattling the glass panes at its centre. And, despite everything they'd done to her and how they'd turned her life upside down, she couldn't have been more relieved to see him.

His cyanic irises lit up, flashing with relief in one moment and in the next they hardened with something dangerous. Something sinister. As he opened his mouth to speak—to warn her—stepping forward briskly with his hand outstretched to her. A gesture she didn't hesitate at accepting as she stepped forward to grasp his hand, three pairs of footsteps thundered upon the wooden veranda, heading toward them.

An arm snared itself around her waist when she moved to close the distance between herself and Niko, dragging her back into the house as she screamed, struggling against the strong arm banded over her stomach. Nyx's eyes widened as her terror seemed to feed Niko's protective instincts. His upper lip curled into a chilling sneer, the blue of his eyes devoid of emotion as he glared at whoever held her and moved closer. The sharp press of a knife to her throat ceased her struggles but enraged him further, his irises flashing with a deathly promise.

Kade appeared suddenly at his side, pulling Niko back from the doorway, ignoring the eerie colouration bleeding into his eyes and the furious snarl that tore from his throat.

Niko struggled against Kade, pushing against his companion whilst his gaze remained locked on her, and the knife pressed to her throat. "If you hurt her in any way. You're *dead,*" he said.

"It hurts, doesn't it?" crooned a voice Nyx wished she didn't recognise. "Knowing that you could lose something you have *finally* let yourself care about."

Nyx didn't want to know what he meant by those words, but as Niko's eyes narrowed and Kade's boyish features twisted into something sinister, she understood the implications of his words better than she would've liked to. Niko refused to stop struggling against Kade's grasp, trying to sidestep his companion with a determination that comforted her. But she knew that over the nineteen years she'd known Amir—that she had grown up around him—that he never lied.

This time was no different.

She knew he wouldn't falter. Not even in the presence of Niko and Kade, holding strong as she knew only he could.

The calm of Ryder's unrelenting and disdain-filled storm.

XLVIII.

Nyx

Nyx's feet slipped upon the hardwood floor, her eyes wide and brimming with betrayal as she struggled against Amir. He dragged her away from the open door, shifting his grasp on her to pull the front door closed with an ominous *thud.*

The whine of distressed wood echoed across the room, and Nyx couldn't fight the satisfaction searing her insides as anticipation crackled throughout the house. Her lips pulled into a dark grin when Amir paused on the antique-looking rug stretched across the lounge room floor. She shifted in his grasp as a thunderous *bang* sounded. Splinters of wood and shards of stained glass skittered over the floor, colliding with her feet as the wooden door tumbled to the floor. Kicked off its hinges by a tall, fuming blond with churning cyanic irises, whose lips twitched with a formidable snarl. At his side stood Orion and Kade.

Orion's gaze nestled upon Nyx. Like he was saying, 'there you are'. Where he portrayed a flawless mask of zeal, Kotori glowered from behind Niko's right shoulder and Kade's hazel irises blazed with bloodlust.

Nyx's gaze lingered on Kade, flickering to Niko and to Orion *holding Niko back,* his palpable rage rippling off him like the heat of a blazing inferno.

Amir chuckled, his stare surveying the quartet with steely calm. "Well, c'mon in," he said.

Ryder's bitter scoff startled Nyx. Her head whipped towards him and the blood staining his face, shirt, and hands. He loomed beside his younger brother like Orion, Kotori, Kade, and Niko loomed in the open doorway when she turned back to them.

"But we both know whose house this is. And you'd be vulnerable the moment you step through that doorway," Ryder crooned, delighting in this assumed weakness.

Niko's lips curled, twisting into a sneer as the melodic timbre of his voice deepened, plunged with something dangerous. "Who said that was a myth?"

"Is it?" Ryder asked.

"Regardless, we'd still kill you," Niko shot back.

"Like I said, c'mon in then," Amir drawled, removing his hand from Nyx's waist, and lazily gesturing to the surrounding room.

"We might want you dead, but we're not *stupid,*" Kotori said, his hand clamped down on Niko's shoulder.

Tension hung thickly in the air as Orion purposefully stepped forward and patted Niko's chest, warning him with the simple gesture, eyeing her for the barest moment before he turned the full weight of his gaze upon Ryder and Amir. Kotori, Niko, and Kade loomed behind him like the quartet had planned it, flanking him, and simultaneously reminding Ryder and Amir of the power they held.

The power Ryder and Amir *didn't* have.

"What's it been?" Orion mused, entrapping Ryder and Amir with the steeliness of his voice. "Twenty-five years? And you're *still* on a *vampire-hunting* rampage?" he paused, cocking his head to the side, "Tell me, *boys*. What's your motive? Because no one holds onto a *hobby* like that without one."

Ryder scoffed, "Of course, *you* don't remember," he said.

Nyx waited, watching as Orion turned his head toward his companions, who shared a look amongst themselves before he turned back to Nyx and the knife pressed to her throat. *His* serpentine knife.

"You're going to have to be more *specific*, bud," drawled Niko, his eyes ablaze as Ryder turned his stony scowl upon him.

"It's been thirteen years," Amir stated, adjusting his grip on the knife pressed to Nyx's throat. "We'd taken the twins down to the boardwalk and were on our way home when a commotion caught our attention."

"It turned out it was a woman *begging* in the alleyway two stores up," Ryder swallowed thickly. Like it took everything in him to continue talking. "Amir took the boys home, and I went to see what was going on. To intervene if I had to."

Niko eyeballed him, unmoved.

"He came back about an hour later. Blood staining his clothes and this … frantic look in his eyes," Amir continued, smoothly picking up the story from where Ryder couldn't make himself finish. His dark irises strayed to Kade and Niko, lingering on Kade and the elaborate patches of his tattoos. "You tore her to pieces whilst they watched."

Ryder swallowed the lump in his throat as Nyx turned toward him, noting the emotionless mask before he continued from his brother with a waver to his voice. "She'd gone looking for us. Wondering why we weren't home yet with the twins … she begged for her life. Told you she had a family. You didn't care."

"You killed her as she begged you to spare her. As she told you, she had two sons waiting for her," Amir said, the words falling from his mouth like stones.

Although he watched them, he missed the flicker of recognition in Orion's eyes as Orion stared at Nyx and she stared back.

Nyx watched the serene mask of nonchalance cinch into place over Orion's face, clipping together like magnets as he leant into the door frame and toyed with the cuffs of his leather gloves. Pretending not to notice the sudden shift amongst his companions as, one by one, they remembered the woman. Nyx couldn't remember Alexander and Tobias's mother—Sophia Montes—past the memory of her laughter and the maternal comfort of her arms, but she supposed that made sense, considering she would've been five when they'd lost her.

When their mother had been murdered by the men Nyx had now come to love.

She knew they were monsters, that they revelled in the bloodshed. But some foolish piece of her had hoped there was a line they wouldn't cross. A line she realised *didn't* extend to or protect women. Even if they'd always protected her. Even if she'd heard Kotori, Niko and Kade speak about not wanting to harm innocents, they still had. And, as that thought jangled loudly inside her head, she found she couldn't hold any of their gazes. Ignoring the weight of four gazes upon her as her mind echoed Ryder and Amir's words back to her, replaying on a never-ending loop, drowning her with horror.

"Motive enough for you?" questioned Ryder, throwing a pointed glance in Nyx's direction.

Nyx wished for death beneath that gaze, keeping her eyes locked on the hardwood floor and her attention on the metallic blade pressed lazily to her throat. As the rustling of fabric and the scuffing of boots drifted past her ears, her gaze strayed from the floor to the doorway where Orion watched her with his steely irises.

"But what does *this*," Orion gestured to her with a lazy sweep of his hand, the authority edged in his words rippling over the room with the ease of someone who knew they were powerful—*dangerous*—and didn't care, "achieve?" he said.

Amir grinned; a dark, sharp smile that matched his knife, "You took someone we cared about. So, we're going to take someone *you* care about. Unless, of course, we *misunderstood* your intentions over the years we've watched you," he said.

The weight of Orion's gaze settled upon Nyx like bags of sand, anchoring her to this moment when all she wanted to do was disappear. To go back in time and stop herself from meeting them. From finding comfort in the dark descent they nurtured like a spark waiting to ignite amongst kindling. But she couldn't do that, and she knew it. But she wouldn't let it be the reason her father, uncle and the twins died at their hands.

She w*ouldn't* let them be a casualty of her war.

"What makes you think I care whether she lives or dies?" Orion drawled, arching snowy brows.

Nyx hissed through gritted teeth as the serpentine-imbued blade pressed deeper into the soft flesh of her throat and three pairs of eyes zeroed in on her. The blade nicked her skin enough to draw blood and for the crimson liquid to bead upon it, trickling down the column of her throat.

"You might not," Amir mused before gesturing with a jut of his chin toward Kotori, who held an enraged Niko back, and Kade, "But they do."

Niko shoved at Kotori's hands holding him, his eyes wild with something frantic. They lightened, and the jangling of his bracelets filled the air. "You're *dead* when I get my hands on you," he said. He whirled on Kotori, and then Kade, who stepped forward to intervene. "Let me go! Kade ... *please*."

"Niko—" Kade began, only for Niko to dismiss him with erratic shaking of his head.

"No!" Niko tried to bat Kotori's hands away, struggling against his companion with his gaze locked on Nyx, "*No!* We're not doing that!" he cried.

"Niko, listen to me." Kade pleaded, grasping the dirty-blond's face in his hands, forcing Niko to look at him.

"No. *You* listen to me," Niko stated, cutting Kade off, "We almost lost her less than twenty-four hours ago, and I *won't* lose her again." His cyanic eyes held her entrapped when they darted to her from over Kade's shoulder, his voice waver-free and suddenly, oddly calm, "I *refuse* to lose her," he said.

Orion hummed, nodding slowly after a moment of contemplation, and turned back to his companions before he flicked his wrist, and Kotori's grasp tightened on Niko's shoulder. Niko thrashed against Kade, fighting like a cornered wolf whilst they dragged him away from the front door. Orion glanced back at her and darted his gaze pointedly to Ryder and Amir.

Nyx's brows furrowed with confusion, mind whirling. Then it clicked, as Ryder's face split into a satisfied grin and Amir's grasp wavered, what Orion wanted her to do. What she *needed* to do to save her loved ones in the other room.

So, without allowing herself a moment to convince herself this was a bad idea, she used Ryder and Amir's distraction to her advantage. Ignoring the burning pain across her throat when she turned her head ever-so-slightly and leant forward. Biting down into the bared flesh of Amir's forearm until the coppery tang of blood filled her tastebuds.

His sharp exclamation of pain rang out across the room as he tugged his arm free, and the serpentine dagger clattered to the floor at her feet. Her mind short-circuited for a second or two, rioting at the bitter metallic taste on her tongue like she desperately needed it. A jarring reminder of what she now was—what she *could* become—if she heeded those instincts urging her to complete the transition from human to vampire.

But she *couldn't*.

Not while her father, her uncle, her brothers—Alexander, and Tobias were in the next room.

As overwhelming instincts screamed at her, some piece of her being was desperate for more blood than what coated her tongue when she had swallowed the red liquid and she whirled on Amir, pressing her palms into his chest and knocking him back. Amir quickly righted himself before he lunged for her with the same arm she'd sunk her teeth into. Nyx stooped and swiped the bloody dagger from the floor, narrowly avoiding him as she stumbled out of his path.

Her eyes darted back and forth between Ryder and Amir, the serpentine hilt of the dagger clutched tightly in her hand as she widened her stance and deftly inclined her chin closer to her chest. Positioning the dagger at the ready like a dangerous shield between herself and them. Leaving her left hand to hover beside her collarbone, her wrist turned inward, with her back to the open doorway and the men looming before her silently, awaiting her next move with eager anticipation.

Ryder strode forward with a scowl twisting the corners of his mouth and Nyx straightened her spine, lifting her chin defiantly, and holding her ground as he approached. Ryder appraised her, eyes darting over her shoulder to the men who bared their teeth like wolves before Ryder lunged.

She stepped forward, keeping her movements light and concise. Meeting him halfway and quickly slashing his left bicep from the elbow up, narrowly avoiding his face as he staggered. She watched as he pressed his hand to the gushing wound with wide, surprised eyes. Nyx lithely darted around him and his feeble attempts to grab her, coming face to face with Amir and his dark eyes. She paused long enough to survey him, eyes darting over the weeping bite mark on his forearm before she cautiously crept closer to the raven-haired man blocking her path across the room and to her father, uncle, and the twins.

"Move," Nyx ordered, throwing a swift look over her shoulder at Ryder before she turned back and readjusted her hold on the dagger.

"No," Amir said as he stepped forward purposefully, like a cat toying with a mouse.

"No?" Nyx said in disbelief.

"*No.* You go through me, or you don't get to them at all," he said.

Nyx hummed, considering his words with false interest before she darted forward. Lunging toward the right side of his body that he seemed to favour with the sharpened blade of the dagger, the ornate hilt digging into her palm. Amir moved with precision, deflecting the dagger with the swiftness of his hand wrapping around her forearm. Destabilising her offensive pursuit before he spun her toward himself. Nyx drove her left elbow into his stomach, tearing her arm from his wavering grip. A chuff of air slipped past his lips as she analysed him closely and he glared up at her before stooping down and swiping her legs out from underneath her with practised ease.

Nyx screwed her eyes shut as her head collided harshly with the hardwood floor and the dagger skittered over it, disappearing beneath a leather armchair at the edge of an antique-like rug. As she blinked back ringing pain in the back of her head and she pressed her palms to the floor, Amir stalked closer with a malicious curve to his lips. Nyx's eyes widened with realisation before she scrambled back, struggling to create enough distance between herself and him so she could push herself up and grab the dagger. Amir's boots swiftly closed the space between them and his fingers gripped her hair, dragging her closer to the dagger beneath the armchair.

Her hands shot up to relieve the burning pain over her scalp, fingernails clawing at his forearm, whilst her face contorted into a silent grimace. Nyx used the dragging momentum of her body to tuck her knees beneath herself, tightening her grasp around Amir's wrist as she unbalanced him, and she staggered up from the ground. She spun toward him then, around his side, beginning to stand. Ignoring the bite of pain from her scalp and the dull throbbing at the back of her head, she slammed her knee into his groin with as much force as she could muster.

Amir dropped to the floor, releasing her hair as an agonised groan of pain tumbled from his lips and his knees collided with the floorboards. Nyx swiped the dagger from beneath the armchair. Her appraisal paused on Ryder and the blood seeping between his fingers, a pained scowl twisting his features.

Orion's grin looked serpentine, like a snake ready to strike as he toed the threshold of the lodge house and then stepped inside. His head dipped curtly and, before Kotori, Kade or Niko could approach her, she pivoted on the balls of her feet and darted toward the dimly lit entrance of the dining room.

The wolves in the pursuit of a definite kill.

Nyx forced herself to tamp down the racing of her heart and the fraying edges of her nerves as she strode through the dimly lit doorway of the dining room and to her father, Asher, Alexander, and Tobias. She shushed her father before she turned to Asher and faltered. A choked sound, part sob, part scream tumbled from her lips when her mind registered the blood staining Asher's shirt and the gaping laceration across her uncle's throat. Nyx's mind whirled, the breath fleeing her lungs as Azeil's irises zeroed in on her and he grasped her forearms, scrutinising the blood weeping slowly down the column of her throat.

"Nyx, hey. Nyx," Azeil murmured, his hands cupping her face, forcibly tearing her gaze from Asher. "Breathe, okay?"

"I … can't," Nyx sobbed, her gaze darted, thoughts spiralling, "How?"

"I'm not going to answer that, Night. Not right now," Azeil said softly, his bottom lip split like Amir had hit him to retrieve the dagger.

"But—"

"No," he said.

Nyx straightened, sucking in a deep breath of air as she wrestled with her anguish-driven thoughts and focused on freeing the twins from the rope around their wrists. Her heart ached when neither of them moved, unconscious to the world around them. She supposed maybe it was a good thing. She peered up at her father as Azeil rubbed the reddened skin of his wrists, "Go," she said, glancing over her shoulder at the doorway. "Take the twins with you and get them to a hospital."

"I'm not leaving without you, Nyx," Azeil stated firmly.

"You either run, or you die. Right here," she said, looking at Asher's body. "Which will it be?"

Azeil didn't argue further, crouching down to hoist Tobias's arm around his shoulders despite the continuous glances he tossed toward his brother's body. A crease etched along his brow whilst he waited for Nyx to lift Alexander with red-rimmed eyes. He was a dead weight and she could only drag him awkwardly toward the kitchen doorway. Her eyes darted around the darkened room with unease, guarding her father's back as they slowly trekked into the sunlight trickling in through the kitchen windows. She gestured for him to watch the doorways leading into the kitchen, quickly rounding the kitchen table, and pushing open the back door. Alexander's weight pressed heavily against her before she grabbed a chair from the table to wedge the door open.

With a swift wave of her hand, she ushered Azeil toward the open door. Her father slipped through, his grasp around Tobias's waist and arm firm as he trudged down the wooden veranda to the front of his house with Nyx at his heels, casting terse looks over her shoulder back to the kitchen.

Nyx laboured with Alexander, grimacing as she headed for the well-loved Land Cruiser, tightening her grasp as Alexander's weight pressed upon her exhausted body. She turned to her father as he paused beside the car, urging him to go on.

Azeil hoisted Tobias into the backseat before he turned back to Nyx and lifted Alexander into the seat beside Tobias, sweat clinging to her skin as she rolled her shoulders to ease the ache of her muscles.

Blinking back tears, she crossed the front yard to the house's front steps. The car door closed with a solid thud when she turned back to her father, who rounded the back of the four-wheel drive and pulled the driver's door open.

Azeil paused with his hand wrapped around the door frame, looking at her, the guilt in his eyes palpable from the distance separating them before his lips moved and he mouthed two simple words, "I'm sorry."

Nyx dismissed his apology with an easy wave of her hand as her tears spilled and she ushered him to go—to survive. He ducked into the red Land Cruiser and the shifting of gears drifted through the sky and to her ears a moment later, her blood trickling slowly down her neck.

She lowered herself to the stone steps and sat staring with her elbows digging into her thighs, relief making her bones ache. Nyx's lips moved to mouth, three words left unspoken between herself and her father. Three simple words that held so much meaning, left to hang in the air like the rust-coloured dust.

I love you.

XLIX.

Nyx

"Let go of me, *leech*," Ryder exclaimed, bucking like a wild stallion against Kade's grasp crumpling his shirt, their footsteps echoing loudly in her ears.

As she turned her head, peering up at the malignant quartet from the stone steps before, her irises locked on Ryder and the blood staining his chin and forearm, trailing from his features to the bloodied retractable knife that clattered to the floorboards. She lingered on the stain the blade left on the wood, as the cooling body of her uncle poisoned her thoughts. His blood had been left to pool and dry. The blue of his eyes, once like the crisp blueness of the sky, were now glazed and dull, staring without seeing. Eternally frozen in the frigid embrace of death.

Nyx focused instead on the darkening horizon as she blinked back tears. The metallic glint of the dagger left forgotten beside her reflected the sunlight, striking her chest like a punch as it glittered in her peripherals. She stared, gaze unfocused, as Kade dragged Ryder down the steps and toward the awaiting motorbikes. Niko followed at his heels, the cyanic-blue of his stare flickering to her as he continued to tug Amir to the stripped-down bikes. Her gaze dropped to the stones of the gravelled driveway, wet with her tears.

She *couldn't* cry. Not now. Not with the towering and equally intimidating presence of Orion and Kotori at her back, watching and waiting like the predators they were. And, if she tried hard enough, she could picture Asher's soft smile as though he stood before her. *"Don't cry, little terror."* The softness of his voice echoed in her head. Like the gentle look in his eyes that comforted her in the caverns of her mind. *"I wouldn't want you to cry for me. Because I could never deserve your tears. Not in this life, or the next."*

Orion's cold and levelled voice split the illusion she'd crafted, jarring, and yet welcomed. "Where are they?" he said.

She turned her head to him, "Gone," she said.

The intensity of his gaze darted over every inch of her face as he stared down at her, "*Gone*?"

Nyx nodded as her palms pressed into the stone steps and she pushed herself up from the floor, swiping the blood-encrusted dagger from the floor and tucking it into her back pocket without a second thought.

"Gone," she repeated, voice as cold as his. "I told Azeil to leave because if he stayed, you'd kill him."

Her gaze flickered to Kotori, his dark eyes trained on the blood coating her neck. An unmistakable cloying scent of the forest amid the warmth of spring suddenly swept into her nostrils, muddling her senses as he towered above her. Nyx's eyes met Kotori's. A warning and a question tied together before he slowly tilted her head back, baring her blood-stained neck to his gaze. A drawn-out hiss of air slithered out from Nyx's clenched teeth, her forehead creasing into a grimace when the movement tugged at the shallow cut across her neck.

Without thought, he leant down and her heart stuttered in her chest before Kotori's tongue lathed over the weeping wound along her throat. An odd tingling feeling like her skin was stitching itself together rippled over her throat.

"He'll be at the hospital, right?" Orion crooned, tearing her attention from Kotori. "I can just send Kade and Niko there to pay him a visit."

Nyx's gaze flashed with something dark. Her feet moved before her mind could catch up before Kotori gently pulled her back to his side.

"Leave him *alive,*" she said, eyeing Orion carefully, and the darkly riveted shifting of his gaze. "You owe me that much."

Orion seemed to find immense satisfaction in this. He waited, seemingly interminably before replying.

"We got ... *partially* what we came for, anyway. And their blood will spill regardless," his gaze slunk to Kotori. "I think it's time to go now."

Kotori's deeply timbred chuckle reverberated in her eardrums. "I think that's for the best. Niko and Kade won't wait any longer than they have to. And we both know how ... *antsy* they both get."

Orion scoffed, shaking his head, "Antsy is one way to put it."

Nyx turned toward the stripped-down motorbikes, Niko and Kade nowhere in sight when she turned and peered up at Kotori, "Where did they go?"

A soft smile stretched across Kotori's face, his arm warm around her waist as he led her down the stone steps and their shoes crunched upon the gravel stones, "They're going for a little *joy ride,*" he said.

Her frown deepened; eyes locked on the mischievous duos' bikes, "But their bikes are still here."

Orion chuckled; his stride imbued with something predatory, his head shaking with smug satisfaction as he swung his leg over the back of his bike, gloved hands on the handlebars, "You still have *so much* to learn, little dove," he said.

As Kotori's bike roared to life, Nyx's hand rested palm-down upon his broad, jacket-embellished shoulder, using it as a handhold whilst she swung her left leg over the back of the idling bike and her thighs rested against his hips. Nyx's arms wrapped around Kotori's waist before his ring-clad hand grasped her thigh and pulled her closer to his back, vanquishing the space between them with ease.

"Don't let go, *kleintje,*" Kotori drawled over the thunderous rumble of the bike's engine, disengaging the kickstand with a deeper meaning to the playfully spoken words.

"Never," Nyx whispered, doubting he'd hear her response over the idling bike and the unspoken understanding lacing her tone.

"Good girl," Orion said.

Nyx's head whipped in Orion's direction; the malignant drawl of his voice unmistakable in the caverns of her mind.

Orion winked at her and in the next moment, they were off.

Kotori's deeply timbred voice caressed her thoughts, *"You have the power to do many things, Nyx. Some good. Some bad."* His large hand twisted the throttle, revving the engine before the bike lurched forward, *"But it will* always *be up to you whether you act on them. I promise you that. So, will you avenge your uncle's death or continue to fight for mortal lives?"*

Nyx worried her bottom lip between her teeth, grasp tightening around Kotori's waist as she *thought* her response instead of speaking it aloud. *"I can't—"*

"You can," came Kotori's quick, soothing response.

"What if what I want makes me a bad person?" she thought.

"Good does not mean that there is always evil. Nor does it mean that everything bad comes with a silver lining. But why have one, when you can have both?" Kotori said.

"But—"

"Life is merely the art of dying, kleintje. It's how you choose to die that truly matters."

* * *

Oceanic shrubbery swayed in the buffering winds of Elveszett Bluff, pulling at Nyx's curls like fingers idly skittering atop the ripple-free surface of a pond. Waves lashed the limestone cliff face, filling her eardrums with its rumbling song when the thunderous roar of motorcycle engines fled her eardrums, swept out to sea like the plume of grey-white smoke. Nyx frowned, craning her neck to peer over Kotori's shoulder and to the beaming duo bathed in tangerine firelight, impending bloodshed thrilling them as they waited and she wondered *how* they'd gotten here without their motorbikes.

Nyx's gaze dragged from Kade and Niko to the two men at their feet, the brothers' knees were sunk in the rocky expanse of land that later plunged to the sea-lashed rocks, to the mercy of crumbling limestone crudely jutting out from beneath the shifting waves. For a moment, she wondered what satisfaction she'd garner from pushing them off the cliff's edge. A satisfaction slandered by their bound wrists and the crusting blood over their skin—tributes to her terror that'd bled into a rage. What Nyx loathed the most was the reminder of her uncle's body. Asher dancing through her head like a cruel and morbid film made to torture her the longer she gazed at Ryder and Amir.

With some effort, she tore her gaze harshly from the brothers—*backstabbers*—and to the soft pinks, purples, blues, and yellows of the darkening sky. Asher's delighted smile as he had watched the sunsets, flickered before her eyes, his hand holding hers or an arm slung affectionately over her shoulders, guiding her through the patrons of the boardwalk whilst he told her stories of his life in Celacali or the wonders he'd seen in the last town he'd been to. He'd always returned to spend time with her, eager to shower her with gifts and elaborate stories. She'd never longed to see the wonders he'd spoken about until now, staring out at the horizon with nothing but memories of him from their life before Celacali.

A small part of her found comfort in the thought that with every sunset—every *beautiful* sunset—she could see and be surrounded by him before dusk gave way to twilight. A simple and small slice of elysian in the darkness of her newfound world.

Her boot-clad feet carried her numbly over the rocky terrain, mind stuck on thoughts of Asher as Kotori's arm wrapped around her waist and he guided her toward the dancing flames. And while she allowed Kotori to lead her toward Kade and Niko, her mind raged with conflict. Torn between wrong and right. Good and bad. Angelic and demonic. Vengeance and forgiveness. Life and death.

Tha-thump, tha-thump, tha-thump.

Half of Nyx reminded her that this was wrong—what the quartet intended to do was wrong—but the other half shoved back against the voice of logic, poking, and prodding her with barbed memories of what Ryder and Amir had done. And as she angled her head toward them, her gaze clashing with theirs, she couldn't quiet the bellowing scream of her instincts that shoved at her. Crooning salacious promises of revenge laced in their blood to the forefront of her mind before justifying it with the whispered reminder of the blood that already stained her hands. The dark and warped path she had stumbled down, seeking to pull her in deeper; never to let her return to the *rightness* of the world.

Tha-thump, tha-thump, tha-thump.

"Any last words, *boys*?" Orion crooned. His pale eyebrows arched tauntingly, satisfaction dappled his eyes like he revelled at the thought that nobody would hear their screams or find their bodies. Niko and Kade towered behind the men like two ravenous wolves.

Amir's dark gaze, like Tobias's, settled on Nyx, "Do you know what happens to a fledgling without a pack?" he said.

Ryder scoffed, shaking his head as he glared up through his eyebrows with blood crusted over his chin and around his nose, "Oh, don't be so *polite*, Amir. She's a *halfling*. Not quite human, not quite a vampire."

Kade chortled, nudging Ryder with the toe of his boot, "What's your point, dead man?" he said.

"Was he talking to you, *bloodsucker*?" Ryder snapped, turning his head as he nudged Kade's boot away from him with his elbow.

Niko took a menacing step forward, his irises lighter and tinged with a golden hue. "*Watch it, bud*," he said.

Nyx's forehead creased, redirecting the conversation; her gaze locked on Amir. "What are you talking about?"

Tha-thump, tha-thump, tha-thump.

"The pack is stronger together," Amir murmured, conspiratorially.

Ryder turned away from Kade to peer up at Nyx with disdainful certainty. "And without it, *halfling*, you'll transition into something *worse* than them."

"Driven mad without their guidance," Amir continued, a sudden weight to his words that filled her with a sense of foreboding, "And without a pack, a *fledgling* won't survive."

"It wouldn't know how," Ryder stated, snickering as Nyx's frown slipped and her heart stuttered in her chest. "I wonder how long *you'll* last?" he said.

She blinked down at the men. Wondering—for the first time since Orion had begrudgingly told her what he'd done—how she could survive this. Because how could she when she knew *nothing* about the transition? And what would it cost her? She'd never admit it out loud, but the thought terrified her. An immortal life filled with bloodshed terrified her, but a small, misguided shard longed for the safety of the darkness and strength this life offered.

Nyx wondered what would become of her in years to come *if* she completed the transition. Would she recognise herself, or would she loathe the person she'd become? And she could've sworn a voice that sounded like Asher's urged her to choose the path *she* wanted. A path that *she* could walk—no matter how dark or twisted it was—and feel at ease. At home among whatever, or w*hoever,* she found security in.

Tha-thump, tha-thump, tha-thump.

Orion gestured to Niko and Kade with a flick of his wrist, the stark blueness of his irises lingering on her for several seconds before Kotori's grasp around her waist tightened. Whether to keep her in place or to comfort her, she didn't know. Her stare tracked the roughness of Niko and Kade's grasps on Ryder and Amir's shoulders, tugging the brothers up from the ground and swiftly snapping the rope around their wrists.

As the darkness to Kade's grin and the malicious sneer upturning the edges of Niko's lips registered in her mind; she found she couldn't look away. No matter how loudly the naïve—*good*—half of her soul screamed, raining its fists upon her skull in a feeble attempt to stop her. To make her stop them. To save the men who'd both played a part in Asher's death. She wouldn't listen, wouldn't heed its desperate call. She sought noise instead, like a river's rapids before the plunging drop of a waterfall. Nyx's onyx gaze darted between Ryder and Amir like she couldn't decide whose death she wanted to see more.

Tha-thump, tha-thump, tha-thump.

But why choose one? She would see them both die at the hands of two men in whose dark company she found comfort. Nyx wondered if this was warped at all, her head spinning with the notion that it wasn't. Because who decided if it was? Was it her? Or was it beliefs passed down and then reshaped by society? Beliefs everyone was raised with but shunned for, the moment they made something for themselves—to find themselves in something or with someone society deemed *wrong*. Who was anyone to decide who she should and shouldn't be? Who was society to say that she couldn't watch Ryder and Amir die, and *not* be anything but a murderer? And why did it matter what people wearing rose-coloured glasses thought of her—of *anyone*—when they weren't even willing to look in their own backyards.

At their own warped beliefs.

Tha-thump, tha-thump, tha-thump.

And like Orion, Kotori, Kade, and Niko could hear her thoughts, or she was projecting them through whatever telepathic link she now had, Orion gestured subtly to Niko, to wait. Orion seemed satisfied with her morbid interest, to watch her as she watched Kade impishly taunt Ryder. Kade's head tipped back as his riveted laughter echoed across Elveszett Bluff to her ears and then out over the darkening horizon. The patchwork tattooed blond silhouetted by the golden hue of the sky and the dancing flames of the bonfire.

Tha-thump, tha-thump, tha-thump.

As Kade's Roman features sharpened—the bone structure of his face jutted and sinister in the shifting firelight—he stalked closer to Ryder. Delighting in the terror engulfing Ryder's face with white-gold irises ringed by crimson around his pupils, Kade's gaze wandered to her for several lingering seconds before his grin grew. The golden-curled blond closed the distance between them without truly trying—like this was all a game to him—snatching up the fabric of Ryder's shirt in his fingerless-gloved hands and yanking the trembling man to him.

Kade stooped down, whispering something into Ryder's ear that made his eyes widen and for him to thrash against Kade's unrelenting grasp.

Tha-thump, tha-thump, tha-thump.

The corner of Kade's eyes crinkled, dimples appearing in both his cheeks whilst his gaze flickered from Ryder to her and then back to the struggling man before him. His head angled eerily, peering down at Ryder in a way that tolled in her head like a gavel. Staunching Ryder's fight for a moment before Kade bared his elongated fangs mockingly and his grip tightened, clutching the hunter's arms before he sank his teeth into the soft flesh of Ryder's neck.

Ryder's harrowed scream of anguish echoed in her ears, his hands pushing and grasping at Kade's clothes to free himself from Kade's hold. The hunter's distress seemed to entertain the quartet, their encouraging hollers urging Kade on before he pulled away and peered down at Ryder with a lazy grin.

In a flash, Niko embedded his fangs into Amir's shoulder without remorse. As quickly as Nyx's eyes darted to him and she heard the chilling bellow of pain from Amir's mouth, Kade's wrist twisted, and a resounding *crack* of bones snapping drew her attention back to Ryder. His forearm was contorted at an odd angle as he shoved against Kade's chest, bellowing in pain.

Orion tutted, "Finish it, Kade. There's no need to prolong his life any longer," he said.

"Aw c'mon, Orion," Kade drawled, his brows furrowing with mock disappointment whilst blood clung to his skin. "I was having *fun*."

"Kade," Kotori warned, adjusting his arm around Nyx's waist, and levelling the other man with a scolding look.

Kade shook his head, feigning disgust as the golden-hued depths of his irises were replaced by the softer, more innocent brown Nyx knew well. "You're both buzzkills. You know that, right?" he said, sighing.

Orion rolled his eyes, gesturing pointedly to Ryder, "*Go.*"

"Alright," Kade exhaled, chuckling before he stalked toward the crawling man and hoisted him roughly from the sand.

The tattoo-embellished blond set Ryder on his feet before one gloved hand went to his chin, and the other grasped the top of his head, twisting Ryder's head with the swiftness of a falcon plummeting to snatch its prey from the ground, the sickening *crunch* of bones mashing together echoed in Nyx's eardrums.

Nyx blinked—shocked and confused—staring down at Ryder's lifeless body and the wrongness of his neck without truly understanding. His neck, broken by Kade, whose eyes darted nervously to her and any bravado he possessed fled.

He shifted the weight of his body from one foot to the other before he jolted like someone had shouted his name and he dragged Ryder's limp body to the crackling flames of the bonfire.

"Ryder!" Amir bellowed, his dark gaze brimming with anguish as he broke free of Niko's grasp and hurriedly searched the fabric of his clothes. He whirled on Niko and pulled a crudely sharpened stake from the waistband of his pants, plunging it into Niko's chest with a ferocity and rage that resounded in Nyx's ears. Something in her urged her feet to move before she could comprehend her actions. It confused her why Kotori and Kade hadn't moved until she turned her head in search of Orion and she couldn't find him beside her. Nyx's head whipped back to Niko and Amir at the same moment that Amir raised his arm to plunge the stake into Niko's chest again. The killing blow registered in her mind as something clicked in her head, and she struggled against Kotori's hold. Her actions were rushed and panic-driven, as if, if she didn't do *something*—anything—to prevent Amir from killing Niko, then she'd lose what semblance of security and comfort she'd found with him.

Tha-thump, tha-thump, tha-thump.

Everything seemed to move in slow motion, at least in her mind. One minute she was thrashing against Kotori's arms around her waist, desperate to save Niko from Amir's crudely sharpened stake and the absolution in Amir's eyes as the hunter's arm moved and Niko's eyes widened, darting to Nyx before his jean-clad knees collided with the sand. Niko's blood stained the hand pressed against his mid-section as the other curled in the sand, half-hidden by the gritty soil when Amir wrenched the stake from his mid-section and drew back as if to plunge the stake a third time. But in the next minute, in a rustling of black fabric, Orion loomed behind Amir.

His gloved hand wrapped around Amir's wrist before he tugged harshly and sent the wooden stake tumbling to the floor. Then it shot forward and Niko forced himself up from the ground, grasping Amir's shoulder in his hands in the same breath that a wet *squelch* reverberated in Nyx's ears and Orion's leather-clothed hand glinted in the firelight. The ivory-skinned vampire's fingers clutched around Amir's heart before he pursed his lips and tossed the once-beating organ into the flames.

Niko nodded his head slowly, as though processing the events prior and what could've happened if Orion hadn't intervened. Nyx glanced toward Kotori and Kade before she slipped from Kotori's arms and past Kade, who stood watching her and the determined set of her shoulders as she approached Niko. Her stride felt rushed—desperate—as she watched Niko toss Amir's body into the dancing flames beside Ryder's blistering body before he turned away from the bonfire and his gaze collided with hers. Relief sparked in her chest with the soft reassuring smile that spread across Niko's face. And though the cloying stench of burning flesh and singed hair filled her nose—tangling with the comforting scent of sea salt and the barest whiff of Orion's cologne—she all but collapsed in Niko's arms.

A jittery anxiousness that unnerved her coiled around her heart and lungs, constricting her breathing and the beating of her heart for those few seconds she thought Amir would kill Niko. But it didn't seem to matter anymore as Niko's arms wrapped around her waist and his head rested atop her shoulder. The familiar smell of him filled her nose with each inhale; weed, sea salt, and the subtle undertone of his cologne. Like a cool balm to the frayed mess of her nerves and the jittery instincts that believed this wasn't real. That Niko had died, like Asher, and this was some illusion she'd crafted to comfort herself. But she knew, as his arms tightened around her waist, and he turned his head to press a lingering kiss to her temple; that this wasn't a dream.

That he was alive.

Despite everything—whether she realised it or not—she *needed* them. A part of her whispered of the unspoken feelings between herself and Niko, whose arms held her, and the emotions evoked by Kade who watched them. But for now, she was content that Niko was alive.

"I'm right here, chica," Niko's melodic voice soothed her mind, without him having to speak as Orion's gaze settled upon her and she shoved her thoughts aside. *"I'm not going anywhere."*

Nyx pulled away enough to peer up at him, and for Niko to reluctantly lift his head to gaze down at her. *"Promise?"*

"I promise," he leant down, pressing his lips to hers in a kiss filled with the weight and conviction of his words. *"I'm* not *going anywhere, anytime soon."*

Tha-thump, tha-thump, tha-thump.

Loud, mocking applause startled Nyx. Her heart stuttered in her chest as she pulled away from Niko and her head turned toward a tawny-blond-haired man dressed in a pinstriped suit, his dress shoes covered in sand. The sinister leer of his smile rankled something deep in Nyx's chest. Niko's arms tightened around her waist as Kade, Orion, and Kotori bracketed her in, shielding her from the newcomer's sight with matching expressions of disdain, like whoever the man was—was no one good.

As Nyx turned her head back to Niko and peered up at him from beneath her lashes, she dreaded finding out who he was and what he wanted. A soft sigh spilled from her lips before she closed her eyes and rested her head on Niko's chest. Wondering if there was any point in the promise Niko had made, or if it would all be for nothing.

Empty words to an empty promise.

L.

Nyx

Firelight plunged Nyx's closed eyelids with red, bathing the side of her face and Niko's with warmth from the crackling bonfire. Nyx's mind was stuck on the whirlwind of thoughts and emotions that'd plagued her since she'd stumbled upon the quartet's true natures, the beasts' lurking inches beneath their skin. She sighed, frustrated by the never-ending cycle of 'what-ifs' darting through her mind, opening her eyes with the slow rise of her head.

Her eyebrows furrowed when she turned, and her gaze nestled upon Orion, Kotori, and Kade's backs. The muscles along their spines and shoulders were coiled like taut wires, angled in front of her with the poise of wolves protecting their alpha as they stood around her. Nyx sniffed with amusement at the thought of being *their* alpha. Despite herself, she couldn't ignore the varying protective semi-circle bracketing her into Niko's chest. Where the gesture should've comforted or soothed her, it instead only fed a festering unease and discomfort trickling into her bloodstream, enticing her heart to beat faster and adrenaline to leak into her consciousness. She gritted her teeth against the sensation and turned in Niko's arms, craning her neck to peer over Orion and Kade's shoulders before her gaze found the tawny-blond-haired man.

The man's pinstriped suit had the look of discoloured, crumbling concrete, tailored to his broad shoulders and formidable height. His hair was combed neatly, but in the steady breeze that danced over Elveszett Bluff, it'd become mussed. As she appraised him from the safety of Niko's arms and the semi-circle Orion, Kotori and Kade had created, Nyx couldn't dislodge the deeply rooted feeling of something being *wrong*.

The man's stare drifted to each of the men surrounding her, landing first on Niko over the top of her head and then onto Kade, Kotori, and Orion. His eyebrows raised as if in challenge, but when none of them moved or ceased their glaring, he heaved an obnoxious sigh, folding his arms over his chest and drumming his fingers atop his forearm.

"Is this any way to greet your father, boys?" he said.

Nyx almost choked. *Their father*?

The man hummed patronisingly, "I thought I raised you better than this. With some *manners,* at least," he said.

Kotori scoffed, a sound so unlike the silent and brooding brunette, "*Father*? Is that what you're calling yourself now?"

The suited man's gaze slid ever-so-slowly to Kotori, like Kotori's bitterly snapped words disappointed him, "Is that not what I am?" he said.

"You're the furthest thing from a father anyone's *ever* heard of," Kade's upper lip curled into a sneer, his head angling in a gesture that screamed 'patronising.' "What have *you* done for us? *You* turned Orion as good as a millennium ago and then left. *You* turned Kotori after Orion brought him to you and *begged* you to save his life. And *you* turned Niko and me *after* it suited you," he spat.

Sitting on the edge of her metaphorical seat, heart jolting in her chest, Nyx looked from Kade to Orion as his fingers brushed against her arm to calm her and the quickening pulse of her heart.

The man tutted, his lips pursing, "What have *I* done?" He gestured to them all with a lazy flick of his wrist, "Look at yourselves. What you are is because of *me*. Did you think you could've been *half* of what you are without me? I *saved* your lives when no one else cared enough to try." He shifted his stance in a flickering sort of way, so that suddenly his eyes found Nyx. An unnerving, disconnected quality glimmered in his eyes. "Now, *step aside, boys*."

A menacing growl rumbled in the depths of Kade's chest, and Nyx stared as Orion and Kotori stiffly stepped aside. Like everything in them protested the order, but they couldn't stop themselves from obeying. Nyx realised she should've delighted in their forced actions at the hands of a sire-bond command, but she couldn't, not when that sire seemed intent upon her.

Her protective semi-circle was broken and now staggered to either side of her. The intensity of the man's gaze rankled over her skin, angering, and terrifying her at the same time, dribbling over her skin like the juices off a rotting corpse. Yet, despite her flighty instincts, Nyx forced herself to meet his stare head-on without flinching or faltering, unwilling to let even a *fissure* of her unease show.

The man's moss-green irises trailed over her, appraising her silently from head to toe before a low hum emitted from his throat and his eyes darted to Orion and then back to her. The corners of his lips curled up into a salacious grin, shadowed by the flickering light of the bonfire and the ghostly glow from the full, waxing moon cusping the horizon. "Now, was that s*o hard*?"

A muscle ticked in Orion's stubbled jaw; his gloved hands clenched at his sides from his fractionally shifted position in front of her. Somehow maintaining his protective stance whilst his companions could not. "What do you want, *Leon*?" Orion drawled lazily, as if the other man's presence bored him.

Nyx's eyes flickered between the two men and her attention lingered on Leon for a moment *too* long, as something shifted in the air. Realisation slammed into her and stole her breath before she moved without thinking, focused on the plunging feeling encasing her heart and the terror that gripped the beating organ. Niko's arms tightened around her stomach like iron bands to keep her in place, his head dipping so his chin brushed over her shoulder.

"Don't do it, chica," Niko urged, whispering the words into her skin.

Nyx struggled in his arms, heart slamming against her ribcage as Orion turned slowly toward her. His glacier-like irises surveyed her closely, a deep frown carving itself into his forehead. But she didn't notice or care whilst she pushed against Niko and her instincts stopped screaming at her to run. Instead, they bellowed at her like a mantra that didn't want to be forgotten, urging her to *stay*. To put herself between Leon and Orion, Kotori, Kade, and Niko. To *protect them* from the malicious will of their sire and the warped plans turning through his head.

"*No,*" she breathed out, an eerie calm to her softly murmured and yet brayed exclamation. "*You* don't get to decide *my* fate … or theirs."

Leon's gaze bore down upon her. His grin grew and then grew some more. It seemed to stretch endlessly, like the unknown depths of the ocean and the fear of not being able to see the ocean floor or what may lurk beneath its ever-changing tides.

That same fear clutched Nyx in a vice-like grasp, sinking its claws into her skin as Orion's gaze darted between her and Leon. His irises darkened as the pieces seemed to click into place in his mind—as the warning in her eyes registered—jaw ticking as his expression turned lethal. Moving with the swiftness, grace and calculated edge Nyx had grown accustomed to, he partially blocked much of her body from Leon's view before Kotori mirrored Orion's actions and bracketed her back into Niko's chest, his be-ringed hands on her hips. Kade's fingers curled through the belt loops of her jeans a moment later as Niko manoeuvred himself in a way that allowed Kade to sidle up against himself and Nyx.

Now they were five.

Each of them glared coldly at Leon, challenging him. Despite the terror embedding its claws into her heart, Nyx couldn't deny the exhilaration and power that rippled through her bloodstream with its steadiness. Having *four dangerous men* at her disposal was empowering, after all. It felt *right* in an unorthodox way. Knowing that whatever Leon did to her or to her pack *would* have repercussions.

If he didn't think so, *she* would ensure he regretted the day he'd ever laid eyes on her.

Leon tutted at the protective circle encasing Nyx, eyeing his 'sons' with the barest sneer before he pushed an otherworldly edge into his voice. "*Let's go, boys*. We have much to do and *so little* time to do it."

As the siren-like quality of Leon's command hung heavily in the star-smattered sky, Nyx pursed her lips with distaste. Her eyebrows slanted as she recalled the dome-like prison that had encased her senses when Orion had ordered her to comply, and how the ethereal layering of his command had cut all her ties to her mind. Fraying her control over her actions like Leon frayed theirs. Their menacing snarls reverberated in her eardrums as she turned toward them, eyes trailing over each of them before terror engulfed her.

Nyx's eyes widened, her hands grasping at their jackets and shirts as if it'd be enough to stop them as their sire-poisoned minds forced them to move, to walk toward Leon's villainous and deceptively pleasing side. That same self-satisfied grin plastered his face as he angled his head and his lacklustre-green gaze remained on her.

His sons' eyes shone as though with rage, resentment and pain.

"*Stay,*" Leon ordered. Commanding them like dogs as he started toward her.

Orion's upper lip twitched, as he tracked Leon, following each step Leon took.

Nyx fought against the urge to step back and away from him, tipping her head back to peer up at him as the trueness of his hunkering height dwarfed her, and he seemed to consider her with that habitual tilt of the head she had come to know in the four men who stood by her. Her hands quivered at her sides, unnerved and unsure as he slowly raised his hand to brush a stray curl behind her ear, the tips of his fingers brushing feather-light over her cheekbone.

"Oh, but I'm afraid I *have to* do this," he said, fake regret in his voice as he stared down at her. "Boys need discipline, and they've broken my rules with their new addition."

Orion's lips curled, appearing to bare his teeth as his eyes flashed and Leon's hold over him wavered. "You're supposed to be *dead,*" he said.

Leon hummed, barely acknowledging the retort.

Every muscle tensed in Nyx's body when Leon's hand lifted to her face and cupped her cheek. Caressing the flesh with an unsettling gleam that seemed almost savoury, like he didn't want to forget her. A shudder begged to tear down her spine the longer he stared, and the crackling of the bonfire twined with the stench of burning flesh filled her nostrils, scattering her crumbling nerves.

"That might be true, Orion," Leon finally mused, without turning, "But I'm afraid she must pay the price for that mistake."

Nyx's heart jolted in her chest at Leon's words, the thudding beat filling her ears before Leon's gaze tunnelled into her with eerie satisfaction. As if the sound of her panicked heart delighted him. Her eyes darted frantically to the quartet behind him, over his left shoulder, as she saw their eyes flickering between white-gold to blue or brown.

Suddenly, Orion shouted, part growl, part guttural scream, managing several enraged steps forward before his face distorted into a painful grimace and his legs crumpled beneath him. One gloved hand grasped his abdomen like he'd been stabbed, and a low groan of anguish tumbled from his lips.

Kotori's jaw worked as he clenched and unclenched it, and Kade's fingers toyed anxiously with the bejewelled, bird-like charm hanging from his left ear. Niko's cyanic irises simmered. It seemed none of them could break free of their sire's commands like Orion could, the power of the *true* head vampire unmoveable than if it was Orion enforcing the orders.

Nyx shoved back the hysteria clutching at her throat as she spoke, imploring Leon, "Please, don't do this. I didn't ask for this."

Leon tutted, shaking his head as though she'd disappointed him. His demeanour, irked and laced with aggravation, "I know, young one, but it *must* be done. How else would I teach a lesson?" he said.

Her anger rose. "Is it a lesson you wish to *teach them*? Or is it just another way for you to kill them slowly without them being able to fight back?" she said.

It was Leon's turn to bristle, metaphorical hackles raising as his irises sparked with anger. Turning, he sniffed indignantly and peered down at Orion, still on his knees. Leon clicked his tongue, "Orion ..." he drawled, a truly menacing glint flickering throughout his moss-like irises as he stooped down to retrieve the forgotten stake, half-buried beneath the sand. He twirled it casually in his hand. *"Order your halfling to drive this stake through her abdomen."*

"You're *dead.* Mark my words, Leon," Kade snarled, his hazel irises flashing gold as he stepped forward and Niko's hand wrapped around his forearm, pulling him back.

Leon turned to Kade, shrugging his shoulders before he lazily waved off Kade's concern, "I guess my death depends on your *dearest* Nyx now, Kade," he said, his hand lifting to his face, rubbing the underside of his chin with dark interest, "Orion, I think it's time to test Nyx's aim."

Nyx swallowed thickly, tracking Leon's theatrical retreat and the ungodly drug called power he wielded. Orion rose from the sand and met her stare head-on.

"Nyx—" Orion said, his jaw clenched, his glacier-like eyes flashed gold, bleeding with unbridled resentment and rage, directed at Leon. His pale eyebrows screwed together against the grasp of the command before his lips parted and Leon's grin grew. The poison of his command forced the unwanted order from Orion's mouth.

"Drive the stake in Leon's hand through your abdomen," Orion said.

Nyx numbly stepped forward, her body acting on commands and prompts that weren't her own whilst she battled against the familiar glass-like dome slowly lowering to encase her mind. Her legs trembled with each step, the urge to continue walking as the receding part of her will *knew* this wasn't her, bellowed its protests. But, unlike the times before, she saw a frisson of regret spark and die in the depths of Orion's irises. Despite everything he'd done, his commands had never *truly* been malicious or endangering to her. They'd been no better when they'd stripped her of her free will, but he'd *never* forced her to do something that would endanger her life. She silently thanked him for that as her feet carried her toward Leon and the wooden stake he extended.

"Don't fight it, Nyx," Leon crooned tauntingly, twirling the wooden instrument in his hand when she stopped several paces away from him, "It's so much better if you don't fight it."

She glared up at the grinning man, her feet stumbling as she gritted her teeth against the searing agony of fighting Orion's command, and she forced herself to stay—muscles locked—where she stood. With an exasperated huff, Leon strode toward her and snatched up her clenched fist, prying her fingers open whilst she defiantly stared him down and he forced her fingers to dazedly wrap around the crudely sharpened stake. Nyx knew, as he pulled away and his forest-like gaze flickered to her face, that her refusal to comply enraged him. But she'd promised him, and herself, that he wouldn't dictate her fate. Not like he'd dictated her father's. Her mother's. Xander's. And Asher's before her.

Asher.

Nyx's heart twisted painfully in her chest like salt rubbed into a fresh and bleeding wound. And it seemed, as she straightened her spine and squared her shoulders, that the least she could do was upset his plans, if only by a little. She managed a defiant step backward, ignoring the pain blooming over her body as her legs crumpled beneath her and the rocky sand dug into her jean-clad knees. Her fist clenched painfully around the stake, eyes screwing shut against the blinding agony tearing at her insides. Splinters of wood pricking uncomfortably into her palm reminded her that this wasn't a dream—a *nightmare*—as she fought against Leon's command.

Panic seized her heart when her hand shakily lifted, and the sharpened point of the stake brushed against the bandages wrapped around her abdomen, the saline-encrusted wind whipping her curls around her back. A choked sob ripped from her throat as vicious snarls rippled across the night, echoing loudly in her eardrums, deafening and resolute in their wrathful glory.

The stake trembled, tremors of maddening terror wrapping around her throat as Nyx fought to somehow shift the dome-like prison from her mind whilst she numbly lined the crimson-stained stake up with her stomach, seeming to cement her *unwilling* fate into stone. Nyx shook her head and glared up at Leon as her arms moved without her control and drove the sharpened stake into her stomach with a harrowing *squelch*.

A clarity engulfed her mind like fog clearing as a garbled gasp tumbled from her parted lips and pain unlike any she had known slammed into her. Blinding and pulsing through her abdomen and the torn stitches. Nyx dropped her gaze from Leon and to the pale-wooded stake lodged in her stomach, blood sluicing onto the sand. *Her* blood.

The sound of him sniffing the air sharply got her moving. He was smelling her blood, her life essence as it flowed out of her. Smelling her death.

It can't end like this! The pain afforded her senses urgency as she pressed a blood-slicked hand into the sand and pushed herself up from the ground. Wincing against the white-hot burst of pain that zinged through her nervous system, tearing around the jutting piece of wood lodged in her abdomen, unbelievable pain.

Leon tutted, mockingly scolding her as he pursed his lips, and rubbed his hands together with baneful zeal. "I wouldn't do that, halfling," he said. He peered over his shoulder at each of his sons trembling with rage and resentment before he turned back to her with an exaggerated sigh. "Welcome to the family, Nyx. I wish it'd been under better circumstances, but life isn't that simple. Death is far kinder than the life you would've been forced to live," he said.

Nyx's legs trembled, and then her knees reconnected with the dirt, teeth sinking into the flesh of her bottom lip to push away from her suffering. Her bloodied hand bathed in the steady trickle of her own blood slipping through her fingers, the crimson-red stark against the pale wood of the stake. "What makes you believe I won't survive this?" Nyx scoffed, shaking her head. "I *will* survive this. And when I do, I'll hunt you down and make you regret *ever* laying eyes on me."

"I *doubt* that, little halfling," Leon said, his mossy stare flickering pointedly to her bloodied hands.

Nyx fought to blink away the sudden weariness creeping in, her mind clouding with the unrelenting weight of her blood loss. Her hands trembled, heart stuttering in her chest as Leon purposefully stooped down on his haunches and nudged her with his hand, smug as her centre of gravity shifted, and her groggy senses sent her tumbling to the sandy floor. The side of her head collided harshly with the blunt edge of a rock before she blearily blinked up at his face, continuing to fight against the allure of unconsciousness and the intensifying pain rippling through her—stronger than when Ryder had staked her as a human.

He turned away from her then, boredom schooling his face as his footsteps crunched in the gritty sand. Striding past Orion, Kotori, Kade, and Niko to the moonlit forest several metres away, calling back over his shoulder with that otherworldly command; lighter and less prominent, but still present. "*Come now, boys*. Let's go home."

No one moved.

Not one of the quartet heeded their sire's loosely uttered command, staying rooted to their spots several paces from Nyx's dazed and blood-stained body as Leon's footsteps retreated. It seemed he knew they'd be forced to follow him, regardless of how far he wandered. It hurt more than the stake lodged in her abdomen as Kade and Niko refused to meet her gaze. Their faces were awash with guilt, regret, and self-inflicted blame. Niko's nimble fingers toyed with his bracelets, his eyes red with a sheen of tears, he furiously blinked back. Kade shifted beside his blood brother, fuscous irises darting back and forth between her and the ground as his teeth gnawed at the pad of his thumb—his habitual source of comfort.

Kotori stared into the wind, his ebony locks billowing around him like a dark halo of a veritable god of vengeance, his ring-clad hands clenching and unclenching at his sides. Where Kotori radiated silent fury, Orion's was the only gaze that stayed frozen on Nyx, the muscles of his body locked firmly in place.

"It's not your fault," Nyx assured, her brows furrowing with confusion. Not understanding *why* she felt the need to reassure them it wasn't their fault.

"How *isn't* this our fault? You're bleeding out and we can't even *help you,*" Kotori gritted out.

"Life is just the art of dying. It's how you choose to die that truly matters," Nyx said as her lips pulled into a soft smile, echoing his words back to him. "It's not your fault, but you need to go before he makes it worse."

Niko angrily stepped forward, his gaze smouldering as Kade shadowed him. "No, chica. We're not leaving you," he said.

"Go, Niko," Nyx said as she eyed Kade and Kotori pointedly, forcing herself to ignore the bolt of pain to her heart when Kotori moved and grasped Niko's right arm. "Don't make this harder than it has to be."

Niko's bellowed protests seemed to fade as the beating of her own heart seemed to get louder. She turned to Orion, ignoring the bitter sting her thoughts left behind. Because, where she *needed* them to learn to survive—to thrive—in their world of death and the darkness that cloyed in her being, they didn't *need* her to survive.

Whether Orion could read the turmoil in her face, she would never know, but his words were weighted, "We'll come back for you, little dove. I *promise.*"

Then he turned and followed his companions, leaving her beneath the full moon and the thunderous lonely roar of waves crashing against the cliff face of Elveszett Bluff.

Nyx supposed it was a peaceful and beautiful place to die. Surrounded by the screeching cries of owls, wind whooshing through the coastal grass, and the symphony of cricket song, but a larger piece of her mourned her life—of what she'd lose. Or had already lost.

Her heart shattered as a pup-like howl echoed up through the cave below, her eyes beading with tears that she furiously blinked away. *Ares*. Her little warrior would die just as surely as she would, abandoned and left forgotten in the labyrinthine tunnels of the cavernous home. She tried to shake the image of a grinning Asher walking into the kitchen with Ares clutched to his chest as her eyelids fluttered and her palms wavered around the stake, seeking to plunge her into the abyss of unconsciousness.

Not quite human. Not quite a vampire.

Both and neither at all as her eyelids slid shut and her heart sluggishly jolted with panic. The crisp, saline-imbued air of Celacali caressed her skin and tried to cool a new anger. Although she lay among the shadows of the night, her blood staining the earth, hair splayed messily around her, and the stars glittering above, she didn't feel *alone*. Not with her mind churning with a newfound purpose—with vengeance—with a direction. She had finally found a target for her rage: Leon.

Leon controlled Orion, Kotori, Kade, and Niko through the power of their sire-bond and the title he held as their patriarch. But he could only keep them on a leash for so long. Nyx knew, like he must know, that the wolves would remember—would wait for the perfect moment—to turn on him, plunging Leon into the maws of ravenous beasts denied their freedom for too long. They craved his blood, she was sure of it.

Power came with consequences, and she would *revel* in bringing Leon to his knees. Bowed at the mercy of her.

And *her* wolves.

DO NOT CROSS POLICE

CRIME SCENE DO NOT CROSS

CRIME SC

CRIME SCENE

CRIME SCENE DO NOT CROSS

DO NOT CROSS

CROSS POLICE LINE DO

Acknowledgements

I'd say I was sorry for leaving you hanging like that, but then I'd be lying. I enjoy endings like this way too much and I can't promise there won't be more in the future because I'm a sucker for chaos. They say it takes a village to raise a child and I won't disagree. However, this baby took a *city* like Celacali it to pull off.

Some of you know the inspiration for this book because I've made no move to hide it. *Shadows of the Night* means the world to me, it's a slice of my favourite movie altered and changed into something else—something different. I'm very proud to say this book was inspired by the film *The Lost Boys (1987)* written by Jeffrey Boam, Janice Fischer and James Jeremias, and directed by Joel Schumacher. Thank you for bringing these characters to life in a way I'm not sure anyone else will *ever* be able to, for gifting me with something that started as a seed of thought, an acorn of possibility, and turned into … well, this tree of night.

Thank you to my editor, Agatha Whitechapel, for all her help and the perfecting of my references. I couldn't have asked for a better person to work on *Shadows of the Night* with. I also couldn't be more grateful for her patience with my whirlwind of questions and the pointers she provided … and our conversations with plenty of *dark* undertones.

Thank you to my map designer, Natalia Junqueira, for bringing my crazy sketch of my city of Celacali to life. It's something I continuously stare at just to remind myself that this is all real, that I really did create an entire world from the caverns of my mind. I adore that map so much.

To Betthina Eriella for the artwork of my characters and the GODLY cover she designed—*god damn*. A goddess when it comes to art, it's not often someone can bring someone else's idea to life the way she can, and the art she created means more to me than *anything*.

Thank you to my lovely beta readers, Mars, Ophelia and Phoebe, for everything you did. From your notes and feedback to the unhinged conversations we had. It's been an honour to work with you, laugh with you … and cry with you (I'm looking at you, Mars). Your support on this journey has been invaluable! And to my ARC readers, I truly *lived* for your messages and reactions as you were reading … and the potty comments whenever you rooted for the villains (as you should!) These got me through the weeks and months of rewrites!

To Chey and Rowan for commenting on my Wattpad all those months ago when this was all just a hobby because I'm not sure what I'd do without you now. You've managed to ingrain yourself in my life so intently that I'll never be able to remove you. Your unwavering support and pep-talks are the reason I'm grateful for talking to strangers on the internet.

Thank you to *The Lost Boys* fandom, you've had my back from my little fan fiction days and there's not one that goes by that I'm not grateful for. You guys latched onto *Shadows of the Night* in a way I never could've predicted. And when I think about that, it makes me want to cry because you get it, and this book is for all of you that do.

Mum, Dad—it goes without saying because I don't need to say anything for you to know. I shouldn't have to, but … *thank you*.

And last, but never least, thank you to my readers. Every single one of you. I wouldn't be here without you. I can't express how much this means to me and I don't think I'll ever be able to. I just hope that if there's someone out there who didn't realise they needed this book until now, that they find a home in the city of Celacali and the allure of its darkness.

Like I did.

It'll always welcome you, no matter how much you might disagree.

About the Author

Charlize K. Kelly writes dark, paranormal romance with unorthodox characters and adventures of the deliciously corrupt kind. She's a villain's villain and quests for the ethereal of eighties glam rock, bridging the then and now in every chapter.

When she's not creating fictional worlds, she spends her time reading, hanging out with her dog Satan, and blasting Def Leppard, Mötley Crüe and Bon Jovi from the coast to the Wheatbelt. Charlize lives in Western Australia and dreams of the day somebody will bring the eighties back with a modern edge.

Follow Charlize K. Kelly for teasers, news and chaos!
Website: charlizekkelly.squarespace.com
Tiktok: @charlizekkelly
Instagram: @authorckkelly
Add to Goodreads: Shadows of the Night by Charlize K. Kelly

www.ingramcontent.com/pod-product-compliance
Lightning Source LLC
Chambersburg PA
CBHW060812120726
47909CB00006B/1894

* 9 7 8 0 6 4 5 7 3 3 5 0 1 *